Family Business

Renny deGroot

Toadhollow Publishing
88 Elder Avenue
Toronto, Ontario
M8W 1S4

Contact Renny at
http://www.rennydegroot.com

2nd print 062014

ISBN-10: 1494233231
ISBN-13: 9781494233235

Dedication

For all the 'J's and 'M's' in my life
Each one of you has helped me to find my voice

"What is it, to be one's self?"
Peer Gynt, H. Ibsen

The Meijers: 1929—1934

I

Spring 1929

Johan's clear blue eyes were wide as he stared at his brother. "How in the world will you tell Mama that you have a girlfriend?"

André shrugged. "She must have known that someday we would find girls and have families."

Johan wasn't so sure. He was fifteen and just starting to think about girls, but not much. He was too busy cycling with his friends, or playing ball when he wasn't working in the shop or busy with his studies. Of course, lately he wasn't seeing much of his friends with the way the hours in the shop had been increasing.

Johan looked away from his brother and stared down at the little walled courtyard where their three chickens and rooster searched endlessly for kernels of grain or seeds. It was a grey, closed-in little spot where the sun only slipped through for an hour or two on its daily tour. They lived in the heart of Amsterdam and it was uncommon to keep chickens, but his mother liked fresh eggs, and what Agatha Meijer wanted, she got. Today, in the chill of a March morning, it was greyer than usual, and the chickens seemed to shiver as they pecked the hard ground.

Johan turned back to his brother, sitting on his own narrow bed in their tiny shared room. They were good friends and used to spend a lot of time here, talking and dreaming. Now that André was nineteen and finished school, his work in the factory and shop didn't leave as much time for those chats.

"How did you meet her?" André's thoughtful and quiet way had made it hard to connect with girls and Johan was surprised that he would have a relationship so far developed that he was talking about bringing the young lady home to meet Mama.

"She is the daughter of Mr. Pol. I met her about six months ago when I went to pick up an order."

Johan wrinkled his brow as he thought of the wool company. "I thought they had some middle aged lady working there—I never heard about a daughter."

"I know. One day she was just there and when I think about it even now, I can't believe how that simple errand changed my life forever. There she was, this lovely girl. I tell you, Johan, I never saw such white teeth or straight posture before!"

"So what was she doing there? Isn't she in school?"

"Tiineke…that's her name, was in school but she's started working full time in the family business."

"So you met this girl, and just like that, you asked her out?" Johan's voice betrayed his surprise. André was often awkward, Johan knew. Johan sometimes thought that André's long slim nose and small round glasses made him look more like an artist or a writer rather than a fabric manufacturer. With his unruly curly hair and his lanky six foot four height that often left a gap between the bottom of his trousers and the top of his socks, André didn't generally have much luck with women.

"It wasn't quite that simple, but the order was running late so she gave me a cup of tea and a *speculaas* cookie and we just started talking."

Johan laughed. "Ah, she bribed you with *speculaas* cookies. That explains it."

"We got on right away. She asked me about my pocket watch so somehow I ended up telling her about how I inherited it when Papa died last year, and I asked her about her name, which is apparently Finnish, and…I don't know. We just talked."

"And now here you are, with a girlfriend that none of us knew about."

"Yes, here I am."

"Does she understand business then?"

"She's trying to learn. She studied art in school and does beautiful water colours." André bubbled with excitement, his voice high and words tripping over themselves. "She's been taking some lessons in bookkeeping because she needs to help her father, but really she's meant to be an artist. She's determined to learn the business, though, and I know she can do anything she sets her mind to doing. Mama is bound to respect that, because she's the same way herself, isn't she?" André couldn't hide his anxious tone.

"Perhaps, yes. Mama is definitely determined."

At that moment, the door opened at the bottom of the narrow stairs leading up to their room.

"Are you coming for breakfast?" Their mother's call was less of a question than a demand. Without waiting for an answer, the door closed with a solid 'thunk'—not quite a slam, but enough force to let them know her mood. Leaping up, they threw their jackets on and scrambled down the steep, narrow staircase.

The kitchen was warm after the chill of the unheated room above. The earthy smell of cooking porridge or 'pap', as they called it, mingled with the morning smell of brewing coffee. Still, it was not quite as welcoming as it might have been. Even after a year it was hard for Johan to get used to not seeing his father at mealtimes. The rest of the day he was busy and could forget for whole moments at a time that his father was long dead of a heart attack, but at mealtimes his place stood empty, echoing better times. They bowed their heads as their mother said grace aloud.

Agatha Meijer was a tall, spare woman. Even in her youth she had not carried any extra fat and would never be accused of looking jolly. There was a permanent furrow carved on her forehead between stern eyebrows. She wore no-nonsense steel glasses and her mouth was set in a grim line even now as she ate her breakfast. There was no conversation as they spooned the porridge. The faint sounds of the adjoining factory floated through the window as the large sewing machines started up. They could hear Mr. Van Loon standing outside, greeting the men as they came in. They couldn't hear his words but his tone was friendly.

Johan felt his brother fidget and wondered if he'd say something about that girl, Tiineke, coming over for tea. He heard André take a breath but, almost as if their mother sensed there was something unpleasant coming, she launched into a list of errands and priorities for the day. Johan would be going to school; this list was for André. There would be another list waiting for Johan when he got home at three o'clock.

"André, you need to pick up a replacement wheel for the machine that broke down yesterday. While you are on the way to Herengracht you can stop and place an order for more cotton at Van Smit's. I expect you to be back here by noon. André, it seems that you take longer and longer over some of these simple errands."

Johan blinked *No, don't mention Tiineke now. Mama will figure out that there have been a lot of detours on the errand trips.* He glanced at André to see if he was thinking the same thing. The excited look had faded from his brother's face. He, too, had decided there might be a better time than now to introduce the idea of a girlfriend to his mother.

Johan gathered his books, kissed his mother on the cheek, waved good-bye to his brother, and jumped on his bicycle to join the throng of other students on their way to school.

Left alone with his mother, André again considered mentioning Tiineke. It had to be done sooner or later. Tiineke was keen to meet the family. As he shrugged into his overcoat, he stepped into the kitchen, where his mother was washing the breakfast dishes.

"Mama, I'm thinking of inviting a friend of mine to tea." *There, that wasn't so hard.*

Agatha turned sharply to face him. "Invite a friend to tea? Why? You boys don't bring friends home for tea. We're not in the business of feeding and giving tea to the community—unless it's a new customer?"

André understood that, in his mother's mind, this was the only logical reason for providing refreshments to strangers. "No, not a customer. In fact, she is the daughter of a supplier."

"Ridiculous." With that pronouncement, Agatha turned back to her chore, effectively dismissing her son. As far as she was concerned, this was an end to the conversation.

With a sigh, André retreated from the kitchen. Without further ado, he turned up the collar of his overcoat and left to start on his rounds. Today there wouldn't even be the opportunity to stop in to say hello to Tiineke.

When André left, Agatha poured herself a rare second cup of coffee and sat down. She wasn't as calm as she may have looked to André. *This is the beginning.* She had had this conversation before, except then it had been between herself and her own mother. Agatha curled her hands around her cup as she remembered. Twenty-five years previously, she herself had met someone and had to endure the lecture from *her* mother. Her mother had insisted on a different man for her, and Agatha now felt that it had been the right decision. Her mother had been a wise woman, despite her one mistake in life, the mistake that had created Agatha. Her mother's bitterness at being left alone and pregnant had been hard for Agatha as a child, but she now believed the experience made her strong and determined. She, too, knew what was right for her sons.

Agatha stood up and gulped down the last of her cold cup of coffee. It was time to open the shop.

II

Spring 1929

André went about his errands that morning in a mechanical way, his mind on the problem of Tiineke and his mother. Usually he enjoyed being out in the heart of the city. It was so alive these days. There was construction going on everywhere with affordable housing being the main development. He went past the new building at Hembrugstraat now and paused for a moment to admire the unique blend of rounded ends, courtyard, and flat facings. He imagined himself and Tiineke shopping for a home. He would continue to live in Amsterdam, of course, so he could be near the business, and he wasn't quite sure how he'd be able to afford a home since he didn't actually collect a wage at the moment, but that would all change once he was married. He was sure in his heart that Tiineke was the girl for him. He loved her. He thought about her all the time—the way she did her dark blonde hair into glossy arrangements, or the way her smile made her green eyes light up. He was determined again as he set off to complete his errands to speak to his mother later. He would have Tiineke over one way or another. His mother couldn't dismiss him (and her) so easily. He pedaled his big black bicycle with renewed vigor, weaving in and out of traffic in the morning bustle.

There was spring in the air. The purple, yellow, and white crocuses were in bloom in window boxes. The flower vendor stalls were a riot of colour with their pails and baskets of tulips and daffodils.

The spicy perfume of hyacinths and freesias enveloped André as he rode past small cafés with pots of the flowers on their tables. The sun filtering through the clouds on this March day gained strength and he opened the top buttons of his overcoat.

"Hey, good morning!" André called out to an acquaintance cycling the opposite way. The man saluted him and lifted his cap with a smile and a nod as he went by. It seemed the whole world was blossoming in the spring air. It felt good to be alive.

It was almost noon and, really, he should have been on his way back, but he was drawn to the street where Pol's wool shop was. If he cycled very quickly and stopped only for five minutes he could still make it back and only be a few minutes later than planned. It was worth it.

He leaned his bike against the wall by the front door and strode inside.

"André! I didn't expect to see you today." Tiineke's delight was genuine.

"I know. I shouldn't really have come, but I just had to see you."

Tiineke's eyebrows raised hopefully. "You spoke with your mother?"

"Well, yes I did."

"So is it set that I will come over on Friday evening? I told my father I was going out."

"Yes, it's fine. Friday is all set. Mama is looking forward to meeting you." *That's it, then. I have two days to get Mama used to the idea.*

Tiineke bit her bottom lip and tilted her head. "Is there anything I should know or do to make sure she likes me? I've heard Papa mention before that she is a very...strong woman."

"Just be yourself. Once she knows that you are working in your family's business, I'm sure she'll be pleased to meet you and to get to know you."

Tiineke smiled. "I can't wait. Speaking of business, shouldn't you be getting on with yours?"

André caught his breath, noticing the time. He touched her hand and with a guilty grin, wheeled around to leave.

"I'll see you Friday, then," Tiineke called as he leaped on his bicycle and peddled off.

André cycled back with a heavy heart. *How will I manage this?* His mother had made it clear that she would not support his having a friend over for tea, yet he couldn't just spring Tiineke on her. That wouldn't be fair to Tiineke. His mother would not hesitate to make it clear she wasn't welcome. No, he would have to figure out how to at least get his mother to allow the invitation, and after that he was sure his mother would love Tiineke without any sales work from him.

How did I get myself in this position? He hadn't meant to fib to Tiineke. It had just happened. Perhaps Johan would have some thoughts on it. He knew how to handle their mother far better than he did. Johan was always the conciliatory one, while André was stubborn.

Agatha stood at the doorway of the house and pointedly looked at the watch clipped to her waistband, then back at André as he parked his bike in the shed. Wordlessly he hustled into the plant with his arms laden with purchases. The rest of the afternoon was spent in the factory. He was apprenticed to Mr. Van Loon and was learning the business from the ground up so he would manage it one day. His mother could have taught him most of what he needed to know but she was also busy in the shop and left the day-to-day management to Mr. Van Loon. Today's lessons were on the mechanics of fixing the machines.

"Most of the repairs that need to be done can be done by someone who is generally handy." Mr. Van Loon explained. "You need to learn how to do these small repairs yourself otherwise you will end up spending a fortune calling in the mechanics."

André was afraid he wasn't 'generally handy' but gave his full attention to the task. He was willing to learn, but often seemed all thumbs when it came to these sorts of things. He was better at the office work, but he couldn't just do that part of the job—he needed to understand textiles, mechanics, business, and worst of all, staff management.

The needle pricked him and André shook his hand before sticking his thumb in his mouth to suck the blood. "Darn it!" He peered at the needle he had just broken on the machine he was attempting to fix.

Mr. Van Loon frowned. "It won't do any good if you fix one piece only to break another."

André blew out his breath. "Yes, I understand that." He shook his head then lowered his voice. "I'm sorry, I didn't mean to be rude."

Mr. Van Loon's neck was turning red and André could see he was trying the old man's patience. "I think I'll finish this myself today. Perhaps you should go up to the office and review the shipping order book for the rest of the afternoon."

André escaped with a sigh of relief and made his way to the office. Here he could sit in peace and think while he checked the books. He supposed he'd have to mention the broken needle to his mother, which would just make her even more annoyed with him. If he didn't, sooner or later Mr. Van Loon would, and that would be even worse.

———

Johan was counting inventory in the shop late in the afternoon and looked up at the welcome distraction when André came in. The sunny spring day had turned into a typical grey end-of-winter day and now the cloudy afternoon had turned to rain as evening fell. It spit against the window with an angry popping sound. Mama was in the kitchen making supper. They always ate around seven o'clock after the shop was closed, and although they rarely had customers this late in the day, it was always Johan's job to work the last couple of hours in the shop and close up. André went around and straightened up some stacks of sheets. Johan worked in silence until finally his brother spoke quietly.

"I told Mama about Tiineke."

"Really?" Johan was astounded. "How did it go?"

"Not great." André admitted. "Well, actually I just asked if I could have a friend over for tea, but she knew very well that it had to be someone special for me to even ask. Mama didn't even bother to say no—she just said it was 'ridiculous', as if the very idea that I might have a girlfriend and would like my family to meet her was out of the question."

Johan wasn't really surprised. He had had a feeling that Mama would not like the idea. Anything that took them away from her and the business wasn't usually met with encouragement. Even his football matches or the odd cycling excursion was disapproved of.

Johan rested his hands on a stack of thick towels. "Remember how Papa used to coax Mama into letting us do things?"

"Yes, he was always the encouraging one. Mama never was, was she? Too bad he can't help me now."

"I think he used to be proud of the way I could handle a football, but to Mama it's all just a waste of time. I miss him." Johan exhaled, pursed his lips, and focused on his brother. He was intrigued with the idea of this girlfriend and was keen to meet her. "So now what?"

André hesitated and then blurted out, "I was hoping you'd have some ideas. I better tell you the rest of it. I'm in a bit of a pickle. I saw Tiineke today and somehow I told her that she *could* come to tea. She and I had tentatively talked about her coming over on Friday and now I've told her that. It's all set."

Johan lifted his head. "What in the world made you say that?"

"It just came out. She jumped to a conclusion and I didn't have the heart to tell her the truth."

"*This* Friday?"

"Yes, day after tomorrow."

Johan thought for a minute. "So did Mama actually say 'no'?"

"Well, not the actual word 'no', but it was pretty clear that's what she meant."

"So you have to take it as if you didn't understand that she meant no. It's about all that you can do. If you like, I can bring it up at supper and see how it goes."

"You're right, it's about all I can do. She'll know it's nonsense, but she can't say that I disobeyed her."

The old clock chimed and Johan began to close up shop. He turned over the wooden sign on its chain in the window. He and André closed and latched the wooden shutters in the windows.

When all six shutters were secured and the door locked, they went through the adjoining door into the house. The smell of potatoes and sausage greeted them and they went into the kitchen to wash up before sitting down to eat.

As soon as supper began, Agatha pointed her fork at her eldest son. "I see you broke a needle today, André."

André tuned out as she lectured him about his carelessness and lack of attention. Instead, he glanced over to Johan.

"Mam." Johan used her occasional shorter pet name. "André was telling me about his friend, Tiineke." Johan sounded casual and lighthearted. "She sounds nice. I'm glad she's coming over for tea on Friday evening; I'm looking forward to meeting her."

Mama sat up straighter and glared at André. "What does he mean? I told you she wasn't to come."

"No, you didn't say that, Mama—is that what you meant when you said 'ridiculous'?" André attempted to sound innocent. "I just thought you meant that the idea of me having a girlfriend really surprised you. I'm sorry I misunderstood you, but I ran into Tiineke this afternoon and already told her that it was fine that she should come over. She's now told her father as well, so it's all set." André stretched the truth a little, knowing that she wouldn't do anything to lose the respect of a business colleague. If she made him cancel now, everyone would know.

Agatha's voice was frosty. "You know very well what I meant, André. I'm not at all happy about this, but since you've gone ahead and confirmed it, there isn't much more to be said about it."

"I'll help prepare things while André is collecting Tiineke, Mam," Johan said. "It won't be any work for you at all. It's a long while since we had guests. It'll be nice."

André threw his brother a grateful look.

Agatha sniffed. "Your father was altogether too fond of having company. That's one thing I don't miss since his passing."

"Mama, this girl is very special to me. You'll like her if you give her a chance. She's works with her father in the family business—you know, Pol's Wool. I'm sure you'll find you have a lot in common."

"I doubt it, but it seems I don't have a choice about meeting her or not, so we'll say no more about it."

They finished their meal in silence, giving André a chance to think more about Tiineke. He knew her real love was her art and she intended to go back to that someday, but he trusted that his mother and Tiineke could find some common ground. André caught himself smiling, then saw his mother's sharp glance and hastily finished his meal so he could escape to dream in private.

———

Friday evening was clear, the stars already bright as André and Tiineke walked from the tram stop to his house. André's heart pounded when he looked at Tiineke. Her soft hair, the way her teeth sparkled as she laughed at something he said. She took his breath away. She had her arm linked through his and he felt like a king as they walked along. Coming into the house through the back entrance leading past the kitchen, they could hear Johan busy with cups and saucers. They stopped in the passageway so André could hang her coat, then as Johan came out of the kitchen, André introduced them.

André grinned when he saw Johan's reaction. *He looks amazed.*

Johan made a small bow to Tiineke and she laughed as she took his hand. "I know we'll be good friends. André has told me so much about you. You must tell me about your football team. I love football!" She burbled with an enthusiasm that they weren't used to in this house.

Leaving Johan to finish bringing in the tea things, André took Tiineke in to the sitting room where his mother waited. Agatha sat stiffly in her tall wingback chair. André noticed she had put a lace collar on her dark dress, as if she couldn't decide between wanting to make a good impression and insisting on remaining plain and stern. She lifted her hand to Tiineke, but didn't rise. Tiineke moved closer and took Agatha's hand. She held her shoulders straight and smiled despite Agatha's cool reception.

Tiineke swallowed. "I'm so very glad to meet you."

Agatha released Tiineke's hand quickly and folded her own on her lap. "And how is your father? I believe I met him once or twice at his shop or at a reception for the Amsterdam Textiles Group. I don't really recall where it was." Her tone was vague and indifferent.

Tiineke nodded. "He's well, thank you. I think he is worried a little about business, but I'm sure it will get better again."

"Please sit." André gestured to the red velvet chaise lounge while he took the leather chair that once belonged to his father. He would have been glad to sit beside Tiineke but thought that he should remain neutral during this first visit, halfway between the two women.

Johan bustled in with the teapot under its wool cozy sitting on the silver tray they only took out for special occasions.

Agatha frowned. "Johan, that tray should have been polished first if you were going to insist on using it today."

"Mam, it's just fine. See? I covered it with a doily so it wouldn't be so obvious. Tiineke would never have noticed if you hadn't said anything." Johan winked at Tiineke.

"All I can see is that everything looks beautiful and I feel quite honoured." Tiineke's lips twitched with a quick smile.

The evening progressed with Agatha refusing to relax. She quizzed Tiineke in abrupt, shotgun bursts. Tiineke responded warmly, unruffled, her smile firmly in place. André was proud of her, and although he interjected occasionally with responses or clarifications in an effort to soften his mother's questions, for the most part he let the two of them converse on their own. Johan served the tea and routinely offered comments and questions of his own. At nine o'clock sharp, Agatha stood up.

Everyone stood up and Tiineke set her cup down, the last sip of tea remaining in the bottom. Already she knew there was no question that it was time to leave.

Johan walked with André and Tiineke to the door and shook her hand. "I'm looking forward to seeing a lot of you around here."

Tiineke smiled in return, touching his arm with her free hand. "I'm looking forward to being here."

André put his arm around Tiineke as they walked together to the tram stop. "Well, you survived."

"Barely."

He pulled her closer. "No, you did really well. Mama is a strong woman herself and she admires others who are too. You'll get used to each other."

Tiineke turned to face him as the tram pulled into sight. She stood up on her toes to kiss him. "As long as you think the evening went well, I'm happy."

He watched the tram disappear into the night and turned for home, his heart full.

———

The next morning, André was up early as usual. The factory and shop were both open for a half-day on Saturdays. He was down before his mother and had the coffee pot on when she came down.

"Well, you're full of energy this morning."

"So Mama, what do you think of her? Isn't she great?"

Agatha set down the plates she had taken from the sideboard. "André, you need to be sensible now. She's a very nice girl, there's no question of that, but she is *not* the girl for you. By all means, have some fun. You're young and you would like to go out now and then, but understand the business comes first. She is an artist, for goodness sake, and the moment her father lets her go from his business, she will go back to that. You must see yourself that this is not a long-term relationship for you. There really is no more to be said for it. As I knew it would be, it's unfortunate that you brought her home, because now she'll read more into your friendship than she should."

Agatha turned her attention to laying out the bread while André stood in stunned silence. He had been so certain the evening had gone well, that his mother would approve of Tiineke. He didn't know what to say. He shook his head at her back. He didn't want to get into an argument. He was wise enough to realize he needed to consider his approach and he would talk it all over with

Johan before he dug himself a hole he couldn't get out of with his mother. At least that was one positive thing—Johan seemed to have genuinely liked Tiineke.

At that moment, Johan clattered down the steps and blew into the kitchen like a storm. "Brrr! It seems colder again. I thought winter was truly over when I saw the crocuses out, but today it seems like a last blast from December."

Johan poured himself a coffee, seeming oblivious to the cold right in the kitchen. Only after he sat down did he appear to notice the heavy silence.

"What's up?"

Agatha jutted her chin towards André. "I've just told André my thoughts on Tiineke and I can tell you, too. She's a very nice girl but not for this family." Agatha turned her attention to cutting her bread into bite-size pieces.

Johan set his coffee cup back on the table. "Really? I thought she was quite sensible and the fact that she is taking a course for book-keeping once a week is good, isn't it?"

André nodded. "Yes! She's very interested in her father's business and is determined to help bring it back to the success it was before the war."

Agatha cut another piece of bread, saying nothing.

———

Later that day, after the shop was closed, Johan lay stretched out on his bed, his schoolbooks lying around him in a heap. He watched André getting dressed in his good shirt and a bow tie.

"So you're really taking Tiineke out for a meal?"

"Yes, we're going for Indonesian in that new place just off the Kalverstraat. In fact, I believe we will have a *rijstaaffel* for two."

"How did you manage to squeeze the money out of Mama for that?"

"She seems to think that I'm going to let Tiineke down gently and break it off with her, that this is a farewell dinner of sorts."

"And is it? A farewell dinner, I mean?"

"Not at all. Mama can think what she likes. I tried to be above board and share what's going on in my life with her, but she clearly doesn't want to know, so perhaps from now on I'll just keep things to myself. Well, aside from you, of course."

Johan could understand that. Who knew, the relationship could wear itself out after a bit anyway and if Mama didn't know about it there wouldn't be constant arguments.

"Well, that's probably a good plan. Have a great evening." Johan picked up his book to study for his upcoming history exam.

André gave his already shiny black shoes another buff with a soft cloth, put on his Sunday hat, and turned to Johan with a rakish grin. "Don't wait up, little brother."

Johan heard him leave by the side door instead of the usual back kitchen door and knew that he purposely wanted to avoid their mother. He wouldn't want her to see that he was in a good mood rather than unhappy.

An hour later, Tiineke was waiting for André by the window in the front room where she could watch the street.

Ah, here he was at last. He came cycling up with a big bunch of flowers in his carrier. That was a good sign. She sprang up and was at the door before he had his bike parked in the front garden. The bouquet brought a feeling of spring to the house, the fragrance of the freesias subtle but spicy, and the tulips and daffodils a riot of colour. She reached for the flowers but André pulled them away.

"Not for you, I'm afraid—these are for your mother." He winked. "Besides, you don't need flowers—you look as beautiful as a garden yourself."

Tiineke blushed. She had dressed carefully in a lilac sweater and chocolate-coloured skirt with pale purple stripes.

She led the way along the narrow hall to the back kitchen where her parents sat in companionable quiet, each with parts of the newspaper. The room was really like a kitchen and casual sitting room combined. At one end were the countertops and sink, at the other end a table, four chairs, a large coal stove, and a low sofa by a window.

Tiineke's father was sitting at the table and her mother on the sofa. When André entered, her father stood up.

"Mr. Meijer, it's good to see you again." The two men shook hands. "Let me introduce my wife, Elsa Pol."

"Mrs. Pol, it's a pleasure to meet you." André presented her with the bouquet.

"Oh, how beautiful, thank you so much! Tiineke, get the Delft vase from the sideboard, please, and put the flowers in." Her mother handed the flowers over to her daughter then shook hands with André.

Tiineke left the room. André was alone with her parents but she wasn't worried. She could see that André was already comfortable with them. His voice was easy as he and her mother talked.

"Where are you going for supper?"

"I thought I'd try the new Indonesian off the Kalverstraat."

"What a great choice. We've heard a lot of good things about it. I'd like to go there, myself. I'll look forward to hearing if it is as good as people are saying."

Mr. Pol spoke up. "How is your mother? I've met her several times at various functions and meetings in the business community. She is very knowledgeable about the textile industry. She really was a help to your father in running the business, I think. I knew him also, of course, and liked him very much. We were all sad to hear of his passing. I probably never took the opportunity to tell you before now and I'm sorry for that, although I did send a card to your mother at the time, of course."

From the kitchen, Tiineke could hear her father's words. He had told her the same thing and now she wondered if André was surprised to hear all this.

She returned with the vase and flowers. The blue of the traditional Delft vase set off the colours of the bouquet and her mother was clearly delighted.

"Thank you so much, Mr. Meijer." Mrs. Pol took the vase and set it in the center of the table.

Mr. Pol snapped open his pocket watch. "Do you have time for a small drink before you go?"

"I'm sure we do." André glanced at Tiineke who smiled her agreement.

Mr. Pol left the room, returning in minutes with a tray and four small glasses filled with Genever. "*Proost!*" He raised his glass and the four glasses clinked together musically.

"To health and happiness!" André tossed back the clear liquid.

Tiineke smiled to see the flush on André's face as the Dutch gin warmed him. He looked comfortable and at home.

They continued to chat. Mr. Pol pointed to a photograph of the post office in the newspaper. "What do you think of this new style of building? They are calling it the *Amsterdam School.*"

"I like it. The rounded corners, the colours of the brick—it's new and modern and I really could imagine myself living in a building like that, maybe raising a family there. They are building play areas right in the courtyards of the housing complexes. I was looking at Het Schip the other day." Het Schip was the complex on Hembrugstraat he liked so much. "It's very family-oriented."

He stopped and swallowed as if he had said too much. He jumped up. "We should go, I think, Tiineke. Are you ready?"

Tiineke hastened to get her coat and hat. As she pinned on her small fawn-coloured felt hat in the hall mirror, she studied André as he stood behind her. Her eyes held his and she smiled. He returned her smile. It was a moment of perfect understanding.

———

They had tall glasses of draft beer with their supper. It went well with the spicy Indonesian food but left André even tipsier as he studied Tiineke. The soft lighting in the dark restaurant made him mellow. He watched her as she finished picking pieces of chicken from the last of the fried noodle dish.

"I can't eat another bite."

"Really? Not even to share a portion of *Pisang Goreng*?"

"Oh, well, I must admit I do love fried bananas. Alright, twist my arm." She laughed.

They ordered dessert and coffee from the smiling server who whipped plates from the table with a speed that left André dizzy.

"Are you alright?" Tiineke put her hand on his forearm.

"I've never been better or happier in my whole life."

She smiled. "You just seem very quiet all of a sudden."

"Tiineke..." He hesitated, then grasped her hand in both of his. He felt her quiver like a small bird. His heart pounded and he gasped a little.

She stroked the back of his hand with her free one. "What is it?"

He started again. "Tiineke, this is probably crazy since we haven't known each other that long, but I *feel* like I've known you always. I feel like part of me recognized you and knew you immediately the very first day we met.

"*Pisang Goreng*!" The server set down the platter of fried bananas alongside a pair of small plates. He poured them each a coffee, then disappeared with a smile and a bow.

André held out his hand again across the white tablecloth and Tiineke took it again.

"Tiineke Pol, I have never loved anyone before. I never even imagined that I would find a girl as beautiful and fun and interesting as you." He felt he was getting lost and stopped again.

Tiineke squeezed his hand and her eyes were shiny with tears.

"I don't know if it would be possible that you could feel about me the way I do about you, but if you could—if you do—well then, would it be too soon for me to ask you to marry me?"

"Oh, André, I've only gone out with a couple of boys before, but I can tell you this: no one ever made me feel anything as you do. You make me laugh, you make me think, you make me see things in a different light. Very often as I'm falling asleep, I feel myself smiling because of something you've said. André Meijer, I would love to enjoy those feelings forever, so yes, I *will* marry you."

Her voice was soft. They were in a halo of candlelight. They were alone in the world.

André's breath caught. He was lost for words as he gazed at her.

She pulled her hand away again. "Now, let's eat our dessert before it gets cold." She smiled at him and dug a fork into the banana fritter.

As they relaxed over their coffee and dessert, André and Tiineke skipped from topic to topic, making plans and dreaming together.

"What did your Mam have to say after I left?"

André was evasive. "She isn't good with change. I've never brought anyone home before so she really needs to get used to the idea."

Tiineke shrugged and left it there. "Where shall we live? Apartments are so expensive."

"Well, we have lots of time to look around and think about it. "André didn't want to go into details right now about how he didn't really get a regular wage from the business. His mother just gave him some pocket money when he needed it.

"You're right. We'll make it work, wherever it is." Tiineke sighed into her coffee cup.

———

It was late when André left Tiineke's house and climbed on his bike to head home. He whistled as he cycled. He had never felt so excited and happy. His heart thumped and the blood coursed through his body. He only stopped whistling when he broke into a grin.

He parked his bike in their shed. "Thank you, Lord," André whispered when he saw that his mother had gone to bed by the darkness of the sitting room window. He could defer that conversation until tomorrow. Tonight he would just enjoy his happiness.

He slipped into the house, locking up behind him, and extinguished the lamp. He crept up the steps in his socks, carrying his shoes with him, and went to bed feeling that the world was his to take—well, his and Tiineke's. Together they would grow both businesses—the Meijer's and the Pol's. He wasn't quite sure how yet, but the future was bright and exciting, that much he knew.

III

Spring 1929

André rose early the next day, but when he went downstairs, Agatha was already up and had finished looking after the chickens. Leaving his mother to get breakfast ready, André went into the shop and wandered around while his mind mulled over the night before. He straightened up stacks of linen and, although it was Sunday and the shop was closed, he opened the shutters, letting the weak early morning sun filter in. He felt at peace. He enjoyed the shop and he could see a future with Tiineke by his side, working in the family business. He went back through to the house where his mother now had fresh eggs frying on the stove and Johan was sitting at the table with a book by his elbow.

"I have a big English test tomorrow." Johan glanced at André before turning back to his book.

"Breakfast looks good, Mama." André inhaled the scent of the food as she set the plates down.

Agatha sat down across from André and studied him for a moment.

"You're very cheerful this morning. How did it go last night?"

"Well, I might as well tell you both. No time like the present." André took a deep breath. "Last night, I asked Tiineke to marry me and she said yes."

The morning light came through the window and glinted on Agatha's small, round glasses. The reflection obscured her eyes as ice on a river, but her black brows drew even closer together than usual. Her hands holding her knife and fork were suspended in the air and she seemed turned to stone.

Her icy stare became molten as she found her voice. "You did what?"

"Yes, Mama, that's right. I asked her to marry me. I know that you feel that she isn't right for me, but I know—I *know*—that she *is* the right girl for me. There is no point in waiting and meeting other people. She is the one I want, and she wants me." His curls bounced as he nodded emphatically.

"Are you completely mad? Do you have *any* idea what it means to be married? You can't support a wife, and what if you have a family? You have only just begun to learn about running a business. You have to focus on that if you ever expect to actually grow the shop and make it a proper success. I have a vision for you boys." She stopped and blinked, biting her bottom lip, then got up and carried her plate to the sink.

For once, André wasn't rattled by his mother. He knew he was right and somehow, after the storm blew over, he would make it all work. He turned his back to his mother and faced Johan, folding his arms across his chest and tilting his head to see what his little brother was reading. "So, what are you studying?"

"Charles Dickens, *David Copperfield*. English is a strange subject. The language is difficult, not always logical, and then some of the things they do, or at least did, in Dickens's time were strange. Did you know that a person could bring his whole family to jail to live if he was thrown in for debt? Can you imagine? The whole family living together in prison? I suppose it would give them a roof over their heads."

André put a hand on Johan's arm and grinned at his brother.

Johan gave a small smile in return. André could see his brother was hesitant, but André wasn't worried. Time would prove him right. It would all work out.

Agatha heard Johan prattle about his studies, but his words were a jumble to her. All her thoughts were on André. How dare that boy do this? The girl had to be behind it. She had bewitched him. He had always been a stubborn boy, not like Johan, who could listen to reason and find a compromise, but even André had never gone so completely against her wishes before. She wondered if it was too late to be undone. If he had truly made the proposal then it would be difficult to back out of it without good reason.

She went back to the table with a fresh cup of coffee. "Johan, go to your room to study, and then get ready for church."

Johan got up, threw his brother a sympathetic glance, and disappeared.

"What do *her* parents think of this?" Agatha glared at her oldest son.

"I don't know what Tiineke's mother thinks of it. She had gone to bed when we returned to her house after supper. I asked Mr. Pol if I could speak with him while Tiineke made some tea." André smiled as he talked. "So I told Mr. Pol that I had an important question to ask him. I'm sure he knew, because he was already smiling before I said anything else. 'Mr. Pol, Tiineke is the most important person in my life,' I said. 'I would like to ask your permission to marry her.' Just like that. I knew I sounded very formal, but that was right, I think."

"And I suppose he just said 'Yes, wonderful' without asking any questions? Didn't he care about how you could actually support his precious daughter?"

André scowled. "Yes, of course he cares and yes, he asked."

"And you said what, exactly?"

"I explained that this was a family business and I talked about yours and Papa's plan. I told him that I would manage the manufacturing side and the overall operations and Johan will run the sales and business side of things. He wasn't worried that both of us will be running things. He knows Johan and I get along well."

"And did he ask how much money you actually make?"

"No, of course not. He trusts that the business is stable enough to support us. He has his own business. I'm sure he knows what kind of money can come in."

"And go out."

"So you see, he asked some questions, but really, I'm sure it was just a matter of form. We get along well and he knows Tiineke is happy. All the other details will be worked out as we go along." André was sanguine about it all.

"The fact that you don't get a salary doesn't seem to bother you or anyone else." Agatha frowned, shaking her head.

"Well, Mama, of course that will have to change now." André smiled condescendingly.

Agatha's mind had already moved ahead to find the best solution to this disaster. She would have to make the best of it. Perhaps it would be possible to take the girl and shape her into a proper wife. She was young enough that perhaps there was some hope.

"Well, André, the fact is there simply is not enough money coming in to pay you any kind of salary that will allow you to get a place of your own."

André was stricken. "How can that be?"

"Goods are just not selling as they used to and we have slowed down on production. It is the way of the world. Right after the war everything was in go-go-go mode while people were rebuilding and expanding, but now it's slowing down." Things weren't quite as dire as all that, but Agatha could see the truth of her declaration was not far off.

"But I was thinking of looking at one of those new homes in Het Schip." André frowned.

Agatha grasped at the possibility. "Well then, you should postpone this silly marriage while you still can, and we can look at five years from now when there will be more money for fancy homes."

"*No.* We will make this work. If we need to save for a while before we have our own home, we'll do that. Tiineke will understand. One way or another, we will get married."

Agatha's stomach lurched. "There isn't some reason that you want to get married so urgently, is there?"

André's mouth dropped open, then he scowled again as understanding dawned. "No, Mama, there is no baby on the way, if that's what you mean. We just love each other and don't see any reason to wait for years before we can share our lives." His face was flushed.

"Alright then." Agatha was resigned "Perhaps we can look at the loft above the warehouse and see if we can modify some of the space to accommodate a couple of rooms for you." Agatha was practical enough to know that if she didn't make some conciliation, Tiineke's parents probably would, and that would be worse. She needed to keep André close and if that meant keeping this girl close as well, that's what she would do.

André grinned and he took a big breath. His eyes glistened and he blinked. "Mama, yes, that's just the answer. Thank you. I knew you'd come around once you got used to the idea. You'll love Tiineke when you get to know her, and I promise she'll be such a great asset to the business as well as the family. Honestly." He appeared more like a schoolboy looking forward to an adventure than a man on the cusp of being married.

"I don't know about loving her, but I'm sure she'll earn her keep, one way or another."

———

Over the next few weeks, Johan helped André in the evenings to carve out two small rooms above the warehouse. The work was dirty and exhausting after a full day of school or work in the plant, but Johan didn't mind. André was so happy and he was a pleasure to be around.

"So Tiineke really doesn't mind moving in here?" Johan surveyed the rough framing of the bedroom.

"Definitely not. I think she sees it as easing in to our married life. She's used to having family around, and this way we have the best of both worlds: our own place, and with family. She'll still be working at her dad's shop until her brother, Hank, finishes school next year, but that's no problem because it's only a twenty minute bike ride away."

André could only see the wonderful side of things. Johan hammered in silence for a few minutes, putting up boards to make the new wall of the room. "How will this work, then? You guys will have your meals just like now except at the end of the evening, instead of coming to our old room, you both come here?"

"I suppose so. I haven't given it lots of thought, but yes, I imagine that's right."

Johan tried to imagine what the evenings would be like with a new person there in the living room. His mother liked to read pieces out of the newspaper to them and get them to discuss the implications of the articles to the business. Johan wondered if Tiineke would enjoy that. The rooms here in the loft would be cold in winter and hot in summer, much like their own small bedroom was now. The boys had never spent a lot of time in the room, usually choosing to do their homework at the table instead, near the stove.

"Has Tiineke been here to see how it progresses?" Johan waved his hammer at the new walls.

"Well, no. I haven't asked her to come over. I thought it would be good to see it when it is more…organized." André stood back to admire their work. "It'll be a wonderful surprise."

"I would have her in to see the place when we finish the walls." Johan cocked his head and looked around the room with a frown. "She has an artist's eye and perhaps she might like to have some say over the paint."

"Great idea! We should be done with the rooms in another couple of weeks I'd say, so perhaps we'll make a date for that Sunday for her to come after church. Perhaps, in fact, she can come for dinner."

André whistled as he returned to his work, sawing the next piece of board for Johan to nail in place. With the sound of his sawing and Johan's hammering they didn't hear their mother climbing the loft steps.

"Well, this is coming along." Agatha surveyed the work completed so far.

The boys stopped, glad for an excuse to take a break.

"Mama, I'd like to invite Tiineke for Sunday dinner in a couple of weeks." André put his hand on his mother's arm. "We should have the rooms pretty much finished by then, except for the trim and small things like that, but it will be a good time to have her in so she can decide how to decorate."

"Decorate—what more are you planning than a coat of paint?" Agatha looked puzzled.

"Well, pick out the colour of paint for the walls. Perhaps we could find a wallpaper border to put along the top."

"Nonsense. There is old paint already available from when we built the office in the plant. That is perfectly serviceable and will not be wasted. You are certainly not going to spend more money on paint and paper when we have this already on hand."

"Isn't that sort of an olive green-grey colour?" Johan furrowed his brow. "Didn't we get that cheap from some place in France that supplied the military, after the war?"

"And what's wrong with that? It's perfectly good quality paint and should be used up." Agatha folded her arms across her chest.

"Yes, of course. That makes sense." André seemed unwilling to create an argument when things were going along so well. "I'm sure Tiineke will be able to brighten it up with some pictures and things. It would still be nice to have her over for dinner. Is that alright, then?"

"Fine. I hope she's not a picky eater. I can't abide fussiness and I'm not going through any more trouble than I normally would for a Sunday dinner."

"Yes, yes. That's great, Mama, thank you."

———

April thirtieth was wet and cooler than usual. The rain had been steady since early morning, smearing against the windows in a greasy sheet. Johan felt trapped in the house, but he didn't dare leave. He knew André was a bundle of nerves. They had finished the last of the walls two days previously and André had cleaned the floors with bleach to lighten them. Together, they had put the first coat of the grey-green paint on the walls and it looked as Johan had imagined it would—like a receiving room at an institution. Johan dashed through the rain to the warehouse and climbed the stairs to the new suite. André was running his fingers over the walls.

"Still tacky. It takes forever to dry in this weather."

"Are you going out to fetch Tiineke?"

"No, I promised I'd help Mama get dinner ready, so she'll just get here on her own." André consulted his pocket watch. "In fact, I better get down there to start peeling potatoes and onions."

The boys made their way downstairs and back through the driving rain to the house. Agatha had just returned from church. She always went to the second service while the boys went to the early one. Sundays tended to be a little more relaxed, with time for reading and catching up on correspondence. Today, though, there was an air of expectation and tension in the house.

"André, I thought you would have started this already." Agatha plunked an empty pot on the counter with a clatter.

"We have plenty of time, Mama. Tiineke goes with her family to the second service as well, so she won't be here before noon."

André glanced at Johan. Clearly Agatha was just looking for things to complain about. She was making it obvious that this whole dinner was annoying her.

———

Tiineke arrived at the house soaking wet. She wore a long grey raincoat but still the rain had penetrated her clothing. Her grey pleated skirt smelled earthy like only wool could. The white cotton blouse was rumpled under her sky-blue cardigan. She slipped her feet from the rubber galoshes that covered her shoes. Her woollen stockings were wet and mud splattered above her ankles and her dark gold hair was slicked closer to her head than usual, and yet, to André, she was beautiful.

The tip of her nose was reddened from the chill, but when she smiled her face glowed. "I'm so glad to be here."

"Come in, come in." André handed her wet coat to Johan to hang.

She took a clean white handkerchief from her pocket and dabbed at the water still dripping from her nose and chin. "I must look a wreck."

"You're lovely."

She smiled again.

Over dinner, Tiineke and André talked of the weather, the road conditions, and other general topics. Tiineke often drew in Johan to the conversation, asking him about his school. Agatha ate her own meal in silence; refusing to join in.

André plied Tiineke with food. "Help yourself to more chicken, and please, have some onions and sauce, you haven't had any yet."

"Oh no, thank you." Tiineke held up her hand. "I can't eat onions, I'm afraid. I know they add a nice flavour to dishes, but they just don't agree with me."

André caught Agatha glowering at Tiineke from beneath her black brows and saw that Tiineke had also seen the look.

"Everything is delicious." Tiineke helped herself to a small piece of chicken.

André moved the bowl with onions and sauce away. "No problem."

Tiineke took a second helping of potatoes as if to make up for her rejection of the onions. "Thank you for the lovely meal. It really is good." Tiineke gave the extra potatoes a determined look and took a large forkful.

"Well, we eat plain here, and *we* eat everything on the plate."

Tiineke glanced over to André. He looked back and smiled.

Johan's expression was puzzled as he watched the conversation. He glanced between his mother and Tiineke, then gave a small shake of his head and continued his meal.

When they finished, Johan turned to André. "Listen, why don't you take Tiineke up to see the rooms?" Usually it was their job to clear up the dishes after a Sunday dinner while his mother had the afternoon off. In this case, Johan thought, surely it would be alright with his mother to help out with the dishes. "Go on. Mama and I can do the dishes today." Johan stood up and started to gather up the plates.

"Yes, alright, terrific! Thank you." André turned to Tiineke. "I've been waiting to show you this. I just know you're going to love it. Come, let's go." With that, he pulled Tiineke, laughing, from the table and they skipped out through the kitchen door, dashing across the small interval to the safety of the warehouse.

"You were quick to offer my services with the dishes." Agatha continued to sit at the table, brushing imaginary crumbs together.

"Come, Mama, it's a special occasion. You relax at the table for a few minutes while I get everything organized." Johan cleared away the dishes in front of Agatha as if he worked at a fine restaurant.

Upstairs in the warehouse, André showed Tiineke the rooms that were to be their future living area. He draped his arm around her shoulder, as proud as if he were showing off a mansion.

"Well, Tiineke, what do you think? Will you be happy here?" His voice betrayed a shadow of uncertainty.

Tiineke turned to him and gave him a small kiss on the lips. At that moment, they heard the distinctive *clump-clump-clump* of Agatha climbing the steps.

Tiineke raised her eyebrows. "I thought she was going to do the dishes."

André shrugged. "I guess not." He dropped his arm and stepped back as Agatha entered the room.

"Does it meet with your approval?" Agatha's arms were folded across her chest and she nodded towards the room.

"I've hardly had a chance to take it all in yet." She looked around. "Yes, yes, it's going to be great." She took André's hand and gently squeezed it. "It's going to be wonderful."

André squeezed her hand in return before dropping it as well. He could feel his mother's gaze on him. "I know the colour isn't perfect, but you can make it look good, can't you?"

"Well, it isn't a colour I would have chosen, but yes, we can make it work, we'll make it our own."

"You're very lucky we made this apartment for you. If you plan to live with this family, you'll have to learn to be more grateful for what we have." Agatha's voice was sour.

Tiineke flushed. "I am grateful and when I'm a part of this family, I hope you'll come to see that."

Agatha sniffed and turned without comment. To the sound of her retreating *clump-clump-clump*, Tiineke again squeezed André's hand before they too went down the stairs.

IV

Spring 1929

Jan Pol sat smoking his cigar beside the cool stove. He was waiting until the visitors were scheduled to arrive before adding more coal. It was almost summer, yet the last few days had been unseasonably cool. The heat of the cigar warmed Jan slightly. He watched as his wife bustled around the room, tidying and straightening a room already tidy, preparing for their visitors.

"The place looks fine," he said. "Stop fussing!"

"I would have liked to have some pastries from Smit's Bakery. Having those little tarts would have been much nicer than just my plain homemade honeycake."

"Your honeycake is just fine, much nicer than any storebought pastries. Besides, you don't need to impress that old battle-ax. In fact, I don't think there is anything we *can* do to impress her, no matter what. I don't know how poor old Wim Meijer put up with her all those years."

"Now, Jan, be nice, for André's sake. After all, soon they'll be part of our family."

"Yes, yes," Jan shifted in his seat and twitched his shoulder. "Of course I'll make an effort. For Tiineke's sake, I'll make an effort. Anyway, I like André. Despite his mother, he turned out to be a nice boy. I would have liked him to have a bit more backbone though."

"Tiineke has enough backbone for both of them."

Tonight was to be Agatha's first visit to the Pols, to finalize details for the wedding. It was to be a simple affair, but the choice of church for the religious service was a sticking point. Agatha insisted that the service should be at her family's church, while Tiineke, of course, believed it should be at her family's church. André supported Tiineke, naturally, but Agatha was still being stubborn.

Tiineke's brother, Hank, came into the room, carrying a copper coal scuttle. "They're coming, I think. I can see three bikes coming along the path."

"Good, I'm ready to be a bit warmer." Jan rubbed his hands together.

After loading up the stove, Hank just had time to take the dirty coal scuttle out the kitchen door when Tiineke called from the front parlor.

"They're here, they're here!" She cast a last glance around the room. "Mama, don't be worried if Mrs. Meijer is a bit cool, it's just her way."

Jan put his arm around Tiineke's shoulders. "Don't worry about your mother and I. I know how to handle Mrs. Meijer, and your mother's honeycake will sweeten even the sourest person."

Tiineke's mother laughed. "Papa's right. Stop fussing and go welcome our guests."

The Meijers came in from the cool, but beautiful, sunny afternoon.

"It's a perfect day!" André said as they came in.

"Hello, Mrs. Meijer," Jan Pol steered Agatha into the room with a wave of his hand. "Let me introduce you to my wife, Elsa Pol."

Hank came back in the room, freshly scrubbed He went around the room shaking hands with everyone. When he came to André, he gave him a gentle punch in the arm. Agatha frowned. When Hank was introduced to Johan, Hank nodded in recognition. "Oh, I've seen you before! You play football on Sunday afternoons sometimes, don't you? I don't play myself, but I like to watch. You really have some fancy footwork."

Johan was pleased at the compliment and the boys began discussing football strategy and the merits of one team over another. They had each found a soul mate.

Tiineke and her mother spent several minutes carrying in the tea things. The warm honeycake filled the air with a delicious fragrance.

"This is my mother's homemade honeycake" Tiineke tipped the plate slightly to display the brown, sugary slices. "It's quite famous around here. At Christmas, people look to receive one as a gift."

Elsa Pol took the plate from her daughter and offered it around. "Tiineke, please, just serve the tea,"

"Well, I'm glad you didn't overdo it today." Agatha gestured to the food. "Some people tend towards being ostentatious with all sorts of fancy delicacies. I can't stand that sort of nonsense." She lifted a slice to her mouth and took a bite. "The cake is very good. Hopefully, Tiineke knows how to bake it, also."

After a few moments of quiet enjoyment, Agatha launched into the sore point of the plans without preamble.

"We need to settle on the church and then you can write out invitations."

Tiineke set her cup down. "No, Mrs. Meijer. We don't need to settle on the church because we know what church we will be using. I just thought it would be nice if Mama could explain to you why the church is so important to me. Mama, do tell how we came to go to the English Church."

Elsa lifted an old English Bible onto her knee and stroked the worn leather cover. "My mother was Scottish. She was brought here as a child, along with the rest of her family, and they always went to that church from the moment they arrived. My mother's brother went on to be a minister at that church, so it has always been a central part of our family. Both my mother and her brother are gone now, but the church and the Begeinhof are like a little piece of home for us. My uncle's wife lived in one of those courtyard houses after my uncle died, and we spent many happy hours there. My mother could speak Dutch fluently, of course, but she always insisted on calling Jan 'John' in the English way, rather than our way with the hard 'yuh' sound. It was a small quirkiness she had."

Jan smiled. "Your mother was one of a kind and I didn't mind what she called me. Her laughter was music in our home."

Tiineke touched her mother's hand. "So you see, Mrs. Meijer, the church is not just a church to my family and I. It is a part of our history almost, and it is so important for me to be married there. Luckily, André understands."

"Meijers have been going to Westerkerk for several generations also. I really don't see the difference, and considering that you will be going to our church once you are married, it makes sense that you would be married there, too."

André turned to look at his mother. "Mama, that very reason is why I agree that we can have the wedding in her church. It's almost a send-off. Mama, please don't make it uncomfortable for us. Our decision is made."

Agatha pursed her lips and set her tea cup down on the table. "Well, it seems that there is nothing further to discuss, then."

"Let me fill up your cup again." Elsa hastened over with the tea pot.

"No, thank you." Agatha held up her hand like a policeman stopping traffic.

"So how is business going with you?" Jan jumped into the silence that had descended.

Agatha looked at Jan coolly. "It's slow everywhere, so it is for us also."

"Not so bad as what is happening in America though, is it?"

She shook her head. "No, although some of our big customers are in France and Germany and they are having the same kind of problems. With the devaluation of their money last month, they are saying they can't pay in guilders any more. It's too expensive." Agatha softened. Discussions about business were always of interest to her.

"Will Hendrik Colijn and his anti-revolutionaries make a difference in our government, do you think?"

"I hope so, but as long as our customers can't buy our goods, I don't see how anyone can help us."

"Aren't we here to celebrate?" Elsa lifted her hands in the air. "All this gloomy talk of business. We have it all week long! Today, let's just enjoy thinking of something nice, for a change."

"Imagine my sister, a wife!" Hank spoke up. "That'll be an end to your painting and music, I suppose."

"I should hope not!" Tiineke threw a small cushion at her brother. "André supports my art and we both love music, so I'm sure we'll always find time to go and enjoy a concert once in a while."

Agatha looked at her. "Art? Your brother is quite right—you'll have to give that nonsense up once you are married. You will be expected to help out in the house and shop. Of course, there isn't anything that you can do in the plant, but certainly there will always be plenty to do otherwise. Johan needs more time to study than he has had and now he'll have it once you take over some of his work."

Hank looked stricken. "I was only kidding. Painting is part of Tiineke." He pointed to a small watercolor landscape hanging on the wall. "You can't give that up, Tiineke!"

"It'll all work out," Tiineke leaned over to pat her brother's knee. "Don't worry, little brother. I won't give up what's important to me. I'll find time." She looked fondly at Hank.

Jan watched the exchange between sister and brother. "Tiineke, you'll miss seeing Hank every day, won't you? Luckily we won't be so very far from you and I'm sure you won't be slaving from sun up to sun down. You'll find some time to do the things you and André enjoy, I'm sure."

Agatha sniffed but didn't say anything while Tiineke threw a grateful glance at her father.

The conversation moved along in fits and starts about general topics, often drifting back to the state of the economy and unemployment. It was especially bad in Germany and there were marches being held to protest. People were going hungry and being evicted from their homes. All around, it seemed the world was in a state of unrest. Finally, André removed his glasses and began to polish them with his pocket handkerchief. Jan watched his daughter smile as André polished his glasses. She obviously was already familiar with this habit.

Hank looked at André's glasses. "You and your mum have exactly the same glasses. Do you ever get them mixed up?"

André looked surprised. "No, of course not. They're always on my nose so we could never get them exchanged. Well, we better be off. So Tiineke, you'll do the invitations, then? Mama, Johan, shall we go?"

They all shook hands in a flurry of good-byes and thank-yous. Agatha remained stiff and formal as she took her leave.

"Good-bye. We will see you on June twenty-ninth, then, at the town hall." It was clear that Agatha did not anticipate any further social interaction between the two families until the wedding itself.

Jan inclined his head in a gesture that was partly nod and partly bow. "Indeed, we shall see you then."

Elsa stood with her arm around Tiineke's shoulders and waved from the front door as the three Meijers mounted their bicycles and pushed off. She shivered in the late afternoon spring day and held Tiineke tighter for a moment as if to cling to her daughter while she still had the chance.

Jan stood behind his wife and daughter. Such big changes were coming.

They went back in the house and he closed the door behind them.

V

Summer 1929

"Watch out!" A man glared at Tiineke as he cycled by, narrowly missing her. "Don't stand right on the bicycle path!" He kept going, followed closely by two children on their bicycles.

André took Tiineke's hand and pulled her forward so they stood at the top of the steps leading down to the beach itself. They stood together for a moment, simply gazing at the sight. The blue and white stripes of the mobile bath houses, children running and calling, people swimming or just standing knee-deep as the waves swirled around them. Tiineke looked at André, and they smiled. André was now a married man of twenty years old, yet at that moment, he felt the pure delight of a child. The wedding had gone off without a hitch although his mother had been grim and quiet throughout the day, and they had travelled to the coastal village of Zandvoort for their wedding night. André had been here once before as a child with his family, but Tiineke had not. Everything was new and wonderful to her and André was pleased to be able to show her around, although in truth, he didn't remember much about the town other than the beach. They were staying in a small hotel within a few minutes' walk to the shore, and now here they were, on a picture-perfect summer day, soaking in the sun and sights of the beach.

"It's so busy!" Tiineke swiveled her head back and forth to take it all in. "Where in the world have so many people come from?"

"From all over. Germany, France, even England. Let's walk along for a bit and look at how the rich people live."

They walked hand-in-hand north along the pedestrian walk until they came to the massive Grand Hotel. They stood in awe for a moment to admire the distinctive brickwork, turrets and the three fluttering flags, before turning back south in the direction of the beautiful watertower with its café high in the air. . They stopped now and again to watch as people climbed in and out of the bathing houses or emerged from the villas along the waterfront. Although there were clearly rich people and poor people, the seaside was a great leveller. People who had little money could still come for the day with their families and enjoy the free entertainment the sea and beach provided, escaping the prison of their worries for an afternoon.

"I should have brought my paints." Tiineke. said. "How beautiful it all is—the colours, the excitement of it all. Thank you for bringing me here." She turned suddenly to André and kissed him. "I just know we are going to have a long and happy life together."

André could feel a flush on his cheeks as he saw people turn and smile to see the two young people in love. He wasn't used to demonstrative affection and wasn't sure how to react.

"Yes, I think you're right." He smiled down into her eyes. She was so lovely. Today, she wore her hair loose over her shoulders, held away from her face with a tortoiseshell comb.

As they settled on a bench overlooking the beach, he let his mind wander to the night before.

They were both a little shy, he more so than her. She was natural and as he stood uncertainly by the dressing table in their room, she went to him and turned her back.

"Will you undo the zip for me?"

His hand trembled as the dress opened to reveal a silky corset. The flimsy fabric was warm to his touch. Tiineke slipped the dress off her shoulders and let it drop to the floor. He held his breath for a moment as she stood there for a second, her back to him. The shape of her long neck and the way her back fanned out where the outline of her rounded bum pressed against the silk and lace of her drawers hypnotized him. There were a couple of inches of white leg showing before her white stockings started. André quickly pulled off his tie and undid his shirt as he stared at Tiineke. She turned to face him, then stepped out of the dress and bent to pick it up and throw it over the back of the dressing table chair. She lifted her leg to rest it on the chair, undid the garter and rolled her stocking down her leg. André pulled his suspenders off his shoulders and tore his shirt off, flinging it on the floor behind him. He watched, enthralled, as Tiineke pulled off one stocking, then shifted her weight to roll off the second. Her breasts swayed as she bent over the chair. She turned her eyes up to meet his gaze and he blushed. She smiled and held his gaze as she finished removing the second stocking. As she straightened, she pulled the silky corset over her head. André undid the buttons of his trousers and pulled them off, then stepped over to Tiineke and took her in his arms. The warmth of her breasts against his chest was like nothing he had felt before. His hands slid up and down her back, feeling the softness of her skin. His penis was hard, pushing against the fabric of his underpants, and he was embarrassed by his need.

"I'm a little nervous." Tiineke pushed back from him to look in his eyes.

"So am I." André's breath was fast and shallow.

Tiineke laughed softly. "We'll figure it out together, then."

Tiineke bent down and slipped off her drawers and stood before him, naked.

In one movement, André pulled off his own clothing and flung back the bed covers. Lying down together, André grew bolder. He kissed his new wife deeply, his tongue probing her mouth. She arched against him and he left her mouth to let his tongue stroke her neck, then down further. He tasted her nipple and felt it grow hard in his mouth. He heard her catch her breath. When he put his hand on her and slipped a tentative finger inside her, she moaned.

"Am I hurting you?" André withdrew his finger.

"No, no. Don't stop." She took his hand and put it back on her.

Slowly he explored her, his fingers probing, enjoying the warmth and wetness of her. Finally, he positioned himself above her and penetrated her. She uttered a small cry as he pushed himself inside, but by then he couldn't stop. He slid in and out of her, trying to go slowly. Her body was rigid beneath him until she began to relax. Despite himself he began to thrust faster and he watched Tiineke's face so close below his own. Her breath quickened with his.

"Oh my God, André—don't stop!" She moaned.

He could feel her muscles clenching him inside her. His body took over and he pumped.

It didn't take long and with a groan he spent himself inside her.

The second time that night went more slowly. They explored each other with tongues and fingers, delighting in the journey and the discovery.

André shook himself back to the present.

Tiineke was watching him with a smile. "Later, my darling. Come, let's keep walking."

They wandered along, gazing in wonder at the Kurhaus, with its huge rounded front entryway.

"Imagine, this is the new Kurhaus. The old one that got torn down was even grander than this." André craned his neck to look up at the elaborate brickwork. "It's too bad there are no concerts here today. Wouldn't it have been wonderful to listen to music in such a place?"

"We'll have to come back. Perhaps we can come to celebrate our anniversary every year."

They strolled back into the village, away from the shore with its bustle of crowds, and poked along the Kerkstraat, looking in the shops. They made plans and picked out all the things they would buy when, someday, they had the money, and their own home. For now, they would be leaving later in the afternoon to go back and were stretching out their little holiday. Neither one wanted to talk about the reality of what going home would mean.

They'd agreed that, while there wouldn't be much time for Tiineke's painting, there would always be Sunday afternoons, the time they could really spend together.

They checked out of the hotel later that afternoon and André paid the bill from the money his mother had given them as a wedding gift. It wasn't much, but it was enough for the hotel, meals, and train fares. He would even have a little bit left over to put into a savings pot. There had been no cash from the Pols but they had paid for the wedding lunch. André sensed it was all that they could afford. Tiineke had never asked about financial arrangements, probably assuming André was getting some sort of salary that would allow them to save a little money each week. André wondered if he should mention now that this wasn't quite the case, but decided to leave it. After all, looking after the financial affairs of a family should be the husband's duty.

———

Johan opened the door as André and Tiineke coming up the walk. Kiss, kiss, kiss—he brushed Tiineke's cheek three times—right, left, and right again. He shook André's hand while grasping his shoulder with his other hand. "Welcome home."

Tiineke's stomach was fluttering now that this really was her home. They set down their two small cases and Johan walked ahead into the sitting room.

Agatha looked up from the newspaper without a word of welcome. "Did you eat supper already or will you have some bread and cheese? Johan and I ate already."

André shook his head. "We ate at the station, Mama, thank you, but a cup of tea would be great. I'll go and put the kettle on."

Tiineke hovered uncertainly, not sure if she should go with André or sit and converse with Agatha. Johan was at the table, closing up some schoolbooks.

Agatha flapped her hand at Tiineke. "Well, you might as well go with André to see where we keep the tea things. You'll be making tea often enough from now on."

Tiineke fled to the kitchen with a sense of relief. She and André spent a few minutes in the kitchen with André doing a grand tour of the crockery and supplies. She was suddenly shy and feeling homesick. This kitchen didn't feel home-like with its extreme neatness and organization. She just knew that any changes she might like to make would be unacceptable. This would be the house she lived in, but it could not be her home. But at least it wouldn't be for long, only until they could save up for a place of their own. Times were tough everywhere and she should be grateful just to have a nice home to live in.

"I'm so glad we have our own rooms over the warehouse." She laid her hand on André's arm. "We'll really make a nice little nest of our own over there, won't we?"

A small furrow appeared between André's brows. "Yes, definitely, but we can't be spending all our time there. Here is where we *live*, that is where we sleep."

"Yes, yes of course." She pursed her lips and nodded, knowing she'd stretch out that time as much as possible.

They carried in the tea tray and the four of them sat together. Johan wanted to know all about Zandvoort. He had been very young when they went there together as a family. He held his chin in hand and gazed up at the ceiling. "I remember the shell collector with his cart and pony going along the beach, gathering up big pails of shells that he sold to people for their front gardens." He looked back at Tiineke. "Did you see anyone like that this time?"

Tiineke laughed. "No, it was packed with people bathing and sitting in the sun. I imagine that sort of work would be done when it is quiet."

She was glad to have Johan there. He was easy to talk to. André had subsided into a quiet mood, he and his mother both drinking tea and listening without speaking. It felt like André was awkward and uncertain. He kept glancing at his mother, as though searching for a clue as to how he should behave.

When the tea was finished, Tiineke stood up. "I'd like to unpack my case, André, before everything gets too creased. Will you help me?"

He stood up and again, glanced at his mother. "I should move some of my things over as well, I suppose. I haven't done that yet."

Agatha pointed to Johan. "Johan, go and help your brother."

"We can manage on our own." Tiineke held her hand up to stop him. "Don't worry, Johan, you relax."

Johan looked at his mother and she jerked her chin towards him. Johan stood up. "It's no problem, I'll help."

"Well, I'll just go up to our rooms, then, André, while you men collect your things from your old room." Tiineke knew she had been put in her place. Mama was in charge and if she said 'hop', people were expected to hop.

Tiineke smiled at Johan to let him know she understood, although it felt strained even to her. Glancing one more time at Agatha, she saw the slight twitch of Agatha's lips in a self-satisfied smile just before she lifted a newspaper before her face.

She thinks she knows what's right for her sons and that together they are building some kind of an empire, but she better just get used to me. I'm here to stay. Tiineke turned and made her way across to their apartment, deep in thought.

She stood in the rooms that would be her refuge for the fore-seeable future. She had hoped that André and she would climb the stairs together and enter it for the first time as a married couple side by side. It wasn't their own home, but it was the closest thing to it. She felt lonely again, as she had in the kitchen. She put her case down on the old wooden floor. The wide planks had been scrubbed and bleached and looked as nice as they could, but a small piece of carpet would make it homier. There was an old table with a single drawer; it would serve as a dressing table. On it stood a dark grey ceramic wash basin and jug filled with water. Two shelves had been mounted on the wall above the table, along with a small mirror. On one shelf stood a vase with some fresh daisies. The simple white and yellow flowers brightened the room, and Tiineke knew that Johan must have collected these to welcome them. They would not have come from Agatha. In the corner of the room stood a straight-backed wooden chair in need of a coat of paint. An old set of drawers completed the furnishings.

She left her case and walked through to the bedroom. This room looked more cheerful. On the bed was a red and blue quilt that had once belonged to an aunt of Tiineke's. Against the left wall was a wardrobe. A window on the right wall let the last of the evening sun in and the room felt too warm and stuffy.

She went and opened the window a few inches. It took most of her strength; the old wood was warped and squealed as she forced it up. She stepped back to sit on the bed, enjoying the breath of air that slipped in, carrying with it sounds of children playing on the street.

Slam.

The window closed with a scrape and a bang. Tiineke gasped and her hand flew to her heart. They would need to find a brace to keep the old window open. She stood up and gave herself a shake.

Come now. The fresh paint on the walls make the room look dark, but clean and fresh.

She would bring a couple of her own watercolours from home and the dark walls would show them off nicely.

I am starting a whole new life with the man I love and that's all that matters.

The rooms would be as nice as her room at home once she was through with it. She got busy unpacking her case and putting her clothes away into the dresser and wardrobe, being careful to leave space for André's things. She still had more to bring from home and would bring things a little at a time on her bicycle. It was all going to be wonderful. She felt her spirits lift and she sang under her breath as she bustled around.

She laid out her brush and comb on one side of the wash basin, leaving room on the other side for André. The set had been her grandmother's. The brush had a silver back and was slightly triangular. Tiineke always laid them slightly in a 'v' together with their bottoms touching and the tops a couple of inches apart. It appealed to the artist in her to see the shape of the brush reinforced by the way she laid them out.

It's the little things that really made a place one's own.

The outside door to the warehouse banged shut and Tiineke could hear André's and Johan's hard-soled shoes on the wooden steps. The sound echoed through the loft.

Tiineke went to the door of the outer room and waited for André. "Welcome home." She smiled.

André smiled back and stopped in the doorway of the room. Without him speaking a word, Tiineke could feel the love as he stood poised in the entryway of their suite, his face flushed.

Johan stood awkwardly on the steps behind André. "What is it? What's wrong?" His arms were laden with jackets and trousers while André had a basket filled with his socks, shirts, and underwear. "Go, will you?!" He nudged André in the back.

André continued on, still smiling at Tiineke. He looked down at the basket and grinned helplessly at her.

The moment had passed, but Tiineke didn't feel lonely anymore.

Johan tumbled into the room after André, barely making it to the bed with his load before the clothing started to slip out of his arms.

"There, you're on your own now." Johan grumbled, but the smile belied his words.

"No, far from it." André patted his brother on the shoulder. "Thank you for your help."

Tiineke reached out also and touched Johan on the arm. "Thank you for the flowers."

Johan coloured, as if caught out in something embarrassing. "You're welcome. You *are* welcome you know." Then, without waiting for a reply, he turned and clattered down the steps.

They were on their own, and for a moment, they were awkward again. Tiineke saw the bundle of André's clothes in the basket and felt unwilling to handle the clothes that were private to him. It was all so new, this intimacy.

"I left you the bottom drawer." She slid it open to show him. "I hope it's enough room. How about you put those things away and I'll hang your clothes in the wardrobe?"

"It's a good thing I only have a few pairs of socks and things, if that's all the room I get." André started to fold his clothes into the drawer. They worked in companionable silence for a while. "It's so hot in here, isn't it?"

"Yes, the window won't stay open. We need to find a brace." She didn't tell him how the window slamming shut had startled her so badly.

André disappeared, returning in a moment with a small block of wood. "One of the great things about being here is that there are all sorts of things available to us within easy reach."

He went through to the bedroom and pulled open the window, which seemed to open much easier this time. Tiineke wondered if he just made it look easy or if he had a knack for opening it after years of living here.

The cool evening air brought a fresh breeze into the room that dissipated the lingering smell of fresh paint and stale air. It was quiet now. The children had gone home for the night. Tiineke sat on the bed and patted the space beside her.

André hesitated for a moment. "Better not. We should probably go back downstairs for a bit, at least to say good night to Mama. I'm sure she'll want to know how we settled in." He held out his hand to help her up. "I would love to just stretch out right now beside you, but..."

Tiineke took the proffered hand. "Alright, but not for long, right? I want to be alone with you."

Agatha and Johan were listening to the radio when André and Tiineke came back into the room.

"Well, that took long enough. I hope you don't take as long over all your tasks." Agatha looked at Tiineke.

Tiineke flushed. "I didn't realize you were waiting for us. Was there something you would like my help with?"

"No. We always have a glass of buttermilk together on Sunday evenings and listen to the news. It's important to know what is going on in the world, not just in your own yard."

Tiineke disliked the inference. She had clearly disrupted the lofty family routines.

"Johan, go and warm up the buttermilk now, will you?" Agatha waved towards the kitchen.

"No, please let André and I do it, since you helped with the room. André, come, show me where everything is." Tiineke turned on her heel and went to the kitchen before Agatha could countermand her and André followed.

"Don't be upset, sweetheart." André's voice was low. "She has to get used to the changes and that's not easy for her."

Tiineke's heart contracted at the word 'sweetheart'. It was the first term of endearment he had used and made her forget her annoyance. A sudden rush of love for him made her think she could put up with anything as long as she had him by her side. While the buttermilk warmed in the double boiler, she took his hand and kissed the palm.

"I'm not upset. I understand. It's a big change for all of us. We'll get into a new routine and it'll be fine."

André laughed a small laugh. "I'm not sure about new routines, but I'm sure you'll soon fit in to the way things work here. You're right, it'll be fine, more than fine."

"Don't let it boil!" Agatha called from the sitting room.

"No Mam, don't worry, I know how to warm up buttermilk!" André called back.

"Mam, Mama, Mrs. Meijer, we never talked about what I should call your mother. My parents told you to call them by their first names, but your mother didn't say anything to me. What do you think I should call her? I can't keep calling her Mrs. Meijer, especially now that it's my name too!"

"I can't imagine you calling my mother by her first name." André looked a little worried.

"No, I can't really either."

"How about Mama Meijer?"

"Mama Meijer." She tried it out to see how it felt. "Yes, I think that would work. I'll try it now when we take in the milk and see what her reaction is." She giggled, feeling like she was being daring with his mother to call her something unexpected.

André carried in the tray with milk and sugar and Tiineke carried in a plate with some *speculaas* biscuits, the same type of cookies she had served André the first time they'd met at her father's shop.

"Mama Meijer, will you have a cookie?" Tiineke held out the plate.

Agatha's hand stopped mid-air as she reached towards the tray.

"Pardon me?" She frowned.

"Mama Meijer, I asked if you would like a cookie." Tiineke smiled and moved the plate a little closer to Agatha.

Agatha's lips pursed and her black brows furrowed as she pulled back her hand. "No, thank you."

Tiineke saw by the frown that Agatha disliked the familiarity, but knew that she really couldn't insist on the continued formality. Tiineke turned away and sat down, satisfied with the tiny triumph.

The small group listened to the world news broadcast in silence, each with their own thoughts, most of which were decidedly on local affairs.

VI

Summer 1929

"**N**o, André, it's not good enough!" Tiineke was angry. They were up in their rooms at the end of the evening. Finally, Tiineke could relax. For the past eight weeks she had been adjusting to the routine of getting up earlier than she had ever done, cycling to her father's shop, working all day, and then home again to help with evening chores before finally getting some time alone with her husband. If they were very lucky, they might occasionally go for a walk in the evening, but often there were chores that she or André were expected to do even after dinner. Agatha was never short of errands to be done.

"I don't know why you believe that someone is coming in here." André looked around. "Everything looks exactly the same, so how can you be so sure?"

"I just *know.*" She wanted him to trust her without having to give the evidence.

"Well, I think you could be mistaken." He sounded tired. He shrugged and rubbed the back of his neck as though rubbing away the strain of the constant friction that existed between his mother and wife.

"Alright, since you won't believe me because I say so, here's how I know for sure." She pointed to her brush and comb set.

André looked at the perfectly aligned set lying side by side on the dresser.

"What am I supposed to be looking at?"

"The comb is straight beside the brush. Did you do that?"

"Me? No. The only time I handle your brush is when you let me brush your hair, which I really love to do, by the way."

He hoped to mollify her.

"Yes, well, I thought so. I always leave them so." She moved the comb and brush back into the 'v' formation she favoured.

"The first time I found them lined up like this"—she moved them back to the parallel way they had been—"I thought I made a mistake, or that you had moved them, which would be fine. I saw, though, that you never do touch them, and you leave the same time as me, so you wouldn't even have the chance to fiddle with my things if you wanted to. Then I knew. Your mother comes up here while we are away and pokes around, at least once a week. It can't be Johan, he's too busy as well, and besides, I can't imagine him bothering. No, I tell you, it's your mother!"

"Maybe she comes in to clean?"

Tiineke looked at him. "You think she comes to clean here, when she has me doing the cleaning in the house on Saturdays? Please, André. No, she has no purpose here other than to see what we are up to."

"Well, we have nothing to hide." André shrugged defensively, but looked sheepish.

"André, I'm not having it. Either you say something to her, or I will. Which will it be?"

"Well, what can I possibly say? That we suspect her of moving your brush?"

"You obviously don't want to say anything, so I will."

"Not now." André held his hand out to Tiineke.

"No, not now. Right now I am so tired I couldn't go down and back up those steps again if I had to. I don't know why I'm so very tired these days. I'm young. You would think I could manage the extra things I'm doing."

Tiineke climbed into bed and sighed as André slipped in beside her. This was the best part of the day for both of them. They lay beneath a cotton sheet, the quilt folded and lying on the chair. It was still warm and the heat lingered long into the evening in the loft room when other parts of the house were already cool. Despite the heat, they snuggled close together.

Tiineke whispered. "I'm not mad at *you*. Just your mother, and I'll sort it out with her."

André put an arm under her head and drew her close, enfolding her with his other arm. She put her leg over his hip, pulling him as close to her as possible, her arm around him. She trailed her fingers up and down his back.

"Your skin is so soft. It amazes me. I always thought men had rough skin." She felt his body respond instantly to her trailing fingers.

"Mmm." He turned towards her, sighing and stroking her back. "I thought you were tired."

"I am, but somehow a little less tired now than I was. That's what happens when we finally have time to be together." It was her turn to purr as she curled closer to him.

He brought his hand around from her back and slipped it under her cotton summer nightdress. He gently grasped a breast, letting the weight of it rest in his hand.

She almost pulled away. "Oh, I'm so sensitive. It must be coming near my time of the month. In fact, I'm overdue, now that I think of it."

André looked puzzled for a moment but then seemed to forget she'd said anything. He stretched out and after a moment of tenuous touching, Tiineke took over and left him in no doubt about what to do. He pulled her nightdress over her head and looked down at her.

"I think your breasts are getting bigger. Is that possible?"

"At certain times they are bigger, but don't get used to it. They get smaller again." She smiled.

He slid down, kissing her shoulder, then her throat, then continued to trail kisses down until he reached her nipple. He gently ran his tongue around it.

"Oh my God, I can't believe how sensitive I am." She shivered. "I like it."

After making love, they lay together in the cooling evening. A breeze whispered across their damp skin. André's breathing deepened and Tiineke knew he was somewhere between awake and asleep. His unique scent comforted her, made her feel complete.

Suddenly, she sat straight up in bed.

"What is it?" He sat up as well, wide awake again.

"Overdue. I'm overdue."

He flopped back down. "Yes, I know, so you said."

"I'm never overdue."

André looked helplessly at her. "It's bound to happen with all the changes in your life. You aren't a train. What does it matter if you're a little late?"

She looked down at him, suddenly nervous.

"You're right. It's probably nothing." She lay back down.

André turned his back to her, settling for sleep.

Tiineke cuddled close to him, spooning him. She'd make an appointment with the doctor first thing tomorrow. Surely women didn't get pregnant so quickly, did they? Her mother had once told her that they had 'tried' for years before she had become pregnant. Tiineke had imagined it would be the same with her and had never asked about how to *not* get pregnant.

She listened to André's soft, rhythmic breathing as he drifted off to sleep. She tried to breathe with him. In, out, in, out. His breathing was slower than hers and she couldn't keep it up. What would happen if she was pregnant? Would he be happy? Could they continue to live here? What would Mama Meijer say? Well, that one she could predict.

Finally, the heat and hypnotic sound of André's breathing lulled her into a restless sleep.

———

Morning came and they walked together to the house. Tiineke was tired after a night of tossing and turning, but André had slept well.

The kitchen window was open and the aroma of coffee and frying eggs wafted out to them. Tiineke felt a wave of nausea wash over her.

"Ah, smell that coffee." André inhaled deeply as they approached the back door. "So are you really planning to say something to Mama about coming in to our rooms?" André rested his hand on Tiineke's shoulder.

"Yes, I have to, but don't worry, I'm not going to have a tantrum."

He glanced at her. "Are you alright? You seem a bit pale."

"I'm not feeling a hundred percent." They entered the kitchen together and she went to sit at the table. "I don't think I'll have an egg today, Mama Meijer." She put two fingers over her lips to stifle her nausea. "I may just have a slice of bread."

Agatha turned from the stove and studied Tiineke for a moment.

"There's nothing like a fresh egg for keeping up your strength." She reached for one.

"I *really* do not want one." Tiineke pressed her hands flat to the tabletop.

"Mama, leave it. It's the heat, I'm sure." André looked worriedly at Tiineke.

"Fine. I won't waste the egg, then."

Tiineke helped herself to a slice of bread as she gathered her courage. She waited until both André and Agatha were seated and eating. She took a deep breath. "Mama Meijer, I'd like to ask..." Tiineke hesitated.

Agatha looked up from her breakfast. "Well, what is it?"

"Do you come into our rooms when we aren't there?" Tiineke hoped not to have to explain the evidence of the brush and comb.

"Yes." Agatha continued with her breakfast.

"Oh." Tiineke hardly knew what to say.

André set his fork on the table "Why, Mama?"

"Why? Why not, I should say. I go in there as I go in to any room in my house: when I have a need to do so. Last week, I went in to see if André needed more socks. I was going to the Hema to buy socks for Johan because they were on sale and I looked to see if André needed some also. Simple."

Tiineke was taken aback and her nausea was forgotten. Her mind whirled.

"I don't think you need to worry about André's socks any more. Isn't that the job of a wife?" Tiineke tried a small laugh but it came out hollow sounding.

Johan ate his breakfast silently and quickly, looking only at his plate. It was obvious he was determined to stay out of the discussion completely. André picked at his breakfast, not looking at either his wife or mother.

"That would be fine, if the wife had money to buy the clothes. As far as I know, you aren't in a position to do so."

"We'll use some of André's wages when we need things."

"André's wages?" Agatha was scornful. "André and you live here at my generosity. André cannot support himself, let alone a wife. That was understood before the wedding but obviously he didn't make that clear to you."

Tiineke looked at André. He flushed and kept his gaze on his plate. She continued to stare at him until he looked up at her, then blinked and looked away. Tiineke's heart throbbed. She was betrayed.

Choking back tears, she stood up and ran from the kitchen and up to their room. She flung herself on the bed, sobbing.

Bang. The door downstairs slammed. André ran up the stairs, taking two steps at a time. The bed squeaked as he threw himself down beside her and tried to gather her into his arms.

"Please, sweetheart. Don't. Don't."

She sat up. Her face felt hot and she knew it would be blotchy. She brushed back the strands of hair falling from the pins that had been so neatly arranged just half an hour previously.

"Why didn't you tell me? Are we just playing house here? We can never be independent if you aren't even making a wage that we can save!"

He sat beside her with his arm around her shoulders. His white shirt was creased and tie slipped askew.

"I assumed I'd be getting a wage and by the time I found out that the business can't afford it at the moment, we were already engaged and making plans. I know it was selfish. I should have said something, but I love you so much and just wanted to be with you. It won't be for long, just while we are in this low period. It always comes around again and when business picks up, I will get a wage and we'll save for our own place. In the meanwhile, it isn't *that* bad, is it?" André chewed his bottom lip and his eyes were worried behind the small round lenses.

"Oh, André." It was all she could manage. She couldn't tell him how bad it might be until she had seen a doctor.

"I'm late." She rose from the bed and pulled her dress straight. "I have to get going." She took the washcloth from the side of the basin and poured water from the jug over it. She rinsed her face and rearranged her hair.

André watched from the bed and thought the worst was over.

VII

Summer 1929

The doorbell tinkled and Johan looked up from the stack of tea towels he was sorting.

"Hank, it's great to see you!" Johan moved around the wooden counter to greet Tiineke's brother.

Hank grinned at Johan, reaching out to shake hands. Hank's arms were tanned and muscular under his short-sleeved white cotton shirt and his trousers seemed to hang loosely on his hips. He had been working as an apprentice at a warehouse for an import/export company and had lost some weight over the past months.

"You looked great on the field on Sunday, Johan. I'm sorry I couldn't stay until the end of the match to talk to you, but I had to help my father with some repair work at the house."

"No problem. I didn't see you leave. Did you catch the final goal that Haarlem scored against us?"

"No! What a shame, it looked like you had it won. They looked really tired in the second half." Even though these teams were just friendly amateur teams, the inter-city rivalry was fierce. Football was gaining in popularity, especially since Amsterdam had hosted the Olympics the previous year with Uruguay and Argentina putting on such a spectacular show for the gold medal. "Speaking of football, that's why I'm here. I was talking to a fellow I work with at the wool warehouse and his uncle coaches a new team, youth football for ages fifteen to eighteen. This is a serious team and they plan to play against cities not only in the Netherlands, but Belgium, France, and Germany as well. My friend is going to talk to his uncle to see if we can go to some practice matches. What do you think? Would you go along if I can get in? It's the next best thing to watching Ajax play." Ajax was their favourite Amsterdam team.

"Well, since neither you nor I can afford to go watch the first division play, that would really be fantastic. So absolutely, depending on when it is, of course. I'd need to get someone to cover for me in the shop if it's when I'm working."

"I'm sure Tiineke would cover for you." Hank waved his hand dismissively. "I'm supposed to hear tomorrow so I'll swing by and let you know."

Hank strode out of the shop and as Johan watched, he pushed off on his bicycle with one foot, the bike already gaining speed before he was seated. Johan went back to his work, whistling while his mind was on football.

Later, at supper Johan nudged Tiineke,. "Hey, your brother was here today."

"Oh yes?" Tiineke looked surprised. "He knows I am still working for Papa, why would he come here?"

Johan laughed. "Sorry to disappoint you but he came to talk to me. He might be able to get us in to watch a new youth football team, so he just wanted to know if I'd be interested."

"Johan, it's already too much that you are playing that child's game. You aren't going to start wasting even more time by going to watch it as well." Agatha sat back in her chair, knife poised in mid-air.

"Mam, it's far from being a child's game. Grown men are playing it. Look how popular Ajax is! There's money to be made in sports, Mama. I know you would never consider coming to watch me on Sundays, but I'm actually pretty good. If Hank can get us in to watch the youth matches, I'm definitely going. I could learn some great tips to take back to my team."

"You should grow up and if you have so much free time, spend it doing something useful like learning bookkeeping, so you can help André in the office while he spends more time learning the manufacturing."

Tiineke jumped in eagerly. "Mama Meijer, I can help André with the bookkeeping. You know I've already offered this. If Johan wants to play football, he should go ahead. There's little enough time to just have fun." Tiineke glanced over to Johan and smiled. He returned her smile with nod of thanks.

"You're over your mood from this morning, it seems." Agatha dark eyes seemed to pierce Tiineke.

Tiineke flushed, then lifted her chin. "I make the best of every situation, even if it isn't exactly what I would like."

"I'd much rather have Tiineke help me than Johan, anyway." André leaned sideways to dig his elbow in his brother's side, diffusing the tension.

Agatha crossed her arms across her chest. "If you have so much free time, I have other things for you to do as well. There are a pile of socks needing to be darned just waiting for someone."

Tiineke sighed. "Well, let's wait and see if Hank comes through and we'll take it from there. I'm not lying around reading novels or looking for things to do. In fact, I'd love to have an hour of time to spend on my painting again. I'm just willing to squeeze in a bit of time to help Johan if it means he can go out and enjoy himself a little."

Johan looked gratefully at Tiineke. "Yes, let's wait and see."

———

The next day, Johan was just closing the shop when Hank returned, calling his name as he entered.

"We're on! Tomorrow afternoon at two o'clock at the Olympic stadium. Meet me at the tower."

"Brilliant! Man I'm glad to see you. Friday evening used to be one of our busiest times but people just aren't shopping as they used to, are they? The evening seems to last forever." Johan put the last dust cover over a display with a flourish. "Let's walk a bit." He grinned as he pulled his soccer ball out from under the counter and tossed it to Hank.

Johan went around closing the shutters and finally locked up. He sighed as he escaped into the warm summer evening.

Toe, flip, kick over to Hank—the ball went easily between them as they danced and skipped along the street to the green on the corner. Johan never missed as the ball scooted back to him. Slap against his ankle, up in the air with his toe, a gentle slap with his instep and the ball went back to Hank. Hank was not as agile and often had to chase the ball is it slipped past him.

"Stop, give me a rest!" Hank was panting. "After all, I've been working in the warehouse all day. You've just been lounging around the shop."

Johan picked up his ball and carried it under his arm as they walked side by side more sedately. He looked up at Hank. "You're seventeen, right?"

"Yes, a big two years older than you." Hank patted Johan on the head.

"So will you be going back to school in September?"

"No. That's why I've been working as an apprentice. I'll be going to work with my father a year sooner than we first planned."

"Because Tiineke got married?"

"No. The first plan had been that, just like you, I'd be working in the shop so I'd take over from Tiineke. Now, though, my father has decided that he has to let our warehouse help go. He and I will do the job between us. My mother will take over from Tiineke at some point."

"A real family business."

"Yes, although between us, I'm not sure how much of a business there is in it anymore. Hardly anyone is buying. Even your mother has cut her orders quite a bit over the past year."

Both boys were silent as they came to the end of the street.

"I'll see you tomorrow at two o'clock then." Hank turned one way while Johan turned to retrace his steps. He dropped the ball and dribbled his way back home.

"Go then!" Tiineke laughed. "You're like a cat on a hot tin roof. You've seen a thousand matches, why is this one different?" She took a stack of towels from Johan and tucked them under her arm as she stepped behind the cash register to review the sales for the day, waving him out of the way.

"It's just that these are fellows who might be training for Ajax. They aren't your average guys on the Sunday afternoon pitch."

"Well, since it's a half-day at my dad's shop, I was free anyway, so get changed and be on your way. Since André is still working I might as well be working too." Tiineke pushed Johan towards the door.

Johan turned for one last parting comment. "You could be darning socks instead, of course, so I'm very grateful to you for helping me."

"No doubt the socks will be waiting for me." Tiineke grimaced.

It didn't take long for Johan to change into his casual clothes and a few moments later he burst free of the house and jogged the first few minutes towards the stadium. He was actually a bit early, it just felt so good to be out in the unusually warm late August afternoon. Sometimes he felt like a caged lion that just needed to exercise his muscles for the sheer pleasure of it.

Johan was gazing up at the Marathon Tower, which had housed the Olympic flame in 1928, when Hank joined him.

Johan lifted his arms to encompass the sight. "It's quite a place isn't it? I've been inside before but just for a tour. I'm really looking forward to this."

"It's just a practice, don't get excited. It's not like watching an actual match."

"I know, but still. It's inspiring, don't you think? I wonder how it feels to be playing on the same field as those big matches." Johan could see the field stretching ahead of him beyond the shoulder of the guard sitting on a stool in front of them. The guard's eyes were riveted on the field, and he scarely noticed Hank and Johan, only speaking to them over his shoulder.

"Yes?"

The guard was no older than they were and wore a blue and white striped football jersey. His hair was shorn in a brush-cut. He sat with his back propped against the brick wall, turned towards the field where twenty or so young men were lined up in two rows, kicking balls between them.

"We were told we could come and watch the practice." Hank gestured towards the field.

"Names?" The guard finally tore his attention away from the field and looked at a clipboard sitting on his lap.

"Hank Pol and Johan Meijer."

"Okay, go ahead. Sit anywhere in section A, but don't shout at the fellows on the field or throw anything. Just sit and watch."

Johan and Hank craned their necks to take in the massive oval as they skirted along the perimeter to the stands. The players on the field were clustered at one end and while Hank looked at the stands, Johan was already mezmerized by the action on the field.

"Hey, there's my friend from the warehouse. Let's go sit with him." Hank waved to his friend as they walked over.

"Cor, this is Johan."

Cor engulfed Johan's hand in his large brown one. His blue and white jersey fitted snugly around his barrel chest. He was about twenty years old and his muscular arms were the well-developed arms of a man who did physical labour for a living. His short, dark hair was streaked from the sun and his face was red.

Hank tugged on Cor's shirt when they were seated. "The fellow at the gate had the same shirt. What is it from?"

"It's the shirt of the Blauw-Wit football club—the Blue-White club. The team uniform is blue and white."

Hank nodded. "Yes of course. I should have realized that. I'm so keen on Ajax that I don't follow the Blue-Whites so much."

"The fellow at the gate is one of the team members. They have to take it in turn to mind the gate, carry water, look after uniforms, and whatever else needs doing." Cor pointed to the field. "Look, the practice match is about to begin. They've been here for an hour already doing exercises. At halftime I'll introduce you to my uncle."

On the field, a whistle blew. The white-bibbed side immediately took possession of the ball.

Johan punched the air and shouted. "Great move!" His eyes were glued to the players as the inside right kicked the ball deep to the corner where his midfielder charged in to take possession.

Johan took a quick glance at Hank and caught him grinning at Cor. Johan shrugged and turned back to the pitch, leaping to his feet to track the play as the ball went up and down the field.

Hank held a finger to his lips but smiled at Johan. "We're supposed to sit here silently. Remember the instruction."

"Impossible! Oh!" The boy groaned. "Pass it! Pass it!"

Thunk. They could hear from the stands as the ball hit the goalpost after a hard corner kick.

When the whistle blew after forty-five minutes, it was a tie game of 1-1.

"My shirt is stuck to me." Johan looked sheepish. "I can't help but get excited. They play well—for kids."

Cor rose and stretched. "Come on down and I'll introduce you to my uncle." Cor rose and stretched.

They clambered down the steps and over the wall separating the field from the stands.

"Heads up!" A ball came flying in their direction. Johan leaped and headed the ball back to the one who had kicked it over.

"Well played." Cor's uncle stood leaning against the boards, waiting for the boys. He was of middle height, slightly balding, slim, but wiry. He wore light-coloured trousers and an orange jersey. A whistle hung on his chest. The team sat or sprawled on the grass behind him, drinking cups of water. The boys who hadn't yet had a chance to play continued to kick the ball around, taking advantage of the empty field.

"Uncle Ton, this is my friend from work, Hank Pol, and his friend, Johan Meijer. Guys, my uncle, Ton Wils."

"Do you play?" Ton nodded to Johan.

"Only with a pick-up team on Sunday afternoons, but we do play inter-city sometimes, so it's good fun."

Again, the ball came towards them and Johan ran into the field a few steps to take possession. Knee bent, he hit the ball with his foot, bounced it up to his thigh, and juggled it for a moment before letting it drop back to his foot and kicking it over to the boy who stood, waiting.

"Show-off." Hank sounded good-natured.

Johan felt himself flush. He had been showing off, it was true.

"Well, that was a good audition. You seem to have pretty good eye-foot coordination." Ton looked thoughtful. "Are you interested in kicking the ball around a bit with the team?"

"Absolutely!" Johan couldn't hide his delight.

"I'm short a forward at the moment. Put on a bib and we'll bring you in as a substitute during the second half." He turned to the white-bibbed team. "This is Johan. Give him a bib." He blew the whistle and the teams organized themselves for the second half.

On the field, Ton blew his whistle again and pointed to the forward, then to Johan.

"Yes!" Hank called out as Johan feinted to freeze out his opponent.

In possession of the ball, Johan ran down the front third of the field, looking to shake his marker. Pass over to the midfielder who had moved up. Pass back. Change of pace from a slow dribble to an all-out spring as he blew by his marker and a hard kick sending the ball straight into the net.

"Goal!" Both Hank and Cor were on their feet.

Johan ran around in a circle, arms in the air. His teammates surrounded him, slapping him on the back.

The whistle blew and play was resumed.

For the next fifteen minutes, Johan passed, faked, and flew around the field, noting his teammates, watching openings, pacing himself, then bursting with speed, arms and elbows snug to his body, shielding the ball.

Final score: two to one for the white bibs!

The teams formed a line-up to shake hands. Everyone was eager to talk to Johan. "Well done!", "Great game!", "Can you show me that step-over you did?"

Suddenly Johan was shy. He hoped he didn't look like a show-off again.

Ton called out. "Johan, come over here for a moment, will you?"

Ton put his arm around Johan's shoulders and they paced together away from the group. "That was some pretty skilful playing. I'm looking for another forward for the team. What do you think, would you be interested? You can see it isn't any more glamorous than the team you're on now. The boys have to help out with everything to make the team work and you need to be in school and keep up with your studies. That is the prerequisite. Should I talk to your parents?"

Johan looked down, hesitating, then turned to face Ton. "I'd love to, I really would..."

"But?"

"My father died last year and my mother really needs me. I'm just not sure if I would have the time." *And my mother thinks playing football is nonsense.*

"Why don't I come by and speak to your mother and we'll see if we can work something out. The team could really use you if you think you'd like it."

Johan's grin was genuine. "I'd love to be on the team."

"Tell me when and where to go, then."

Johan set the time for Sunday afternoon as the most likely for his mother to be in a relaxed mood. Then he and Hank bid Ton and Cor farewell, and set off for home.

Hank's face was full of admiration as he threw Johan a sideways glance. "You were pretty great out there, better than a lot of them."

"I was surprised, I thought they'd be really good. Better than me." Johan shook his head.

"They were good, but you're better than you seem to realize. Did you ever consider football as a career?"

"You're kidding, right? My career path is laid out for me. No, this was just a fun afternoon. Now that I'm away from the stadium I realize that it's a waste of time to even have Mr. Wils speak to my mother. She'll never allow it. End of story. I shouldn't have let him talk me into allowing him come to see Mama."

"You're probably right, but no harm in trying. You're a great footballer and you should be allowed to use your skill." Hank crossed his arms in front of his chest. "Just like Tiineke is really a talented painter, and I hope she finds the time to keep it up. That was one thing about my parents. They always encouraged her. I don't have any of these hidden talents, unfortunately, so I'll just work away at whatever is necessary. Mind you, I wish I could have finished my last year at school. I was enjoying studying business." He let his arms drop and shrugged. "Never mind. I can always go back when things get better again."

They reached the corner to go their separate ways. Johan reached out impulsively and shook Hank's hand. "Thanks for arranging this. It was brilliant."

Hank grinned back. "It was fun. I'm looking forward to watching you play regularly."

"Hmm. Maybe." Johan lifted one shoulder, then waved and turned to make his way home.

———

It was evening by the time Johan got back to the house and made his way in to the living room.

Tiineke looked up from the socks she was darning. "Well, was it a good afternoon?"

Agatha sat at a small desk, reviewing invoices, André by her side. She was giving instruction on the proper filing method for the different types of invoices. Materials here, repairs there, transportation so. They both looked up as Johan hesitated.

"Yes, fantastic!" He could feel his face was flushed from the sun and his heart pounded. He sat and picked a sock from Tiineke's basket, mindlessly poking his finger through the hole in the heel.

Tiineke held out another sock to him. "Did you want to take over?"

"What? No." He flung the sock back in the basket.

Agatha studied her youngest son from under her black brows. "What's wrong with you?"

"Nothing's wrong. In fact, it was a great afternoon. I was asked by the team coach—Mr. Wils—to join in during the second half of the match. I did well. I scored a goal."

"That's great, Johan!" André made a circle with his forefinger and thumb. "Good man."

"And?" Agatha knew her younger son like the back of her hand. There was something more.

"Well, he thinks I should join the team, and he's coming here tomorrow to talk to you about it, Mam."

"What nonsense. Why did you invite him to come here? You know perfectly well that you don't have the time to add more sports to your life. I knew this was a foolish thing that would lead to no good when you were so excited about going today."

"Mama, I was thinking about it all the way home. I would give up my Sunday team in order to help out as I'm needed around the house or for bookkeeping or whatever. That would make up for my time for practice and matches."

Agatha slapped her hand on the desk. "Sunday is not when you are needed in the shop, and *that's* your job."

"But like today, maybe Tiineke could take over my Saturdays."

Tiineke looked alarmed. "I'm not sure about that, Johan. Once is okay, but I'm not sure about all the time." Tiineke shifted and the basket of darning fell to the floor.

"Look, could we just talk about it?" Johan held out his hands. "This is important to me."

"There's nothing to talk about." Agatha turned her attention back to her paperwork.

"Well, Mr. Wils is coming tomorrow regardless, and I don't know how to reach him to cancel." Shoulders hunched, Johan stalked from the room.

They heard him slam the door as he went upstairs.

André touched Agatha's arm. "I'll talk to him."

"I don't like sulking," Agatha said to no one in particular as she stacked the invoices. "I think we've done enough for today. I'll leave these here and tomorrow you can finish them. I'll review to make sure it is done properly." She looked at Tiineke and nodded. "You can leave that for now."

"I don't need to be told twice." Tiineke set aside the basket of sewing she had collected back together and stood up, stretching and rolling her head.

André stood up. "Come, let's go for a walk before supper." He held out his hand and Agatha watched as the two of them trotted out the kitchen door.

Agatha groaned as she stood. The small of her back often bothered her these days and she massaged it to ease the pain.

She moved from the straight-back wooden chair at the desk to the old wing chair by the window. Years of sunlight had faded the floral pattern, but it was comfortable with a high back that she could lean her head against. Left alone, she indulged in some time to simply think. Johan. *What will I do about him?* André had been so much trouble lately with his rush to marry, and now Johan, too, seemed to be rebelling. Why? *Where am I going wrong?* She let her mind drift back to when she was Johan's age. Fifteen.

"You're always so angry!" her mother had accused her. *"Can't you just cooperate with me once in a while?"* Her tone wheedling now. *"It isn't easy to raise a child alone. I hope you never know what it's like."*

"I am what you've made me!" Agatha had flung back. *"You're always telling me that people will take advantage if they are given half a chance, or that you need to make your own way in the world because you can never count on others. Well, I have learned the lessons, and I am making my own way!"*

"But you don't need to go against me!" Her mother had protested, but by then it was too late. *"You have a hard shell like a crab. I can't even talk to you anymore!"*

Life was a constant battle of wills from her early teens onward. At times Agatha won, and others—most times—her mother dominated.

Finally, when Agatha became engaged, tensions eased and, as if there was no longer a reason to keep up the fight, her mother had died a couple of years later.

Where am I going wrong? I've been careful to be firm with the boys but I'm not bitter. I'm not my mother. Agatha wanted the boys to have something solid when she was gone – something of their own to build on and be proud of. She wished they could see that.

"Mama?"

Agatha's eyes flew open. "I didn't hear you come in, Johan. You were much quieter than when you left the room."

"I'm sorry about that, Mam. I lost my temper. It's just that...I know you think the football is a waste of time, but it's important to me. Mama, I know I have to help in the house and business. I will, honestly. When you talk to Mr. Wils tomorrow, he'll tell you that the rules are quite strict about keeping up with schoolwork and I'm sure I'm not the only one who helps out at home or at a job. Will you just listen to what he has to say before you make up your mind?"

Agatha sighed. "I'll listen."

"Thank you, Mama!" Johan's face glowed. "What can I do to help with supper?"

Agatha could see that he was determined to prove himself already.

Agatha reached out her hand and Johan tugged her out of the chair.

She touched his hair. "You were always my cheerful boy."

Johan furrowed his brow at the unusual display of affection and skipped ahead of her to the kitchen to pull out the pail of potatoes from the storage area. "I'll start with the potatoes, will I?"

And the moment passed.

VIII

Fall 1929

The smell of onions assaulted Tiineke as soon as she walked in the door. Her stomach heaved.

"Oh God in Heaven." She was going to have to say something soon. The doctor had confirmed her pregnancy but she hadn't figured out how to tell anyone yet.

I thought the sickness was only a morning thing. She tried to breathe shallow through her mouth as she went into the kitchen.

Agatha gestured to the pot of onion stew. "We're having *hachee* for supper."

It was too much. She'd never manage it.

"Mama Meijer, I don't eat onions."

Agatha continued to stir the pot without even looking at Tiineke. "They were on sale and since we are feeding a larger family these days, we take advantage of what is on sale"

"Well, you don't have to worry about feeding me today, then. You've saved yourself some money." Tiineke whirled to go up to her room, but the sickness was too much, and she had to bolt for the toilet. A moment later, she emerged, shaking. "You see, it isn't my imagination. I really can't abide onions."

"We haven't been having onions for breakfast and yet it seems to me that you can't abide breakfast these days either."

Tears burned in Tiineke's eyes and her throat had a lump the size of an egg. Any second she'd burst out crying. Agatha knew.

Tiineke ran out to the warehouse and up the steps. She was dimly aware of André standing in the storage area with Mr. Van Loon, counting bales of material, as she rushed past them. Upstairs, she threw herself on the bed.

André came in softly, closing the door behind him. "Tiineke, are you alright? Shhh." He stroked her back. "Shhh, it'll be alright. What has Mama done now?"

Snuffling, she sat up. "Nothing, really. She's making *hachee* for supper when she knows I don't eat onions."

"Is that all? Mama probably didn't even remember about the onions. Don't worry, we'll make you an egg for supper, instead." André started to get up. "Mr. Van Loon is waiting for me."

"Wait, that isn't really it." She reached for his hand. "André, I'm sorry, I don't know what I should have done, I'm not sure..." She was fumbling for the words.

"Tiineke, what is it? I really should get back." He started to pull his hand away.

"I'm pregnant." Tiineke burst out with it, then sat, frozen, watching his face. She had his hand gripped in both of hers.

He stared at her, immobile. "Are you sure?"

"Yes, the doctor confirmed it."

André blinked as he absorbed the news. His mouth opened, then closed again, and he frowned slightly.

Tears again. Tiineke's vision blurred as her eyes filled. It wasn't the same explosion as before but a slow flooding that spilled down her cheeks.

André pulled his hand free and she was bereft as she felt the connection broken. Then arms, strong arms, were around her, pulling her tight to him. The smell of dust and cotton in his hair. The taste of sweat from his neck as her mouth was crushed against him in the awkward clutch.

He whispered against her hair over and over. "A baby, our baby, our own baby." His voice was full of wonder.

She was trembling. "Is it okay? Are you alright with it?"

"It's a miracle!" He pushed back from her and took her hands in his. "Are *you* well?" Suddenly worried. "You're always so tired. Will you be alright?"

"Yes, yes, I'll be fine. Apparently it's normal. The sickness and tiredness should go away in about another month. So, really, we'll make this work?"

"Of course we'll make it work. I'm not quite sure how, mind you, but yes, we'll figure it out." He sprang up. "Can I tell people?" He glanced at the door as though he wanted to run right out and tell Mr. Van Loon, who could still be heard grumbling and shifting things in the warehouse loft, just a few feet away from their rooms.

"We better tell our families first." Tiineke laughed. Suddenly, the world was sunny. "Finish your work before Mr. Van Loon complains to your employer. As soon as you are finished, come back and we'll go together to tell your mother."

André flung open the door and Tiineke could hear Mr. Van Loon exclaim. "God Almightly!" She could picture him standing, hand on heart, glaring at André, and André looking back at him with the big grin on his face.

Getting up from the bed, Tiineke closed the door and surveyed the two rooms that made up their little apartment. If the table that served as the dressing table were pushed further along and the chair placed beside it, one wall would be freed up to have a cradle and eventually a small bed. They would need more storage for baby clothes. There wasn't a fraction of space available in their wardrobe. Perhaps it could be built in under the child's bed. Tiineke made plans with a burst of energy she hadn't felt in weeks.

When André finished his work a few hours later, he came back for Tiineke. They went down the steps together and across to the house, her mood becoming more subdued with each step. She reached for the steady warmth of his hand and felt her own shake. "I don't know if my stomach is turning because of that god-awful smell of onions, or if I'm just afraid of your mother."

André squeezed her hand. "Don't worry about Mama. She always comes around, and she'll be an Oma! What woman doesn't want to be a grandmother?"

"Your mother doesn't strike me as the grandmotherly type."

Agatha waved her hand towards the table when she saw them. "Here you are, finally. Sit down at the table, please. Supper is more than ready. Johan is already here, waiting."

Tiineke took a deep breath. "I'm just having some bread and butter, Mama Meijer. I apologize for snapping at you earlier."

"Suit yourself." Agatha sniffed as she removed the dinner plate from Tiineke's place. She clattered down the smaller bread plate and immediately bowed her head to say grace.

"*Amen.*"

"And Dear God, thank you for the miracle that you have given us. *Amen.*" André added while all their heads were still bowed.

Johan raised his head. "What does that mean?"

Agatha sat back and crossed her arms, then made her hand into a fist and raised it to her lips. A few more seconds, and she seemed in control of herself again. "I knew it." Agatha looked at Tiineke. "You're pregnant."

"Really?" Johan swivelled his head looking from his mother to his brother. "Is that true?" He seemed uncertain about whether it it was good news or bad. His forehead was wrinkled and mouth twisted.

"Yes!" André was bursting, oblivious to his mother's glare. "You're going to be an uncle! How does that feel? I suppose you'll have to teach him football, since I'm hopeless at it."

Tiineke smiled. "It might be a girl, you know."

"Well, then she'll learn how to darn socks instead." André laughed, and turned to Agatha. "And Mama, what do you think? Can you imagine a little one calling you Oma?"

Agatha's voice was harsh and cold. "What I think seems to be irrelevant in this house anymore. If you had asked me before you made such a foolish mistake I would have told you that there is no money to bring a child in to this family. The world is a shaky place right now and the last thing we need are even more mouths to feed. What you need is to learn and become proficient at the business, not have even more distractions."

André shivered and reached for Tiineke's hand, resting it on his thigh. "Mama, I'm sure that people through the ages have said that there isn't enough money to bring a new baby into the family. If that was always heeded, there would be no new babies. We are having a baby and we will figure it out. I'll work extra. If necessary, I'll get another job outside of Meijer's."

"Are you blind?" Agatha spit out the words. "There are no jobs to be had. You can't just walk down the street and get another job. Everywhere people are *losing* their jobs. You are ready to work extra? Good, because I've known for a month that we would have to let people go and I've been holding off as long as possible. You will do the job of Mr. Van deMeer in receiving and completely take over the shipping so we can let Mr. Van Loon do all the mechanical work. That way we can let the part-time mechanic go, also." Agatha stood and carried her half-eaten supper to the kitchen, slamming the plate on the counter with a force that should have cracked the dish.

Sweating now, André's hand over Tiineke's was slick, his grip suddenly loose. She pulled her hand away and looked at him. His neck was red, making his face look white and pasty. He wiped his hand on his pants.

Tiineke touched his arm. "Are you alright?"

"Yes, fine." He attempted a small smile.

Johan's fork scraped against his plate and he looked up guiltily. "I was hungry."

André gave his brother a small smile. "You're right, of course. Eat. We should all eat. Tiineke, you especially. Have some bread." André buttered a slice and put it on her plate, nudging it closer to her. "Eat." He pushed away from the table and stood. She started to get up also, but he laid his hand on her shoulder, gently pushing her back down, and shook his head.

André walked to the kitchen where his mother stood, staring out the window.

"Mama, I'm sorry you are so upset over this. I'll do whatever I need to do to help and cover the extra expenses. Do the others really need to lose their jobs? Is there no other way?"

Agatha kept her blank gaze focused out the window. "No other way." Her deep sigh was almost a moan. "You boys just don't seem to understand."

She left him standing looking after her while she went out to the small courtyard to throw a handful of grain to the chickens.

"I'm sorry, Mr. Van deMeer. We've paid you until the end of the week, but you're free to leave now, if you wish." André held out an envelope to the man.

Mr. Van deMeer stood with his arms at his sides, not reaching for the envelope. "Please." His voice trembled.

Oh God, don't let him cry. I couldn't bear a middle-aged man crying. Why did Mama make me do this?

"Please." Mr. Van deMeer tried again. "Don't do this. I have a family to feed. Three young children…"

Agatha stood by André's side but said nothing.

Mr. Van deMeer turned his attention to her.

"Mrs. Meijer, I've been a good worker these past years. When your husband was alive, I helped him with many special projects and long hours. I've always been loyal to this business. Please."

When André said nothing further, Agatha sighed. "Yes, you have been a good and loyal worker. When business picks up, Meijer's will be happy to take you on again, but at the moment, there just is not enough work. My son's wife is having a baby"—she lifted her hands and shrugged—"and we need to cut costs."

She makes it sound as though it's Tiineke's fault.

Mr. Van deMeer's honest face fell. His eyebrows lowered. He looked at André, his skin ashen. "Congratulations."

He finally reached for the envelope and stuffed it into his pocket. He took his jacket from the hook on the wall and jammed his flat cap on his head, pulling the brim low, obscuring his eyes. He picked up his lunch-pail. He had come to work that morning a tall man with a ready smile. Now, shoulders slumped, he shuffled to the door, beaten.

André pulled the door closed, his hand slick on the door knob. "I feel sick."

"Yes." Agatha agreed, and left André to take over Mr. Van deMeer's job.

———

Tiineke's stomach rumbled and she looked at the clock. Seven o'clock. Supper was laid, but André had not come in yet.

Agatha glanced at the ticking clock, then waved Tiineke towards the kitchen. "Put a plate together and put it in the oven to stay warm. We'll eat without him."

"I can run out to see where he is. Perhaps he's almost done." Tiineke started to get up.

"No. He won't be done for a good hour yet, I'm certain. Put a plate in the oven." Agatha poured milk out for the three of them. "This is the life you are choosing for yourselves. You better get used to it."

Tiineke did as she was instructed, and the family—minus André—ate their supper for several minutes in silence.

Tiineke straightened her shoulders. *I refuse to let her get me down.* She smiled at her brother-in-law. "So, Johan, you've been to three training sessions now. Are you enjoying it as you thought you would?"

Johan grinned and nodded. "You can't imagine how much I love it. I'm so grateful that you are covering my shifts for me, and I rather like learning the bookkeeping side of the business. It's true that I have to spend time in the evenings to learn the accounting work, but that's alright because it's something I can do in my own time instead of being held to the hours of the shop.

"I know my schoolwork comes first, but it's amazing how much studying a person can get done while cycling. I just find that I'm more organized now and don't waste time talking while I'm having lunch or whatever. If I use my time better, I get it all done!"

Agatha tapped the side of her dish with her knife. "Eat your supper, Johan. All this chatter. If you have extra time, you can help your brother, since today he has taken on a whole new job. Maybe you can help him sort out the receiving paperwork."

"New job—what does that mean?"

"We let Mr. Van deMeer go today and André has taken over that job, as well as managing the shift."

"Oh no." Johan's shoulders slumped and his face fell.

Tiineke touched his arm. "Don't let it ruin your pleasure. It's not your fault."

He looked at her with a small smile. "Still, it does make football seem irrelevant." He turned back to his mother. "I'll go in right after I eat."

Tiineke caught the tiny twitch of Agatha's mouth as she stopped a smile of triumph. Tiineke's brow furrowed. "I can help him."

Agatha stood and started to clear the table. "I need your help here. After we clean up the kitchen I want to rearrange the display in the front window."

Tiineke glanced at Johan and lifted a shoulder in a small shrug. *Sorry.* It was clear Agatha would get her way this time. The boys would work together.

It only took Johan a few moments to eat and disappear into the plant. *My fine system needs to be adjusted.* How could this new twist be accommodated? Johan rarely fought against new burdens put on his shoulders, just reassessed and figured out what he needed to do to make it work.

Inside the office, André sat at the desk in a nest of papers.

"Hi." Johan slipped into a straight-backed wooden chair opposite his brother.

There were documents strewn all around the desk and on the floor. Johan looked around the small office. Black binders stood on shelves in a wooden bookcase against one wall. On a shelf that pulled out from the desk sat a black typewriter, the key faces stark white against the black metal of the machine. It was dusty. What did Mr. Van deMeer ever type? On one corner of the desk was a Burroughs adding machine, its tail of white tape hidden by the layer of yellow and pink papers. The 'in' box beside it was also buried.

"Hi. How was supper?" André leaned back in the wooden swivel chair making it squeak in protest. He ran his hands through his hair, pulling on it so it stood on end like the hair of a curly-headed rag doll.

"No one ever leans back in that chair."

"No, probably not. It doesn't like me sitting here. It's used to Mr. Van deMeer."

"Was it awful?"

André knew instantly what Johan meant. "Yes. Mama made it sound like the only reason we were letting him go was because Tiineke was having a baby. I thought he might cry."

Johan stood up and gestured to the desk. "Tell me what you're doing here and then let me carry on while you go eat your supper."

"Would you?"

"Yes, of course." Johan moved around the desk to look over André's shoulder. "It looks like a mess."

André explained the filing system as he understood it, and left Johan to it. "Just a short break."

Johan was already immersed in the puzzle of paperwork. "Go."

When André returned half an hour later, the piles of paper everywhere had been reduced to many neat stacks on the desk, some clipped together, others piled criss-cross.

André picked up one bundle and flipped through it. "Wow. You seem to have it under control already."

Johan leaned back in the chair, making it squeak again. "It surely wasn't so messy when Mr. Van deMeer left it, was it?"

"No, it just seemed to get worse and worse as I tried to understand it all."

"Well, I haven't done that much, really, but as a start, I just put all the same things in bundles, see? Pink with pink, shipping lists that he had stamped with 'Received' here, and so on."

André nodded. "You have a knack for this."

"I think Tiineke should be doing this, you know. Why does Mama seem so adamant against her helping in the office? She already has some training. You would think Mama would want to use it. You, on the other hand, are really good with customers, and maybe not so good with this sort of thing." Johan chewed his bottom lip, hoping he hadn't hurt his brother. But really, it was true.

André flung himself down on the hard wooden chair in front of the desk. Now it was he who sat on the opposite side while the younger brother worked. "I think Mama just doesn't want Tiineke to know the inner workings of the business. She just has this bee in her bonnet that you and I will run this business and Tiineke is fine as some kind of casual help, but not to actually know what goes on. It'll have to change because Tiineke is here to stay."

"Yes, you're probably right. It really seems that Mama can't accept having Tiineke around. I like it–I mean, I like *her*." Johan flushed and swivelled restlessly.

"I'm glad. Already, I can't imagine being without her." André laughed. "Of course, you get along with everyone."

"Mama will come around, I'm sure. Meanwhile, I'll help as I can." Johan put the last of the papers into a tray. "But for now, I better go and get my homework done, and then I have to show Mama the ledgers I brought up to date. I like doing the bookkeeping, but I sure can't take on shipping and receiving, too." Johan sighed as he stood up.

André rose as well and put his arm around Johan's shoulders. "Thank you for your help. You've already got it organized for me. Don't worry. I'll get the hang of it. You should be out having fun, not worrying about the business."

Johan shrugged. "What's family for?"

André called out as his brother left. "I'm glad that it's working out for you with the football!"

Johan turned and grinned before leaving André to muddle along.

IX

Fall 1929

Water slithered under Tiineke's collar and crept down her back. Icy cold sleet. Tiineke used one hand to pull her raincoat closer around her as she steered her bicycle with the other. Her teeth chattered. *Thank God I won't have to do this everyday anymore.* She had told her father she was giving up working for him She just couldn't do it anymore.

I wonder what's for supper tonight. It seems like there is nothing on sale these days but onions and more onions. Luckily I have no appetite anyway. All I want to do is sleep.

Tiineke continued to pedal sluggishly through the rain.

I had hoped that Papa would give me a bit of money for the work I've been doing. The first couple of weeks he did and then nothing. I wonder if I should have just asked. Well, it's at an end now anyway, so there's no point in thinking about it anymore.

Hunching her shoulders, water dripping from the tip of her nose, her stockings soaked through and feet like blocks of ice, she was finally home. "At last." She pulled in to the lean-to beside the house where they all kept their bikes, then went through the shop, passing her mother-in-law. "Mama Meijer, I'm making some cocoa to take out to André. Will you have a cup?"

Agatha frowned. "I had expected you would take over for me here. I need to meet with a supplier in half an hour."

Tiineke stifled a sigh. "Yes, I'll be here. It will only take a few minutes. I'm chilled to the bone and need something hot."

"Well, get on with it then. I don't need anything."

Tiineke continued into the kitchen without another word. *So much for trying to be nice. The heck with her.* Tiineke enjoyed the steam rising from the warming milk as she stood over the stove. By the time she had mixed the cocoa and walked over to the office, she was almost feeling relaxed.

"Hi there." Tiineke held out the mug of steaming cocoa to him.

"Ah." André took a deep sip. "What a treat."

"I felt a bit guilty walking past everyone at the machines. Is it alright that I bring this to you?"

"Oh yes. They had a break about half an hour ago. Don't let them intimidate you."

"It seems quiet, though. Are there fewer people working than last week?"

"Yes." André stood, sipping his cocoa and looking through the glass window of the office before turning back to Tiineke. "We let someone else go on Friday. Really, we only need three workers these days. The customers just keep cutting their orders and we can't keep people on when there isn't enough work. I hate it. The tears, the pleading. What can I do?" He shook his head and tipped up his mug to finish his drink.

"Poor you. I guess your mother has handed that over to you completely now?"

"Oh yes. It's part of running a business, I'm told."

"Speaking of mothers, I told mine today that I wouldn't be going back to Dad's shop anymore. I just can't keep going back and forth like that."

"I'm glad!" André reached for her hand. "It won't be so hard on you just being around here. How did your mother take it?"

"She understood. She knew it was coming, but still I think she's sorry."

André laughed. "Well of course. Now she'll have to take over."

"No, not just for that. I think she'll miss seeing me everyday. I'll miss seeing her, I know that."

They were quiet for a moment, then Tiineke tipped her mug to drain the last of the cocoa. "I better get down to the shop. Your mother is waiting." She scurried out, leaving her husband to his papers.

The stiff back and rigid way Agatha held her head told Tiineke that, although she had only been fifteen minutes, she was, nevertheless, overdue.

Tiineke smoothed her skirt with shaking hands. "I'm sorry. André and I got talking and the time ran away from me."

"Yes, of course, that could be predicted." Agatha marched out of the shop, leaving Tiineke in her wake.

A middle-aged woman, examing a stack of tea towels, looked up at Tiineke. "You're André's wife, aren't you?"

Tiineke pasted on a friendly smile. "Yes, I am. Are you a regular customer here?"

"I am. I have a small cafe and I go through linen at a shocking rate. I don't suppose she's a picnic to live with." The woman nodded her head in the direction Agatha had gone.

"She's alright. We're still getting used to each other. Now, what can I help you with?" Tiineke knew that whatever her issues might be with Agatha, she wasn't about to discuss them with customers. One never knew who you were talking to, and how things got around.

Disappointed there would be no gossip, the customer handed over the money for three tea towels, and left the shop.

Later, at supper, Tiineke again resolved to work at getting along with her mother-in-law. After all they'd be spending a lot of time together. *But I won't be intimidated.*

"The pea soup is delicious, Mama Meijer. Isn't it, André? It's just perfect on a night like this."

A gust of rain splattered against the window as if to emphasize the point, and Tiineke and André laughed together.

"Yes, delicious." André buttered a piece of bread to mop up the last of his bowl.

Agatha tilted her head, glancing from André to Tiineke. "You seem in a very good mood this evening."

"I think I feel better, knowing that I don't have to do the long day at Papa's shop anymore."

Agatha sat poised with her spoon in mid-air. "So you've given it up already."

"Yes. Now I can focus on helping more here. I know it has been a stretch with Johan's new schedule."

Johan looked up and raised his eyebrows. "That's great! Won't your Papa have a hard time, though? Will Hank have to work more?"

Tiineke smiled, knowing he was wondering if his friend would be less available. "I don't think Hank will be bothered. It really means that my mother will have to help fill in more. I think they might cut down on the hours a little anyway since there are never people in the evenings. They can just close up at five everyday and not lose a customer. It's quite common now."

Agatha pushed her empty dish aside. "Not at Meijer's."

Tiineke began to gather the dirty dishes. "No, no, I wasn't trying to suggest that it should be. After supper, let's work out the new roster. Johan, you'll be able to focus more on your football, and Mama Meijer, you might even like to take it a little bit easier, at least for now. I know that when the baby is born I won't be able to do as much, but for now, I can. I can even help with the bookkeeping, André."

"You work in the shop. André manages the operations, and Johan will continue to look after the books. It will be a help, though, that I can spend more time trying to get more business in." Agatha sounded grudgingly pleased.

"Very well, but if I'm finished in the shop and André still has work to do, I will help him." Tiineke stood up and stacked the dishes, taking them into the kitchen.

The sound of clattering dishes came from the kitchen as Tiineke started the washing up. Johan went in to help with the drying.

Agatha stayed at the table, lost in thought. *If she thinks she can start running things here, she has another thought coming. A little bit of bookkeeping knowledge and she's ready to take over Meijer's.*

"Take it easy indeed." Agatha spoke to no one in particular. "Does she think I'm ready to retire?"

André was exasperated. "Mama, she didn't mean anything by it. She just wants to pull her weight. Isn't that what you wanted?"

"Everyone needs to pull their own weight, but I think she doesn't understand how much work there is to running an operation like ours. She thinks it is like her father's, a small-time business. He's about to go under, by the way."

André's voice lowered. "What? What are you talking about?"

"So I've heard at the market." Agatha couldn't help the superior tone in her voice.

André bit a fingernail. "But that's terrible. Couldn't we help out? Buy a couple of extra shipments ahead of time?"

"As if we have money to spend on materials we don't need. All his stock will have to go up for auction, anyway, and perhaps I'll get some then at a better price."

"Mama, that won't help him! By then it will only be creditors that get paid. We should buy now to help him stay afloat."

"There would be no point. He can't stay afloat. André, be sensible. Meijer's comes first, always." Her voice grew softer. "It wouldn't be a kindness, André. Don't get me wrong. I like Mr. Pol. He was a good supplier to us and he's a hardworking man, but in this economy, not everyone makes it."

"Should I tell Tiineke, I wonder?" André looked at Agatha. He was a boy now, asking his mother for advice.

"I would wait. It is the Pol's family business. Let him do it on his own time." With that, she got up and went to the kitchen.

Agatha's voice floated back to André at the dining table. "Did you put away the rest of the soup into the cold room?"

André didn't listen to Tiineke's answer. He knew she did things as they should be done, but his mother just couldn't stop herself from asking, demanding, quizzing, always with the critical tone. He blocked them out and thought about the Pols. What would happen to them? He looked around the room, for a moment wondering if they could move in with the Meijers before dismissing the idea as ludicrous. Did they own their house? No, of course not. Most homes in their area were long-term leases. People lived their whole lives without owning their house or apartment.

He'll get another job.

But how? Jobs were impossible to find these days. Hank was working, at least, thank goodness. Hank had stayed on at the warehouse even while he was helping out in his own family business. So far they had kept him on, but the hours weren't full-time. Could he support himself and his parents on that one income? André rested his chin in his hand, his head throbbing.

Tiineke came back in the room. "Come on, lazy lump! Why are you sitting here still? You know your mother will find work for you to do if you look so aimless." Tiineke stopped and studied him. "Is something wrong?"

"No, nothing. Just taking advantage of the quiet moment." He smiled and stood. "I was thinking about how you said you'd miss your Mam. We should go see them on Sunday. Take her some flowers, maybe."

"Flowers to make up for not having me. Am I so easily replaced?" Tiineke smiled and took his hand. "That's thoughtful, and yes, that would be nice."

"And we should have them here for supper once in a while."

A small frown furrowed Tiineke's forehead. "I'm not sure that either your mother or my parents would really enjoy that."

He squeezed her hand gently with both of his. "Perhaps you're right." They hadn't gotten together since the wedding in June and he couldn't see making it a regular event now.

They settled together on the settee.

Tiineke had the basket with darning beside her. "Give me a little elbow room here!"

André slid over and picked up the newspaper.

X

Winter 1929

Tiineke shifted in the bed, getting comfortable. "Do you realize it has been four weeks already since I stopped working at Papa's shop?"

"Is it?" André was enjoying the best part of the day, lying together, hip to hip. He touched the swell of her belly. "When will I be able to feel the kicking, do you think? You've been feeling something for a week already, why can't I?" He was disappointed and not sure he really believed that she could feel something. Like butterflies, she had said.

"I don't know. I think in the next couple of weeks. I'm so glad I'm not going back and forth anymore."

André thought of Tiineke's parents. There had been no word about them closing the business. Hopefully it had just been a rumour.

Aloud he said, "Yes, I'm glad too. Your parents seem to be managing alright. At least, they didn't say anything when we saw them a couple of weeks ago."

"Yes, they seem good, but they were very quiet, weren't they?"

"Perhaps. I don't know them well enough to judge. Anyway, despite my mother's pessimistic mood, everything is going just fine isn't it?"

"Yes." She stroked his soft, curly hair. "Sinterklaas is coming up soon, the feast of St. Nicholas. This is really a fun time, although I love Christmas itself, too, with the carol singing and church services.

Imagine: next year we'll have our own small child to have fun with on Sinterklaas. We can make poems and toys just for him or her. What fun it will be. Meanwhile, I'm busy writing poems for Hank and Johan and thinking of what surprises I can make for them."

André had woken up a little more and lay with his arms behind his head. "Johan has really taken to the football, hasn't he? You can make a poem about that. I always knew he liked it, but he has developed a real…passion, I'd say."

"Hank tells me that Johan is very good and if he keeps with the youth team, he might even be picked for Ajax some day."

André shifted again to prop himself up on one elbow. Looking down, he brushed a strand of hair from Tiineke's face. "I can't imagine that happening. When he finishes school next year he'll be working for Meijer's, and that won't leave much time for big league football. Even now I can't imagine how he does it all. I think Mama keeps watching for something that he neglects so she can use it as a reason to tell him to quit."

Tiineke reached for André's hand and held it against her stomach. "He's very determined. Maybe he'll decide that Meijer's isn't what he wants to do with his life."

"Not work for Meijer's?" André hadn't ever considered that possibility. "It's preordained."

Tiineke looked at him to see if he was serious. "I think it's time to sleep." She sighed and turned, pulling the quilt up around her shoulders.

André cuddled close to her back and reached around to caress her belly as they both drifted off to sleep.

The next morning, Tiineke had a good appetite as she went down to the kitchen. Eggs for breakfast. She was glad to have one and thought it was probably good for the baby. It was warm and fragrant in the kitchen. *It's actually starting to feel like home here.* The thought was surprising.

Johan had already eaten and left for school. He went early these days to finish his schoolwork in the classroom. André had poured his coffee and was sitting at the table.

Tiineke rubbed her hands together and smiled at Agatha. "Gosh, it's cold up in the room above. It's always so good to come down here to the kitchen in the mornings. It's really cozy here." Tiineke felt that she didn't make enough of an effort, at times, to let Agatha know she was grateful for the things that were done for her.

Agatha sniffed. "Well, don't get too comfortable. As soon as breakfast is finished I need you to wash the shop windows. They're grimy after last night's storm."

André glanced at Tiineke with a frown. "Don't overdo it."

Tiineke smiled at him. "Don't worry, a little window washing won't kill me."

Agatha set a plate down in front of Tiineke, then sat down to her own breakfast. "I should say not. I worked everyday until each of you boys were born and then I only took a couple of weeks off until I was recovered enough that I could return to work. André, are you planning to go to work today or just spend the day gossiping?"

André finished his coffee in a hurry, coughing as the hot liquid went down. The last piece of bread was forked into his mouth. His mother had the effect of always making one rush. She continued to drive everyone, despite the fact there was less work to do these days.

Tiineke blew on her own coffee between small sips. "How do you plan to celebrate Sinterklaas, Mama Meijer?"

"We have a quiet dinner together. It's just as any other day for the most part."

"And what about gifts and poems?"

"We do usually exchange small gifts after supper, but certainly not poems. We stopped that by the time the boys were ten or twelve." Tiineke could hear the hint of a sneer in Agatha's voice.

"Well, my family always does the whole thing: gifts, poems, special things to eat. I plan to write poems this year too."

Agatha sniffed. "You will *not* write a poem, or even give a gift, for that matter, to me."

Tiineke shrugged. "I won't argue with you, but it's too bad. It's always fun."

"Fun. Life is not all about having fun." Agatha brushed a few tiny crumbs from the table on to her hand.

"What is it for, then?" Tiineke was genuinely curious.

"It is about making a place in the world so that you can leave something behind. It's about raising your family properly. It's about minding your own business." Agatha rose from the table. She emptied the crumbs from her hand on to her plate and picked up the dish. "And now I am going downtown to get some new yarn. We have an order that requires orange embroidery and we don't have the right colour. I leave you to open the shop." Having finished her speech, she exited, as though from a stage.

There were a few blissful moments of peace when her face suddenly reappeared in the kitchen window. "Don't forget the shop windows."

"Don't worry."

As if I could forget. Tiineke watched Agatha's tall, straight form, enshrouded in a black winter coat, make its way down the street. *There's no fear of her having too much fun in this life.*

Tiineke heaved a pail of warm, sudsy water outside, and began on the front windows.

XI

Winter 1929

"Stop! Stop! I have a pain in my side from laughing so much." Tiineke sputtered and wiped the tears from her cheeks. They had opened their Sinterklaas gifts and her poem to Johan had been about football. Now he was telling stories of his team.

Johan could hardly stop laughing himself. "Come on, I have to tell you the rest."

Tiineke held up her hand to stop him for a moment longer. Her other hand was on her chest as she tried to catch her breath. "Okay, wait. Alright I think I'm better now. So you were saying that your pal had scored his first goal and he was so happy that he tried to pull his shirt off while he was running around the field and it got stuck? Why would he even do that?"

"Yes. Why? Who knows. He saw someone do it once and I suppose he thought it added drama to the moment. So, yes as I was saying, his shirt got stuck and his shorts were slipping, so he was running around the field with his shirt tangled up over his head and all we could see was a long stretch of skinny white ribs and belly, like a fillet of sole waiting for sauce." Johan danced around the room, waving his arms in the air, demonstrating.

Tiineke gasped out words between laughter. "And then?"

"Then he felt his shorts slipping even more and tried to get a hand free to pull on them, but that was too much, and he fell in a heap after tripping over the corner of the net."

Agatha had had enough. "Johan, sit down! You'll break something with all this bouncing around."

"Sorry, Mama." The boy tried to bring his face to seriousness as he caught his mother's disapproving glare. Johan snorted. The effort was too much and his big grin broke out as he and Tiineke started laughing all over again.

Tiineke poked André in the ribs. "How can you sit there so serious?"

"Because he's sensible!" Agatha shook her head, her mouth drawn in a grim line.

André shrugged. He so rarely laughed with such abandon that he wasn't sure he even could anymore.

"You need a good laugh sometimes. It feels so great." Tiineke took another deep breath and rested her hands on her belly. "What a wonderful storyteller you are, Johan."

"We do have fun at football. It's serious as well, and when the coach is teaching us something, no one fools around. We need to be ready for the coming year. We are going to start playing teams from France and Belgium. Sometimes, though, especially after practice, we're all so hyper that we really kick up."

Agatha picked up a piece of wrapping paper from the floor and folded it neatly for reuse. "Johan, you were sixteen last month. Isn't it time you thought about giving it up?"

Johan's face paled and the grin slid from his face. "Mama, no. Don't ask it of me. We are really settling together as a team, and the fellows need me. I don't mean to sound like I have a big head, but I can play quite well and the team needs me."

Tiineke jumped in to support Johan. "Mama Meijer, we are managing quite well with the schedule. I think it's good for Johan to be part of the team."

André added his voice. "It's true, Mama. We're managing fine as it is."

"And when the baby is born? What then?" Agatha stood up, holding all the folded paper. She turned and put the paper on the desk. The room was tidy again.

"That isn't for a few more months. We'll figure it out then."

"Oh, for goodness sake. I was only suggesting you think about it." Agatha took her seat again and reached for her knitting bag.

There was a collective sigh of relief, but the festive mood was broken.

Johan crossed and uncrossed his legs restlessly. "Anyone for a game of cards?"

Tiineke reached beside her and lifted the large book on to her lap. "No, I think I'll look through my new history of Rembrandt."

André picked up yesterday's newspaper. "Not me."

Agatha had already begun knitting, continuing with a scarf she was making for André. "Turn on the radio."

They all listened in silence to the news about the decline in share prices on the Amsterdam market. Exports and prices continued to fall in the chain of events started by the Wall Street crash. Each one of them knew that falling prices meant tightening the belt even more.

———

A little more than three weeks later, André and Tiineke were visiting her parents.

"Oh, Mam! It's just beautiful, isn't it, André?" Tiineke held up the tiny yellow sweater with matching cap. "Thank you so much. It's the start of the baby collection. There are so many lovely things in the shops, but homemade is so much nicer. It's easy to see this was made with love."

"I enjoyed making it. It took my mind off other things to imagine our coming grandchild." Elsa sat down beside Tiineke, ignoring the puzzled look her daughter gave her. "How was Christmas? I missed having you by my side at the midnight service at the English Church."

"I missed being there with you all." Tiineke took her mother's hand in hers. Even now, Tiineke felt a prickling behind her eyes as she remembered how alone she felt sitting beside her stiff-backed mother-in-law on Christmas Eve. "Westerkerk is such a huge church, so different from our small, cozy church at the Begijnhof." Tiineke shivered, then pulled herself back to the present. "Don't get me wrong. The service in André's church—my church, I mean—was quite beautiful, but it wasn't the same."

"Well, Jan, how are things with you?" André turned away from the baby clothes and sniffles of his young wife and her mother.

Jan Pol looked at Elsa, but didn't respond. André turned back to look at Elsa also. At the silence, Tiineke looked at her father. She saw the glance between her parents as if they were communicating silently between themselves.

André picked up the baby sweater again, biting his lip as if he was sorry he had spoken.

Even Tiineke knew something was amiss in the long silence. "What is it?"

Jan began. "We didn't want to say anything before now. We didn't want to spoil the Christmas season."

Tiineke found herself squeezing her mother's hand tightly. "Say anything about what?"

"We are closing the business. We've been going downhill for the past year, and just can't manage any longer. Maybe in a year we can think of reopening..."

"You know that isn't true, Jan." Elsa pulled her hand away and crossed her arms. "Tiineke and André need to know the truth."

"Yes, alright. It isn't likely that we can ever reopen the business. We've lost everything and wouldn't be able to start up again. Certainly not at our age."

Tiineke's voice trembled. "But what will you do? How will you live?"

"We've been talking to my cousin, Rit, who lives in Rotterdam. We went to see her a few weeks ago. She is getting older, and she is a widow without children. She has a rather large house—enough room for us as well as herself, anyway—and she would like us to live with her to help her out. She can't manage the garden and shopping and all those sorts of things."

"To Rotterdam?" The words were muffled as Tiineke put both hands in front of her mouth.

"I'm so sorry to hear of the difficulties." André leaned over and placed his hand on Jan's arm. "But I'm glad that you have such a good solution arranged."

"Good solution? It's Rotterdam!" Tiineke leapt up and glared down at André, her hands splayed.

Elsa stood up and put her arm around Tiineke's shoulder. "André's right, Tiineke. Don't be so upset. We're grateful that we have a place to go. So many people these days are in the same boat and don't have anyone to fall back on or anywhere to go."

"And Hank, what will happen with him? He's surely not going to Rotterdam as well?" Tiineke shook her mother off and stood before her father, her hand pulling the skin of her throat.

"No. Luckily, he still has his job at the warehouse, although that's little enough. He will take a room and send us some money to help as he can. He has a friend in Haarlem and I think he plans to take a room in his house. It's further to go to work, but it's quite cheap and he's a big, strong fellow. It will be good exercise to cycle the extra distance every-day." Jan stood and led Tiineke back to the sofa, pushing her down gently.

Tiineke blinked. "I just can't take it in." She picked up the little sweater again and tears fell on the yellow yarn.

"I know, little girl." Jan sat on the arm of the sofa and pulled her into a hug.

Tiineke sniffled. "Hardly a little girl." The words were muffled against his chest.

"Always *my* little girl." He pushed back the loose strands of hair from her forehead as she sat back and tried a small smile.

"When? When are you going?"

"We'll give notice now that we have told you. It will take some time to make all the arrangements, so probably April."

Tiineke gripped her mother's hand. "You'll stay until the baby is born?"

Elsa stroked her daughter's hand. "No need to panic. One way or another, I will be here when the baby is born." She pulled her daughter close and murmured in Tiineke's ear. "Don't worry, I won't leave you alone with that jail-keeper mother-in-law."

Tiineke tried to smile and failed. Instead, she hugged her mother tightly. "I should be the one comforting you. Your whole lives are being turned upside down, and instead all I'm doing is worrying about myself. I'm so sorry."

André leaned towards Jan. "What can we do to help?"

Jan stood. "You can have a sherry with me."

"It's not quite a celebration."

"It's a celebration of all the good years we had."

The two of them went together to the kitchen to fetch glasses. The smile slid from Jan's face. His eyes filled with tears as he faced André and put his hand on his son-in-law's shoulder.

"She is my little girl, you know. I always thought I would be close by to look after her, if need be. Now I can hardly look after her mother and I. So I am handing the job to you."

Jan's face was serious and André hardly knew what to say.

"Yes, of course. That is the promise I made when we married, and I will."

"I need to say this to you." Jan gripped both of André's arms in his hands. "Don't be angry, but she counts on you for her happiness, and you need to be sure your mother isn't getting in the way of that."

André flushed. "My mother does her best, and after all, we are living in her home so we all need to find compromise, but don't worry. Tiineke is my first priority."

"Very good."

They collected the glasses and bottle of sherry when the front door banged shut. Hank was home.

"You're just in time." Jan set another glass on the tray as Hank poked his head in to the kitchen. "Come and have a drink with us."

Hank nodded to André and then raised an eyebrow to his father.

Jan lifted the tray and headed back in to the living room. "Yes, we've told them the news."

Hank followed his father and André, raising his hand in greeting to his mother and sister as his father handed around the glasses.

"To the good business that kept this family for so many years." Jan held his glass up for a toast.

They all clinked glasses, murmuring, "The good business."

"Well, Sus"—Hank called Tiineke the derivative of 'sister'—"can you imagine Papa retired and living an easy life?"

"No, I can't." Tiineke turned to her father with a smile. "You'll have the gardens reworked into a showpiece."

André felt his breath catch and his eyes burn as he watched the family while sipping his drink. He envied Tiineke's relationship with her parents and brother. He couldn't imagine hugging his mother, or even holding her hand. He smiled as Hank put his arm around his father's shoulder, teasing him about his retirement. They were working hard to get into a positive spirit about the disaster which had befallen them. They were all able to show their feelings. *How do you get like that, I wonder? However it happens, that's what I want for our baby. Tiineke will have to teach me.*

He wanted to join the conversation. "You'll have to get to know your way around all the shipyards so that when we send our son to you for holidays you can entertain him with sailing stories."

"Or daughter!" Tiineke rubbed her belly.

Elsa smiled. "Well, I'll have that much more time to make clothes for him or her. One thing we are not short of at the moment is wool, and you can be sure I'm keeping enough to knit all sorts of sweaters, hats, socks, everything and anything that can be produced by knitting will be made."

They laughed for a moment before the effort became too much. In the sudden silence, Elsa sniffed and pulled a handkerchief from her pocket. Jan tried to smile at her and then turned away to look out of the window.

Elsa shook herself. "Come, Tiineke. Let's you and I make some tea." Elsa rose and gave Tiineke her hand to pull her to her feet.

They went arm in arm to the kitchen. Left alone, the men dropped the cheerful facade. Suddenly, Jan looked years older.

"I never thought it would come to this. Leaving my business and living on someone's charity."

Hank shook his head and put his hand on his father's back. "Papa, you can't think like that. It's what family does, and I'm sure Rit will be glad for your company and help. I doubt if she sees this arrangement as charity."

"Whether she does or she doesn't, that's what it is. Well, it can't be helped. For now, I need to see what I can salvage. We'll need to take inventory and start selling off the stock and equipment." He seemed to shake off his depression as a dog shakes off water. The rest of the visit was spent making practical plans for the weeks to come.

Two hours later, Tiineke and André were on their way home. The tram wheels screeched, metal against metal. The jerking motion made Tiineke ill. Her upbeat attitude was gone and all she felt was sadness. She fought tears as they sat together in silence.

"We'll see them regularly, I promise you." André held her hand. It lay lifelessly in his.

"This will kill him."

"No, he seems resigned to it all, and he's just the kind of man who will make the best of things."

"Do you think so?" She looked at her husband.

"Yes, absolutely. Your father doesn't give up."

Tiineke turned and stared out the window of the tram. "Look at those people picketing outside that factory. There must be twenty of them. What do they hope to gain with their marching?"

"I don't know. Their jobs back, I suppose." André peered over her shoulder out the window.

"Where are the jobs going? Why is this happening?" It was as if it were the first time Tiineke really was aware of the problems all around her.

André answered truthfully. "I'm not really sure. My mother could probably explain it better than I can."

"Perhaps I'll ask her."

But both knew she wouldn't. Tiineke didn't want a lesson on global economics. She wanted her parents close by, happily working in their business.

When they arrived home, they found that Agatha had prepared a list of chores that they were to tackle during the upcoming week. Sitting in the living room, Tiineke couldn't focus on the conversation.

Agatha tapped the paper she was reading from and glared at Tiineke. "Are you listening?"

Tiineke lifted her head. "I'm sorry, what did you say?"

André ran his hand down Tiineke's arm, letting his hand rest on hers before turning to look at his mother. "Mama, Tiineke's had a shock. We just found out that her parents are closing their business and moving to Rotterdam."

"Ah. It had to come sooner or later."

Tiineke snatched her hand away from André and pointed at Agatha. "What do you mean?"

Agatha smoothed her list on her lap. "We've known for quite some time that this was coming."

"Who is we? I certainly didn't know."

André could feel himself getting hot. He tried to catch his mother's eye, but she ignored him.

"I knew. Many people in the trade could see it coming for a number of months. I spoke with André about it a few weeks ago."

Tiineke turned to André, her face pale above a deep red flush on her throat and neck. "You knew?"

He crossed his arms, then freed one hand, reaching for Tiineke. The hand slid back under his folded arm when Tiineke refused to take it. "I only knew the rumour, and there was no point in upsetting you with rumours."

"Maybe we could have done something to help, to prevent it from happening!" Tears slid down Tiineke's cheeks.

Agatha's voice was sharp and brittle. "Don't be silly. What could the two of you have done to prevent this? So many businesses are going under."

A gust of cold air blew in as Johan bounced in to the room. He stopped, seeing Tiineke crying. The grin slipped from his face as he glanced between his mother and sister-in-law. His eyes shifted back to the door as though he would like to turn and leave again, but instead he threw himself into a chair. "I had a great practice today."

"The Pols are going out of business." André nodded towards Tiineke.

"No! I don't believe it." Now it was Johan's face that paled and his brow furrowed. "I was talking to Hank yesterday. He never said a word. Are you sure about this?"

"Yes, we just came from there."

Tiineke pointed first to her husband, then to Agatha. "They knew. André and your mother. They knew it was coming."

André was defensive. "I couldn't have stopped it."

"Does Hank know?" Johan looked at Tiineke, his eyes wide.

"Everyone knew except for me, apparently."

Johan shook his head. "And me. So what will they do?"

André explained the Pols' plans.

Johan turned to his mother. "Can this happen to us, Mama?"

Agatha nodded. "It can happen to anyone who isn't prepared. I have always been looking ahead, though, and taking the necessary steps to make sure it doesn't happen to us. You boys can count on me, don't worry. We will be alright for the future, as long as we work together as we have always planned."

Tiineke gripped the arm of the sofa, her knuckles whitening. "Are you trying to say my parents caused this for themselves? The lost customers? The poor economy?"

"I'm not saying anything about your parents. I'm talking about Meijer's. This is the only business I know, and what I can say is that I have an eye on the future. What I know is that the boys and I need to continue to be vigilant, because things will get worse before they get better. The more we can rely on ourselves, the better it will be for us."

"I think I need to lie down for a while." Tiineke stood up. "André, are you coming up as well?"

André flipped out his pocket watch. "It's a bit early yet. You go ahead and I'll be there shortly." He turned to his mother. "Will we put the radio on for a while?"

Tiineke stood staring at André, her mouth open, then she snapped it closed and whirled on her heel to leave. There was a click and a buzz as the radio came on. André watched as she left the house to cross to the warehouse up to their own room.

Tiineke lay on the bed, fully clothed. Her dress, which had felt so pretty when she put it on to go out, was rumpled. Shivering, she unlaced her shoes and dropped them beside the bed before pulling the blanket over her. It was itchy and damp, and smelled musty. Why hadn't she noticed that before? Probably because André was usually there and his scent was always warm and comforting. The feather pillow felt hard and lumpy. She sat up and punched it a bit. Then punched it again. The tears spilled. Another punch. Another.

What am I doing here? Her parents needed her, and here she was, by herself, in a cold room in a warehouse.

I should be at home, comforting my mother.

Punch, sob. Finally, she stopped punching the hard pillow and groped in her pocket for her handkerchief. Home. *This is my home now. Even though it's a home where I'm always an intruder, always unwelcome.*

She lay down, clutching her white cotton hankie. The tears leaked and she dabbed at her eyes and cheeks until sleep brought release from her loneliness.

Darkness. Tiineke was dimly aware of André pulling back the sheet and blankets to slip into bed. He must have seen that she was still dressed and lying on top of the sheets, just under the top blanket because he switched on the bedside lamp.

"Tiineke, come to bed properly."

She awoke more fully, but still groggy and confused with a slight headache.

"Where were you? I needed you." She got out of bed to pull off her dress and shivered in the cold evening air.

André climbed back out of bed, his striped pajamas looking like a cartoon prison uniform.

"Come, let me help you now." His voice was contrite.

He pulled her flannel nightdress out from under the pillow and held it for her while she stepped out of her slip and underclothes. He slid the nightdress over her head. Like a child, she meekly stood and let him help. He flipped back the sheet and blankets and she slid into bed while he went around and climbed back in on his side, sliding close to her. He took her in his arms and positioned her head on the soft part between his collar bone and shoulder.

He stroked her hair with his free hand. "I'm sorry."

"For what?"

"For not coming sooner. For my mother's hard words. For your parents' problems."

"You're here now."

André stretched back for a moment and turned off the light, not letting her go.

Tiineke sighed. She was home.

XII

Spring 1930

The steps creaked and groaned. Even with the metal legs folded in, the bed hit the walls a couple of times as they carried it up the narrow stairs leading to André and Tiineke's rooms.

"Watch it!" The bed bumped painfully against André's shin.

"Sorry, but I can't see very well from down here, you know." Hank's voice was tired and grumpy. Over the past few weeks they had been slowly clearing out the Pol's house and shop. "Are we nearly there? My arms feel like they're going to give out."

"Nearly there. Now I need to go around the corner, so push up more if you can."

Pushing and pulling, they got the *opklapbed*—a folding bed—into the front room. This was to be the child's room. They had rearranged everything to make space for the new bed.

Hank leaned gratefully against the metal frame for a moment. "It'll be a long time before the little one can use this, I should think."

"I know. We're getting a cradle from someone Tiineke knows from school. That'll do for a while and then we need to get a cot of some sort. Tiineke's asking around."

"This was Tiineke's bed for her whole life before moving here." Hank patted the mattress.

"I know. I think that's why she was so keen to get it even though it'll be a while before it gets used." André dusted off his pants, then looked at Hank quizzically. "How are you managing?"

"I've taken a few things as well. Yes, it's hard to let all these things go. I'm trying to not think about it. I'm telling the folks to sell every last pot, if they can. They need the money."

"I know."

There was nothing more to say. André moved things around a little more to set the bed against the wall. The legs folded tight against the bed so it only took up a few inches of floor space when not in use. "Great inventions, aren't they? I'll make a shelf to go above it and we can put a curtain across to hide it."

"You're making yourself a regular little apartment here." Hank leaned against the wall, glancing around the room. "It's pretty comfortable. Or at least it would be, if it wasn't so cold."

"You get used to it. And it'll be spring soon, so then it's fine. I'm going down to the cart to get the easy chair as well. Tiineke just had to have it, even though it's going to make it pretty crowded."

Hank shook his head and grimaced. "I tried to talk Tiineke out of it, but she was determined. When no one bought it at our auction last week, she said she wasn't prepared to donate it to charity."

"I'll make it fit." André grinned. "Who needs walking around space?" There was a moment of silence. "How are your parents managing, stopping with their friends at the moment?"

"It's hard on all of them, but it's only for a few more weeks. Once they know Tiineke and the baby are alright, they'll be gone." Hank shrugged.

"I know Tiineke and your Mam are cleaning the house now. When is it actually getting handed over to the landlord?"

"Next week. Hank paused, sticking his hands in his pocket. "It's the only house I ever knew before now."

"It must be very strange in your room in Haarlem. Have you actually slept there yet?"

"No. Last night I slept on this bed at the house." Hank pulled his hand out of his pocket and again touched the bed. "Even though the place is three quarters empty, it still felt better than going to stay in a strange room."

André looked at the bed. "So I guess tonight you go to Haarlem, now that the bed is gone."

"There is still a pile of blankets there." Hank grinned. "I'm not leaving before I absolutely have to."

André and Hank went together to wrestle the armchair up the narrow stairs. "Hey, it's exciting about Johan, isn't it?" Hank's words were almost lost in the scraping noise as he slid the chair against the wall. He immediately plunked down on the chair, stretching out his long legs.

André looked up at Hank as he pushed the dressing table a little further into the corner in an effort to make room for all the furniture. "What do you mean?"

"Well, the team is going to Antwerp for their first real serious match. He must have told you."

"No, he didn't mention it. André perched against the edge of the dressing table. "I wonder why not. When is this supposed to happen?"

"In two weeks, I think. I've been so wrapped up in this whole thing with my parents that I haven't paid too much attention, but yes. I think it is in two weeks."

Before André could consider this, they heard Tiineke climbing the steps. At eight months pregnant, she had to stop a few times to catch her breath these days. The light trot of a few months ago was now measured and heavy.

"Well, it's finished." She gratefully took the easy chair that Hank relinquished to her. "Everything is clean and ready to hand over, and most things are gone except for those few bits you still have there, Hank."

André fussed over her, wiping a few beads of perspiration from her forehead. "How are you doing?"

"I'm alright." Her voice was low and tired sounding. "I suppose I'm used to it by now, and I'm just glad it's done. It'll be good for Mam and Papa when they get settled with Tante Rit." She gave her mother's cousin the respectful title of 'Aunt'. Tiineke stretched her neck and rolled her shoulders. Her face was pale with weariness. "These past few weeks have just been awful. They are like lost souls right now, staying with the neighbours. At least in Rotterdam they will have two rooms of their own. A little like we have here." She looked around. "It's not so bad, really. I'm so glad I got this chair. I can see myself sitting here with the baby, feeding and talking to her. It makes it feel a bit more like home for me, even though it's very crowded now."

André smiled. "I don't mind it crowded. You're right, we needed a proper chair here anyway."

Tiineke picked up the small yellow sweater that her mother had knitted. It had been lying on the dressing table since that horrible evening. "It's so soft, isn't it? Mama is a lovely knitter. I'm not nearly so good at it. She's taking wool with her and once she knows if we have a boy or a girl, she'll make some more outfits."

"Mama is good at it too. Her fingers really fly when she's knitting. Funny that she hasn't made anything for the baby yet." André leaned over to also touch the tiny garment.

Tiineke looked up from the sweater. "Yes."

Hank straightened up. "Well, I better get going. I'm meeting Mama and Papa to have some sandwiches at the house. Good bye, Sus. I'll see you soon."

Tiineke struggled to get out of the chair but gave up and stayed where she was. "Will you still have time? You'll be spending so much time cycling back and forth all the way to Haarlem."

"It's only seventeen kilometers, or so they say. I haven't actually measured it." Hank laughed. "It'll be very good for me to clear my mind and body from working in that warehouse." He leaned down to give his sister a quick hug and, waving at André, he left them alone.

Tiineke folded the small sweater and put laid it on the armrest. "So much change in one year, isn't it?"

"Yes, and the coming year will be a lot as well."

Tiineke shivered and pulled her sweater a little tighter, hugging herself. She leaned back in the chair and looked up at André.

He tilted his head and smiled at her. "What are you studying so carefully?"

"I hope our baby has your nose. You have a lovely, thin, straight nose. I also hope that they get your wavy hair."

André perched on the arm of her chair. "I don't know. I think you have beautiful hair. My hair is a curse."

She sighed. "Come. Help me out of this chair. We better go downstairs before your mother sends a search party up for us."

Tiineke gave one more glance around her small apartment and squeezed André's hand before they went down the stairs and into the house to the fragrance of cooking.

The meal was one of Johan's favourites. Brown beans and bacon.

"Delicious, Mama." Johan forked in another mouthful. "I was starving. This really hits the spot."

André looked over to his Johan. "How is the team doing, anyway?"

Johan glanced at his brother and wondered if Hank had told him about the trip to Antwerp.

"Good."

The sound of forks scraping the plates sounded loud.

"Well, great, really." Johan took a breath. "Actually, the team is going to Antwerp for their first international match. The weekend after next, the team is taking the train to Antwerp and staying overnight."

Agatha peered at Johan. "You don't think you're going, I hope."

"Mama, I have to go. I'm the star. Well, the main forward, anyway. How can I not go?"

Agatha put her knife and fork down on her plate. Her jaw was rigid. "I knew it would come to this one day. You pleaded and harassed me to let you join the team with the understanding that it wouldn't take you away from your responsibilities. How do you propose to go away for a whole weekend and not have it affect your work?" Agatha's voice was shaking with anger. "I knew this infatuation with football would cause problems. You boys have no vision. You need to be putting your energy towards your future, not silly pass-times like football. Well, what do you have to say?"

"Mama, I'm not quite sure yet, but I'm working on a plan. If I can cover my shift, can I go?"

Agatha took a deep breath and exhaled slowly. When she spoke she seemed more controlled. "What about the cost? I'm sure that you can't take a train and stay in hotels for free. I'm not giving you one guilder towards the cost of this."

Johan broke out into a big smile. "No need, Mama. Some of the fellows from well-off families don't like helping with team chores after practice, so they've been paying me to do them. With all that, I've saved up my share, and the rest is subsidised by the Royal Netherlands Football Association." Johan glanced at André, who nodded.

Agatha's face was pale. "So you have been getting money and not contributing to the family."

Johan crossed his arms. "Mama, it isn't much. And I contribute by working."

Agatha stood and started clearing the table. There was nothing further she could say.

Johan leaned closer to André and Tiineke. "Will you guys help me?"

Tiineke lowered her voice and gave Johan a conspiratorial smile. "If I'm not in the middle of having a baby."

André nodded. "Yes, of course. Good man for having the money part sorted. Aren't you so very clever."

"Actually I'm not, it just worked out."

Johan got up and went through to the kitchen. "Mama?" The door to the garden courtyard stood open. *Oh oh.* That was a sure sign Mama was upset. She always went out to talk to the chickens when she needed time to think.

"Mama? Are you alright?" He stepped out into the small yard.

"I'm fine." Agatha let a handful of grain trickle through her fingers to the excited fluttering of the chickens. The rooster pecked and crowed at the chickens to let him through as they crowded around their mistress. She looked at Johan briefly, then turned away again. "Johan, you have no vision for your future." Her voice was low and she looked down as if she was speaking to the chickens. She brushed her hands together to loosen the last few seeds from her damp hands. "You just can't seem to understand that you need to be thinking and working on things *now* in order to be successful in the future. All I can do is keep working as best I can on your behalf and hope that you grow up one of these days and understand." She looked at him sadly. "I'm fine, but yes, I am disappointed in you right now."

Johan looked at his mother. He was taller than her now, yet she was strong and wiry. The dark hair scraped back into the usual hard knot on the back of her head showed a few grey threads. He realized she had always frightened him a little. Her glasses and hair, her black wool dresses and stern lace-up shoes—together they were like a suit of armour. She was a general, always ready to do battle.

While André had often tried to rebel against the regime, Johan had always tried to compromise. His way was to find the small chink in the armour and win his point through cajoling and persuasion. This time, though, something inside Johan flared.

"Mama, you're *wrong*." His voice sounded strong, more a man's voice than a boy's.

Her head snapped back on her neck as if he had struck her. "What does that mean?" Her eyes narrowed and lips pursed.

"I do have a vision for my future. It may not be the same vision as yours but I do have one, and in my opinion, I am working on achieving it."

His mother's voice was cold and sarcastic. "Oh yes. And would you like to share that vision with me?" Her black eyebrows pulled together in a frown that must have ached.

He slid his hands in his pockets. "I plan to be a professional footballer."

"What nonsense." She spit the words at him. "That *vision* tells me just how much of a boy you really are. There are sixteen-year-old boys out there working for a living in these hard days, and here you are, still playing children's games. Grow up." She pushed past him to go back in the house, shaking.

"Mama Meijer?" Johan heard Tiineke's voice as Agatha swept past on her way upstairs.

"I'm busy." Agatha's voice was muffled as the door banged closed behind her. Johan stormed in to where André and Tiineke were finishing up the dishes.

André put his hand on Johan's arm to stop him. "What's going on?"

Johan's voice shook. "She won't take me seriously."

André laid his tea towel over Tiineke's shoulder, looking at her. "Will you be alright on your own for a bit?"

"Yes, of course. Go." She nodded towards the front door.

"Come, brother. Let's go for a walk, you and I." André reached for both their jackets from the hooks by the back door and tossed Johan his.

André had taken to wearing a bowler hat versus a cap, and set that on his head, while Johan threw his cap over his blond curls. They were the same height, but André's thinner build made him look taller, while Johan's strong muscular build made him look more formidable.

Tiineke watched their receding backs from the kitchen window and sighed. If even Johan and his mother were arguing, there was no hope for a happy household.

After finishing washing, drying, and tidying the dishes, Tiineke sat down in the big wing chair in the sitting room. It was rare that she had the room to herself, so she didn't often sit in that chair.

It's not a bad room. It always felt so uncomfortable because of the atmosphere, not the furniture. The realization was surprising.

Kick. Kick again. The baby was active tonight. Tiineke sat, dreaming for a few minutes, trying to imagine what it would be like once the baby arrived and they all sat here in the evening. Would Mama

Meijer become mellower with a baby in the house, or even more of a sergeant-at-arms?

There was movement above her head in the small room that was used as a storage room of sorts.

Should I go and offer my help with whatever it is? She decided against it. Agatha would have no problem shouting for her to come and help if she wanted it. It seemed odd, though, to have these few minutes alone without a task to do. Remembering back to when she lived at home, there were often evenings like this. Not needed by her parents, she would take out her paints and spend hours creating. She enjoyed doing landscapes and would either use old sketches or just imagine a place she had seen and try to recreate it. She hadn't taken out her paints all these months that she had been married. Where had her dreams of being an artist gone? Would she ever find the time to paint again? With a baby on the way, it seemed even less likely.

The noise from upstairs was louder. What in the world was Agatha doing?

Tiineke pushed herself up to go and get the basket of darning. She switched on the radio to muffle the sound of boxes and trunks moving around above her head. World news. The United States of America was in a full-blown depression. More people had jumped out of buildings as their stocks plummeted. In the Netherlands, the shipping sector was suffering because exports were down. Everywhere it seemed that people were suffering.

Thank goodness Mama and Papa are going to Tante Rit. This was a complete reversal of what she had thought previously, but she now felt that at least they had a roof over their heads. They wouldn't need to worry about where their next meal would be coming from. She was suddenly grateful that Mama Meijer had let her and André make a home for themselves here. It wasn't perfect, but it was secure. She stood up and went to the door to upstairs.

"Mama Meijer, shall I make you a cup of tea?"

"Yes, put the kettle on. I'll be down in a few minutes." Agatha's voice echoed down the stairwell.

Well, she sounded in better humour, anyway. *I'll make a big pot, just in case the boys are back soon.*

By the time the tea was made, it was dark outside.

Agatha came in to the sitting room. "Where is everyone?" She dropped an armload of clothes on to the sofa.

Before Tiineke could answer, the door opened, and the boys came in with a gust of cold air. They were laughing and Johan's cheeks were rosy from the spring night. André's glasses fogged up and he took out his large white handkerchief to polish them and wipe his dripping nose. While Johan looked fresh and healthy from being outside, André looked pinched and chilled.

Tiineke smiled at them. "Just in time. I've made a pot of tea. Come, André, and help me carry it in."

Although their voices were low, Tiineke could hear as Johan spoke to his mother. "Mama, I'm sorry I upset you earlier. I know you only have my best interests at heart. I need to try this for myself, though. I am very good at football and need to see where it can take me. I do realize, though, that I can't put all my eggs in one basket."

Tiineke wondered if Agatha caught the reference to her beloved chickens.

"I am going to continue to work as hard as I can for Meijer's as well, at the same time as my football. Just as I have been doing."

"I suppose André talked some sense into you." Agatha was thawing slightly. She glanced at André as he and Tiineke came in to the room carrying the tea things.

"He didn't have to talk sense into me, Mam. I always intended to continue to work on both things. What he reminded me, though, was that you are always working for our good, and maybe for a moment I forgot that part, so I'm sorry if I was sharp with you. I wish you would come see me play sometime, Mama. Maybe then you would understand better."

Agatha sniffed and pursed her lips as she turned away from Johan. "I don't have time for games." Agatha looked up at her daughter-in-law. "Tiineke, I pulled out clothes that I still had from when the boys were babies." Agatha gestured to the pile of clothes.

"Ah, that's what I heard. You were digging in the trunks upstairs." Tiineke sorted through the clothes. "Let me see. How wonderful that you saved these things all these years. This is nice." She held up a small sailor suit to show André. "You must have been adorable in it." She continued rummaging through the pile. "I'm not sure about this, though." She held up a woollen one-piece sleeper with buttons. It was yellowed and had a stain on the front.

"It'll be fine when it's washed. The child won't notice a small stain on it." Agatha sat sipping her tea, watching Tiineke handle the garments. "You don't have the money to turn down perfectly good baby clothes."

"No, I'm sure we don't." Tiineke set aside the clothes and picked up her own tea.

André folded the small sleeper and put it back on the pile. "Let's take them all with us after we have our tea and sort through them up in our room." He looked at Tiineke, his eyebrows raised. She could see he was pleading with her not to start anything with his mother. André gave Tiineke a small smaile when she nodded and he turned to his mother. "Thank you for digging these out for us, Mama."

"Yes, Mama Meijer, it was very good of you. I'm sure if we have a boy, they'll really be put to good use." Tiineke nodded towards the pile.

"Are you saying that if you have a girl you won't use them?" Agatha put her tea cup down.

André tipped up his cup, finishing his tea in one gulp, and started to gather the clothing. "I'm sure that isn't what Tiineke meant."

Tiineke glared at André, then turned to Agatha. "What I'm saying is that while this sailor suit is lovely, no, I wouldn't put it on a girl."

"What a silly, wasteful girl you are, then. At that age, it makes no difference."

"Can we just wait and see before we get into a big debate about it?" André stood up and rolled his head tiredly.

Tiineke gathered up the clothes and stood, nodding to Johan and Agatha. "Good night."

No more needed to be said.

Over the next few days, Tiineke washed and hung the small clothes out to dry in the early spring afternoons. The days favoured her with sun and a crisp breeze.

Later that week, she showed the clothes to her own mother. "We'll hope for a boy."

Elsa studied each piece. "For the most part, they're fine, although there is no doubt they are boy's clothes. Never mind. Here is something to help the wardrobe." Elsa smiled as she pulled a small parcel from her bag.

"Oh, Mam." Tiineke held up the tiny white sweater with green ducks swimming across the front and matching green pants. "It's so beautiful. Whether I have a boy or a girl, this will look beautiful, and the yellow sweater you made before will go with the green pants as well."

Elsa glanced at the clock. An hour had passed since they had come up to see the clothes. "It's chilly up here. We should go downstairs before Mrs. Meijer thinks we are very rude."

Tears welled in Tiineke's eyes. "I never get to be alone with you anymore. I just want to keep you for myself."

"Come now. No tears. You'll have me plenty of times yet over the next few weeks." Elsa stood and pulled Tiineke up with her. Together, they headed downstairs.

Elsa rubbed her hands together as she entered the living room. "Mrs. Meijer, the clothes you gave Tiineke are wonderful. How nice that you kept them all these years. I'm sure the baby will get good use of them."

"Yes, I'm sure also. If Tiineke will use them."

"I will. I'm sorry if I didn't seem grateful for them before. I am, of course." Tiineke sank onto the sofa.

Before Agatha could offer any further comment, the shop doorbell tinkled, and Agatha went through to serve the customer.

"At least there are still customers coming here, then." A shadow crossed Elsa's face.

"Yes, but not all that many. I think they do more business with exporting to a couple of big customers in Germany and France than people coming in off the street. I don't really know, though. Mama Meijer doesn't let me get too close to the business."

Elsa was surprised. "Why ever not? You were so good with the bookkeeping after you took the course. You could be a help here."

"Johan does the bookkeeping under Mama Meijer's supervision and André is managing the plant. Anyway, soon I will be busy doing other things." Tiineke smiled and rubbed her belly.

"Have you found a midwife yet?" Elsa also touched Tiineke's belly.

"Oh yes! She's so nice and kind. I'm to call her 'Tante Miep'. She checked out our room and, while she's not entirely happy with it because it is pretty far from the hot water, she said she's seen worse places, so we'll be fine." Tiineke nodded. She didn't really want to think about the actual birthing process. She preferred to think about having it done and over with and the beautiful little baby in her arms. Tiineke took her mother's hand and held it in both of hers. Her voice shook and she blinked back tears. "Mama, will you come to be with me when it's happening?"

"Yes, of course! That's why we are staying until then. I'll be with you. You just need to send André or Johan to us when your water breaks and then I'll come as quick as I can."

Tiineke's voice dropped to a whisper and she leaned close to her mother. "You don't think Mama Meijer will want to be there, do you?"

"Oh, I don't think so. Besides, a girl's mother has precedence, and there certainly isn't room there for all of us, so if she tries to come in, I'll chase her away, don't you worry." Elsa smiled and stroked her daughter's hand.

Bang bang bang.

Elsa heard her husband muttering. "Who in the world can that be at this hour?"

They flipped on their bedroom light. It was one o'clock in the morning. A dog barked inside a neighbor's house, its voice muffled but audible in the silence of the night. Jan slid open the window and looked down where Johan stood on the doorstep.

Elsa could hear the boy's voice. "It's time!"

Jan waved once to acknowledge Johan. "Oh! She'll be right down."

Elsa could hear Jan go down and open the door as she threw her clothes on. His voice floated up to her. "You'll have to wait a few minutes while Elsa pulls herself together. Has Tiineke been in labour long?"

Elsa came down the stairs to see Johan shrug. He seemed confused and his eyes were wide and frightened looking.

"Here she is now." Jan patted Johan's shoulder. "Don't worry, these things always work out."

"Go back to bed." Elsa gave her husband a peck on the cheek.

"Are you sure you don't want me to go over with you? It's very late and these days there are some very undesirable people wandering around at night." Jan looked up and down the quiet street.

She gestured to Johan. "Look at this strapping boy."

A strapping boy who was starting to look more relaxed now that Elsa, so calm herself, was with him.

Jan looked up at Johan. "Yes, you've really grown this past year. I suppose you can probably look after my wife's safety better than I can these days. Alright. I'll be over in the morning to see what progress there is." Jan kissed his wife. "Give her a hug for me."

Johan climbed back on his bike, nodding to Jan as he waited impatiently for Elsa. "Well, good bye then. We'll see you later!"

Elsa pulled her own bicycle out from the small lean-to where all the household bikes were locked up. Johan put his foot on his pedal. "Ready?"

"Ready!" And with that, the two of them set off.

Light spilled out into the night from several windows as they arrived at the Meijers' house twenty minutes later. They had hardly spoken on the ride over, each quiet and busy with their own thoughts.

Elsa nodded to Johan as she rested her bicycle against the house. "I'm going straight up."

"Yes, go. I'll lock the bikes. Go." He practically pushed her towards the warehouse door.

Elsa ran up to André and Tiineke's rooms, walking straight through to the bedroom. "Sweetheart, I'm here."

"Mama!" The relief in Tiineke's voice was apparent. "Oh my God, my back hurts."

André sat perched on the edge of the bed, rubbing his wife's back as she lay on her side. He looked up, his face stricken and pale. Sweat beaded his forehead and his hair was damp. "What should I do?"

The midwife nudged André with her elbow. "I've already told you that you should go down and join your mother and brother. We can manage this ourselves. She doesn't need you here right now."

André shifted but stayed by Tiineke's side. "Tiineke? Do you want me to go or stay?"

"Mama's here now. It's okay. Go on." Tiineke's voice was high with stress.

André sprang from the bed. "I'm right there if you need me." He leaned down and kissed her forehead.

He whispered to Elsa as he passed on his way out. "I'm so glad you're here."

Elsa smiled. "It'll be fine. Don't worry."

His footsteps clipped down the stairs and out of the warehouse. *Running to his mother.*

Elsa turned her attention to Tiineke and the midwife. "How long has it been?"

"Hard to say for certain, but her water broke several hours ago now." Tante Miep looked at the watch she wore on a chain tucked into the waistband of her white apron.

Tiineke lay on her side, breathing shallowly, tears trickling down her cheeks.

116

Elsa took up the spot André had left and began kneading Tiineke's back. "There, there, sweetheart. In a few hours, this part will be over and you'll have a beautiful baby in your arms."

"Let it be over soon." Tiineke whimpered and then gasped as another pain engulfed her.

"Try not to push yet." Miep straightened up from examining Tiineke. "You are only five centimetres and should be eight before you start to push. Puff-puff-puff, like so." She made a puffing breath. "Don't push. Easy, easy. Good. Still eight minutes apart. You have a way to go yet. Why don't you get on your knees for a few moments? That will help to ease the pain in your back a little bit."

The hours went by with Tiineke shifting position every few minutes. Laying on her side, on her back. Up on her knees, then standing and walking around the two rooms for a little. Elsa went down and got a thermos of tea for her and Miep. Tiineke had some water, and then threw it up.

At long last Tiineke was on her back and straining to push, gasping between painful contractions. "Never again!"

"Push, push, push." Miep tugged gently on the emerging baby. "You're nearly there."

With a scream and a grunt, Tiineke gave one last mighty push. Elsa gripped her hands tightly, and then released. It was done. A thin mewling cry, and the baby was laid on Tiineke's breast. Miep pushed down on Tiineke's body to help finish the last stages of delivery but Tiineke hardly seemed aware of it.

A boy. A perfect tiny boy.

Tiineke felt a physical wrench when the baby was lifted away and washed in a basin of warm water her mother had ready.

The clean-up finished, Tiineke sat propped up against the firm feather pillows, dressed in her favourite pink flannel nightgown, and weeping on the baby's small, soft head. She couldn't have explained why she was weeping. "He's so beautiful, he's so beautiful."

There was a tentative knock on the door. "Is everything alright?" André's voice was shaky.

Tiineke gestured to her mother without looking up from the baby. "Oh Mama, bring André in. André, come!"

She looked up long enough to see André come through the door.

Elsa smiled and squeezed his shoulder. "Congratulations, Papa. You have a beautiful baby boy."

He came to the bedside.

"Look André, look at our son." Tiineke looked up at her husband with eyes still blurry with tears.

The world stopped. André couldn't speak as his heart swelled and breath caught. He perched on the edge of the bed but found he couldn't see very well, so slid over, closer to Tiineke.

"He's perfect." André held his forefinger out to stroke one of the baby's tiny, pink hands. He gasped when the baby grasped the finger. André's eyes widened. "He's strong already. Tiineke. Oh Tiineke." He looked away from the baby and into his wife's eyes. "You and this baby. You are my future. You are my dreams. My future." He swallowed and chewed his top lip. He shook his head, unable to say all the things he felt.

Tiineke gazed back at him and then down at their son. She didn't speak. She didn't need to.

Tante Miep cleared her throat. "And now, I think my work is done, so I'll be leaving you all to celebrate. Perhaps, sir, I could just speak with you a moment."

It was painful, but André backed away from the bed a few steps before turning to follow Miep out to the hall.

She picked up her medical bag. "I'll return in two days to check on them, but everything went very well, and I'm sure both mother and son will be just fine. So now the small matter of my bill..."

"Your bill, oh, yes, of course. Please come with me. My mother handles the family finances."

André led the way downstairs and over to the house. Daylight had broken and birds were chirping. The rooster was crowing from the back garden. The world was alive and fresh and full of song. They went in to the sitting room where both Agatha and Johan were sitting, reading the morning newspaper.

André grinned at his brother and mother. "It's a boy!"

Johan jumped up and pumped his brother's hand. "Congratulations!"

Agatha folded the newspaper on her lap and nodded. "A boy to carry on the Meijer name. That's good."

"Can I see him, or is it too soon?" Johan flushed.

André smiled at his brother's sudden shyness. "Yes, of course, come." Already André was a proud Papa, anxious to show off his new son. He gestured to the midwife. "Tante Miep, I leave you to my mother."

With that, the two brothers raced to the warehouse together.

"What are you naming him?" The boys stood in the bedroom together looking down at the small, sleeping baby cradled in Tiineke's arms. Elsa had dragged the easy chair from the front room to beside the bed.

Tiineke looked up at André. "André, are we still agreed on what we want?"

"Yes. His name is…" The moment seemed awesome and André hesitated for a second before continuing. "Willem Jan Meijer, 'Wim' for short."

"After the two grandfathers." Tiineke smiled at her mother.

Elsa reached across and took Tiineke's hand, giving it a squeeze. "Your father will be so pleased."

They sat together, André on the bed beside his wife and sleeping son, Elsa in the big chair that once presided in her own living room and Johan on the wooden chair from the dressing table. They spoke little, just watching the sleeping baby as one might gaze out at a breathtaking view, until Johan started to nod off.

He snapped awake with a jerk and rubbed his eyes. "I'm sorry, but I think I'll go and lie down now that the excitement is over."

"Yes, do, and Johan, thank you for your help in going for my mother." Tiineke smiled at him, then looked down at the baby. "Oom Johan will see you later, Wim."

Johan blushed and tilted his head, looking at Wim. "Yes, I am an uncle – an Oom." He paused "I'm going to be the best uncle around."

André smiled at Tiineke at the solemn vow his brother was making to the baby. He stood and rested his arm on his brother's shoulder for a moment. "Johan, when you go down, let Mama know that she can come up now, if she likes. She probably thinks it's so crowded here that she hasn't wanted to come up yet."

Tiineke and her mother exchanged a quick glance before Tiineke nodded. "Yes, of course she's welcome, and could have come up any time this last half hour."

Johan grinned. "Yes, of course. I'll go down now."

Johan found his mother in the kitchen. "Mama, I'm going to lay down for an hour. André and Tiineke say that you are welcome to go up and see the baby." Best he leave it to them to tell her the name.

Agatha shook her head. "And if I go up, who will be here to open the door when Mr. Pol arrives?"

Johan combed his fingers through his hair and straightened his shoulders. "Well, if you want to go up, I'll wait."

"No, you were up half the night. Go and lay down. I'll wait until he comes. I'll have plenty of chances to see the child." Agatha went on with preparing some coffee and buttering bread.

Johan yawned. "Well, if you're sure." He waited until she nodded again and turned gratefully to go to his room.

———

Tiineke heard hurried footsteps on the stairs. There was a knock on the door and it was pushed open without waiting for a response. Jan burst in the room and crossed the floor with long strides.

"Shh, Mam's asleep." Tiineke nodded to her mother, crumpled in the big chair, softly snoring, her mouth open.

Jan smiled and crept closer. André slid off the bed to stand and shake Jan's hand. "Congratulations, Opa. How does it feel to be an Opa? A grandfather is a big responsibility, you know." André's eyes crinkled. "Especially when your grandson carries your name."

Jan tore his gaze from the baby and looked at André "What? What is his name?"

Elsa awoke at the sound of her husband's voice and murmured, half-awake. "Willem Jan."

Jan sniffed and blinked a few times. "Willem Jan. A fine name."

Tiineke gently stroked her baby's head. "Wim will be his everyday name."

Jan sat on the bed and stroked the baby's cheek. At the touch, Wim opened his eyes and looked at Jan solemnly. His eyes were a dark, shining blue and his white-blond hair against his pale skin made him look almost bald.

Jan cleared his throat. "He's lovely. Almost as beautiful as his mother."

Wim screwed up his face and balled his fists. He took a deep breath and let out a cry that made Jan jump off the bed. "Well, pardon me if I said something to insult you." He turned to Elsa. "I think perhaps we should leave them alone, and Agatha sent me with a message to say that she would have breakfast ready for anyone who will have something."

Elsa reached out and touched André's hand. "Your mother is very practical." She stood and stretched. "To tell the truth, I am ready for something, and I think after feeding the baby, you should get some sleep, anyway, Tiineke. We'll be back later this afternoon."

"Thank you for being here for me, Mam. I couldn't imagine being without you."

André let Jan and Elsa pass him and then turned to Tiineke. "I'll bring you up some breakfast. You'll take something?" His voice was tentative.

"I'm starving!"

André continued to linger. Tiineke tilted her head towards the door. "Go on. You can't leave your mother alone to entertain my parents." Tiineke gave him a last glance, then focused on her baby. She settled him against her breast, feeling the tug as he began nursing.

In the kitchen, André's in-laws were already seated at the table with his mother. Jan was talking to Agatha.

"And what do you think of young Wim?"

"Wim. Is that what he's called?"

Jan looked at his wife and then over at André. "I'm sorry, I didn't realize that she didn't know yet."

"That's alright. Mama hasn't had a chance to meet him yet." André slipped in to a chair, reaching for the coffee pot.

Jan looked flustered. "And here we are, expecting you to look after us instead of being upstairs, meeting your new grandson. I'm sorry. Elsa, we should go."

"Don't be ridiculous. You've just started your breakfast. I'll have plenty of time to see him later." Agatha's stern tone allowed for no argument.

"So, yes, Mama. His name is Willem Jan." André looked up from stirring his coffee to his mother.

"Well, your father would have been very proud, I'm sure. It's a good name to carry on the business into the next generation."

Elsa laughed. "You have big plans for such a little boy."

"André understands the importance of making plans." Agatha's back was stiff. "It's the only way to succeed."

Jan's face flushed at the indirect allusion to his failed business. "Yes, and now I think it really is time to go, Elsa, if you have finished." Jan set down his cup and stood up.

Elsa drained the last of her coffee and stood also. "Mrs. Meijer, thank you for keeping us nourished through the night and this morning. It was very thoughtful and generous of you. We will be back later this afternoon, but will not disturb you. We'll go directly up to Tiineke and Wim on our own."

Elsa shook hands with Agatha formally, then turned to André and pulled him to her in a big hug, kissing him three times—right cheek, left cheek, then right again. "He's beautiful and will be a wonderful credit to you both, I know, whatever he might do in the future."

Jan stood with his hat in his left hand and shook hands with Agatha also before turning to André and shaking his hand.

"A beautiful, beautiful boy. Goodbye, son, for now."

André stood at the door, watching them off, then turned back in to the kitchen. "I'm making up a tray for Tiineke, Mama. Would you like to come up with me to take it to her?"

Agatha continued clearing the table without a word.

"I'd like you to meet Wim."

"Yes, of course. This can wait." Agatha set the stack of plates down beside the sink and followed her son up the steps to the apartment, standing back until André had settled the tray on the bed near Tiineke.

"Isn't he a picture of perfection?" André looked at his son sleeping on the bed. Tiineke had been dozing but now woke up with a smile.

"Ah, good. I'm ready for a cup of coffee." She set the tray on her lap.

André couldn't help himself. He picked up the small bundle and stood, cradling him, angling the baby so Agatha could see his face.

Agatha looked at Wim impassively. "All babies are lovely, especially when they are sleeping." Despite her sharp words, she stroked his downy cheek and looked at André. "But yes, some are prettier than others, and he is very pretty."

"Would you like to hold him, Mama?" André stretched out the bundle to his mother. There was a catch in Wim's small, snuffling, sleeping noises, and for a second, his small face wrinkled, as if to cry.

"No, he isn't a plaything to be passed back and forth. He should be in his cradle beside the bed so he can get some proper sleep. It's what he needs. Eating and good sleep. Too much coddling is not good for a baby." Agatha shook her head and looked at Tiineke. "Congratulations, Tiineke. He's a lovely little boy. Now, I have work to do. I'll leave you in peace."

André saw in his mother's glance towards him that she expected him to follow. He looked down at the baby in his arms and tucked him closer against his chest. "I'll stay here for a bit. Until Tiineke finishes her breakfast, anyway, and then I'll bring the tray down. I've been up all night too, though, so I may just have a short nap. You don't have anything urgent for me to do, do you, Mama?"

Agatha sniffed. "No, nothing urgent. I'll see you later, then."

In the kitchen, washing the dishes, Agatha remembered André's birth. *None of this business of people crowding around to visit and pass the baby around then.* Agatha shook her head. Her mother had said 'Don't coddle him' and she was right. It had taken a few weeks of listening to André cry and then he'd settled nicely into a routine.

The sooner the Pols go to Rotterdam, the better. I'll get Tiineke into a proper routine then. Her boys had turned out well and Agatha was quite certain Wim would as well. Wim. At least they'd chosen a sensible name for the boy. She'd been half afraid Tiineke would insist on some silly, romantic name. Perhaps there was hope for the girl yet to become part of the family.

———

Wim was a week old and Agatha watched as Tiineke tickled his feet as the family sat together after supper, listening to the radio.

Agatha slapped her knee. "For goodness sake, put Wim in his buggy."

"Mama Meijer, I see nothing wrong in holding him sometimes. My mother told me that she and Papa used to often sit for a whole evening with us as babies on their knees, just to talk to us and hold us."

Agatha frowned. "That's ridiculous. You could be working on some sewing instead of constantly playing with his feet and hands. Put him down and he'll go to sleep."

André wiggled his fingers on the baby's belly and smiled to see his eyes widen. "He'll sleep when he's ready, Mama, and then he can be put down."

Agatha folded her arms across her chest. "You're like children with a new toy."

Tiineke continued to gaze down at Wim. "I think I need to hold him as much as he needs me."

"What does that mean?"

"I miss my parents now that they've really gone to Rotterdam. Holding Wim helps to keep me from thinking about them. He distracts me."

"Well, I can tell you that you'll spoil him with all this constant picking up and fiddling with him."

"Mama, I just can't believe that holding a baby so young can be bad for him." André looked down again at where his son lay on Tiineke's knees. With arms and legs waving, his hands balled into fists, Wim was exploring his new world. "He's ready to take on the world."

"Well, we obviously can't agree on this. Just don't complain when he has you running after him like a little lord." Agatha grumbled and flipped the newspaper up in front of her face.

What do they know? Agatha raged behind her paper, staring at the page without reading. She'd raised two boys, yet they thought she knew nothing. Didn't they understand that you needed to give a child the security of solid walls around him, even if the walls were just those of his cradle? He'd feel safe then.

Well, I won't waste my breath. I'll just have to be sure to have enough time with him to counteract this foolishness.

Tiineke could see the newspaper shaking slightly and knew that her mother-in-law was angry. *She won't dictate to me how my baby will be raised. Mama and Papa always made us feel so loved, and that's what you'll feel too, little one.* She looked at Wim. He had dropped off to sleep, his hands loosening into curls instead of fists.

"Alright, I'll take him up to bed and read for a bit upstairs." Tiineke squeezed André's hand before gathering up her bundle of baby and blanket and standing up. "Good night Mama Meijer."

"Good night." Agatha rattled the paper, as if deeply absorbed.

XIII

Summer 1930

"Look at Meijer run! It's a breakaway. He has a clear shot at a goal. And he scores!" Johan held six-month-old Wim in his arms and dodged around the displays in the shop.

"Johan, stop that racket!" Agatha stepped in to the shop from the house.

Wim shrieked with laughter and bounced in Johan's arms.

"Oh, Mam. There are no customers, anyway. We're having fun, aren't we, Wim?" He tickled Wim's stomach and Wim squealed again.

"Give him here and I'll put him into his playpen in the living room." Agatha plucked Wim from Johan's arms. "When is Tiineke expected back from her dentist appointment?"

"I'm sure she'll be back any time now. She thought he'd sleep most of the time while she was gone, but since he woke up I couldn't just leave him in his carriage."

Agatha turned to glare at Johan. "He probably would still be sleeping if you didn't constantly go and stare at him." His mother disappeared in to the house with the baby.

From in the house, Wim cried as he was set down in his playpen. Johan closed the connecting door between the shop and the house.

———

By the time Tiineke arrived home, Wim was sound asleep in his playpen.

"You see? He's quite fine in there." Agatha had a note of triumph in her voice.

"Yes, I see that." Tiineke tried not to sound irritated. "I know it's a good and safe place for him Mama Meijer. I do use it quite often, you know."

"Not often enough." Agatha's voice was sharp. "I think you should start helping more again, now that he is big enough to be left with one of us. You could take over doing the shopping in the mornings."

Tiineke brightened. This was new. "I'd love to do the shopping for you. I can go right after Wim wakes up from his morning nap and we could make a regular outing of it."

"No, you can leave Wim with me. You need to get out early enough so that you can buy the freshest produce before it's all gone. It's not efficient to have a baby along, anyway. No, you'll leave him here with me while you do the shopping, and I can work on my paperwork while I'm minding him."

Tiineke wasn't terribly disappointed. She had felt free today being out alone, even if it was just for an appointment with the dentist.

"Thank you, Mama Meijer. That'll be fine."

Later that night, while they were getting ready for bed, Tiineke spoke to André.

"What's behind this, do you think? Why now all of a sudden am I allowed to do the shopping? I was never trusted before."

André shrugged. "Mama's just starting to realize that your young legs can do the running around better than hers. Why not? That's what I would do, if I were her."

He whistled as he hung his clothes in the wardrobe. He took another quick peek into the crib where Wim lay, breathing softly, then pulled Tiineke into bed.

He held Tiineke against him and stroked her silky hair. "I'm so happy. My son is happy and healthy. My wife and mother seem to be getting along better. Life is good. If we could start to get the business back on track, it would be even better, but all in all, it's good, isn't it?"

Tiineke cupped her hand against his cheek. "Yes, it's good. If we could ever get a place of our own it would really be even better."

"One of these days."

The next morning Tiineke got ready to go out early.

"Wim is sleeping in his carriage, Mama Meijer. He might not even wake until I get back, but if so—"

Agatha waved at Tiineke. "I know how to look after a baby. Leave him to me. We'll be fine. Here is the list, and here is the money. I've estimated what it should cost, so you should have enough."

Agatha counted out the money into Tiineke's hand as though giving a child an allowance.

Tiineke glanced at the list. Agatha had itemized right down to what store to go to for what item. *She's going to make sure I don't make a mistake. I wonder what would happen if I bought sugar at the wrong store.* Tiineke opted not to try it, or it would be her first and last shopping trip.

Picking up the shopping basket and slipping on her grey raincoat to protect her from the chilly drizzle, Tiineke went out with a cheerful bounce to her step.

———

It was an hour later. Her legs were wet and her damp hair dripped cold rain down her neck.

I'll have to warm up my hands before I pick Wim up.

Hanging her wet coat on the hook and stepping out of her shoes, she stood in her stocking feet in the kitchen.

"Mama Meijer, I'm home. Shall I put everything away?" She went into the sitting room. "Mama Meijer?" No answer. No carriage. Tiineke went through to the shop, even though these days they only opened three afternoons a week. Empty.

There was a hollow feeling in Tiineke's stomach. She wriggled her damp feet back in to her wet shoes, throwing her wet coat over her head and shoulders like a cape, and hurried across to the plant where André was busy in the office.

"André, have you seen your mother and Wim?"

"No. They aren't in the house? Maybe upstairs?"

Tiineke's voice was high with anxiety. "No, the carriage is gone. They've gone out somewhere."

"Don't worry. She's probably just taken him out for a walk or to the shop. There's nothing to be worried about." He touched her arm.

"I know, but why would she take him out in this weather? She sent me out to do the shopping, so there is no reason for her to be at the shops"

"It's not that bad out, is it?" There were no windows for him to check the weather.

"It's been pouring, but I guess it *is* starting to let up." She sighed and turned away. "Alright, I'll go back and put the shopping away. I thought she'd want to check what I got, that's all."

"Make yourself a nice cup of hot tea. You looked chilled."

Tiineke left her wet shoes on, unable to settle. She sat in the big easy chair by the window and had her tea, constantly craning her head to peer up and down the street.

Forty-five minutes later, when she saw them coming along the sidewalk, she jumped up and opened the door.

Tiineke reached to take the buggy from Agatha. "Where have you been?"

Agatha stopped in the middle of taking off her coat and studied Tiineke. "I had a letter to post, and decided to deliver it instead since it wasn't too far. I thought that some fresh air would be good for both Wim and me. Why? What's wrong with you?"

"Nothing. I just wondered, that's all." Tiineke's voice was low now and she didn't meet Agatha's eyes. "I thought Wim would be here when I got home, and I missed him." She tried to minimize the trembling of her voice.

"Well, you can see that he's just fine. If you don't trust me to look after him for half an hour, then just say so."

"I trust you, of course I do. I'm just not used to being apart from him." Tiineke finished removing Wim's small hat and felt her heart return to normal.

"It's high time you get used to it." Agatha pursed her lips. "By the time each of the boys were six months old, I was already back to work and the boys were put in the carriage out in the plant. It's about time you get busy again."

"Yes, I'm sure you're right." Tiineke straightened up and turned away from the baby. "Well, I did the shopping." She rooted in her pocket. "Here is the change."

Agatha counted it carefully in her open hand, then looked sharply at Tiineke. "I thought you would have more change left."

Tiineke flushed. "I'm not stealing from you, Mama Meijer, if that's what you're implying."

"I'm not implying anything other than surprise. Please take me through the list and tell me what each item cost. I do this for budget purposes. In fact, from now on, when you are doing the shopping, please write down the price of each item. That will be easier than trying to recall it later."

Tiineke choked back her anger and took Agatha through the list and prices.

"I see. Sugar is more expensive again this week. Where will it end?" Agatha asked herself more than Tiineke. "Did you go to the stores I told you to go to?"

"Yes, Mama Meijer."

"Well, there's no help for it, then. I'll have to budget for the higher price."

Each day after that, Tiineke went out with her list and made the rounds. Butcher, baker, greengrocer.

Most of the time, Agatha and Wim would be away from the house when she returned, but the wrench she had first felt subsided. She knew Agatha would look after him.

"Mama and Wim were over with me most of the morning." André unzipped Tiineke's dress as they prepared for bed one evening. "It was great to have him in the office with me while Mama and I looked over the books."

"Why would she do that when I was at home on my own most of the morning, baking bread?"

"Maybe she thinks you can do with some time alone."

"Maybe." Tiineke sat on the edge of the bed frowning.

The next morning, before going out, Tiineke spoke to Agatha. "Mama Meijer, don't feel obliged to take Wim out all the time. I'm perfectly content to look after him, you know."

"Yes, of course. I should hope so, you are the boy's mother. Do you have a problem with me taking him out?"

"No, it's not that. It just seems like you are taking him with you more and more these days." She trailed off, not knowing how to articulate what she was feeling.

Agatha sat silently, looking at Tiineke. Finally, "Well? Are you going to do the shopping today or not?"

"Yes, I'm leaving now." And Tiineke left with a sigh.

———

Over time, Tiineke became accustomed to the growing role that Agatha had taken on with Wim. She had more errands to do herself as Agatha tasked her with much of the baking and cooking as well as the shopping.

"Supper is delicious! The red cabbage and apples are one of my favourites." Johan particularly seemed happy with the change of chefs. "I like your cooking, Tiineke." He smacked his lips. "Not that I don't like Mama's cooking, it just makes for a nice change."

Tiineke smiled at Johan. "I enjoy doing more in the kitchen, although I do miss having so much time with Wim."

André teased his mother. "I think Mama enjoys having the day with Wim, don't you, Mama? Admit it. You're having fun being a grandmother."

Agatha didn't smile and her voice was serious as she replied. "We all have a job to do in this family, and right now, I think my job is to help set Wim on the right path for his future."

Tiineke tilted her head. "His path for the future? Good heavens, he's only a few months old. I don't think there is any rush for him to decide what he would like to do with his future." She laughed.

"It isn't that there is a decision to be made. It's making sure that he is trained properly, and that starts in childhood."

Tiineke glanced at André. He shrugged and smiled at his wife. Don't worry about it, in other words.

"If you're finished, Mama Meijer…"

Agatha looked at Tiineke.

"I mean, if you're finished with your plate, I'll clear it away."

———

Later that night, in the quiet of their room, Tiineke sat with Wim cuddled in her arms in the big easy chair that once belonged to her parents. André sat on the edge of the bed in their bedroom and looked through the door at his wife and son. The doorway framed them in a peaceful tableau.

André held his arms open to encompass the scene. "This is my favourite time. I love having the two of you to myself. Just watching you with Wim makes me happy. You're so good with him."

Tiineke looked over Wim's head at André. "It's my favourite time, too." She kissed the baby. "You know who to look to for your cuddles, don't you, Wim?"

The baby settled more comfortably against her, sucking his thumb and reaching up with the other hand to twist a strand of Tiineke's hair. He tilted his head back so he could see his father and smiled at him around his thumb. André smiled back.

"Yes, son, you do know, don't you?" He stood up and joined Tiineke and the baby, stroking his son's soft, fuzzy hair. "It's funny."

She glanced up at André. "What is?"

"I never could have imagined being this affectionate. We were never an affectionate family, but now it seems the most natural thing in the world."

"That's because, despite what your mother claims, touching actually *is* a natural thing, and I think it's necessary."

"Yes, I think you're right. You're teaching me to be different. I like it."

"Right, young man. Into bed you go." Tiineke laid Wim into his crib.

André put his arm around her waist, and together, they watched their son drift off to sleep. Wim awoke as a muscle spasm startled him, but seeing his parents watching over him, he was soon snoring softly again.

André was mesmerized. "He's getting so big, so fast."

"Yes. It won't be long before we'll be packing away the crib and he'll be using my old bed."

They went to their own room and André watched Tiineke brushing out her hair. "It's great the way Mama is really developing a relationship with Wim, isn't it?"

Tiineke stopped brushing for a moment, seeming to be deep in thought. "Yes, it is. I wish he could develop a relationship with my parents, too. I know they send him postcards almost every week, but it's hardly the same, is it?"

"Don't worry, he'll get to know them just as much. Next summer, we'll go down and spend a holiday with them. He'll be big enough then to really understand." André wanted to be assuring, although in his heart, he knew it wasn't the same. He was glad that his mother was here to be with Wim everyday. "I know my Mother can seem hard sometimes, but she means well, and she won't be teaching Wim bad ideas."

Tiineke hesitated before answering. "Yes, I'm sure you're right. Sometimes I just feel a little bit overwhelmed by her, though. I sometimes feel as if she's trying to take over my son."

"Oh, no. I know that isn't true. I think it's partly because she's used to being so busy, and with business so slow, she needs something to help fill her hours. That's all it is. Really, you'd be doing her a kindness to let her spend the time with Wim with no fuss."

"Yes, I suppose I hadn't really considered that. Alright, I'll let Wim entertain her and stop being so grumpy about it."

André patted the bed and Tiineke joined him. He felt all was well with the world and the future looked bright as they drifted off to sleep.

XIV

Spring 1934

"Oma?" Wim pulled on his grandmother's skirt. "Oma!" At four years old, he was used to getting Agatha's attention as soon as he called her, but this morning she sat on the kitchen stool, gazing out of the window.

"Oma—egg!"

Finally, Agatha looked down at Wim. She seemed surprised to see him standing there.

"Come and sit with me for a moment." She reached down and pulled him up on her lap.

He wriggled, unaccustomed to her arms around him holding him in a stiff hug, her chin resting on his blond curls.

"Egg." He patted his stomach for emphasis.

When he didn't get a response, he remembered the manners Oma was always talking about and tried again. "An egg please, Oma." He touched her face, his small hand resting against her bony cheek.

Agatha put Wim back on the floor, stood up, and walked to the window. Removing her glasses, she polished them with her hand-kerchief for a moment before responding. "No eggs today Wim. No more eggs."

Wim looked up at his grandmother, puzzled. When his father walked in to the kitchen, he ran to him and looped an arm around his leg.

"No egg, Papa."

André looked down at his son and patted him on the head.

"Mama, what's wrong?" He was surprised the coffee hadn't been started yet and no sign of breakfast preparations.

Agatha spoke without turning from the window. "The chickens are gone."

"Gone?" André didn't understand. "They can't just be gone. They don't fly."

"No they don't fly, but they can be stolen." Agatha set about measuring out coffee, exactly what they would need for three cups. Johan was already gone for his early morning football practice.

André unlaced Wim's small arms from around his leg and walked out to the courtyard. The wooden gate had been wrenched open and now hung on a broken hinge. A few feathers eddied around in the morning breeze. The chickens and rooster had probably had their necks broken quickly to minimize the noise before being carried away.

"No more chickens, Papa."

André turned to scoop up his son and carry him back inside the house. "No Wim, no more chickens."

"Why?"

This was his favourite question these days. Oddly enough, Agatha seemed the most patient with him, giving him logical answers nearly every time.

Setting Wim back on the kitchen floor, the boy turned back to Agatha. "Why no more chickens, Oma?"

She rested her hand on his head briefly. "There are many, many hungry people in Amsterdam, Wim, and I think that someone must have stolen the chickens to feed their family. Come now and have your milk and bread."

"I'm sorry, Mam." André shook his head, wrinkling his brow. "I'll fix the gate."

"Yes, do. It isn't safe with it open as it is. See if there is a strong board in the warehouse to make an extra bar. We should have done that before."

"Mama, I think that no matter what we did, it was bound to happen. There are so many people out of work now, especially in this area. The sound of the chickens was probably driving someone mad, if, as you say, they had hungry children at home."

"Yes. Well. What's done is done. Is Tiineke coming down?" Agatha's eyes were shiny behind her glasses.

"She's going to lie in for a while longer. This new baby is really making itself felt. She hardly slept all night because of the kicking and indigestion. You don't mind watching Wim, do you? It's not like we open the shop in the morning anymore."

"It's fine. Wim can stay with me. We'll go for a walk since it isn't raining for a change, and then we'll go to the market."

The three finished their breakfast together and André got ready to leave for a meeting with a local thread supplier. As he put on his hat, he could hear his mother speaking to Wim.

"Come, climb up on your stool here so you can help me with drying the dishes."

André heard the effort in her voice and he gave a small smile at the picture of the two of them together. He closed the door behind him, leaving his mother in charge of his son.

———

Later that morning, Agatha stood before the small hallway mirror and slid the long pin into her hat, securing it firmly to her head. She tucked a grey wisp under the brim, and her scarf into her long grey coat, then bent down to retie Wim's shoelaces, pulling them tight around his woollen stockings. He wore a dark blue jacket with jaunty white sailor stripes on the collar with matching knee length pants. Giving him a last glance and feeling secretly proud of her handsome little grandson, Agatha held out her hand. "Come then."

As they walked along, she kept up a steady stream of conversation, pointing out buildings and reading out street names to him. Agatha firmly believed that every walk should be a time for teaching.

They passed a line of people waiting outside a red brick building, and the little boy pointed. "Football!" He had been to see his uncle Johan play football a few times and always associated lines of people with waiting to get in to the stadium.

Agatha held his hand a little tighter. "No, Wim. Those people are waiting to report in to the government."

"Why?"

"They have no work to go to, and must report in twice a day to the government in order to receive money to buy food." She pulled him past the line quickly.

They passed a boy in the line-up, close to Wim's own age. "Hello." Wim smiled at the boy and gave a small wave.

The boy was standing with his mother, along with two more children. The child wore a dirty plaid jacket torn at the elbow and short socks with his knee-length pants. His thin white legs were scabbed at the knees. Despite his thin build, both the jacket and his pants were too tight for him. The boy said nothing to Wim in return. All the children stood silently, turning to follow Agatha and Wim with large, darkly circled eyes. Wim turned back to stare at the boy and Agatha jerked on his arm to pull him along.

"Eyes forward, please."

Wim stumbled, and Agatha realized she had been pulling him along at a pace that forced him to trot beside her.

"Oma, tired." Wim whimpered.

She slowed down so Wim could walk again.

They crossed over the bridge of the Westemarkt. "Let's stop here for a moment. Look, you can see our church there." Agatha pointed out the Westerkerk in the distance.

As Wim chattered about the boats and ducks, scooting back and forth, picking up small pebbles to throw into the water, Agatha took a deep breath. *All those out-of-work people. Stealing my chickens. How dare they come in to my very home.*

She was shaking when she felt Wim put his hand in hers.

Agatha glanced down at the little boy. "Don't worry Wim. I'll protect you." She took a deep breath to steady herself. "Come. We'll go to the market and then right home."

She needed her home with her sons around her. She gripped her grandson's small hand firmly in hers and marched on to the market.

She stood, in shock, before the boarded-up window of the greengrocer's shop. She rattled the door handle but the door was locked.

"What has happened here?" Agatha asked a passing woman. "Was he vandalized?" She thought of her own loss just this morning.

"No, just closed down." The woman stopped and looked at the boarded window with Agatha. "Yesterday afternoon he came out and put up the boards. He said he was going to his daughter in Friesland. A pity. It's hard to find good produce these days."

"We'll have to go to the Edah, I suppose. I don't like those big shops, but I suppose we have no choice now." Agatha shook her head and frowned.

"Yes, there aren't too many places to choose from anymore." The woman nodded to Agatha and went on her way.

———

"Look at these." Agatha held up two small potatoes to Tiineke. "It's outrageous that they can charge good money for these things." Agatha was glad to be back in her own kitchen.

Tiineke took one of the potatoes and turned it over in her hand slowly. "Imagine how people with no money feel."

Agatha didn't respond to that, not wanting to remember those long lines of people. "Is Johan back?"

"Yes, he's gone over to help André. They're sorting through some scraps of wood to repair the back gate."

"Ah, good. The sooner that's fixed, the better. I'll go and see what they're finding."

"I'm sure they're able to fix a gate on their own, Mama Meijer." Tiineke finished putting the few groceries away as Agatha turned to go outside.

"I'm sure they can, but I intend to ensure that no one comes or goes by that gate again."

Agatha felt Tiineke touch her arm and she turned back again. "You're closing up the gate so that it can't be used anymore?"

"Yes. We don't use it that often, anyway, so we might as well bar it completely and just use the house door to go in to the back garden. In fact, perhaps now that we have no more chickens, I'll put in a small vegetable garden so we can have some proper vegetables instead of the poor excuses for vegetables that can be bought at the shop." Agatha nodded as she developed her idea. "The chicken coop will make a fine garden shed with a bit of effort. I'll miss my fresh eggs in the morning, but a garden really would be nice."

Tiineke looked doubtful. "I'm not sure you'll get much sun back there."

"Well, we can give it a try anyway." Agatha whirled out of the house.

Tiineke listened as the hammering and sawing went on all afternoon.

———

First it's the back gate. The windows and doors will be next. Soon she'll have us all locked in here like some kind of Noah's Ark.

At five o'clock Tiineke stepped out into the back garden herself. "I'll make supper, shall I, Mama Meijer?" Tiineke shouted to make herself heard over the noise out in the yard. The gate had been completely boarded over and the whole back fence had been heightened using pointed boards. Wim sat off to the side, surrounded by small scraps of wood that he was stacking.

Agatha shouted back. "Yes, of course. You can see I'm busy." She was handing nails to André as he worked on converting the chicken coop into a garden shed. It was being raised so a person could comfortably stand up straight inside. Agatha had cleaned it out already. All signs of the chickens were gone, other than the lingering smell. Johan was busy tacking the wire that had once fronted the coop to the top of the now pointed fence, making it even more impassable.

"Wim, will you help me make the supper?" She looked down where he sat in the dust.

The little boy reached to pick up another piece of wood and added it to his pile. "No. Helping Oma."

Agatha stepped closer to the child. "Leave him. He's fine where he is."

Tiineke sighed and went in to prepare supper. At least, for a change, there would be no onions to pick out.

The hammering had just stopped as Tiineke gave the stew a final stir.

"Supper is delicious." André smiled at Tiineke.

Agatha patted her lips with her napkin. "Bland."

Johan smacked his lips. "I'm starving. It tastes great to me."

Tiineke laughed. "You're always starving."

"You boys have done good work today." Agatha nodded to her sons.

Tiineke fought the excluded feeling. "Your cheeks are a little sunburned, Mama Meijer."

"Working in the fresh air with my boys felt good. We made a strong fence, didn't we, boys? No one will break in here again."

Johan grinned at his mother. "Mama, you would make a good foreman, I think. All these years bossing the workers in the plant around has made you a natural. I think you miss it, now that we are only down to a couple of part-time workers."

"I do miss the work."

"What is the news on you joining Ajax, then, Johan?" Tiineke waved her fork at Johan.

André pushed away his empty plate and turned to his brother. "Yes, you were supposed to hear from the Amsterdam football team this week, weren't you? I remember they were out watching you and a couple of your mates a few weeks ago."

Johan sat a little straighter in his chair and laced his fingers together in front of him. "Alright, well, I wasn't going to say anything because of the sad news of Mama's chickens, but since you are asking me..."

"You're in!" Tiineke dropped her fork and clapped her hands.

Johan nodded. "I am. I'll only be in training, of course, until the start of next season, but at least I'm on the team."

André leaned over and shook Johan's shoulder. "Congratulations, Johan! You've been at loose ends since you turned twenty and really finished with the youth team last year. What terrific news."

"Why is this such wonderful news?" Agatha folded her arms across her chest. "From what I can see, it's no different than your other team. You still won't be making any money at it, will you?"

"Well, no, they don't pay anything, but there is talk of the team going professional one of these years." Johan shrugged one shoulder.

"One of these years. A complete waste of your time."

"Mama, the business doesn't need me anyway right now, so there's no harm in me continuing on, is there? I can learn so much, and who knows? Maybe someday I'll play in England where players get paid good money."

Agatha gave him a hard look.

"Or maybe the Dutch will form their own professional league. Meanwhile, I get to meet all my football heroes!" For a moment, Johan was the same excited sixteen-year-old who had first joined the youth team. "Mama, please, you won't object?"

"You'll do as you want anyway. There's no point in objecting." She waved her hand, her face pulled into a pinched look.

"Thank you, Mam." Johan beamed as if his mother had been enthusiastic. He turned to his little nephew. "Well Wim, won't it be exciting to go and watch Oom Johan playing football with the big boys?"

"You're men, not boys." Wim shook his head as if to say 'Silly Uncle Johan'.

With the exception of Agatha, they all laughed, André tousling Wim's hair. Wim looked puzzled but pleased.

Agatha stood up and started to clear the dishes. "Come Wim, time to help Oma with the dishes."

Wim slid off his chair and trotted after Agatha. Johan also got up to help.

Tiineke watched her little son. "He follows her around like a puppy. He hardly even wants to spend time with me."

"It's just a phase he's going through." André rubbed the back of her neck for a moment. "It's a good thing right now that he does because it lets you rest more without worrying about him. When the baby comes, you'll be especially happy that he's willing to be with her."

Tiineke stretched her neck under André's massaging hand. "Maybe. Yes, I'm sure you're right. I'm just tired and cranky." She sighed and lowered her voice. "Mama won't be here this time for me when the baby comes, and I'm missing her."

"I know. It's hard for them to come here, but as soon as the baby is born and you're both strong enough, the four of us will go down for a visit. Your Tante Rit said that somehow the room would be found for a couple nights' stay."

"We'd have to ask your mother for the bus fare. Do you think she'll give it to us?" Tiineke tilted her head and raised her eyebrows.

"Yes, I'm sure of it. It's been a year since we were last there. She can't object." André sounded confident.

"Well, that's the dishes done." Johan came back into the dining room followed by Agatha. He reached towards the radio as they all moved to the more comfortable chairs in the lounge area. "Mama, will we listen to the world news on the radio?"

"Yes, put it on." Agatha settled in her chair. "Lately I haven't felt like listening to it, but we really should know what's happening in the world."

Johan fiddled with the dial until they heard a strident voice in the middle of a tirade.

Tiineke frowned. "There's that Adolf Hitler, shouting again. What's it about this time?"

They listened for a few moments as Hitler ranted about how the Nazi party would do away with unemployment.

Johan looked at his mother. "Do you think he really could achieve that?"

"I don't trust him. I think he tells a good story, but there was something fishy last year when the Reichstag was destroyed in that fire. They blamed the Dutch man, van der Lubbe, but I think there was more to the story than people heard. Hitler used it as an excuse to take a lot of control. Mind you, I'm all for a man of action who will help to tackle unemployment, but I don't think this fellow is the answer. Next year, Germany is having elections, and that's what all this ranting is about—trying to convince people to vote for him. Turn it off, Johan. I think we've heard enough for one night." Agatha picked up the paper instead.

"Papa, fix, please." Wim handed his wooden train to André. One of the wheels was missing.

Andre took the train and examined it. "I think this needs a new washer, son. Come, let's go to the plant and see if we can find one to fit and then it's off to bed with you."

Tiineke stood up herself. "Bed sounds like a good idea." The three of them left Agatha and Johan alone together.

Agatha watched the small family leave and then she set her newspaper down and studied Johan. "You know, I've been corresponding with the naval base in Den Helder about a possible order for sheets and towels. If we need you, can I count on you, or will you be too busy with this new football team of yours?"

Johan put his hands on his knees and leaned forward. "Mama, if you need me, I'll always be here for you. You know, though, that André is more than able to handle an order of that size. He'll bring back a couple more machinists for some time; they'd be happy for the work. But yes, of course, if you need me, I'll be here." Johan stood and stretched. "I'm off to bed as well and I'll be gone for a practice early tomorrow, so I'll see you at supper. Good night, Mama." He leaned down to kiss her cheek.

She patted his arm. "I do need you, Johan. Don't think that I don't."

"What a funny mood you're in, Mama." He squeezed her shoulder fondly before going upstairs to bed.

———

The next morning Tiineke was surprised to see that Agatha wore a long brown apron over her high-necked blouse and grey skirt.

Tiineke finished putting away the last of the breakfast dishes. "Mama Meijer, you look like you are ready to tackle a big cleaning job today." *I hope she's not expecting me to help rearrange the shop.* That was often what Agatha did when she found herself at loose ends.

"Yes, I'm clearing out the room above today."

"The small store room?"

"Yes, that room. There are many old things there that should either be given away or used somehow." Agatha picked up the broom and dustpan.

"Would you like my help?" Tiineke leaned against the counter.

Agatha sniffed and raised her eyebrows. "You would barely fit in that room along with me in your state, let alone be of any help."

"Well, if you're sure." Tiineke smiled. *She must be restless, but as long as I don't have to be part of the job, she's welcome to it.* "I'll take Wim out to the park to keep him out of your hair."

A shadow crossed Agatha's face. "Don't go far."

"Just down the street. Wim loves that little park."

"There seem to be some rough people in that area these days."

"We'll be careful. The fresh air will do us both good."

For the rest of the week, Agatha kept busy clearing out the upstairs room. She put on the brown apron after breakfast and disappeared upstairs. Her shoes clumped up and down the stairs all day as she made trips to the garbage bin, or out to her new shed.

She had Johan and André move one of the larger trunks to the loft above the warehouse.

André questioned Tiineke one morning when he came in for a cup of tea. "Has she said what her master plan is for this room she's clearing out?"

"Not a word. I asked her, but she just mumbled that she is still making plans."

"Maybe a sewing room?"

"Maybe, although why would she need a room for that? We both just sit in the living room to do the sewing."

André shook his head. "I suppose she'll tell us when she's good and ready."

———

Tante Miep, the midwife, was back, having a cup of tea in the living room with André while Tiineke lay in bed in the loft.

Miep sat back in her chair with her tea. "Although her water broke a few hours ago, it'll be a long while yet."

The sound of heavy furniture being dragged across the floor came from upstairs.

The midwife looked at the ceiling. "What's that?"

André looked up with a puzzled expression on his face. "I'm not really sure. Excuse me for a moment."

André opened the door to the staircase leading to his old room and saw his mother and Johan carrying his old bed into the storeroom.

"What in the world are you doing up there?"

Johan wiped his sweating hands on his pants. "Sorry, old man, you aren't coming back to your old room now. Mama's got me moving your bed out."

"Mama, what are you up to?" André climbed the steps. It had been a couple of years since he had been up here.

Agatha gestured to the small room across from what had been the boys' bedroom. "This is now a bedroom, and Wim can sleep here tonight while Tiineke is having her baby. He'll be frightened by all the excitement."

"Mama, that's such a thoughtful thing to do. I was just going to have him sleep on the sofa until it was safe for him to go back to his own bed." André was touched by his mother's planning.

The bed was settled in the corner of the room. André looked around. There wasn't much space, but it was enough for the bed and a wooden box with a lamp, plus a small chest of drawers he vaguely recalled seeing years before, when he was still a boy. He thought it had been used to store sewing materials. She had even hung curtains in the window.

André was delighted. "Mama, it's a regular small bedroom. He'll love sleeping here tonight, I'm sure. I'll go and tell him, shall I?"

Agatha set a blanket on the bed. "No, I'll bring him up and show him, and let him know that his Oma is right next door if he wakes in the night. You look after Tiineke and I'll look after Wim."

———

"So Mama has it all fixed up there with my old bed in a little room of his own." André folded up Wim's bed as he talked. "There. Now there is more room for you to walk a bit."

Tiineke was only half listening to him as she paced their bedroom, pressing her hands to the small of her back. "It's good that he isn't here at the moment. It was kind of your mother to do all that." She stopped and grasped the top of the folded bed as a pain seized her. "I wish there was some way for this to hurry up and be over. Oooh." She doubled up, her knuckles white.

André helped her back to the bed. "Shall I go and get Tante Miep now?"

"Yes. Why isn't she here instead of down there, drinking tea?"

"I'll send her up right away. I'll leave you now for a bit, but if you want me, I'll be here."

"No, go. Go and keep Wim company. He's probably a bit frightened."

André left, and Tiineke was alone in the little bedroom.

"Oh Mama, why aren't you here?" Tiineke rolled to her side as a pain washed over her.

"I'm here now." But it was not Tiineke's mother, but Tante Miep sweeping into the room. "You're an old hand at this, we don't need your mother." She rubbed Tiineke's back. "You'll probably be faster than you were with the first baby. And isn't he growing into a fine boy? I hear that he's going to follow in his father's footsteps and grow up to work in the Meijer business. Isn't that wonderful?"

Tiineke gritted her teeth. "He'll grow up to do whatever he likes to do. Perhaps he'll be an artist."

"Yes, yes, of course. Well, it's a long way in the future still, isn't it? Time will tell. Alright, we're ready for you to start pushing now. Let's focus on this baby."

———

Down in the sitting room, Wim was grilling his father. "Will I have a little brother soon, Papa?"

André tousled Wim's hair. "What if you had a little sister to play with, wouldn't that be fun, too?"

"No. I want a brother."

"We'll have to see. It is in God's hands. Did Oma show you the room where you'll sleep tonight, Wim?"

Wim pointed to the ceiling. "That's *my* room now."

"For tonight, anyway." André smiled.

Wim nodded. "Forever."

André could hear his mother's steps in the room above. She was probably laying out his pajamas.

"Well, we'll see."

"Oma said."

"We'll see." André pulled out his pocket watch. "Speaking of bed, it's about time you were in it, young man. Shall we go up and I can tuck you in?" André stood and held out his hand to his son.

Wim bounced to his feet and ran ahead of André to the staircase door. Stretching up, he pulled it open and clambered up the steep steps using his hands, as though he were climbing a ladder. "Oma! I'm coming!"

Agatha looked out of the room and watched his progress up the steps.

André followed. "He's excited about sleeping here tonight, Mama. What a great idea you had to clear out the room to make an extra bedroom. Thank you for that."

Wim scurried into the room and climbed up on the bed. Agatha spoke to André as she leaned over Wim to unlace his shoes. "It always was a bedroom before we took over the house. For us, it always seemed easier to have you two boys in the same bedroom and use this for sewing and storage. A little bit of cleaning up, and now it's a bedroom again." Agatha nodded at André. "You go on. I'll put Wim to bed."

"You even have his pajamas and favourite bear here. When did you organize all this?" André looked around the small room with wonder.

"Look, Papa." Wim slid off the bed and pulled open a drawer in the chest. Several articles of his small clothing were neatly folded inside.

André felt his stomach lurch. "Mama, I thought this was an arrangement for tonight."

"It's always best to plan ahead, and I'm sure Tiineke will appreciate having some quiet time to spend with the newborn." Agatha closed the drawer again.

André shifted from one foot to the other. "Well, you're probably right."

"Now leave us to it. He'll never go to sleep if you're standing around here, watching." Agatha shooed him out.

André reached out to enclose his son in his arms. "Good night, Wim. When you wake up, you should have a brand new baby brother or sister. I'll take you up to visit as soon as you're up."

Wim gave André a brief hug, then turned his attention back to his grandmother as she laid his pajamas on the bed beside him. As André descended the stairs to the sitting room, he heard his son chattering away.

Tick-tick-tick. The clock sounded loud in the stillness of the room. Above him, he could hear the muffled sounds of his mother and son talking.

I wonder if I am allowed in the room with Tiineke. He stood and paced into the kitchen, unable to sit still to read. He rinsed out the tea cup Miep had used. *I'll go up and listen outside the door.* He went out the kitchen door and into the warehouse. A moan rolled down the stairs to greet him.

No, perhaps not. He returned to the house, sat again, and stared out the window as day darkened into evening, then realized how bored he was.

He slipped up the stairs and stuck his head in to Johan's room.

Johan stood up at André's entrance. "What's up? Is Tiineke alright? Is she done already?"

"No, I just need some company."

"Sure, no problem. I wasn't doing much anyway." Johan steered André back down the stairs. "I'll make some coffee, will I?"

"Great idea."

They took their coffee into the living room and André sat in his mother's big chair, enjoying the hot drink. "What were you doing, anyway?"

"Just rearranging the room a bit now that the extra bed is gone. I have room for some bookshelves now and I've created a sort of desk with a board and a couple of packing cases. I was just trying it out for size by sitting there, writing a letter."

"A letter? Who are you writing a letter to?"

Johan's cheeks flushed. "A girl I know."

"Ah, a girl! Tell me more, little brother."

Johan glanced towards the staircase door.

"Mama's busy in her room. Come, you're safe to tell me."

Johan hesitated. "There isn't a lot to tell. We're just friends at the moment."

"Alright, well tell me about your *friend*." André smiled.

"Her name is Mary Steen."

"That doesn't sound very Dutch."

"No. Her mother is English, but her father's family is all from around Gelderland. Her parents live in Wageningen."

"How did you ever meet someone from way over there?"

"She's crazy about football, and she and a few others from a youth group she belongs to came to a match I played in a few months ago. She wanted my autograph after the match." Johan was now brick red.

"You're not serious!"

Johan was defensive. "Not *just* mine. It was all in fun. That's all, just fun."

"And so you've been writing ever since? I haven't seen any letters come through to you in the mail."

Johan shifted in his chair. "She has Hank's address. She writes to me there."

"Oh-ho, I see."

"Well, until I knew it was really going to develop into a...friend-ship..."—Johan hesitated over the word—"I didn't want to get Mama wound up. You know."

André grinned. "Yes, I know. Well, good for you."

"What's good?" Agatha came into the room.

André winked at his brother. "Johan was just telling me about some of his football successes." Agatha had no interest in Johan's football stories.

"No word from above, then?" Agatha nodded towards the warehouse.

"No. It sounded like things were progressing, though, when I listened in for a moment about an hour ago." André crossed his legs restlessly.

Agatha gestured for Johan to turn on the radio. "We'll listen to the news, and then I'm going to bed."

The radio hissed and squealed, then settled on the solemn voice of the newsreader.

Agatha pursed her lips and shook her head. "Are they rehashing the whole mutiny on the *De Zeven Provincien* again? Is there no other news? It's something I just cannot understand. Of all people, the military should be models of law-abiding citizens. What did they think they could achieve when those sailors took over the ship?"

André folded his arms across his chest. "Well, Mama, it sounds like the conditions under which the sailors were working were just terrible, and on top of that, their wages keep getting cut. I'm not saying they were right, but I can understand that sometimes you just feel like you need to do something drastic to change the way things are. Sometimes the only way is to just take control, even if it seems extreme. I think they should be shown some mercy."

Agatha shook her finger at André. "I think that the Ministry of Defense knows how to run a ship better than the sailors on board do, and while it was unfortunate that those twenty or so men lost their lives, they brought it on themselves. They should have trusted those in charge to know best. No mercy. Those men made their choice and they have to live by it." Agatha sat back in her chair again. "Now that Colijn is prime minister, I thought we would have had a stronger show of law and order. Instead, I get my chickens stolen. It doesn't seem to make much difference which party or person is in charge."

André and Johan exchanged glances, then André spoke cautiously. "I don't think one man can change the state of the economy, Mama. He can't feed all the hungry people."

"That's the job of the person in charge. To look after those he is responsible for."

Johan drained his coffee cup. "I'm off to bed. André, if you need me for any reason, just give me a shake. Otherwise, I'll see you and the new little Meijer in the morning."

"Yes, I've had enough also. Good night, André." Agatha rose and gave her son a nod.

"Good night, Mama." He reached out and pressed her hand for a moment as she passed.

The news over, the radio began to broadcast a concert from the London Philharmonic Orchestra. André stretched out his legs and closed his eyes.

———

"Mr. Meijer. Mr. Meijer." Miep was calling him.

André jumped. "What? What is it? What time is it?"

Miep was standing in front of him, and he shook his head to clear his thoughts when it all came flooding back.

"Tiineke! Is she alright? And the baby?"

"She's fine. Easy now. It's two in the morning, there's no rush. Congratulations, you have another fine son." Miep smiled down at him.

"Another son!" André stood and, grinning, shook Miep's hand. "Thank you for looking after her. Them. Can I see them?"

"Yes. She was nursing a few minutes ago, but she's ready to see you."

They went up together, André taking the steps two at a time with his long legs, Miep following slowly behind to give them a moment together alone.

André pushed open the door of their apartment quietly and saw through to the bedroom. Tiineke sat propped up in bed, gazing down at the tiny bundle with a gentle smile. André's heart squeezed and his breath caught in his throat.

He hurried over to the bed. "Sweetheart, are you alright?"

"I'm fine. It was easier this time." Tiineke pushed the flannel blanket away from the baby's small face and André watched him nursing, mesmerized by the sight of his wife and son together.

"He's beautiful. Wim is already so big, I had forgotten how tiny a baby is."

Tiineke smiled. "I'm not sure he's so tiny, but yes, he is smaller than Wim was."

"It's the diet. People aren't eating so well these days and I see it everywhere. Babies are smaller than before." Miep had come in quietly and spoke from behind André. "Have you decided on a name?"

Tiineke nodded and spoke without lifting her gaze from the baby. "Yes. He has a big name even if he is a small baby—Andréas Johannes Meijer."

"A fine name. It's good to keep family names, carry on the tradition." Miep rested her hand on André's back. "And now, I believe that my work is completed here and I can leave you alone." She looked meaningfully at André.

André tore his attention away from his wife and child. "Yes, I'll walk down with you. My mother left an envelope for you." He stole one last glance at Tiineke before turning to leave. "I'll be back in a moment. Is there anything I can get for you?"

"No, I think when he's finished I'll try to get some sleep."

André and the midwife went downstairs together and across the living room to the corner where the desk sat to retrieve the midwife's fee.

"She misses her mother." Miep slipped the envelope into her bag without looking at the contents. "Having your mother is not the same for her as having her own." She pulled on her short spring coat and pinned her hat firmly in place.

André tilted his head thoughtfully as he watched her. *She's right. I'll have to organize something so we can see Elsa and Jan.* He was deep in thought as they walked outside together. He brought his focus back to Miep. "Shall I cycle with you to get you home, or have my brother do it?"

"No, no need. I am used to keeping these strange hours." Miep wheeled out her bicycle.

The midwife's dynamo light flickered as she pedalled off. The small generator sounded loud in the stillness of the night, scraping against her back tire. As quiet resumed, André stood for a moment more, enjoying the fresh spring night. Even in the heart of the city, the breeze smelled clean and he was filled with a sense of well-being.

Maybe this is the year that business will turn around and we can start saving for a place of our own.

Suddenly he felt a rush of longing to be close to his wife and new son. He hurried up the stairs, but went in to the room quietly.

Tiineke was awake, waiting for him. "I thought you fell asleep down there."

"No, no. I was just enjoying the night and thinking about what a good year we have ahead of us." He stroked Andréas's cheek with the back of his forefinger.

"You think it will be a good year?"

"Yes. No matter what, it will be good. I have you and my sons, and what more does a man need to be happy?" He now stroked his wife's cheek instead.

"Some money would be good." Tiineke smiled to take the coldness from the words.

André looked solemn and nodded. "Yes, that is a worry. I just feel that things will turn around somehow."

"I'm not sure I agree with you, but for now we'll just enjoy having our healthy baby safely arrived." Tiineke sighed. "I'm going to sleep. Shall I put him in his cradle?"

"No, just let me keep him here between us in bed. I'm not sleepy. I'll watch him."

Tiineke laid the baby down between them and slid down to curl beside him. "You've changed a lot since Wim's birth. You were almost afraid of him."

"You've taught me. You're right, I was afraid then. I was afraid of everything about being a father. I'm easier with it all now." André pulled the quilt up further to cover Tiineke's shoulders.

"I wonder what Wim will think." Tiineke's voice was already tinged with sleep.

"He'll love him."

André listened to his wife's breathing as she drifted to sleep.

He kept vigil, watching his son as he made plans for the future. As the sky lightened to a spectacular pink and violet, Andréas started to wave his arms. His small fists flailed and his forehead furrowed. He yawned and kicked out his heels, stretching his little legs.

At the feel of her baby's movement, Tiineke's eyes opened. "He's hungry." She struggled to push herself up.

André stood and stretched. "I'm going down for a wash and some breakfast. Shall I bring you up a tray?"

"No. I need to move anyway, so as soon as I have him fed I'll bring him down to meet the family."

André tore himself away from his wife and son.

———

The smell of coffee greeted Tiineke. "That smells good. Are you making pap?" She looked into the pot André was stirring.

"I am. I thought a healthy helping of porridge would be good for all of us."

The clatter of footsteps on the stairs announced Johan's arrival.

"Good morning, Oom Johan!" Tiineke held the small bundle up for Johan to see.

"I can't believe you're up and about already! And the baby! Well, what is it? Boy or girl?" Johan peered into the blanket.

André looked at his brother over his shoulder as he continued to stir the pot. "A baby brother for Wim. Please meet Andréas Johannes Meijer."

Johan turned pink. "That's his name? Really?"

André couldn't resist teasing his little brother. "Yes. You've proven that you are a good uncle, so we thought we'd encourage you to keep it up by giving your name to Andréas."

"I won't let you or *them* down." Johan looked very serious.

Tiineke kissed her baby's cheek. "I wonder if I should take him upstairs to meet Wim now. We could wake him up."

"Mama is already with him. She has him in her room and was busy scrubbing him down with a wet face cloth when I came down. He was complaining the whole time, but you know Mama."

"Yes, she doesn't pay any attention." André laughed. "Will you have some breakfast before you go training?"

"Wonderful!" Johan took a bowl and André scooped some porridge into it.

Tiineke watched the two brothers. *I hope my boys are as close as these two brothers are.* "Did you two always get along so well?"

"Yes, I think so." André looked at Johan.

"Oh, I'm sure we argued now and again like anyone does, but for the most part, yes. I always knew that my big brother would be there for me, and once in a while I know that André took the heat for something I did." Johan laughed.

"And I liked the fact that I always had a friend to play with. You were always clever at coming up with games and adventures." André smiled at his brother.

"Speaking of games, I have to go. Thanks for breakfast. And congratulations again with the new baby." Johan picked up his football boots that were tied together by the laces and flung them over his shoulder. A moment later, he waved cheerfully from outside as he cycled away.

"Mama!" Wim came bouncing into the kitchen. "The baby is here! Oma, look, the baby is here!" He wiggled with excitement, trying to climb up on Tiineke's lap.

André placed his hands on the small boy's shoulders, holding him still. "You stand here beside Mama to look at your new brother."

Tiineke put one arm around Wim's shoulders. "He's very small at the moment, but soon he'll be big enough that you can play together."

"Another boy?" Agatha came in to the kitchen.

André's voice was filled with pride. "Yes, Mama. Andréas Johannes."

"And will you call him André or Andréas?"

"We think we'll try Andréas for a while and see how it goes."

Agatha took over the breakfast preparations, ladling out the porridge. Tiineke had just finished eating when the baby started to whimper. She walked around the room bouncing him and patting him on the back.

"Shh, Andréas, shh." She tried to sooth him, but before long, he was howling.

"I'll take him back up. He's probably hungry again." Tiineke looked down at her older son. "Wim, tonight when you are in bed, you might hear some crying like this, but it's nothing to worry about. Babies just cry when they are hungry."

"I won't hear. I sleep there." He pointed to the ceiling.

André put his arm around Tiineke's shoulders, steering her towards the door. "Why don't you take Andréas up and look after him. We'll sort everything else out later."

She shot him a piercing look but didn't respond as she left. They could hear her crooning softly to the baby as she went back up to their rooms.

André took his breakfast dishes to the kitchen and left for the office.

Agatha and Wim cleared the breakfast dishes together then got ready for their walk. "Where is your cap? We'll go past the office to visit Papa for a moment before we go for our walk, shall we?" She helped Wim into his light grey jacket with its wide white collar and matching white cuffs.

She tugged on his knee-high grey and navy socks and tightened the strap of his black shoe. The socks visible through the sandal-like openings of his shoes already had some dirt smudged on them.

Agatha brushed the grit from his feet. "How did you get dirty so early in the day?"

"Don't know." Wim shrugged.

Agatha gripped his hand and they set off to the office.

André smiled at their arrival. "Hello, you two! Where are you off to?"

Wim pointed through the window. "The park!"

Agatha also looked out the window for a moment. "Yes, I said we would go to the park for a short while. We'll see if it seems safe enough."

"Safe enough?" André looked puzzled.

"Yes. There are so many homeless people around, it just isn't safe. We need to take good care and always be on the lookout."

André held his hands up. "Lookout for what, exactly?"

"Violent people." Agatha was dismissive. "The reason I dropped by was to say to you that you should gather some more of Wim's clothes later and bring them up to his room. I don't want to disturb Tiineke by doing it myself."

André shifted in his chair. "I haven't actually discussed this move with Tiineke yet."

"What is there to discuss? It makes sense to leave Tiineke some peace and quiet with the new baby and to have Wim in his own room. We have the space there now, and he likes it, so what could the problem be?" Without waiting for a response, Agatha turned to leave. "We'll go now and leave you to your work."

———

When Tiineke returned to the family living room, she wasn't sure if she was relieved to have the quiet time on her own to enjoy with Andréas or lonely.

"Well, little one, you'll have to wait a little longer to get to know your brother, I suppose. I thought he'd be here but I guess your Oma has taken him out somewhere."

The baby snuffled and made faces in his sleep.

"Shall we go back up and have a little sleep, then? At least upstairs we can be among our own things instead of all this big, heavy furniture of Oma's, right?" Tiineke suddenly felt claustrophobic.

Moving quickly, she carried her small, precious bundle to the other building and up the stairs. She sighed at being back in her own room as she laid Andréas in his small rocking cradle and lay down on the bed, turned on her side so she could look down at her sleeping baby. She felt a sudden urge to cry and wished her mother was here to talk to and help celebrate. Tears trickled down her cheeks and she reached out to lay her hand on the baby's stomach.

The warmth of him and the slight movement of his chest brought her some comfort, but still the lump in her throat and hollow feeling in her chest persisted.

Don't be so silly. What am I crying about? I have two beautiful sons and a wonderful loving husband.

The tears flowed and she felt a rising unaccountable fear. Panic washed over her.

Where is Wim? Why does she take him away so often when I want him here? It isn't right. Her heart raced and her breath came in gulps. *I want my sons here with me.*

Clump clump clump. She heard André's distinctive steps on the stairs. He bounced into the room with the air of a boy playing truant from school, his eyes bright and happy behind his polished glasses.

He stopped, the smile fleeing, before he crossed the room to his wife. "What's wrong? Why are you crying? Is Andréas alright?"

"Yes, he's fine." Now Tiineke was on the verge of sobbing.

"Are you all right? Shall I call for a doctor?" André's voice was raised and breathless.

"No, no. We're both fine."

"Well, what is it then?" His voice was softer now. He sat on the bed beside Tiineke and gathered her into his arms. Her tears soaked his collar.

"I don't really know. I just feel...worried." She couldn't put her feelings into words. The empty, panicky feeling was subsiding and she hardly knew now why she had been so upset. "I just wanted Wim."

"I'm sure Mama thought she was doing a favour by taking him out for a while." André sat back a little to study his wife.

"I know. I can't explain it."

"She wants to help, you know. In fact...that's why she cleared out the room across from Johan. She's made a wonderful little room there for Wim and he loves the idea of having his own place. I said he could stay there for a bit until you and Andréas get into a routine. Is that alright?" André continued to rub her back.

Tiineke's brow wrinkled. "I suppose so. It'll be better for Wim instead of being woken up in the night for the feedings, I guess. I just feel sometimes that she is completely taking over our lives."

André looked relieved. "I'm sure that's not her intention."

"Will you talk to your mother about letting us go to visit my parents? Maybe I'm just missing my own mother."

"Yes, definitely. I'll do it today." André looked at the new baby. "Look how long Andréas is. Was Wim so long? I've already forgotten."

"I think Andréas is longer. He takes after his Dad with those long legs. He's also thinner, though." Tiineke stroked the baby.

"You should get some rest while he's sleeping." André kissed Tiineke's forehead. "Will you be alright now?"

"Yes, don't worry. You're right, I am tired. I'll get some sleep."

André drew a light blanket over her, took a last look at his new son, and left to go back to work.

———

When André came back to the house at noon, he broached the nerve-wracking subject with Agatha.

"Mama, Tiineke and I would really like to go down to Rotterdam to visit with her parents. You know, show off young Andréas and let Wim spend some time with his other Oma and his Opa for a bit. We'd need a bit of money, though, for the train fares, and some spending money while we are there."

The sun reflected off Agatha's glasses, obscuring her eyes. The silence stretched for a moment before she finally spoke. "Are you seriously asking me to give you money for a holiday? You don't think that the extra burden of another child in the house is enough?"

"Mama, be reasonable. It won't cost that much. We'll stay with the Pols so there aren't any living expenses as such, although of course I would hope to be able to buy some of the food while we were with them. After all, you'd be saving that expense while we aren't here." André could hear the pleading tone in his voice and didn't like it.

"Mama, I don't like having to ask you like this, but since I don't have money of my own, I have no choice."

"The answer is no. There is no money for holidays. You have no concept of how little we are bringing in compared to the expenses of this household." Agatha started to turn back to preparing lunch.

André tugged on her arm so she was forced to turn back to him. "Actually, Mama, I do have a concept. Don't forget that I have been essentially managing the business for the past three years. I'm not a child anymore, Mama. I understand that things are hard, but this is important for Tiineke, and actually for the boys and I as well."

"I've said no, André." Agatha pulled away from him and gripped the edge of the kitchen counter, her knuckles white.

"Papa?" Wim had slipped into the kitchen unnoticed by either André or Agatha. His voice was timid and tears welled in his eyes as he looked up at his father's angry face.

André exhaled and stooped to lift Wim in his arms.

"Don't worry, Wim. Oma and I are just discussing things. Shall we go up to see your Mama and little brother?"

Wim wrapped his arms around André's neck and clung to him.

"Okay, let's go."

Agatha pointed to the sandwich on the counter. "I've just made Wim's lunch."

"Well, he can wait a few minutes for it. Can't you, my boy?" He opened the door and stepped out, leaving Agatha alone in the kitchen.

Wim clambered up the stairs, the clip-clop of his shoes echoing through the stairwell. André followed slowly, fuming. *What will I say to Tiineke?*

"Mama!" Wim galloped through the room and flung himself on his mother's bed.

Tiineke gathered him in her arms and hugged him. "I missed you."

"I went to the park." He began to prattle about the birds and boats he had seen.

André took a deep breath to steady his voice. "Are you feeling a bit rested?"

"Yes, and now that I've seen both of you, I feel even better." Tiineke smiled at him.

Small hiccups came from the cradle. André reached down and picked up the baby. "So you're awake too, are you?"

Tiineke slid her legs off the bed. "He's just been fed so I was thinking we should go down."

Wim grinned. "Lunch."

André tousled Wim's hair. "Why don't you run on down, Wim. I'll help Mama, and we'll be down in a moment."

Tiineke reached for André's hand as soon as Wim skipped out of the room. "What's wrong?"

"Nothing, really. I was just thinking about the trip to see your parents. I think it would be better if we waited a few weeks until Andréas is a bit bigger. I heard that there is some sickness going around and I think we should wait to take him out on a train with so many people around until we know he is tough enough. Don't you think so?" André prayed that this appeal to their son's health would put off the proposed trip until he could tackle his mother again.

"Oh, I don't want to put him in any danger." Tiineke's hand flew in front of her mouth. "I hadn't heard of anything, but of course, I haven't been out much these last couple of weeks. I'll write to Mama and let her know that we'll come in the summer when he's a bit bigger."

I just hope Mama doesn't say anything. But André knew his mother well enough to believe that it was a closed issue as far as she was concerned, so she would be unlikely to raise it.

Tiineke changed Andréas and they went down together, all three of them. The bread and cheese were sitting on the table, but Agatha and Wim had already finished eating. André made sandwiches for himself and Tiineke.

Tiineke's voice was polite when she spoke to Agatha. "Thank you for looking after Wim for me."

"It's no problem. He's an easy boy. This afternoon he is helping me in the shop."

"Oh, I thought I'd take both boys out for a short walk this afternoon. It seems like a nice day out." Tiineke smiled at her older son. "Would you like that, Wim?"

Agatha's face darkened. "I've already told him he would be helping me. It's best to stick to a plan once it's made."

"Mama Meijer, I appreciate your willingness to look after him, but I think that being out in the fresh air must be better for a young boy than being in a shop." Tiineke was trying to remain polite.

Agatha was silent for a moment. "Fine. Have it your way, then." She turned to Wim. "I'm sorry, Wim, you can't be with me this afternoon." She rose to go through to the shop, her back stiff and head erect.

André could see Tiineke watching Wim. The boy sat on the floor with his wooden blocks, stacking them listlessly. His bottom lip trembled.

André frowned as he saw his wife's own lip tremble as she looked at their son. "Would you like to stay with Oma, or go for a walk?"

"Stay with Oma." He didn't look up from his blocks.

Tiineke looked helplessly at André.

"I think Mama would like your company on her walk today. Wouldn't you like that?" André crouched on the floor beside Wim.

"Okay." But he did not give his usual happy smile.

"No, don't make him if he doesn't want to." Tiineke shook her head.

"He's four. I'm sure he'd rather be outside." André looked up at his wife, then turned back to his son. "Why don't you go through and keep Oma company while we eat our lunch? That way, you can do both things."

Wim jumped up and skipped through to the shop. His high-pitched voice floated back into the kitchen. "Oma, *I'm* not mad at you."

They ate their sandwiches in silence, then Tiineke sighed. "He's picking up the tension between us."

"Not just between you two. I get frustrated with her, too, so I suppose he's feeling that as well and doesn't understand."

"Why between you two?" Tiineke studied her husband.

André hesitated for a moment. "Nothing in particular." He pulled out his pocket watch and flipped it open. "I better get back to work. I've got a machine completely taken apart over there and don't like to leave it like that to get dust into the parts."

Tiineke watched through the window as André walked back to the factory.

She rocked Andréas in her arms. "Your papa has come a long way since I first knew him. When I think about how unskilled he used to be, breaking needles and incurring the wrath of both your Oma and Mr. Van Loon, look at him now, taking machines apart and putting them back together. What a wonder, isn't it?"

She could hear Wim chattering away to Agatha in the shop.

Andréas had fallen asleep and she set him in the carriage that waited near the door. "I suppose there's no rush to go out, is there? We'll wait until your brother is ready and then we'll go for our walk." She went into the sitting room and settled back in the big wing chair to relax while she waited for her oldest son to return to her.

———

Tiineke was dozing when Johan walked in. He peeked in to the baby carriage where Andréas was snoring before throwing himself on to the sofa, putting his head back and sighing.

His sister-in-law woke at the sound. "What's wrong with you? You look like you just lost your best friend."

"I was just down at the clubhouse and we listened on the radio to the Holland World Cup qualifying game against Switzerland."

"I guess we lost, by the look on your face."

"Yes. The final score was three to two, so we're out of the running now." Johan sighed again.

"It's only a game, Johan."

Johan straightened up, eyes wide. "Only a game? Tiineke, don't you see how it is bringing the whole country together? All the politics and other problems can be forgotten for a short while when everyone is united for the game."

Tiineke nodded thoughtfully. "I suppose I didn't think of it that way."

"Well, never mind. Ajax is still doing well as a team. I can't wait until I'm really part of them. They're set to win the National Championship this year, you know. Next fall, when I'm actually playing with them instead of just training, you'll have to come to some of the matches. Wim especially."

"He'll love it, and assuming we can somehow pay for the tickets, we'll make a family outing of it to watch you in your first game." Tiineke smiled, then lowered her voice, glancing towards the shop where Agatha and Wim were still together. "André told me…do you have a girlfriend?"

"Yes. Her name is Mary." Johan's cheeks turned pink. He wasn't used to talking about Mary with anyone other than Hank.

"Is it serious, do you think?"

"Serious? Yes, I suppose it is, although we haven't really talked about it much and I keep telling Hank we're just friends."

Tiineke leaned forward. "Tell me all about her. After all, she may be my sister-in-law one of these days."

"I'm not sure if she's crazy about *me* or just football. What I do know, though, is that she understands me, and doesn't think my need to play is silly. Her mother is English and we've talked about how the English players get paid. They don't get rich with it, but it's enough for their bills."

Tiineke looked shocked. "Are you thinking of going to England? What about the family business?"

"The business can manage without me. Let's face it, André manages quite well, and if I wasn't around, Mama would for sure let you keep the books and manage the shop while André ran the plant. Mama loves meeting the sales people and doing all that sort of thing.

You don't need me." Johan stopped talking at the shocked look on Tiineke's face.

"I think you and Mary have been talking more seriously than you want to let on." Tiineke was no longer playful. "Your mother will be upset if you go to England for anything, but especially football. You know that, don't you?"

"I'm not needed here." Johan shrugged and crossed his arms. "Tiineke, don't say anything. Promise me now."

"I won't say anything, don't worry. So when do we get to meet Mary?" She gave him an encouraging smile.

"She's actually coming to town next week for a few days with a friend of hers, so perhaps I could invite her around then. She's been saving for months for the trip."

"Oh yes, do!" Tiineke slapped her thigh. "I feel like I've lost track of so many of my old friends. They've either gotten married themselves, moved away, or we just don't have anything in common anymore. Sometimes I'm going crazy here. I would love to have a friend I could write and talk to once in a while."

Johan sighed. "I'll have to tell Mama, I suppose."

"She'll be fine. She won't have to do anything for it. I'll bake something and we'll have tea. It'll be simple. Bring Hank, too. Your mother seems to like Hank well enough and he can distract her. I remember the first time I came over, what pressure that was. Let's make it a little easier for Mary."

"Thank you, Tiineke. André's lucky to have you."

Tiineke laughed. "I'm not sure your mother would agree, but thank you."

———

Saturday afternoon a week later, Agatha sat stiffly in the wing chair, waiting to meet Johan's girlfriend. She wore an unfashionably long charcoal skirt and high-necked black shirt. Her iron gray hair was pulled back more severely than usual and her forehead had a deep furrow chiselled between her eyebrows. Her hands gripped the arms of the chair as if holding on for life.

"Mama, relax." André laughed. "You look so grim, you'll frighten the poor girl. Wim, go and sit with Oma for a few moments and show her the new wooden boat your Opa sent you."

Wim stood obediently and hovered at his grandmother's knee, looking to climb up on her lap.

Agatha held up her hand to prevent Wim from climbing up. "I don't need dusty little boys sitting on my lap." She did, however, take the wooden toy from Wim to examine. "Very nice." She handed it back.

The door opened and Johan stepped aside to let a young woman in before him.

"Hello, everyone. Here we are." Johan poked his head into the living room before turning back to take the young woman's jacket.

Tiineke crowded into the small hallway and smiled to see her brother stepping into the house close behind Mary.

Hank gathered Tiineke up in a big hug. "Hi Sus! How is young master Andréas?"

Tiineke broke out in a big smile. "He's healthy, and I think already grown a little." She turned to the girl who stood shyly beside Johan. "You must be Mary. I'm Tiineke and I'm so happy to meet you. I'm sure we're going to be good friends." Tiineke pressed Mary's small, white hand between hers. Mary felt fragile, like a small bird caught between Tiineke's strong working hands.

"I'm pleased to meet you." Mary flashed a shy smile before entering the living room to meet the rest of the family. Once she shook hands with Agatha and André she returned to stand beside Tiineke. Hank pulled a chair from the table and set it beside Agatha, striking up a conversation about the warehouse where he was working and the problems facing the textile trade. Agatha's face became less grim as they talked.

Tiineke linked her arm through Mary's. "Mary, will you help me carry in the tea?"

Mary smiled. Together, they went into the kitchen, where Tiineke could speak to the girl privately.

"Don't be worried about Mama Meijer. She looks fiercer than she is."

"Thank you. I must admit, I am a bit nervous." Mary's voice trembled.

Once they were all back and sitting in the living room, Agatha began as though Mary were at a job interview.

"So, do you work, Mary?"

"I do. I work in the laundry of a hospital. I supervise the staff of four."

Agatha nodded. "A supervisor. That's a good job, then. Johan tells me you like sports, though."

The word 'though' hung in the air as a rebuke.

"Not all sports. I like football."

"Like?" Johan laughed. "Be honest, you're mad about it. A true-blue fan."

"Yes, that's true." Mary laughed too. "I know it's unusual for a woman to enjoy it so much, but I got hooked during the 1930 Olympics, and now there is a whole group of us that go to as many matches as we can manage."

André nodded and smiled. "You've seen Johan play then?"

"Oh, yes." Mary's eyes lit up and her face flushed. "He's an absolute star, and when he starts playing in the new season with Ajax, I just know he's going to be their champion striker."

Agatha sniffed loudly. "I can*not* understand how people can waste so much time on sport."

"Mary's father works for the city government in Wageningen, Mama." Johan steered the conversation away from football.

Tiineke gave Johan a nod. She too, knew that hearing about Mary's good, solid family would interest his mother more than any conversation about football.

After that, Mary kept quiet for the most part, letting Johan tell her story to his mother. Her burst of animation had been spent on Johan's football. Now she was back to being subdued and shy.

When the clock chimed the passing of an hour, Johan stood up. "Well, we had better be going, hadn't we? Mary, you promised to meet your friend by the Rijksmuseum right about now, didn't you?"

Mary looked gratefully at him. "Yes, I didn't realize the time."

Tiineke and André stood to walk Johan and Mary to the door. Agatha remained seated and Mary went to shake her hand.

"Thank you for the tea. It was nice to meet you."

Agatha's back was stiff and voice cool. "Yes. Enjoy your stay in Amsterdam. Perhaps we'll see you again someday."

In the hall, André lifted his eyes to Heaven and shook his head. "Don't worry. She'll thaw out sooner or later."

———

When Mary and Johan got outside, Johan slipped her little white hand into the crook of his arm.

"You seemed to manage that alright. How are you?"

"Oh Johan, your mother hates me." She was on the verge of tears.

Johan looked at her in surprise. "No, don't say that. She's formal with everyone. She admired you with your good job, and she was interested in your family."

"She didn't admire anything. I could feel it."

"Come, let's not think about my mother anymore. Let's go and have a coffee somewhere, and we do have to meet up with your friends at some point."

Mary looked up at him, her eyes welling. "Not for a couple of hours yet. You knew yourself it was going badly, which was why we left so soon."

He smiled and pressed her hand on his arm. "I could see that you were miserable and I didn't want to waste our precious time being stifled by my mother."

They strolled along arm in arm towards Dam Square where they found a small cafe and sat outside, enjoying their coffee.

"I've never felt so happy." Johan took Mary's hand in his. "I'm going to make a career out of football. I can finally see that as a reality and not just a dream. After I've been with Ajax for the exposure and training, I'm going to see about getting on with a team in England where they actually pay the players." He lifted her hand to kiss it before releasing it. "And best of all, I've met a girl that understands me and my dreams." He hesitated before taking a deep breath. "Mary, I know I don't have any real money at the moment, although I have put some away that no one knows about, money I've made from little jobs here and there for the guys on the team. I've even helped Hank out a few times at the warehouse when they just needed an extra body for a day. It's not enough to live on, but I'm going to keep saving for when I move to England." Johan stopped again for a moment to look at the lovely girl across from him. Her round face and creamy skin were more typically English than Dutch, and the few freckles across her nose and her clear gray eyes gave her an innocent, almost childlike appearance.

Johan reached across to brush from her face a wisp of copper-coloured hair that had escaped the small shell-shaped green hat pinned to her head.

"You're very serious-looking." Mary looked deep into his eyes.

"Mary, I need you with me to help my dreams come true. I know that we'd have to live with my family for a bit while I get the experience with Ajax, but then we'd go to England where you have family anyway and wouldn't be lonely. You've been there before, you could show me all your favourite places and would know how to find a place to live." He knew he was babbling but couldn't find the right words.

"Johan, what are you asking?" Mary looked uncertain.

Johan moved around and knelt on the cobbles beside her chair while she laughed.

"Johan, people are looking!"

"Let them. Mary Steen, will you please marry me?" He'd finally found the words.

"Yes, yes, yes!" Mary stood and pulled him to his feet, wrapping her arms around his neck. Around them, people at other tables began to applaud and whistle.

He continued to hold her. "When?"

"Sit down again and we'll talk it through. Better yet, let's walk again. I can see that the athlete in you can't sit anymore." She laughed.

They spent the rest of the afternoon walking through Vondel Park and making plans. There was no point in a long engagement, they decided, and they would make plans to be married in the summer.

"The only thing I worry about is how your mother will take the news, and if she'll like me. After all, it is her house, and if she doesn't like me, it isn't very fair to live there." Mary's forehead wrinkled in a frown.

"My mother doesn't like too many people at first. She'll get used to the idea soon enough. One thing, though, that I'll need to put my foot down about is that any money you and I might make belongs to us, although of course we'll contribute something to the household expenses. I know you'll be giving up a good job to come here to Amsterdam, but with that experience, hopefully you'll find something else, and that money will be saved for when we go to England."

Mary was puzzled. "Of course it'll be ours. Why do you say that? She wouldn't expect us to hand everything over."

"André and Tiineke have no money of their own. Since they only work for Mama, they have absolutely no money."

"How awful! So they have to go begging when they want something?"

"Yes, and believe me, it's no life." Johan shook his head. "I don't say anything, of course, it's their life, but it's like a prison for them. Come, never mind them. Let's go and tell your friends!"

Johan and Mary walked off, hand in hand, on a cloud of dreams.

XV

Summer 1934

"No, Mama Meijer." Tiineke glared at Agatha. "We've been through this already. I don't want Wim to simply stay in the back garden all the time. He needs space to run and kick the ball around, so we are going out to the park, Wim, Andréas, and I." She hesitated for a moment. "If you would like to come along, you're welcome to join us."

"I am not going out. It's hot and the canals don't smell clean at this time of year." Agatha fanned herself. "I'm sure they are breeding grounds for disease, which is why you shouldn't take either of the boys out there right now."

"Mama Meijer, that's nonsense. They're no better or worse than they ever are, and it's never stopped us in previous years." Tiineke reached out her hand to Wim. "Come, Wim, we'll stop and see Papa on our way to the park."

She strode out of the house without another word.

———

"Honestly André, your mother becomes more impossible every day. She wants to keep the boys, especially Wim, in her sight every minute and I'm not having it."

André watched Wim through the window of the office as the boy chatted to Mr. Van Loon. He turned back to Tiineke and sighed. "Yes, I've seen it myself. She does seem to be a bit clingy lately."

"You would think that with Johan's wedding coming up soon she'd have something else to focus on."

"I suppose there are no arguments there to get her teeth into. Since they are getting married out in Wageningen, there isn't a whole lot that Mama can be involved in. Johan and I are fixing up his room for the two of them, so what can she do?"

"I don't know, but I wish she'd leave the boys and I alone for a change." Tiineke brushed some cotton dust from her skirt. "Well, I made such a fuss over getting Wim outside I better get going. She's probably watching from the window."

André laughed. "Now, now, she's not as bad as all that."

"Yes, André. She is." Tiineke walked out, calling for Wim as she steered the baby carriage out into the warm summer sun.

Wim galloped and skipped along beside the baby carriage, running a few steps ahead and then back again to make faces into the buggy. When he was rewarded with a smile from Andréas, Wim burst into his own laughter.

Tiineke joined in with a laugh and lay her hand on Wim's sun-warmed hair. "It's fun now that your brother has learned to smile, isn't it Wim?"

Tiineke was so engaged in the joy of her two boys, she hardly noticed the small groups of men all around as they entered the park. Now she looked around for a bench to sit on and realized that they were all taken with people sitting and standing in clusters.

Tiineke's brow furrowed. "It looks like we aren't the only ones who wanted to come out to enjoy the day, Wim."

For the first time, she felt a little bit uneasy as she realized there were very few children playing. Two gaunt-looking men joined a group of three others. They were speaking loudly and one punched the air with his fist.

"They can't do this to us!"

"We need to take action, now!"

Wim had taken the football from the rack under the baby carriage and was kicking and chasing it by himself. The ball rolled towards the group of men and suddenly Tiineke was fearful. She pushed the buggy after her son quickly.

"I'm sorry." She could sense their anger as the men turned their attention to her as she approached. "Here, I'll take my son and the ball and get out of your way." She knew she sounded afraid.

One of the men picked up the ball and threw it towards her. "Take your babies and go home, Missus."

He took a step towards her as she picked up the ball and she stepped back. He was unshaven and his hair was too long under his battered fedora hat. His shoes were badly scuffed and the stitching along one side of his right shoe was loose.

"Don't be afraid of me." He stopped and nodded towards the baby carriage. "I have kids of my own at home. That's why I just wanted to warn you. I think there is trouble coming."

His soft voice calmed Tiineke. At least he, personally, was no danger. "What do you mean by 'trouble'?"

"The government has lowered the unemployment support again. We can't live on it. We just want to feed our kids the same as you do. There's a protest coming. You better go home."

"Thank you. I will. Wim, come, we're going now." Tiineke tried not to allow her panic to transmit to Wim.

He ran to her in a zig-zag pattern, laughing, stopping every few feet to grin at her.

"Now, Wim!"

"Not yet!" He whirled and ran away again.

"Willem Jan, you come now!" She was close to tears.

Wim stopped and turned back to her, his smile evaporating. He ran towards her, his arms pumping in the effort.

Tiineke was already bumping the baby buggy across the grass towards the sidewalk as Wim caught up to her. He reached out and grasped the handle of the carriage, holding tightly as they walked, one arm stretched up, his small hand clinging next to her hands. She took her right hand off the handle and held it out to him. He let go of the carriage and grasped her offered hand.

Tiineke knew she had frightened her oldest son, but couldn't comfort him more than this. They walked quickly, in silence, towards home. She saw now there were clusters of people standing here and there, talking quietly, their voices a deep grumble as she passed. It was like the sound of distant thunder. More people were coming out of homes and joining the groups already congregating. One group was swollen to what Tiineke would call a crowd. The distance between the park and home had never felt so far before. Tiineke glanced down to Wim. His eyes were large as he swivelled his head to look at everything. There were tears welling. He knew these people were not waiting for a football match.

The air was thick with rising voices and the smell of sweat.

"Here we are now." Tiineke spoke with an air of forced cheerfulness as they swung through their own gate. She manoeuvred the carriage in to the house and left Andréas sleeping in it in the living room.

"Go and find Oma, Wim, and see if she will give you some milk. I need to go and talk to Papa for a moment, alright?"

The boy ran off towards the shop. Tiineke took the key that always hung from a hook beside the door and locked the door behind her before she went out to the plant.

She began calling for her husband when she was still several steps from his office. "André, André!"

He came to the door and Tiineke began crying as he reached out his arms to her.

"What is it? What's happened?" He enfolded her in a hug and held her. "You're shaking. What's going on?"

"There's something happening. Crowds are gathering outside. The poor people…there's going to be trouble. A man told me." She sobbed.

"What are you talking about? A man told you something?" André tilted back and held Tiineke's arms, his face puzzled. "Take a deep breath and tell me what's going on."

Tiineke told him what had happened at the park and on the walk home. "André, you better close the factory. Mr. Van Loon and Anna should go home." They were the only two workers who were still coming in every day.

"Yes, you're probably right. I'm sure it's nothing, but we'll close for the rest of the day, and tomorrow they can come again."

André went to explain to the workers and watched as they packed up their things and left, then returned to the office with a smile. "A half-holiday is good for all of us." He and Tiineke left together, locking the factory behind them.

They stood for a moment and looked down the street, watching as Anna navigated her bicycle through crowds of people.

André put his arm protectively around Tiineke's shoulders. "You're right. It doesn't look good. Come, we'll go inside." He steered Tiineke back to the house and took the key from her for the house door when her hands were shaking too badly to work the lock.

Inside, Agatha and Johan were listening to the news on the radio. There was a special bulletin telling about the new support cuts. Johan had come home early from his training and had already told Agatha what was going on in the streets.

Johan held up his hands in question. "How are people to live on those amounts?"

Agatha laced her fingers together, her hands restless on her lap. "The National Crisis Committee will supplement it."

"They can't do much. It's been in the paper already that it was a great idea when Princess Juliana set the committee up in 1931, but it just isn't able to support everyone that needs it." Johan stood and went to the window to look out. "Where are all these people coming from?"

Agatha gripped the armrests of her chair. "I think we better put up the shutters in the shop."

"Yes, we'll do it." André jumped up and Johan followed him quickly. The sound of the shutters being closed sounded loud to Tiineke as she and Agatha sat in silence, listening to the radio and watching Wim playing with his blocks on the floor.

André and Johan returned to the living room. "There, that's done. Now people know we're closed for business until tomorrow." He tried to make it sound like this was a normal thing to do in the middle of the day.

"I remember the riots of 1917." Agatha hugged herself. "It doesn't seem like that long ago. The shop windows were all broken. It's why your father had those shutters fitted. Of course, since the shutters are on the inside, the windows could be broken again, but at least we won't feel like anyone can come in. We were hammering up pieces of wood across the openings while people were throwing rocks and all sorts of things."

"They were throwing things at us?" Johan put his hand on his chest, a look of horror on his face. He was too young to remember it.

"No, we were just in the way of their anger. Mob anger. It had nothing to do with us." Agatha shivered. "This has been coming for a while now. I could feel it. I have food in, though. We're prepared and no one will go out until it's over."

Johan was at the window again. "Oh my God."

"What is it? What's happening?" André went to join him, peering over Johan's shoulder into the street. Tiineke moved to sit on the floor with Wim. She picked up a block and set it on top of a small stack that he had started. Wim smiled up at her. It wasn't often she sat on the floor to play with him.

"They're building some sort of barricade out there, closing off the top of the street. Listen." Johan pointed down the street.

The sound of shouting was audible now. Above it, they could hear the clanging of a police siren. André pressed closer to Johan. "Did that guy just throw something?"

Johan craned his neck. "A rock, I think. A paving stone."

"Yes, looks like they're trying to pry rocks up along the road there."

The brothers continued to watch the activity in the street. Johan gasped.

Tiineke looked up. "What's happening?"

His voice shook. "The crowd at the barrier is really huge. All I can see now are the backs of people and waving fists."

André went to sit down close to Tiineke and Wim on the floor while Johan threw himself on the sofa.

As the day crept into evening, they ate a small meal and listened to the radio. No one went out or even suggested it, other than for one trip that André made to go to the warehouse apartment for some clothes and baby supplies. They would all stay in the main house that night, André on the sofa while Tiineke would share Wim's bed. Wim was delighted, feeling like it was a holiday to have so much attention lavished on him.

As darkness fell, the jumping light of a bonfire at the barricade threw ghostly shadows on their walls. As Tiineke and Wim went to bed, the smell of smoke came through when she opened Wim's bedroom window a crack. She closed it again quickly, then turned and smiled at her son.

"I think tonight we'll leave your window closed. It's hot outside, anyway, so it's probably just as cool inside."

She and André had made a bed for the baby out of a drawer lined with blankets. The small room was hot and stuffy with the three of them, and when the baby started fussing a couple of hours later, it was with some relief that Tiineke rose to slip back downstairs. André had pulled a chair to the window and was sitting in the dark, looking out.

Tiineke settled into the big wing chair to nurse Andréas. "What's going on?" The closeness and intensity of the bond with her baby brought her comfort.

"Not too much. There are just a few of them left, but they seem to be passing a bottle around, so that'll keep them riled up, I suspect."

"Maybe they'll fall asleep and it'll all blow over."

The eerie light from outside glinted off André's glasses when he turned towards her. "I wouldn't count on it."

Tiineke stroked the baby's head. "I wish we were far away from here. Somewhere healthy, with a long strand for the boys to play on."

"Perhaps we'll go on a nice holiday next summer when Andréas is a bit bigger." André was peering outside again.

"I don't mean for a holiday."

André turned away from the window and faced Tiineke. He stood and went over to perch on the arm of the chair.

"This will pass. Everything will go back to normal again. You're just afraid at the moment. I understand, and honestly, I'm a little afraid too, but it'll all go back to normal in a day or so. You'll see." He kissed the top of her head and went to stretch out on the sofa. "You should go back up when you're done with the young master and try to get some more sleep."

André took off his glasses and laid them carefully on the end table. He crossed his ankles and folded his arms across his chest. His voice was dreamy when he spoke. "Listening to Andréas reminds me of the sea lapping on the beach at Zandvoort."

He was asleep when Tiineke went back up to Wim's small room.

In the morning when Tiineke came down again, André was still sleeping, but Johan was at the window.

She edged up beside him but he blocked her view. "What do you see?"

He frowned. "There are a good thirty people there. They seem to be waving and burning pieces of red cloth. Oh, I see now."

André woke and sat up. "What?"

"I see what they're waving and burning." Johan gestured out the window.

"Well? What is it?" Tiineke stepped away from the window and sat near André.

"It's that government subsidized clothing. You know, they've made all these special jackets and whatnot, all in red to show that it is government issued."

Agatha came into the room. "Ungrateful."

"Well, I suppose it's humiliating to have to wear those red clothes, telling everyone that it's a charity handout." Tiineke was sympathetic.

"On one hand, they are out there protesting that their handouts have been cut back, and on the other hand they are burning the handouts that they did receive. What kind of nonsense thinking is that?" Agatha glared at all of them.

No one answered and Agatha stomped into the kitchen.

————

As the day progressed, the crowds in the street swelled and became noisier. Wim was frightened and bored in the house. He whined to his mother to take him to the park.

"No Wim, not today. We'll go out in the back for a little and check how the garden is coming along. Papa will come with us, won't he?" Tiineke turned to André, who immediately got up.

"Yes, of course. Johan, are you coming too?"

"Why not." Johan got up to follow.

The three of them walked outside together with Wim in tow, Johan close behind. The brothers stood on the doorstep, watching Tiineke and Wim pulling weeds from the small garden plot.

They could hear the people shouting.

Johan nudged André. "I'm going crazy sitting in. I'm thinking of going out for a bit to see what's going on."

André tilted his head to listen before answering. "Mama will have a fit if you do. Maybe if we both go it wouldn't be so bad." He too was feeling restless. He turned to his wife and son. "Tiineke, come on you two, time to go back in."

When they were back inside, André announced he and Johan were going out to see what was going on.

Agatha grasped André's arm and reached for Johan's hand. Her voice was loud and eyes wide. "No, you're staying here."

"Your Mother is right, it's too dangerous." Tiineke stepped in front of André as he pulled himself free of his mother's grip.

"We'll be fine. No one is after us. It's the government that people are angry with." André took his hat from the hook.

Johan pulled his cap down so that the visor obscured his eyes. "We won't be long, but we can't just keep sitting here, not knowing. For all we know, it's already settling down out there and we're holed up here for nothing."

Agatha held a hand to her mouth and waved towards the window. "You can hear for yourself and see from the window that it isn't settling down." She reached out and took André's arm again.

"Mama, we'll be fine." André gently pushed his mother back.

Johan pulled his jacket collar up. "Back soon!" He was almost cheerful as they slipped out the door.

———

André and Johan made their way along the main road of Westerstraat towards the Noordermarkt area. The streets were busy with people drifting from one cluster to the next. When they reached the square, it was packed with people, with more arriving every moment.

André stopped and looked around. "Let's not go any further. The crowd seems pretty ugly here. Look over there." André pointed out two men who were pushing each other with others shouting encouragement.

"Watch out!" Johan pulled André out of the way as an old shoe flew through the air, narrowly missing André's head. "Yes, let's head back. This is definitely not settling down."

They hurried back, André rapped on the door and a little shriek came from inside.

"It's us! Come, open the door!" He knocked again.

The lock clicked and Agatha's white face appeared as the door opened. The boys hurried back inside.

André threw his hat and jacket on a hook, wiping beads of sweat from his forehead. "It's getting bad out there. There are no shops open at all."

The sound of yelling outside was punctuated by the crackle of breaking glass. Johan raced to the window to look out.

"The house on the corner has a window broken. It looks like people are picking up rocks from the road and throwing them."

André pushed Tiineke towards the stairs. "Tiineke, take the boys upstairs. Wim, you can play in your bedroom today, a special holiday treat." He hustled Wim and Tiineke, carrying the baby, up the stairs. "Mama, you should go up, too."

Agatha dragged her wing chair further into the middle of the room, away from the window. "I'm not being chased out of my kitchen and sitting room. I'm staying here."

The strident clang of police sirens filled the air. A cacophony of sound filled the room. More breaking glass, screams and shouts, rocks striking brick walls.

André laid his arm on Johan's shoulder. "Best stay back from the window. We'll draw the drapes just in case something breaks. At least the room won't be filled with broken glass."

Johan drew the heavy brown velour drapes, putting the room in darkness, the only light filtering in through the kitchen window.

The hours passed with a nightmare quality. André went up every so often to check on Tiineke and the children. Tiineke dozed off and on, and Wim had thankfully fallen into a fitful sleep.

André came up and sat on the bed beside Tiineke. The shouting outside hadn't diminished. Tiineke grasped his hand tightly. "I'm really scared."

He stroked the back of her hand with his thumb. "I know. I've never seen anything like it. It can't last, though. The police will get control of the situation and it'll all be fine again."

"It'll never be fine again."

———

The riot lasted five days. By the end of that, they were nearly out of food, despite the brief trips that André and Johan had risked. There were virtually no shops open in the area and to leave the area was impossible as all access points were barricaded and manned by crowds of hungry, desperate people.

They huddled around the radio. For days the reports had described the riots taking place in several cities in the Netherlands, but none as bad as the one in their own neighborhood. The police and military were harsh.

Agatha's voice was relieved after they listened to the special bulletin on July ninth. "It's finally over."

"Six people were killed." Tiineke brushed the tears from her cheeks. "Right here in our own neighbourhood. Six people killed and so many more hurt."

"No one is hurt here, though. Our family is fine." Agatha had a note of triumph in her voice, as if that was the only thing that counted.

André turned off the radio. "It's unbelievable that neither the house nor factory suffered any real damage, isn't it? I don't count the lumber that was stolen or garbage that needs to be cleared up. We really did manage alright."

Tiineke's face was flushed. "How can you both say that we're alright or fine? We've been terrified and virtually prisoners here for the past five days. How can we be fine after that?" She turned to her husband. "André, I must get away from here for a bit. Andréas is eight weeks old now and big enough to travel. We'll go to my parents for a few days. Please."

André's face flushed as he glanced at his mother.

Before he could say anything, Agatha spoke. "Nothing has changed in the last eight weeks. André, I told you the first time you raised this, and I'll tell you both again: there is no money to be squandered on holidays, especially now, after all of this. We went through a lot of food in the past days and I'm sure prices will be at a premium right now while everyone tries to replenish their pantry."

Agatha's back was stiff as she marched from the room.

Johan reached out his hand to his nephew. "Let's go out for a walk, Wim." Hand in hand, they went outside.

Tiineke looked at André without saying anything for a moment. Then the words came.

"She won't give us the money to go to Rotterdam." Her voice was flat and dead. "You already asked her when I first mentioned it, but you didn't want to tell me when she said no."

André couldn't look his wife in the eye. "I didn't want to upset you."

"You think I'm not upset now?"

Tiineke squeezed his arm and André was forced to look at her. "Yes. I know you are."

Tiineke was shaking. She pulled away and turned to look at the kitchen, then back to André.

She spoke through gritted teeth. "How dare she? How dare you? You kept this from me and let me walk right into that so she could use her iron fist with me. This can't go on, André." Her fists were balled. She took a deep breath and shook her head. "I'm going back to our own rooms, now that I finally can." She picked up Andréas and went upstairs to fetch his things.

André followed her. The bedrooms were stuffy after being closed up for days. He threw open a window to let the warm summer breeze in. It puffed the curtains and they watched the billowing fabric in silence. Andréas had settled in to his cradle and was snoring quietly.

Finally, André touched Tiineke's arm. "What can we do? Give me an idea and I'll listen, but at the moment I don't know what we can do. I'll talk to Mama again. Maybe I can convince her to give us the money for a holiday, but honestly, I'm not too confident."

"No, I'm sure there's no chance. She's made up her mind and that's that. Maybe there is money, maybe there isn't, but it's her decision isn't it? We have no say in the matter."

"It'll get better. Perhaps in another couple of months we can ask again."

"How will it get better? Why should it? You're dreaming. This is our life. You might be fine with it, but I'm not. No, André. I don't know how, but I'm going to think of a way to make changes because I cannot continue to live like this." Tiineke's face was pale with exhaustion. She threw herself on the bed and put her arm across her eyes. "I need to sleep for a while." She turned her back to him.

André sat on the edge of the bed for a moment and then stood. "I'll leave you for a bit, then."

Tiineke didn't respond.

XVI

Summer 1934

"Johan, it was so good of you to pay our train fares to come all the way to Wageningen." Tiineke squeezed Johan's hand. "We had a wonderful trip. Wim enjoyed it so much. What excitement."

André sat back and took another sip of his drink. "Yes, Johan, I can't thank you enough. It's a real holiday for us."

"Especially just being away on our own."

Johan smiled. "It was my pleasure. I've been saving a little here and there and once Mama said she wasn't coming, I knew she wouldn't pay for you folks either. So, since I can't have a wedding without a best man, what else could I do?"

Tiineke gestured towards Johan's bride. "Mary is beautiful. You're very lucky."

They watched Mary cross the lobby of the Hotel de Wereld, where the wedding lunch was being held. She seemed to flutter across the floor like a butterfly. She wore a borrowed wedding dress that reached to just above her ankles. The gauzy fabric floated behind her with the silk sash at the waist making her look even thinner than she was. Her copper-coloured hair was coiled on the back of her head in an intricate braid with a simple flower pinned in at the side.

"Gosh, I feel like such a horse when I see Mary's tiny feet in those silk shoes." Tiineke shook her head and frowned.

André reached across the table and squeezed her hand. "You're no less beautiful than Mary, just different. She has that delicate look of an English girl instead of the solid look of a Dutch girl."

"I'm not sure I like the sound of 'solid', but I know what you mean." Tiineke laughed.

Mary reached their table and Johan stood to encircle her waist with his arm.

He kissed her temple. "How is Mrs. Meijer doing?"

"I'm so happy. What a wonderful day. The weather even cooperated—not too hot. The lunch was lovely, and I'm looking forward to staying in this fine hotel with my husband tonight before going to my new home tomorrow."

André stood up to speak to his new sister-in-law. "Mary, it's so kind of your parents to put us up at their house tonight."

Mary smiled at him. "It'll be a bit of a squeeze with all four of you in my old room, but for one night I suppose you can manage."

Tiineke nodded and then glanced around the room. "It'll be fine. It's just such a holiday for us being away. I haven't seen Wim for the last hour, but I'm sure he's having a wonderful time."

"I saw him not long ago with a couple of my cousins, and while I think he may be getting his good clothes a little bit dirty, he did seem to be having fun." Mary waved towards the garden doors.

Johan pointed across the room. "I'm not sure that your two brothers are having such a good time. They look like they are longing to escape."

"I suppose when you are fourteen and sixteen, a wedding gets pretty boring once the food is cleared away." Mary dropped her arm from around Johan's waist. "I think I'll go and tell them that they can leave if they like. They're good boys and I know they don't want to upset their big sister." Mary slipped off in a soft swish of gauze and silk.

"I'll go along to say good-bye in case I don't see them again before we leave tomorrow." Johan followed his bride, leaving André and Tiineke alone.

Tiineke pulled André down again to sit beside her. "Johan looks so happy, doesn't he?"

"He does, yes. They're sort of an odd pair though, aren't they? Johan is such a big, sporty fellow and she's so fragile-looking."

"I suppose it brings out the protective side in him. She does love football, though."

"Yes, that's true. He's found a soul mate with that."

People were starting to leave and Mary's parents came to collect the four Meijers to take them to their house for the night.

———

"Your home is lovely." Tiineke gazed out the large living room window as they sipped their tea. It felt good to sit quietly and relax. "I love being in the country. Your garden is so wonderful and being so close to fresh produce must be such a treat."

Mrs. Steen followed Tiineke's gaze. "Yes, we couldn't go back to living in a city again. I worry a little about Mary. This is the only home she's ever known. It will be so different for her in the middle of Amsterdam."

"There is so much to do, though, in the city. I'm sure she's going to love it. Johan is looking forward to taking her to all his favourite places." André's voice sounded a little defensive.

Mary's father nodded. "Yes. She'll have Johan and that will compensate, I'm sure."

Mary's mother looked down at her hands and was quiet for a moment. "She had such a good job here, though."

Mr. Steen's voice was firm, but his glance was warm as he looked at his wife. "She'll find another. You need to stop worrying about her. This is her choice, and one of these days, when they move to England, she'll have some good experience to take with her."

André cocked his head. "Going to England?"

"Yes. Don't you know? Johan is hoping one day to get on to an English team where they pay their players." Mr. Steen nodded.

"Ah." André looked over to Tiineke but she didn't meet his eyes. "My mother will have to get used to that idea, but we'll let Johan tell her in his own good time."

Mary's mother sighed. "Just as I have to get used to Mary leaving."

Now Tiineke looked at André "My parents are far away as well. I miss them all the time."

Mrs. Steen leaned over and patted Tiineke on the knee. "Yes, Mary told us. I'm sure you must miss them and they you. Perhaps one day they'll move back to Amsterdam."

"Perhaps." Tiineke stood and started to collect the tea cups. "Let me help you tidy this up before we go to bed."

Mrs. Steen rose also while the men chatted.

———

André and Tiineke, along with both children, slept in Mary's room that night before rising early to meet Johan and Mary at the station for the trip back to Amsterdam.

Mary and her mother held each other on the platform.

"Mam, don't cry. I'm only a train ride away and we'll see each other again at Christmas for sure."

Mary's father kissed her cheek. "You'll write often to your mother."

"Yes, Papa, I promise." Mary smiled through her tears and boarded the train after the others. She waved through the window to her two brothers who were sauntering in the background, trying to distance themselves from the emotional leave-taking.

The return trip seemed to take longer than the outgoing trip. The boys were tired and fussy. Mary fell into a fitful doze in the comfort of Johan's arm, exhausted from the turmoil of the wedding and fare-wells. The freckles stood out more than usual on her pale face, and the copper tendrils of hair seemed dark against the whiteness of her skin.

There were almost there when Mary woke with a start.

Johan stroked her hair. "We'll be there in about twenty minutes.

"I'm suddenly nervous about seeing your mother. I'm sure she doesn't like me. You'll be away so much with your training that I'll be with her a lot on my own." Mary's voice was shaky.

Tiineke smiled at Mary over the top of her youngest son's head as he snuggled in her lap. "It'll be fine. Don't worry. I'll be there even when Johan and André are away."

Mary gave a weak smile in return. "Will you?

"Yes, definitely."

"That helps. I'll be out hunting for a job starting tomorrow, anyway. I'm lucky that I have some good reference letters with me."

"There seem to be quite a few new work schemes being set up these days by the government. Maybe you could get in on something there." André raised his eyebrows and nodded.

Johan shook his head. "I was reading about those last week. I think it's based on the American 'New Deal' programs but I have a feeling most of the programs are in construction and whatnot."

"Oh. I don't suppose that would be your field." André laughed, looking at the pale, slim girl.

Mary fiddled with her lace handkerchief. "No. I have good experience, though, so I'll be hopeful that something will turn up."

Johan gave her a brief hug. "Good girl. I know you'll find something. Any place would be happy to have a girl like you."

The train pulled in to Central Station and there was a flurry of activity as they pulled down their suitcases from the overhead racks and adjoining seats. They struggled their way out through the crowds of people rushing in every direction. They passed the large flower stall by the exit, the air heavy with the scent of freesias and other flowers, and spilled out on to the sidewalk and began the walk home.

They made their way slowly from Central Station, André and Johan carrying Mary's loaded cases. Once out of the train, they felt refreshed and cheerful again. Johan acted as a travel guide on the way. Mary laughed as Johan pointed out the interesting shops and homes on the way.

"Johan, I've been here before, you know."

Johan pouted. "I know, but you've never seen it from the point of view that the neighbourhood is now *your* neighbourhood."

Mary pecked him on the cheek. "You're right. Tell me everything."

They chattered happily, stopping now and again to set the cases down for a brief rest.

Wim skipped back and forth between the two couples, pointing out things that he liked as well. He was already fond of his new aunt, who seemed so different and exotic to him.

When they reached the house finally, the door opened as they approached. Agatha stood, framed in the doorway, wearing a severe black dress despite the warm weather.

"So you're here, then." That was her greeting as the young people crowded up the walkway.

"Oma!" Wim bolted ahead to throw his arms around Agatha's legs. She patted his head.

"Alright, Wim, alright, I see you." Her voice was warmer and her lips lifted in a slight smile.

Agatha stepped back to let in the two couples past her, then put out her hand to shake with Mary.

"You had no problems yesterday?"

Mary's voice was quiet and trembled. "No problems, thank you."

"Good." Agatha turned back to the sitting room. "When you're all unpacked, I'll make some tea."

André had already gone ahead with the case and was carrying it up to Johan's room. Mary stood awkwardly in the hall.

Johan gestured with his head. "Come with me. You'll want to unpack these things right away before it all wrinkles too badly." He steered her towards the steps to their room.

"I'll be going up to unpack as well, so we'll see you shortly." Tiineke gave her an encouraging smile.

"My goodness, Mary, what have you got in those cases?" André was shaking his arms as though they were numb when he came back down the steps, but his grin took the sting from his words.

"My life," Mary replied simply.

André was busy. A machine was in pieces spread across the work-bench in the small mechanics shop that occupied a corner of the factory. He had a jeweller's magnifying glass strapped to his head and was studying a small piece through the glass.

Mr. Van Loon popped his head into the shop. "Do you need my help here?"

"No, I'm fine. There's some wearing here that I'm just going to file down."

"I'm heading out, then. There isn't a lot to do and I heard there might be some fresh potatoes arriving at the grocery shop on the way home. I thought I'd try to get there early."

"Yes, go on." André was already turning his attention back to the intricate work before him. He was once again absorbed in his work when he heard his mother's voice. He turned to look and saw her crossing the floor towards him with a man in naval uniform. André took off his glass and wiped his hands on a rag.

"André, this is Luitenant ter Zee 2de klasse Cuypers." Agatha rolled the man's full title out in a solemn tone. "He is here from the naval base in Den Helder and wishes to discuss a large order for sheets and towels."

"Lieutenant. A pleasure to meet you." André put out his hand and then pulled back slightly. "I may be a little greasy. You just caught me working on the inside of a part here." He laughed apologetically.

The young lieutenant grasped André's hand firmly. "I respect a man's dirty hand when it comes from honest labour."

Agatha handed André a three-page document. "I have the details of the order from Lt. Cuypers, but since he was interested in seeing the operation, I thought I would bring him in and leave him to you, André."

André smiled as he took the form from his mother and turned to the naval officer. "My mother is rather proud of our setup and I suspect was happy that you are interested in seeing everything."

Agatha flushed and frowned. "I'll leave you two together, then."

Lt. Cuypers nodded at Agatha. "I look forward to doing business with you, Mrs. Meijer. Your husband had a good reputation with us years ago, I understand, so now that we are looking at replenishing our supplies, it seemed logical that we come back to the firm with which we had such success. I will personally be involved in these orders, so I am sure to see you again soon."

The tall, handsome officer turned his attention back to André. "You seem very adept with mechanics." He surveyed all the small pieces of machinery spread across the work table, all neatly ordered and organized.

"I wasn't always so." André swept his arm, indicating the shop floor. "If you had seen me with the machines a couple of years ago you might not have had such confidence, but yes, I've had lots of time to develop my skills. There is an upside to business being slow."

André showed the officer around the factory, walking outside with him in the end, where they met Tiineke and the two boys. Wim was wearing his dark blue sailor suit with white piping along the wide collar. When he saw the real naval officer in his crisp uniform standing before him, Wim stopped and stared, then put his small hand to his temple in a salute. Lt. Cuypers saluted in return and André and Tiineke laughed with some embarrassment.

"Aren't you a sharp young man?" The officer smiled down at Wim.

Tiineke's voice was apologetic. "He doesn't mean any disrespect, Sir. His uncle taught him that."

The officer tousled Wim's hair. "No apology required. I can see that he's a fine fellow. Your husband seems like a very capable mechanic, Mrs. Meijer. It's a skill for which I have great respect." He turned back to André to shake his hand. "I'll see you again soon."

He gave a small bow to Tiineke and snapped another salute to Wim who stood watching, wide-eyed, as the officer spun on his heel and strode off down the road.

They went in together where Agatha sat knitting while Mary flipped through a magazine. Agatha put aside the knitting and stood up. "Come and take me through the order."

André led his mother to the desk so she could examine the paperwork. His mother was the most cheerful she'd been in a long while. He glanced up when Johan walked in, but turned his attention back to continue the discussion with Agatha.

"We'll have to bring back two men."

"And order more materials."

Tiineke and Mary rose to go make supper and as they passed Johan, André heard him stop Mary for a kiss and to wonder what was happening.

"What's going on?"

André saw Mary shrug. "Business."

Before André could say anything, Agatha heard and jumped in. "Yes, business. I think we've turned the corner finally and things will start to get better again." Agatha was animated as she told Johan about the day. Tiineke joined in to tell of Wim's fascination with the officer.

Johan looked at his wife. "What about you? Did you have any luck in your job hunt?"

"No, nothing." Her shoulders slumped.

Johan ran his hand across Mary's back. "It's only been a couple of weeks that you've been looking. I think this order we got today is a sign that things will start to get better again. Don't worry and don't give up."

André looked at his mother. "Perhaps we could train Mary on one of the machines?"

Agatha and Mary spoke together. "No."

Agatha shook her head. "We need trained machinists for this order. We can train Mary if she's interested, after hours, but not to work on this."

Mary twisted her fingers. "I don't really think I'm cut out for the work, anyway. I'm trained for institutional services, running the laundry or kitchen. I'd like to find something in that field, if possible."

Johan winked at his wife. "You'll find something. I know you will."

The following week, when Lt. Cuypers came again to finalize the details of the order, he spent some time with André. Dressed in his everyday work uniform instead of his formal-dress uniform, he was less rigid and friendlier. He was about the same age as André himself and they talked comfortably.

"You really have a talent for this, don't you?" Lt. Cuypers gestured at the new set of machine parts spread across the worktable.

André picked up a cog and brushed a piece of cotton fibre off it, almost caressing the piece. "Well, I've come to love these machines. They are like tiny moving puzzles that sometimes you need to solve. Since we are starting up a few machines that haven't been used for a while, I thought it best to take them one by one and service each of them. When they are back together, I'll be able to hear if they are just right or if something is amiss."

The officer watched André work with a tiny screwdriver for a moment. "Have you ever considered leaving Meijer's to work elsewhere?"

"Work elsewhere?" André put the pieces down and wiped his hands on a clean rag. "No, I can't really say that I have thought about it, before now." He hesitated, stroking his chin, then glanced to either side and back to the lieutenant. "Come."

He led the way to the office, out of earshot of Mr. Van Loon, and settled into the seats around the desk.

"What made you ask me that?"

Lt. Cuypers leaned forward. "We have an opening coming up for a senior mechanic at the yard in Den Helder. We have a fellow who has been running the civilian shop there for years, but he's quite old now and isn't well. He's been off on sick leave for the past month and it's obvious he needs to retire."

"So there must be thousands of qualified people who would jump at the chance of such a job."

"Yes. That's the problem. We don't want to advertise this one job because we'll have thousands of people lined up outside our gates wanting to apply. How do we pick from them all? We don't have the time or resources to interview them, and then we're afraid there might be trouble when we do choose one. All those who didn't get it will want to know why and so on. After the bad publicity with the mutiny, no one wants more problems. I've been told to hire someone quietly."

"What about the junior mechanics, aren't one of those fellows able to be promoted? Wouldn't that be better than bringing someone in from outside?"

"None of them are able. They can work under direction, but no, none have either the mechanical skill or the ability to manage others. It would cause more problems than solve them." Lt. Cuypers grimaced.

"Well, it does sound like you have problems, alright. I'm not sure what the answer is." André tented his fingers under his chin and frowned.

"I should be going. You have enough problems and work of your own without thinking about mine." The lieutenant stood. "I'll come back next week if you don't mind, just to see the work starting, and look at the materials you have."

"Yes, of course. You're very welcome to come by anytime." André warmly shook the lieutenant's hand.

That evening, when André and Tiineke were alone together in their rooms, André related the conversation to her.

Tiineke's eyes were alight. "How much money are they offering?"

"I don't know. I didn't ask. Tiineke, I can't leave Meijer's."

Tiineke ignored him. "Would a fellow have to live on the base, I wonder, or could you live in a normal house in the village?"

He shrugged and lifted his hands. "I don't know."

"André, this is it. This is our big chance to go and make a life of our own." Tiineke put her hands on André's shoulders, her eyes looking steadily into his.

"I can't." He closed his eyes to escape Tiineke's piercing gaze, then opened them again. "It would kill Mama. How could she manage?" He turned his head to look at the cradle where Andreas lay sleeping, but he didn't move out of Tiineke's clasp.

Tiineke gently touched his cheek, bringing his gaze back to her. "Johan can step up and take over. He and Mary." Tiineke felt a shadow of guilt even as she said it, knowing that Johan had plans of his own with his football.

André's voice shook. "It was always Mama's dream that I manage the business. She worked so hard for it."

"Yes. That's just it. It's *her* dream. Well, André, I cannot live like this any longer. We're living your mother's dream. We have a life of our own and it's time we started living it. I thought we could do that and have you work for Meijer's, but it's now clear to me that your mother will control our lives as long as we are living here, and since we can never get a place of our own as long as you work for her, then the only answer is that you not work for her. André, I'm telling you that this is our chance. You and I together will meet with Lt. Cuypers when he comes next week, and if the answers are at all favourable, you are taking that job."

Tiineke's stare brooked no argument.

"Alright, we'll talk to him. That's all I'll agree to right now." André's stomach rolled. He almost wished he hadn't said anything.

"You know I'm right. Otherwise you would have told us all about that conversation at supper tonight. You didn't. You waited until now because you know yourself that I'm right." Tiineke's shoulders dropped.

She pulled him by the hand, slipping into bed and turning off the light. She slid close to him and slowly unbuttoned his pajama shirt, running her hand across his chest when André pushed his groin against her. His penis was already hard and sprung out when Tiineke guided his pants down. She grasped him with just enough pressure. As she stroked him, her other hand slid down further, touching, sliding, stroking his inner thigh and testicles. Tiineke seemed completely relaxed and she responded to André's touch with an abandon he hadn't seen for a long time.

When André entered her, she pulled him to her with her strong long legs wrapping around him. Her arms were flung back over her head and she arched up against him. She met every thrust with a tightening of her muscles and had to stifle a small scream as they came together.

"Oh my God. You're a witch." André fell back on the bed beside her. He nodded to the sleeping baby. "How is it that he slept through that?"

"The sleep of the innocent." Tiineke lifted his hand from where it rested on her thigh and kissed the back of it. "André, I love you so much." She hesitated and then left it at that. It was enough. He knew how she felt.

———

When the lieutenant returned the following week, he inspected the materials, saying little over the loud hum and clatter of the machines cutting and stitching. The two machinists worked steadily with heads bowed, getting back into a rhythm lost during months of unemployment.

André spoke loudly into Lt. Cuyper's ear. "I'm going to ask my wife to bring over a pot of coffee and we can have it in the office in a few moments. I'll be right back."

The officer gave André a thumbs up and André hurried out to the house, where Tiineke was hovering in the kitchen.

"Okay, get the coffee and bring it over."

Agatha called from the living room. "How is it going over there?"

"Good, Mama. Tiineke's just going to bring us some coffee before the lieutenant goes."

Agatha stood. "Shall I come over? Will he want to discuss the results of his inspection? I can bring the coffee."

André's eyes widened when he glanced at Tiineke, but his voice remained calm. "No, no, Mama. You're fine. We've been talking throughout the tour and he's fine with everything. You stay and watch the boys, if you don't mind. Tiineke is already working on the coffee and will bring it over."

Agatha sat again, clearly a bit disappointed at not being included in a meeting with the fine young officer, but not willing to undermine her son after she had taken such pains to demonstrate that he was in charge of the work.

When Tiineke carried in the tray with the coffee, Lt. Cuypers and André both stood. André stepped forward to take the tray from her and set it on his desk. He had already brought in an extra chair which Tiineke now dropped in to. André closed the office door as Tiineke handed a cup to the lieutenant.

André cleared his voice. "Lieutenant, I was telling my wife about the conversation you and I had when you were last here. Your difficulty with your retiring mechanic."

Lt. Cuypers coffee cup was poised in mid-air and he raised an eyebrow. "Oh yes?"

"Is the position still open or have you solved the problem by now?" André wasn't sure if he hoped the decision would be taken out of his hands or not.

"No, I'm afraid I haven't made any progress with the issue."

"Could a man support his family on the salary?" André's felt beads of sweat forming on the back of his neck. He had never had a conversation like this.

"Yes, certainly. It isn't a high wage—there are no high wages any-where these days—but yes, it is fair."

"And can a man live in the village with his family or does he need to live on the base?" Tiineke's voice was strong as she jumped into the conversation.

"All our civilians live off of the base in the village, which is an easy walk or ride by bicycle. Are you seriously considering my offer?" The Lieutenant looked from André to Tiineke and back again.

André rubbed the knuckles of his right hand. "Right now we are just talking."

Tiineke folded her arms across her chest and sat up straighter. "He's very serious. When would you need to know?"

"It has been decided that the incumbent is definitely retiring and will not be coming back to work at all, so the sooner the better. There are already some jobs behind schedule. If you don't take it, I need to start looking elsewhere by the end of this week." Lt. Cuypers finished his coffee and set the cup down. "Send me a note one way or another by Thursday, if you please. I sincerely hope you take it. I know that you would be leaving this work behind, but I think your mother is quite a capable woman, and I recall her mentioning that you have a brother in the business as well."

André stood to escort the officer out. "Yes, I do. I'll send you a note."

After the officer had gone, André and Tiineke sat together in the office with the door closed.

André pressed his hands flat against the desk and shook his head. "Tiineke, it just isn't possible."

"Why not?"

"It would kill Mama. She has kept this business going just for Johan and I. The intention always has been that I would run the operations and eventually Johan would take over the customer side from Mama. I just can't walk away from it."

Tiineke was silent for a moment while André shuffled papers around on the desk.

"André, for five years now I've been living with your mother. I've tried to make it work, I really have, but I know now that it can't. Maybe it's me, I just have too much of a mind of my own, but I can't go on having your mother control our lives. I hate living here. That's the truth of the matter. It doesn't get better, it only gets worse. Now I feel every day that she is taking Wim away. I can't live like this, André."

André started to reach out to her, then pulled back when she leaned back in her chair, out of reach. "I'll talk to her. We'll make some changes."

Tiineke's eyes narrowed. "Like you talked to her about us going on a holiday to see my parents? I can't even see my own parents because of her."

André was silent.

"Even aside from your mother, I don't feel that this is a good area to raise the children, André."

"She won't understand."

"We may never get this chance again. André, if you don't take it, *I* won't understand. Or perhaps I should say that I will understand. I'll understand that you choose your mother over your family. I can't settle for that. I *won't* settle for that." She bit her bottom lip as tears welled.

André looked up at her and Tiineke returned his gaze steadily.

"Alright." He took off his glasses and polished them with his handkerchief.

"It'll be hard, but you won't be sorry. I'll make sure you're never, never sorry." Tiineke leaned forward, reached out and squeezing his hand.

André put his hand over hers. "You and the boys are everything to me, Tiineke."

"I know that. Finally we'll be able to be a proper family together and live some of those dreams we talked about years ago." Tiineke gave his hand one more squeeze, then sat back again. "Should we tell Johan first, I wonder?"

"Write the letter first and get all the details and then we'll tell everyone together. I think that'll be best."

"Yes, alright."

André was happy to defer the conversation. Perhaps the naval officer would change his mind and the whole thing would go away.

———

Two days later, he received a note in response to his letter. The navy was pleased to offer him the position and would expect him to report for work in ten days. Included in the letter were a couple of options for houses in the area that could be rented at reasonable rates.

As supper was finishing that evening, Tiineke brought it up. "André and I have something we would like to tell you all. Can we leave the dishes for a few minutes and come and sit in the living room?"

"You can't be pregnant again!" Johan looked towards Andréas who slept in his carriage by the window.

"No, this little one will do me for a while, thank you." Tiineke laughed and took a seat beside André on the sofa and held his hand.

André swallowed and took a deep breath. "Mama. Johan. This is the hardest decision I've ever made in my life, but I—we—have thought it through and think it really is the best thing."

"What is it then?" Agatha was stiff and her brows were drawn together in a deep 'v' on her forehead.

Johan sat beside Mary on the small couch and instinctively put his arm around her, as if bracing for bad news.

André gripped Tiineke's hand and blurted it out. "I'm leaving Meijer's to take a job in Den Helder."

Johan gasped. "What?"

Agatha slapped her leg. "No."

Tiineke's free hand went up as though to stop her mother-in-law from speaking further. "Mama Meijer, it wasn't a question open for discussion. The decision has been made and André has accepted the position." Beside her, André had paled and was breathing heavily.

Agatha stood now, towering over Tiineke. "This is all *your* doing! André would never have even considered such a thing if you weren't poking him and pushing him. You have always been a bad influence on him. I knew it the first day I laid eyes on you." Spittle formed on Agatha's lip as she yelled. She spun away to stare out the window, her back rigid.

"Mama?" Wim had been playing quietly and now crawled on his mother's lap, frightened by his grandmother's shouting.

"Shhh, it's alright, Wim. Oma's upset, but not with you." Tiineke shook as she comforted her son.

"André, let's talk about this." Johan's voice carried a note of desperation.

André found his voice, finally. "As Tiineke said, there really isn't anything to talk about."

"I won't have it. I'm telling you, André, you can't do this. I won't let you make this mistake." Agatha faced her oldest son and held out her hands in plea.

"André, think about it, please." Johan's hand was fisted in front of his mouth.

"We have thought about it. In ten days, I'll be starting as lead mechanic at the naval yards in Den Helder." André shook his head. "It's a good job. We'll have money of our own and a home of our own."

Mary nodded to Tiineke. "I can see why you would like that."

Johan rounded on Mary and glared at her. "Can you see what this means to me?"

Mary flinched.

Johan took Mary's hand. "I'm sorry, I didn't mean to yell at you. I need to get out of here. Come Mary, we'll go for a walk." He wouldn't look at André.

André looked at his mother's back as she stared out the window, silently watching Johan and Mary walk away. As he looked back at Tiineke, she gave him a smile. He felt as though the roof had blown off the house, leaving him exposed, yet somehow liberated.

———

For the next week, Agatha felt her world falling apart.

All my planning and hard work, and this is the thanks I get.

She watched from the kitchen window as André and Tiineke set their suitcases down outside the door. Tiineke's folding bed and big easy chair had been sent on ahead to their rental house. It was all the furnishings they were taking from the Meijer house.

André and Tiineke stepped inside the front hall.

"We'll be going now." André snapped open his father's pocket watch to look at the time. "Our bus leaves in half an hour."

Agatha's jaw was stiff and she spoke through gritted teeth. "You should leave that watch for Johan."

"Why?" André looked at her. "What are you talking about?"

Agatha sniffed loudly. "If you leave today, you are no longer a son of this house."

Johan and Mary sat in the living room, listening.

"Mama, that's nonsense." He put the watch away in his vest pocket and followed Tiineke to the living room.

Agatha stood frozen, watching and listening as the two brothers said good-bye.

André reached for his brother. "Johan, I'm sorry to be dropping you into this, but it's the right thing for Tiineke and I." André shook hands with his brother.

Johan stood and grasped André's upper arm as they shook hands.

"One last time, please, I'm begging you to reconsider. She won't change her mind, you know; she'll disown you." Johan nodded toward Agatha.

André shook his head. "I can't, Johan. Will you stay in touch?"

"Yeah, sure." Johan dropped his hands, his voice cool.

André grabbed his brother and pulled him into a hug. Agatha narrowed her eyes in satisfaction when she saw that Johan stood stonily without returning the embrace.

Mary and Tiineke were hugging as well, Mary speaking softly to Tiineke. "I'll write to you."

Tiineke glanced quickly at Agatha then turned back to Mary. "Do. Look after yourself here. Don't let her eat you up."

"Oom Johan!" Wim was crying. "Come with us!" He sobbed as Johan scooped the child up in his arms.

"I can't come with you, but soon your little brother will be big enough that you can play with him. You won't need me for a play-mate anymore." Johan held his nephew close.

Wim laid his head on his uncle's shoulder, clinging. His tears soaking into Johan's collar.

Johan's voice was choked when he spoke again. "You must keep up with your football practice." Johan set the boy down, then went over and lifted Andréas from his carriage. "Good-bye little one. Grow up strong in all that sea air."

Mary leaned over to kiss the baby's cheek and Johan tucked him back into the carriage.

André leaned over to give Mary a peck on the cheek and then, with one more glance around the living room, he faced forward to the front hall. "We have to go." He took Wim's hand and walked to the door.

"Good-bye, Wim." Agatha leaned down to hug the boy briefly.

André paused in front of his mother. "Good-bye, Mama. I'll be in touch. If there are any questions about the business, just send them to me and I'll be happy to help."

"I won't have any questions for you." Her eyes were icy behind her glasses. "When you leave, you are leaving your family for good. Are you certain that's what you want?"

"Mama, I'm not leaving my family." He half turned and swept a hand around to encompass Tiineke with the baby, and Wim. "Here is my family, and we are leaving together. I'm sorry you can't accept that, but yes, I'm certain it's what I want." He leaned towards Agatha to kiss her on the cheek and she pulled back.

André shrugged and stepped out, picking up the two suitcases.

Agatha, Johan, and Mary watched from the window. Tiineke walked ahead, pushing the carriage, the rack underneath loaded with a heavy box. She had a large carpet bag over one shoulder. Wim went next carrying his own small case, then André with the two large cases.

Agatha turned away and went to the kitchen to make tea.

André and Tiineke: 1934 – 1942

I

Fall 1934

"No, you have to walk, Wim. It's not far now." André pried his son's clinging hands from his leg.

"The trip felt long, didn't it?" Tiineke had to almost shout over the sound of the wind.

"It would have been good if there was a bus that came here directly. It was the change in Alkmaar that made it seem so long." André was studying the note that Lt. Cuypers had sent with directions to their new home. "It's down this way, I think. Yes, here it is. Hoogstraat. Not far now."

Tiineke stopped for a moment to give them all a rest and studied the sign post. "Highstreet. Well, it has a grand name anyway."

They stopped in front of the narrow two-storey brick house and André set the suitcases down gratefully. Tiineke had been carrying Wim's case and the carpet bag was balanced on the baby carriage.

They stood there for a moment and looked at the house. It looked worn out. Constant wind dominated this tip of land jutting out into the sea, sanding down brick and flaying paint from wooden surfaces. The years of hard economic times had seen house maintenance fall to the bottom of priority lists, and this house had that rundown look of neglect. There was no front garden, and the seashells that had once been spread across the tiny square in front of the house had long since been ground down or swept away by the wind, leaving bare ground where dust eddied.

Tiineke poked André in the ribs with her elbow, then rested her hand on Wim's neck, massaging it. "Come on, get out the key and let's explore our new home. Isn't this very exciting, Wim?"

The door creaked open; the hinges were in need of oil. Once inside with the door closed, the sound of the wind was muffled enough they could speak in normal tones again.

Tiineke unpinned her hat and tried to flatten back her hair that had been torn from the pins. "I had no idea how loud wind could be."

Lt. Cuypers had arranged for an advance on André's pay and they used it to rent the house and buy a few pieces of inexpensive furniture. Tiineke's easy chair sat by the front window. There was a plain wooden table and four chairs as well, completing the furnishings in the front room. Tiineke lifted the baby out of the carriage and the family went for a tour. Upstairs, they looked first into the boys' room and found the bed and a small wooden chest of drawers.

"Andréas will have to sleep in his carriage for a bit." Tiineke kissed the top of the baby's head. "It'll be a nuisance having to drag it up and down the steps every day, but we'll make it work."

In their own room was a chest of drawers with a pile of quilts folded neatly on top. André had told Lt. Cuypers not to worry about looking for a bed for them. They would make do with folded quilts on the floor for the time being. He had been worried about spending too much money. In the kitchen were the basic dishes, pots, pans and cutlery and in the icebox Tiineke found a bottle of milk and a pound of butter and six eggs. On the counter sat a loaf of bread.

André squeezed the loaf of bread to check its freshness. "He's thought of everything!"

"Yes, he's very kind." Tiineke put the baby back into his carriage and turned to André, throwing her arms around him. "I know it doesn't look like much. I know you've given up everything to do this for me—for us—but you won't be sorry. We're going to make this work and be so happy here."

Tiineke reached down and picked up Wim and leaned in again to hug André with her free arm, the three of them pulled together into the hug. Wim giggled. They so rarely had shown such open physical contact, always feeling constrained by people around.

Tiineke had taken a few things from the house that she knew Agatha would have begrudged had she asked: some linens, some tea, coffee, and biscuits along with Wim's favourite cup. She unpacked the few items, and then they celebrated their arrival in their new home with some bread and butter and cups of tea. After lunch, they took a walk in the area to become oriented. Their bicycles were being shipped and would arrive on Monday.

A short walk showed them the bridge that crossed the canal and would take André to the naval yards each morning. He would be able to cycle home for lunch each day if the schedule allowed it. If they walked in the other direction, they would get to the Zee-Promenade and the actual seaside within fifteen minutes.

Tiineke waved back in the direction of their house as they turned away from the bridge. "It's a very handy location, isn't it?"

André gave a small nod. "Not quite as handy as just walking across the doorstep to get to work, but still, yes, it'll be fine."

With the first sight of the sea, Wim fell in love. He ran screaming through the long dune grass to the beach, oblivious to the scratches the hard grass inflicted on his bare legs. He plopped down on the sand and peeled off his socks and shoes, flinging them aside.

Tiineke pushed her husband after Wim. "André, go with him!" She was fearful the small boy would run into the sea and be swept away by a powerful wave before they could save him.

André chased after Wim, whose small legs pumped with almost hysterical energy, taking him to the water's edge.

André roared at his son above the sound of the wind. "Wim, you do *not* go in the water without me!"

Wim stopped with his toes just in the water. He glanced back over his shoulder at his parents, his eyes wide and his mouth open in an 'oh' as the water swirled around his feet A wave broke, spraying him with a salty mist and covering his feet with foam. Wim grinned up at his father as he reached him, and André grinned back, hopping as he took his socks and shoes off. He rolled up his pant legs and took Wim's hand. The boy was quickly up to his thighs in water, the bottom of his short pants getting wet. They danced backwards as waves rolled towards them and then scurried forward again as the water receded. Wim laughed and cried up to the seagulls that swooped and circled around them, imitating their calls.

Tiineke stood with the baby in her arms and watched André and Wim.

She whispered to Andréas. "Look at those two boys." Her voice was choked with emotion. The baby gurgled happily, reaching for a strand of Tiineke's hair that the wind had pulled loose from the pins.

An hour of playing and running on the beach was still not enough for Wim. They had a hard time getting him to leave. Later, at home, Wim tugged on his father's sleeve. "Papa, can we go again tomorrow?"

"You can go every day, Wim. I'm not sure if I can go with you every day, but you and Mama can."

Wim turned to Tiineke. "Can we, Mama?"

"Yes, Wim. This is our home now and we can go whenever we like. Next time, though, you aren't going in the water with all your clothes on." She scolded, but with a laugh.

After a small supper of eggs with bread toasted over the stove top, Wim fell into a sound sleep in his new room.

Tiineke pulled the door closed and they went back downstairs. "He's exhausted."

"I'm not much better." André yawned as he settled in to the easy chair. He patted his lap as Tiineke moved to pull a chair from the table. She left the chair and curled up on his lap.

"How decadent, to be sitting here on your lap in the sitting room." She snuggled down against him.

"I know. It's quite appalling."

"I'm seeing a whole different side of you here. You were so..." She struggled for the right word. "So abandoned...with Wim on the beach. You already seem more relaxed than I think I've ever seen you."

"You're right. I feel, somehow, as if all the rules that I took automatically as correct can be rewritten. Suddenly, if I want to cuddle with my wife in the sitting room, it's alright to do so."

Tiineke pushed the hair back from André's forehead. Usually he was so tidy, but today the wind had blown his hair into an unruly mass of curls. "You look like a boy yourself."

He kissed her forehead. "It's a new beginning for us, isn't it?"

"I think it's *the* beginning for us." She stood up and pulled him to his feet. "Let's go see what we can make for a bed up there. We won't bother with the baby carriage, we'll use a drawer from the chest in our room to make a bed for Andréas. He'll be happy enough with that." She led the way up the stairs, carrying the baby. They stopped long enough to peek in at Wim, watching in silence for a moment, then André pulled the door closed with a smile. They went together into their own new room.

———

On Monday morning, André was ready to leave early, carrying a sandwich with him. "I'm not sure how it will go, so don't count on me for lunch. For today, I'll stay there, and then we'll see how it goes. Do I look alright?" This was the third time he'd asked as he stood at the door.

Tiineke put her hand on his cheek. "I can see myself in your shiny shoes, your tie is straight, your hair has been beaten into submission. André, you look perfect. They are interested in your ability, not your fashion sense."

"I know, but I'm going to have men working for me. I think they're going to be upset that one of them didn't get this job." His forehead wrinkled in a frown. "I need to make a good first impression."

"You're going to make a great first, second, and third impression. Now go." She kissed him lightly on the lips, handed him his hat, and gently propelled him out the door.

Tiineke and Wim waved through the front window when André turned back for a moment, as if hesitating to leave the comfort of his family. He waved back, gave a small smile, and set off with a determined step.

Tiineke scooped Wim up and waltzed him around the room a little. "Your Papa is a bit nervous, but he's going to be so great at his new job." She sang a children's song while she danced and Wim sang along in his high, squeaky voice.

Wim pulled on Tiineke's sleeve after she set him down. "Can we go to the beach now, Mam?"

She held up her hands. "We have to wait for our bicycles. When they get here, we'll go out."

An hour later there was a knock on the door. Wim bolted to the window.

"No bicycles." He announced sadly before Tiineke could open the door.

Tiineke opened the door halfway and looked at the postman curiously. "Yes?"

"Are you Mrs. Meijer? You need to sign for this."

Tiineke signed for the thick envelope and barely closed the door before tearing open the letter.

Wim sighed deeply when he saw that it was nothing more interesting than a letter and went back to his spot by the window.

Tiineke spoke more to herself than Wim. "It's from Oma and Opa Pol."

Dear Tiineke and André, You've picked a difficult road for yourselves, but we are sure that it is the right one. Congratulations on your new beginning. You are both brave and strong, and we know that you will make a success of your new life.

Tiineke, we can't be there with you in person, but imagine that I am giving you a big hug right now. We are with you in spirit. You have our love and support, always.

We can't do much for you, but here is a small gift to help set you on your feet. We hope it helps.

Love from your Mama and Papa.

Tiineke's eyes filled with tears as she looked again in the envelope and found the cashier's cheque for money that she was certain her parents couldn't afford to spare. It wasn't a lot, but would allow her to buy some more pieces of secondhand furniture and stock the kitchen with staples.

"Oh Mama." Tiineke bent down and cupped Wim's face in her hands, giving him a kiss on the forehead. "After our bikes get here, we are going to do some shopping."

His face fell.

"Don't worry, we'll go to the seaside as well. We'll do the shopping first and get something nice for our supper and then we'll go, alright?"

The child beamed at her.

Tiineke tucked the cheque into her purse and held out her hand to Wim. "Come and help me set up that corner of the sitting room with my easel."

Together they went to unpack Tiineke's paints. They had been unused for so long, but now she was determined to get back to painting.

By the time André arrived home at five-thirty, the house had been transformed into a home. In the front yard, their bicycles were locked, the two child seats strapped to Tiineke's. The fragrance of baking fish greeted him as he pushed open the squeaking door. There was a piece of cheerful red checked oilcloth covering the table and in the middle, an empty milk bottle held a few wild flowers.

"Papa!" Wim came racing from the kitchen to fling himself at André.

André tweaked the red, freckled nose of his son. "You look like you got some sun today."

"I'm not sure if it's sun or just wind burn." Tiineke laughed as she came in the room to kiss André. "I think the sand is in every little place possible. My ears, nose, hair, the wind drives it everywhere!"

André lifted Wim and swung him in a circle before setting him down again. "Well, it looks like you all had a good day. Was it fun, Wim? Do you like it here?"

"Yes!" Wim nodded vigorously. "When can Oma and Oom Johan come to visit?"

André and Tiineke exchanged glances. "I'm not sure, Wim. They need to stay in Amsterdam and watch the shop."

"Oh." The little boy scuffed his shoe against the threadbare carpet.

"Perhaps Oom Johan and Tante Mary will come on a holiday in the summer, though. We'll see." André looked at Tiineke. "Supper smells wonderful. How did you manage to do the shopping? I thought we'd be doing bread and cheese for supper."

"Look." She handed him the letter from her parents as he sat in the easy chair. Tiineke left him to read while she went back to finish getting the supper ready. When she carried the plates in to the table, he was standing in front of the window looking out.

"Are you alright?"

He turned to her, holding up the letter. "They're so kind. Why can't my mother be supportive like this?"

Tiineke smiled in relief. "I'm so glad. I was a bit worried that you would be upset with them."

He shook his head. "How could I be upset?"

"I was afraid you might think it was charity or something. It isn't, though. They are just happy for us and want to help."

"Yes, I know, and I love them for it." He smiled at her.

They sat at the table and gave thanks for their blessings, then started in on their first real supper on their own. Tiineke used one hand to rock the baby carriage, lulling Andréas to sleep. As with all of them, the unaccustomed sea air had tired him out as well.

Tiineke pointed at André with her fork. "So now, tell us everything about your day, from the first moment when you left us. We want to hear it all, don't we, Wim?"

"I was pretty nervous."

"Mama said you were." Wim piped up.

Tiineke scolded gently. "Hush now, let Papa tell us."

"I arrived early—it's no walk at all from here. I waited by the gate for a good fifteen minutes before Lt. Cuypers got there, but I had time to look around and get a feel for the layout of the place. It's huge. There are three other mechanics there, all of them older than me."

Tiineke's forehead furrowed. "Are they angry that you, a young man, are put ahead of them?"

"That's the wonderful thing. They don't seem at all upset. It's as Lt. Cuypers had said, none of them want the responsibility. They just want to put in their hours and go home. They like to do what they do, fix things, but no one wants the paperwork and headaches that go with being the boss. At least, that's what they all said when we were left alone to talk. They seem like really nice fellows.

"As I said, the place is huge, although I'll spend most of my time in the shop, which is sort of at the north end of the base. But I'll have to go for meetings in the main service building. It's this massive building right on the main jetty, quite a walk from the shop. Thank goodness the bikes arrived today, otherwise I'd spend hours walking everywhere."

Tiineke tut-tutted. "You must be worn out."

"I can't talk about lots of things. I had to sign all sorts of papers about keeping things confidential. I did ask Lt. Cuypers, though, if I could bring my family just to see the place once, and he said yes." André had stopped eating, fork and knife poised in mid-air. His eyes sparkled and he grinned. "Next weekend, he's going to meet us there on Sunday and just take us around a little bit. You won't see anything classified, but you'll see how it's all laid out." André turned to Wim. "There's a huge ship there, the *Cornelis Drebbel*. You'll see it next Sunday."

The rest of the evening was spent making plans. Buying furniture, painting, swimming—they tripped over themselves to talk about all the exciting things that lay ahead of them.

When they cuddled together on their makeshift bed that night, Tiineke asked the question that was still bothering her. "You're not sorry that we made the move?" She needed to hear him say it out loud.

"No, I'm not sorry. It's not going to be easy because we can't live in the style that we had at Mama's place, but the only thing I'm sorry about is that Johan, and yes, Mama, too, won't share our new life with us." He sighed and gave her a hug before pulling his arm out from under her head.

"They might come around after a bit. We just have to give them time." Tiineke stroked his arm. "I am so, so very happy about this. So is Wim. I know he misses your mother and Johan right now, but he's only four, he'll soon get over that. He absolutely loves the seaside and I can see we'll have to go every day or I'll get no peace. The good thing is that he exhausts himself so much that he doesn't argue about bedtime. I'll take him next week to get enrolled in nursery school as well."

There was a snore next to her, and Tiineke stopped talking, going to sleep herself with a smile on her face.

II

Summer 1938

"Are you sure you'll be alright?" André laid his hand on Tiineke's shoulder.

"I'm fine. I'm just tired. I don't remember being this tired when I was pregnant with either of the boys." Tiineke smiled up at him, shading her eyes.

He moved to block the sun for her. "Don't get a sunburn out here."

"I won't. I'll go in shortly, but having a back garden where I can sit in peace and quiet seems like such a luxury that I have to enjoy it for a little. Don't worry, I'll go inside soon. You go. The boys are going crazy waiting for you."

He rolled his eyes. "I know. You'd think we were hunting for buried treasure instead of periwinkles."

He left her and she could hear their voices fading as they walked away, carrying pails made from old tin cans. Wim's voice sounded so mature against Andréas's, whose voice still had the piercing, squeaky tone of a very young child. She could hear it long after she couldn't hear André or Wim. She sighed and closed her eyes in the heat of the sun and enjoyed this wonderful new house.

André had come home six months ago and told her about the house. They had been worried because they were outgrowing the first house with this, her third pregnancy. She had been sad to hear that the previous tenants were leaving because they went out of business. Memories of her own parents' failed business still hurt, but the joy of a large house, with a back garden and close enough to the dunes for the boys to go off to play by themselves overcame any reluctance she may have had. Klaas Duitstraat was quite a bit further for André to travel to work, but he didn't seem to mind. Even back in February, with the bitter wind blowing off the sea, he never complained.

Now, though, the cold seemed very far away. Tiineke sighed again and pulled herself out of the chair to go back in the house. Now she felt too hot and the sweat trickling down her back bothered her. She went to her easel and decided to work at her latest seascape while she had the house to herself. She wondered how the boys were making out on their expedition.

———

Andréas looked up at his father. "Papa, tell us again about the periwinkle."

Wim poked at a tuft of grass with his stick as they walked. "Such a funny name."

André slowed his pace to match his youngest son. "Well, a man at work told me that if you can catch enough of them, they are quite good to eat."

Andréas wrinkled his brow. "Like fish?"

They often went out fishing in the evening. If André augmented their food with fish they caught, it helped stretch the budget, and often meant the difference between a supper of bread and cheese and a hot meal.

André smiled and shook his head. "No, they aren't like fish. They are much smaller."

Wim held up his fingers to measure out an imaginary two inches. "Like shrimp?" This too was something they had collected themselves before.

"No, smaller than shrimp."

The boys exchanged a look. These things must be very small indeed.

"Will we take them home for Mama?" Andréas tilted his head. Already at his young age he showed concern for others, and now he wanted to make sure his mother didn't go hungry.

"Your mama wants us to have a big feast on the beach, and if there is anything left we can take it home to her." André didn't want to say that Tiineke had loathed the idea of eating the tiny sea snails. "That's why we brought the big cans. We will cook them in the can over a fire on the beach."

"Yay!" Andréas ran off to pick up a small piece of driftwood, brandishing it above his head. "For the fire."

"Stay on the path!" Wim waved to his brother and pointed to the path. "Mama says that we should always stay on the paths because the dunes could be dangerous. A person could get lost, or something."

They arrived at the water's edge and set down their things.

André gestured to the windrow of driftwood littering the beach. "Okay, we'll all go and collect some wood for the fire to add to what Andréas already collected."

They combed the beach until they had a good little stack of wood, and André prepared a fire without yet lighting it.

"Now, Andréas, you sit here, and Wim and I will go and find a bunch. They hide in seaweed, so we'll bring you the seaweed and your job will be to pick out the periwinkles."

Andréas sat down obediently.

André rolled up his pant legs and he and Wim stepped into a tidepool.

He instructed his son. "Okay, you pull on the seaweed while I cut it from the rock with my knife."

Wim reached down to grasp the weeds, his torso and legs browned from months in the sun. His blue bathing suit was faded and worn. They cut and pulled a bunch of weeds from the rocks, and then another.

"Here now." André and Wim returned to the fire pit, each with an armload of seaweed, and dropped them on the sand beside Andréas.

"Look, these are the periwinkles." André pulled a small, dark gray snail shell from the seaweed. "See? They can be different colours—this brown one, this green one—they're all periwinkles."

The two boys huddled together as they studied the tiny shells that André pulled out of the weeds. André knew his own curls were thinning slightly and his hair had receded a little in the past couple of years while Wim's hair had darkened into a thick thatch of honey-coloured blond. Andréas, on the other hand, had a mop of white-blond curls. André could smell the sun and sea in the hair of both his sons, and he watched their small hands as they pried the hard shells from the dark green mass, dropping them one by one into a tin can.

The bond between the three of them was an almost tangible thing. He was aware of his blood coursing through their veins. They were a part of him.

André sat back on his heels, his breath catching in his throat. He needed to stand up again and walk. "Can you get them out by yourself, Andréas? If you can, then Wim and I will get some more."

Andréas shaded his eyes from the sun and peered at his father. "Are you okay, Papa?"

"Yes, yes. I have a frog in my throat, that's all." André took off his glasses and polished them on his shirt tail.

"I'm fine, too." Andréas went happily about his task, and André and Wim went to collect more seaweed.

By late afternoon, they had collected about fifty of the small snails in a can. André unwrapped the bread and butter Tiineke had sent along. "Well, shall we get the fire going and cook our supper?"

"Yes, yes, yes!" Andréas hopped about.

André handed Wim the empty can. "Wim, you fill this other can about halfway with seawater." André lit the fire, then sat back and watched the two boys fill and empty the can several times before they decided it was correct.

André placed the can in the middle of the fire. "When it boils, we're going to drop some periwinkles into the water to cook, a few at a time."

Wim picked up one of the small snails and looked at it curiously. "Do we eat the shells?"

"No, see here. With these pins we pull them out of the shells, and then eat them right away with some bread. André didn't want his youngest son to prick himself with the pin. "I was only able to borrow two pins, so I'll help you, alright, Andréas?"

Andréas nodded as he crouched beside the small pile of shells.

The boys watched with big, round eyes as André dropped a dozen of the shells into the boiling water. After about three minutes, he took them out with a pair of tongs and dropped them on to a newspaper between the boys. He sat down alongside them again.

"Here's how it works." André showed Wim how to use the pin to pull the little cover out of the shell before pulling out the meat.

When they had each eaten several, André looked at them both. "Well, what do you think?"

Wim nodded thoughtfully. "It's good. They taste like the sea."

Andréas nodded vigorously. "I like it! Do you, Papa?"

André looked seriously from one boy to the other. "I don't think I've ever had a nicer meal. I know I'll never forget today."

"I'll never forget it either." Wim grinned and then took another bite of bread. .

"Me neither!" Andréas patted his father's knee with his small hand.

They cooked the remaining periwinkles and ate them with the rest of the bread and butter.

Later, André watched as the boys ran up and down the beach, chasing seagulls, while the sun slowly set into the sea.

III

Summer 1938

"Mama's going to die." Andréas wept. He put his hands over his ears to block out the sound of moaning coming from the bedroom upstairs.

"No, she won't. Really, she won't." Tiineke's father leaned down and hugged his youngest grandson. "Why don't we go for a nice long walk and you can show me all your favourite places?"

André rested his hand on Jan's shoulder and smiled gratefully. "Yes, that's a great idea. You three go and I'll stay here, just in case anyone needs me."

André was doubtful if he would be needed and part of him longed to go out for a while with his father-in-law and sons. He knew that the midwife and Tiineke's mother would handle anything that needed doing, but still he wouldn't leave, just in case.

Andréas clung to André. "No. Want to stay here."

"You go, and when you come back, maybe your little brother or sister will be here, waiting." André gently pulled Andréas's arms from around his neck and propelled him out the door to join his brother. "Show Opa where we go fishing." André waved them out the door. "Thank you, Jan."

"It's for my sake just as much as theirs." Jan Pol nodded at André and left with the boys.

Upstairs, the midwife was giving Tiineke instructions. "I know it feels like it's been a long labour, but you're nearly there. The head is crowning. Just a little bit longer...push now to keep him coming, you can do it."

"Mam!" Tiineke cried and her mother gripped her hand tighter.

Whoosh. The baby slid into the waiting hands of the midwife. She efficiently tied off the cord and rubbed the tiny body. A thin wail erupted from the small creature as Tiineke strained to see what was happening.

The midwife gently lifted the baby and placed it on Tiineke's breast. "Congratulations, you have a beautiful baby girl. All fingers and toes are accounted for."

Almost unaware, Tiineke went through the last stages of childbirth with the midwife cleaning up as Tiineke and her mother stared, enchanted, at the baby.

The midwife reached for the little girl. "Let me take her for just a moment and get her ready for company." She took the baby and washed her gently with the warm water in a basin on the dressing table.

Elsa Pol brushed Tiineke's hair and helped her in to a clean gown. "Everyone will want to come and see you soon."

Tiineke held her mother's hand. "Oh Mam, I'm so glad you were here with me. I missed you when Andréas was born."

"I'm glad, too. It's so nice for us to come here to stay for a couple of weeks. At first it seemed so far out of the way, I was worried about you coming to live here. But now I can see why you like it so much."

Above the lusty cries of the new baby came a tentative knock on the door. Elsa Pol smiled at Tiineke, who nodded. "Yes, let him in."

André stepped into the room. "Is everything alright?"

Tiineke was holding the baby, now wrapped in a clean, white cotton blanket.

The midwife handed a basin to Elsa. "Come, perhaps you can help me carry my things downstairs." The two of them left the room and André stepped up beside the bed.

Tiineke pulled the blanket further down from the baby's face. "Come and meet your daughter."

André breathed the word. "Daughter?"

"Yes, daughter." Tiineke laughed. "It shouldn't be such a shock. We had a fifty-fifty chance, you know."

He sat on the bed. "She's not just a daughter, she's a princess, a beautiful princess, like her mother."

Tiineke handed the small bundle to him, and André crooned and nuzzled the baby. "Welcome to the world, Elsa Agatha Meijer."

Noise from downstairs told them the boys were home, and André went down to get them.

Tiineke heard the shrill voice of her youngest son. "Is Mama okay?"

"Yes, she's just fine, and you can come up to see for yourself. You can also meet your little sister."

He led the way back up to the bedroom and stood back to let the boys climb on the bed beside their mother. Jan and Elsa followed and hovered near the door.

Tiineke could not stop smiling. "Here is your sister. Her name is Elsa." She held the baby so the boys could see her face while she glanced at her mother.

Elsa Pol sniffed, and searched for a handkerchief.

"Now, don't snuffle like that." Jan put his arm around his wife's shoulder and pulled her close.

When the boys had exhausted their curiosity and started to poke each other, André shooed them off the bed. "Alright, let's let your Mama rest now."

André nudged his sons back down the stairs. Jan and Elsa had already left the room and were in the kitchen when André and the boys returned. "Soup for supper. Is that alright?" Tiineke's mother had taken over the kitchen and was busy chopping vegetables into a big pot.

André popped a piece of carrot in his mouth. "Yes, perfect. Thank you for your help. It's so good for all of us that you are here. It really means so much to Tiineke and to me, too."

André had been pleased when Tiineke told him that her parents would come for a few weeks to help out when the baby was due. They had hardly seen them at all over the years, although they had gone to Rotterdam to stay with them twice for holidays. This was the first time that her parents were staying with them. They had not had room before now. Now with the third bedroom, they could stay in comfort, and the visit was going well.

Elsa slapped his hand playfully to prevent him from taking any-more of the vegetables and then smiled at André. "It's good for us, too. We never felt that welcome when you were living with your mother."

Jan glowered at his wife. "Elsa!"

"I'm sorry, but it's true. André, I know that Agatha is your mother, but honestly I felt like an intruder when I was there, so it seemed better just to stay away. Of course, we couldn't afford the trips back and forth anyway after we first moved to Rotterdam, but now it's a bit better. Jan has been able to find casual work here and there. It seems to be picking up again."

Jan finished peeling a potato and wiped his hands on a cloth. "Yes, we're much more hopeful about the future. It's fine living with Rit and we'll certainly stay there no matter what, but it's good to get a bit of money in once in a while. I hope I can eventually get working again full time."

André leaned back against the counter. "How's Hank? We haven't seen him in about a year now. He usually comes to visit every sum-mer, but hasn't made it this year yet."

"He's not bad. At least he's always managed to get enough work to keep up his rent. He hasn't got a serious girl yet, though." Jan shook his head and frowned.

Elsa tossed her head. "He hasn't found anyone who's worthy of him yet."

André and Jan exchanged a smile. Elsa caught the look and blushed. "It's true! Now why don't all you men get out from under-foot and leave me to get the supper ready."

———

Little Elsa was only three days old when they took her out for her first trip to the sea. They borrowed bicycles from the neighbours for Jan and Elsa, and with tiny Elsa packed in a carrier harness on Tiineke's chest, they all cycled along the sea promenade to the Lange Jaap lighthouse, a tall cast iron pillar glowing red in the twilight.

They parked their bikes and then Wim started to push his family into positions around the lighthouse. "Now we have to stand with our backs against the wall."

Obediently, they all stood against the old lighthouse with arms outstretched.

Wim gave the order. "Look up now!"

They each gazed up in the early evening darkness and watched the white light flare. Every twenty seconds there were four white flashes.

Elsa's voice broke the silence. "It makes me dizzy."

Wim was quick to respond. "Shhh, Oma!"

A moment more of quiet, but for the waves breaking on the nearby shore, and finally Wim's young voice rang out again. "Alright, we can stop now."

With the fall of darkness, the wind died down. They heard the hum of the lighthouse and crickets.

When they gathered together again on the sea side of the pillar, Wim explained to his grandparents. "It's magic, you see. The light has a magical power to keep people safe, and when you stand like this underneath it, it gives you some of the magic. That's why we had to bring Elsa. She's new in our family and we had to give her some of the magic."

Tiineke wondered what her parents thought of this made-up family lore.

Then her father spoke quietly. "It feels like magic, alright. Thank you for bringing us to share it with you."

———

228

Tiineke couldn't believe how quickly the time had gone. On the last night of Jan and Elsa's visit, André and Jan sat at the table, playing a card game with the boys.

Wim crowed. "I win!"

André groaned. "You did. How is it possible?"

Elsa and Tiineke sat together on the sofa in the living room, content to be together with the new baby sleeping soundly in Elsa's arms.

Elsa glanced at the table, then turned back to Tiineke. "André seems like a different man these days. He was always so serious and stern looking when you lived in Amsterdam. It's wonderful to see him so relaxed and having fun with the boys. He's really good with the baby, too. I couldn't believe it when he changed her diaper yesterday. That's something your father never did once when you and Hank were babies."

Tiineke looked across to her husband and smiled. "He's not a different man, Mama. It's just that now the man I always knew to be inside has the freedom to show himself."

"And does he like his work? He doesn't talk much about it."

"I think he likes it well enough. He isn't allowed to talk about it much. He does seem more worried these days, but I don't know why, really. You know, it's really quite sad because, in fact, he loved his work at Meijer's. He would have been very happy to work there and run the family business."

André laughed and put down another card.

Elsa's voice was low. "Yes. I was afraid he would be angry with you for forcing him to choose."

"He wasn't angry. He knew himself that it was impossible to go on the way we had been. If only Agatha had understood him better, understood that they essentially wanted the same things and that she didn't need to control him to make her vision come true, everyone could have been happy."

"And you tell me that now Johan has taken over running the business?"

"Yes, apparently so, although we really only know what we get from Hank's letters. Neither Agatha nor Johan write, although Mary does once in a while." She sighed. "It breaks André's heart to be estranged from them both. They were such a close family."

Elsa shifted the baby to lay her down on her lap. "Hank told us that Johan has given up the soccer completely now."

Tiineke stoked the baby's hand and was rewarded with the child grasping her finger. "I know. It's such a shame. He had such dreams, and real promise to make them come true."

"I don't know much about Johan's wife, Mary. How does she manage with Agatha?"

"Better than I did, I think, because she doesn't seem to argue about anything. She just lets Agatha run over her like a train. Her letters seem sad. It isn't the life she had expected when she and Johan got married. She and Johan had planned to go to England, you know."

"Really? And instead she's trapped there with Agatha." Elsa shook her head.

"At least she's got a job, so I'm sure that helps. It gets her out of the house." Tiineke folded her hands in her lap when the baby's grip loosened. "I feel badly about how it worked out for them, but I had to put our family first, and for us, it's wonderful."

She looked up at André again when he burst out laughing at something Andréas had said. Tiineke smiled. "He never laughed like that before we moved to Den Helder."

Elsa lifted the sleeping baby a little and nuzzled her neck. "It's hard to think that tomorrow we go home again."

"Well, now that Papa is working, you can come again, right? Maybe for Sinterklaas or Christmas. That would be fun wouldn't it?"

"Yes, we'll come again." Elsa nodded and handed the baby to Tiineke.

———

September sixth was raining and chilly when Queen Wilhelmina celebrated her fortieth jubilee. It was a school holiday for the children and they all went to the shipyards for a celebration. The wind drove the rain slantways and Tiineke clutched her raincoat tight at the neck with one hand while steering the baby carriage with the other. Her hands were numb by the time they reached the services building where tea and biscuits were being served. André was waiting for her, smiling. They stood and watched the boys in their sailor suits slipping through the crowds to peer at the large framed photos of ships and submarines that adorned the walls of the hall.

Tiineke shivered in the chill of the damp hall. "Did you listen to the queen's speech on the radio?"

The smile slipped from André's face. "Yes, we have a radio in the shop."

"She said that we need to keep our 'heads erect' and to 'accept' whatever the future brings." Tiineke turned to look into her husband's eyes. "Will there be a war in Europe, do you think?"

"I don't know. I do know that it's gotten very busy around here the last while. There are more people working and there is a real feeling of urgency everywhere."

Tiineke put the worry to the back of her mind as they joined André's coworkers in waving small flags.

She could feel there were black clouds gathering on the horizon.

I'm not going to fuss about things I can't do anything about, anyway.

Later that month, Tiineke was washing the supper dishes with Wim while Andréas made a pest of himself.

"Don't poke your brother when he's drying the dishes, Andréas. He might drop something and it wouldn't be his fault. Go and pester your father instead of us workers."

Andréas ran off as ordered.

"You're my steady and serious helper, aren't you Wim?" She smiled at her oldest son who stood beside her, patiently taking the plates one by one from the dish rack to dry them. He wore glasses like his father now, and as he looked up at her solemnly, she could imagine André as a boy.

"I like to help."

Andréas came belting in through the kitchen door. "Papa! Mama! Look what I have!" His hands were cupped around something small and alive.

André came through to the kitchen where they all clustered in to see.

Wim tried to pry open his brother's hands. "What is it?"

"A bird. It hit the window and fell down and now I have it. Papa, we need to build a cage for him. Please, please, may I keep him?"

Tiineke straightened up. "No, take it outside."

Andréas held his small cupped hands against his chest just under his chin. "Papa, pleeeease."

André crouched down in front of his son. "Let's first take a look to see if he's injured." André swivelled to reach under the sink and pulled out a carton. He emptied it of the rags and pots of polish.

"Okay, put him in here now carefully and let's take a look."

Tiineke waggled her finger at her husband and son. "If that bird gets loose in the house, you'll all be in trouble."

André held the flaps of the carton close and they all looked at the small bird sitting in the bottom. "I think he's just stunned and frightened. He doesn't seem to be hurt." He gently moved the sparrow's wings. "Yes, I'm sure he's fine." He closed the flaps, then sat back to look at Andréas. "He's a lovely little bird."

Andréas eyes were round and he nodded. "He is, he's beautiful!"

"He's used to having all the sky and sea and trees for his home. Now you would like to make a cage for him."

Wim sat at the table, watching his younger brother.

Andréas pushed his finger under the flap of the box, as if hoping the bird would reach up to touch his small, searching finger. "He wouldn't get hurt anymore."

André nodded solemnly. "That's true. You would keep him safe, I'm sure. Would he be happy to give up the sky and sea to be looked after, do you think?"

The silent moment stretched.

Finally, the little boy's eyes filled with tears. "No. He would like to be free."

André took Andréas's small hand in his and patted it with his other hand. "Come, let's go up to the dunes to let him free. We have a few minutes of light left." André picked up the carton and handed it to Andréas.

Tiineke took the tea towel from Wim's hand. "You go with them, I'll finish here." The three of them went out into the fading light of evening as Tiineke watched from the window. She finished the dishes and went to the sitting room with Elsa to wait.

When the boys returned and André had restored the carton to its place under the sink, he joined Tiineke. They had a small radio of their own now and Tiineke sat, listening to the news.

André stretched out his long legs. "I've sent the boys up to get ready for bed."

"Good. Did it go alright?"

"Yes. He was sad for a moment, but when the bird flew off, both boys cheered. They know what's right."

"Yes, they do. They learn from their father." Tiineke smiled at him. "Come and listen. Premier Colijn is speaking."

Tiineke turned up the radio and they listened as the Premier assured Dutch citizens that there was nothing to worry about, that there was no war coming.

Tiineke breathed a deep sigh and smiled at André. "Well, that's a relief, isn't it?"

"I wish I was as certain as he seems to be." André stood and went up to tuck the boys into bed while Tiineke nursed the baby.

IV

Winter 1938

December 5th, Sinterklaas, was a Monday. André went to work as usual, but hurried home, knowing that he was coming home to a houseful of people.

"Jan, how good to see you again!" André placed his cold, damp hand in his father-in-law's large, warm one, shaking it vigorously. "And Elsa, welcome." He gave her the three traditional kisses and a warm hug.

"And what about me?" Hank stepped in to the sitting room from the kitchen.

"Hank! What a wonderful surprise! It's so great to see you." André pumped Hank's hand.

Wim was demanding Hank's attention, while Andréas hung back slightly. An uncle was a little bit of a novelty to the younger boy.

"Come upstairs and see our room, Oom Hank."

Elsa and Tiineke went back to the kitchen to finish preparing the meal while Jan lifted four-month-old Elsa out of her carriage. He walked up and down the room, bouncing her. "You've grown so much already!" He turned to André. "She reminds me so much of Tiineke at this age."

The evening was full of excitement as gifts were exchanged and poems read out loud. A lot of care had gone into writing the short, anonymous poems that were traditional at Sinterklaas. They poked fun at each other good-naturedly, laughing a lot.

Tiineke finished reading a poem that only André could have written. It alluded to a day on the beach when Tiineke had screamed after a seagull dropped a mess on her from above.

André grinned when Hank gave him a thumbs up. André shook his head. "Once we were both older than ten, we didn't do this anymore at home."

Tiineke poked her husband in the ribs. "Well, you seem to be making up for lost time now."

The boys had made gifts from feathers, stones, and shells. A necklace for Mama, a paperweight for Papa. They sang songs and ate the small, hard, traditional Sinterklaas cookies called *pepernoten*.

After the children were in bed, and it was finally quiet and peaceful, the adults had a special treat of a glass of sherry and toasted each other's health.

André topped up Hank's glass. "So when are you getting married? You need to settle down and have a couple of children of your own. You're so good with the boys."

Hank laughed. "First I need to meet someone. Besides, marriage isn't always as easy as you two make it look. I know some that seem to have a rather hard time of it."

Tiineke raised her eyebrows. "Are you thinking of anyone in particular?"

Hank hesitated for a moment before replying. "I'm not sure Johan and Mary are doing that well. She's pregnant you know."

"No! She didn't write about it. But that's wonderful. Johan must be so happy, isn't he?"

Hank nodded. "Yes, I think he is, but I'm not sure how Mary feels."

"Maybe she's just feeling sick. That can make a person miserable. I know." Tiineke laughed.

"Yes, maybe." Hank shrugged one shoulder.

André studied Hank. "You don't seem sure. Is there more?" He worried about his brother.

"They just don't seem happy. I don't know how to explain it, and maybe I'm all wrong anyway. He just never laughs anymore. You know he used to always be such great fun. I think that was one of the things that Mary liked so much in him. Now he's always...I don't know...not the same." Hank shrugged and turned up his hands.

They were quiet for a moment, then Tiineke picked up the baby clothes her parents had brought. She held up a small knitted yellow dress with matching cap.

"Mama, this is so sweet. You're so handy in your knitting. I'll never be as good as you are."

Conversation turned to more general topics. Deliberately they stayed away from talk of war. Tonight, by tacit agreement, they would keep things light.

———

Hank went home in the morning, but Tiineke's parents were staying until the weekend. The whole family walked with Hank to the bus station. The wind was moaning and drove the rain at them as they braced themselves against it.

"How do you stand this constant wind?" Hank almost shouted to make himself heard.

Tiineke looped a strand of loosened hair behind her ear. "You get used to it. At first I didn't think I would, but now I hardly notice it. It's just something that's always there."

Hank pulled his collar tight around his throat. "I don't think I could get used to it."

They went inside the station and were able to speak normally again. Tiineke smiled. "Now I can't imagine living in the middle of the city anymore. I love the taste of the salt on my lips when I come outside. I need to see the open spaces of the dunes and the sea. I love it here."

"Well, you do seem happy, and I'm glad for you." Hank kissed his sister on the forehead and leaned down over the baby carriage to stroke the baby's cheek before hugging each of his parents. "I'll see you both at Christmas. I'll let you know what train I'm on."

Tiineke felt a small pang as she always did at being far from her parents on special days like Christmas and Easter, but brushed it aside. She had them here now.

On Saturday they went to the train station again, to see the Pols off.

Elsa's eyes were shiny with unshed tears. "We'll see you again next summer."

Jan tickled his granddaughter's chin. "Maybe the little princess will be walking by then."

Tiineke laughed. "Papa, I think you're being optimistic there, but we'll see."

There was a flurry of hugs and kisses, and then the bus was gone in a cough of diesel smoke that left their eyes stinging. They took the long way home. Wim and Andréas ran ahead and then dashed back to point out interesting things along the way. André whistled. Tiineke inhaled the tangy, clean sea air, lifting her chin and breathing deep. André put a hand on the handle of the baby carriage beside Tiineke's.

He nudged her with his shoulder as they walked close together. "Okay?"

"Yes, Okay." She smiled at him.

V

Summer 1939

Arms outstretched, one step, two, and then a third before falling with a 'plop' on her backside.

"Hooray!" A cheer went up from the small crowd around little Elsa.

"I knew she could do it!" Jan's voice glowed with a grandfather's pride.

André picked Elsa up and set her on her feet again. Her dimpled knees wobbled for a moment, then steadied.

André pointed at Tiineke. "Go to Mama."

"Come, Elsa." Tiineke held open her arms.

The small girl stood looking around at the faces watching her. She grinned at her oldest brother, showing off her two teeth. Her sandy blonde hair was like a downy halo, the soft fuzz floating around her head. Ignoring her mother, she reached towards Wim and took two steps before sitting down and flipping to her hands and knees. She crawled to her brother and pulled herself upright by clinging to his shirt.

Wim pulled his little sister onto his lap. "Oh, Elsa, you're drooling all over the new shirt that Oma and Opa just gave me for my birthday." She settled against him with her thumb in her mouth.

Tiineke sat back, resting on her hands. "I think Madam has had enough for the time being. I'll get some lemonade to celebrate."

They all moved off the floor where they had been clustered for the past hour, coaxing Elsa to take her first steps.

Tiineke smiled as her mother helped her pour out glasses of lemonade for everyone. "I'm so glad you were here for this."

"Your father was determined that he would see her walk." Elsa laughed.

"We've been coaxing her for weeks and she hasn't been interested, so it looks like he knew the right encouragement to give her."

After the lemonade, Tiineke ordered the children to go outside and play. "Give us some peace now to catch up on grown-up conversation. Take Elsa in the carriage with you."

The children scurried off.

Jan leaned toward André, resting his elbows on his knees. "All these elections. What do you think of it all?"

André shook his head and grimaced. "It's worrying, there's no question. First the election in July that brought in Colijn again, and with it immediately falling, another election a month later to bring in deGeer. Frankly, I don't have any faith in the Social Democrats."

Elsa flicked her hand dismissively. "I think all these politicians are the same. I'm more concerned about what's going on with Germany."

Tiineke nodded. "I know. We keep hearing that the Netherlands won't be involved in a war, that we'll be neutral, but I think it will still mean problems. Why can't people just live in peace?"

Elsa sat back in her chair and folded her arms across her chest. "It's all about the economy, isn't it? I heard that back in December, the Dutch debt was somewhere close to four billion guilders. It seems impossible, doesn't it?"

Jan wagged his finger in the air. "That's why we need a new government. I think this one will get us back on track." He turned to André. "I hear that Meijer's is doing well, at least. I still have some friends in the business."

André nodded. "Yes, I know. Our friend, Marty Cuypers, mentions the business once in a while. He knows that we had rather a falling out with Mama because I came here, but I still like to hear how they are doing. He told me they were given a big contract for more linen. The navy, and army as well, I understand, are stocking up on things as much as they are allowed. It's good for Meijer's anyway."

Tiineke jumped up, anxious to change the mood. "Let's sit outside while the sun is shining."

They sat out on folding chairs in the back garden, André pointing out some new plants he had put in, when he suddenly broke off. Shading his eyes, he stood up and looked down the street.

"What in the world..."

"What is it?" Tiineke got up and stood beside him.

The trio was coming. Wim carried Elsa and Andréas pushed the baby carriage, but the frame was bent, making it difficult to steer, and Andréas continually corrected his direction as the buggy tried to swerve off the sidewalk.

André opened the gate and walked towards the children. Tiineke ran past him and took Elsa from Wim's young arms.

Tiineke's heart pounded. "What happened?" She searched Elsa for signs of injury.

The little girl smiled at her mother and pulled a pin from Tiineke's hair, causing a large strand to fall into Tiineke's eyes. She flipped her head to clear her vision.

Her young daughter was fine. She turned to the boys. Her voice was louder this time. "What happened?"

André was down on one knee, examining the bent carriage. Jan and Elsa had followed and now Jan peered over André's head at the damage.

The boys looked at each other without speaking.

André glared at the boys and stood. "Your mother asked a question."

Wim started. "You know how we have to lift the carriage and carry it down those steps to get to the Sea Boulevard?" He looked down at the carriage, not able to face the four adults now standing in a semi-circle in front of the two boys.

André's voice was firm. "Yes. We know."

Tiineke gasped, a horrifying image leaping to her mind. "You didn't let it go with Elsa in it, did you?"

"No, Mama, we wouldn't do that!" Andréas put a hand on his hip and he scowled as if offended at the thought they would endanger their sister's life.

André crossed his arms as he stared down at the boys. "Well, go on."

"We didn't let it go." Wim hesitated.

"But?"

Wim scuffed the walk with his toe. "But, we didn't lift it. We let it bump down the steps. It's *very* heavy." Andréas looked up at his father and nodded.

"We held it very tight with Andréas in front and me keeping it from getting away. Elsa loved it." Wim smiled tentatively at the adults.

Andréas threw his arms open. "She was laughing so much."

André's brow was furrowed as he looked from Andréas to Wim. "I find it hard to imagine that this much damage happened from what you are describing."

Again, Wim and Andréas exchanged glances.

"She had such fun." Andréas looked up at his sister.

"That you thought you would take her through it again?" André took Andréas's chin in his finger and thumb to force the boy to look at him.

Andréas continued to look his father in the eye even when André had released his chin. "Well, no. Not Elsa."

Tiineke furrowed her brow, uncertain what was coming, but André guessed. "You went in it yourself, am I right?" André looked at his youngest son.

Andréas looked down at his shoes. "Yes, Papa."

Jan turned away. From the corner of her eye, Tiineke could see that her father was stifling a grin.

Wim gave a little sigh, then spoke up. "It's my fault, Papa. I shouldn't have let him, but I held Elsa while he went down. He was too heavy though, and it went very fast. Faster than we thought it would."

"*Much* faster!" Andréas grinned and his eyes sparkled.

Wim bit his lip and continued. "The carriage really bumped along and then, because it was going so fast, it didn't quite stop at the bottom where we thought it would."

"It went all the way across the boulevard and crashed against a pole. Look." Andréas lifted his shirt to show a long scrape on his back which was already starting to turn blue with the promise of a big bruise. He looked over his shoulder proudly. "I didn't cry."

"You went right out across the boulevard? You were very lucky that there were no autos coming!" Tiineke felt faint at the thought.

"Oh, but there were. They honked a lot at me!"

"Oh my God." Tiineke shifted little Elsa on her hip and held her tightly.

André pointed to the house, frowning at the two children. "You boys get in the house. We will discuss your punishment shortly."

The boys disappeared and he wheeled the crippled baby carriage into the garden.

Jan was laughing. "That boy is fearless."

"And he has no sense." Tiineke shook her head. "It's a bad combination."

"Wim took responsibility, though, instead of just blaming Andréas. He's a good boy." Elsa was quick to defend her eldest grandchild.

Tiineke handed the baby to her mother and stooped to examine the buggy. "The carriage is destroyed. They're equally responsible."

"We can hammer it out again, can't we André?" Jan was examining the frame.

"I'm expected to get submarines working. I'm sure I can get a baby carriage moving again. Don't worry." André patted Tiineke on the arm. "They're just being boys. I can imagine it was exciting, although perhaps a little more than they had counted on." André had a small smile.

Tiineke looked sharply at her husband. "You sound proud!"

"No, no, I'm not!"

Tiineke turned but swiveled back quickly with a glare when she heard her father stifle a laugh. She was sure that André had winked at Jan. Tiineke turned to go in the house with her mother and the baby, leaving him and Jan alone. As she walked away, she heard André say: "He's a brave little man isn't he?"

As part of their punishment for the carriage ride incident, it was decided that both boys would do extra chores for the week. It was a few evenings later, and Wim was peeling potatoes as Andréas was setting the table. Tiineke sat outside with her parents. Elsa was asleep in the restored carriage in a shady corner of the yard.

Tiineke heard the front door close. "André's home."

There was the thunder of little feet as the boys ran out to their father. "Papa, Papa!"

"Hello, boys."

Tiineke could hear from André's voice that something was wrong. She went in to the house and saw him kneeling in front of the boys giving them both a hug.

"André? What is it?"

He stood and gave the boys each a ruffle of their hair. "You better get back to your work." The boys ran back to their chores. André nodded at Tiineke and they went back outside to where her parents sat. "Have you listened to the radio today at all?"

Jan stood up immediately. "No, what's happened?"

"Premier deGeer has recalled all Dutch citizens who are vacationing in the Black Forest, and has ordered border guards to take positions. They're preparing for an invasion."

"No!" Elsa reached for Jan's hand.

André put his arm around Tiineke's waist. "It's only precautionary. It may not mean too much to us."

Jan squeezed Elsa's hand. "André's right. We've been through this before and the Netherlands was neutral. We weren't impacted too badly."

André nodded but continued to look solemn. "Nevertheless, for me it means there will be quite a bit of overtime coming."

Tiineke sat down beside her mother and took the baby back in her arms. "That's not a bad thing." She imagined the new shoes both boys would need when school started again in a few weeks.

"That's right. We'll make the most of it while we can." André put a bright tone in his voice.

Tiineke studied his face for a moment, then went in to get supper ready.

———

Jan and Elsa had gone home by the time the Netherlands declared their neutrality following the invasion of Poland. The boys had just started back to school, and the extra pay had indeed paid for new shoes.

Tiineke switched off the radio after hearing the news and faced André. "I think it'll be alright, won't it?"

"I hope so." André sounded subdued and Tiineke didn't pursue it, just pulled her cardigan closer to ward off the early autumn chill.

The family's small horde of savings grew over the next few months. There was plenty of overtime for André, and while Tiineke was pleased about that, a sense of foreboding was evident every-where. The news reports were gloomy and André often seemed wor-ried. Tiineke felt they should celebrate, to help brighten the mood in the house.

"Let's have a really grand Sinterklaas and Christmas this year. We can afford a nice celebration this year with all the overtime you've been doing."

He kissed her forehead. "What did you have in mind?"

"I'd like to invite my folks to stay right through for the three weeks. Would that be alright?"

"I don't have a problem with the idea, but your father has been working a bit here and there. Do you think he'll be able to take so much time away?"

"Yes, I think he will. It's slowed down for him again and I think he's feeling a bit down about it."

André smiled at Tiineke. "You and your mother already have this all arranged, don't you?"

She shook her head. "No, not quite. I wouldn't do it without your agreement."

André seemed to consider the idea for a moment. "They'll have to bring their ration cards with them. The way your father takes sugar in his tea and coffee, we'd be through our ration in two weeks."

She frowned. "They'll help out."

"I'm kidding. They always do, I know that. I like your folks. By all means, if they would like to come for that long, it would be great to have them. I'm sure the kids would love it, too."

Thus began a flurry of letters between Tiineke and Elsa with plans and proposals. By the time they arrived on December fifth, baby Elsa's room had a fresh coat of paint and her small bed had been moved in to the boys' room, replaced by one borrowed from a neighbor.

"What's in this, Oma?" Andréas studied an oversized box the Pols had brought.

Tiineke waggled her finger at him. "Now, Andréas. You can't ask questions like that. Just take everything upstairs to Oma and Opa's room and leave it there. And no shaking."

"It looks like a small army has moved in!" André laughed as he walked in the door and navigated around suitcases to hug and kiss his mother-in-law.

Jan made a harrumphing sound and shook his head. "We had to hire a porter at the train station."

Elsa poked her husband. "Well, we made it safe with everything, so stop complaining."

"Hello, hello!" Hank walked in. "What chaos!"

"Oom Hank, Oom Hank!" Wim pounced on his uncle. "Come and see how big Elsa is." Wim pulled him over to where Elsa was screeching and banging a wooden block on the rail of her playpen.

"How about a glass of advocat?" Hank waved a bottle of the yellow liquor at André.

"Oh yes, please!" André relieved Hank of the bottle and went to pour out small glasses for each of the adults and glasses of lemonade for the children.

"A toast. To family." André held up his glass. *Clink, clink, clink.* The tinkle of glass tapping glass sounded musical.

"Opa, you didn't clink me." Wim stretched his arm across to touch his glass of lemonade against his grandfather's glass.

Everyone repeated the toast. "To family."

The dining room windows fogged over in the heat of the coal stove, the hot food that was laid out on the table, and all the people. Tiineke glanced to the window and saw, reflected in the glass, her father lifting her daughter high over his head. Elsa giggled and reached for his thinning hair. He caught Tiineke's reflection in the window and smiled at her.

It's like seeing something in a dream. She stood, looking at the image in the window, mesmerized. They were enclosed in this small world, the darkness outside the backdrop.

Andréas was anxious to start the Sinterklaas celebrations. "Come, Mama, can we eat now?"

The spell was broken.

"Yes. Come everyone, squeeze in and let's start!"

———

The weeks flew by, filled with eating, activities and laughter. The oversized box had revealed a new wagon with which the boys were delighted. Hank left the day after Christmas while the Pols stayed on until after the New Year.

"Where did the days go?" Elsa asked as they once again were packing up to leave.

Jan laughed as he fastened a strap around a suitcase. "I'm sure André and Tiineke are counting down the hours to have their house back to normal."

Tiineke protested. "Not at all. I don't know where the time has gone either. It flew. André and I and, obviously, the kids, we all loved every minute of your visit."

"Don't go home yet." Wim tugged on his mother's dress. "Why can't they stay longer?"

Jan tousled Wim's hair. "No, son. We have our bus and train tickets bought. We'll be back in the summer again, God willing."

"I have little Elsa all bundled up and ready to go." André came in to the room as the last suitcase was being strapped up and looked at his sons. "Come boys, on with your jackets and gloves. Be careful now with those cases."

"The wagon is a great idea. Thank you for your help with the luggage. I think there might be a little something for your work when we get to the station." Jan winked at the boys.

The little group didn't feel the cold wind biting as they wound their way to the station. The wagon zig-zagged with Wim pulling it and Andréas regularly re-balanced a toppling suitcase. Young Elsa giggled and sang as her grandmother bounced and jogged her with every step. The baby wore a small cherry-coloured wool hat that her grandmother had knitted for her. It had small ears knitted at the top and with her round face and rosy cheeks she looked like a red kitten.

Jan tickled the baby's cheeks. "Where are your whiskers, Puss?" She laughed.

"I suppose I have to give you back now." Elsa said and nuzzled her granddaughter one more time before handing her to André.

"Now boys, thank you." Jan slipped a coin into the hands of each of the boys as he bent down to hug them.

Tiineke put her hand on her father's arm. "Papa, you don't need to do that. They are happy to help, aren't you boys?"

Wim looked glum. "Yes, Mama"

Elsa nudged Tiineke. "Let him. It gives him pleasure to be able to."

Tiineke sighed. "What do you say to Opa?"

The boys grinned and sang out together. "Thank you, Opa!"

"Thank you, Oma," Andréas wisely added.

Jan patted his wife on the shoulder. "Elsa, they're calling our bus. Come now. It's time."

Tiineke hugged her father tightly. "Papa, thank you for coming. It was so good having you here. Mama." Tiineke could feel the lump in her throat. She hugged her mother and the two women stood, holding each other fiercely. "I love you, Mama."

"And you, sweetheart. We'll see you again soon." Tears were welling in her mother's eyes as well.

"I know." Tiineke was openly crying now. "I don't know what's wrong. I know I'll see you soon."

With difficulty Tiineke let go and her mother gave each of the children one last quick hug before following Jan on to the bus.

A cloud of diesel smoke, and the bus started up. Waving hands inside and outside of the bus. André held little Elsa up and she opened and closed her hand several times in a baby wave. With a gasp and a roar, the bus moved off. They waved at the departing bus until it turned a corner and was out of sight. Still Tiineke stood for a moment.

André stood holding the baby on his hip, his other arm around Tiineke's shoulder. "It's always hard to say good-bye to them, but they'll be back in the summer."

Tiineke nodded and brushed a tear from her cheek. "My head knows that, but my heart is having a very hard time this time. I just feel so sad to see them leave."

André handed little Elsa to Tiineke. "Give your Mama a big kiss. She needs one."

Elsa promptly gave Tiineke a large slobbery kiss on the lips.

Tiineke wiped the kiss away. "Oh André, give me your hankie. Her nose is runny. I'm not sure I needed that."

But she smiled at him and held her daughter close as they turned and set out for home.

VI

Spring 1940

"What is it? What's happening?" Tiineke had to scream to make herself heard over the roar of the aircraft overhead.

"Papa!" Andréas came running into their room with Wim a step behind.

Tiineke pushed past them to run to Elsa's room. She reached down to pull the screaming child from her crib and tried in vain to comfort the sobbing baby. "Hush, sweetheart, hush."

Out in the hallway, André was instructing the boys. "Go and get some clothes on. Quickly now."

Tiineke put Elsa on their bed while she and André scrambled into their own clothes.

"It's an invasion, isn't it?" Tiineke was crying as she fumbled with her buttons.

"Yes. I'll have to go in. I don't know when I'll be back. Stay here. Have the boys help you put up the storm shutters." André spoke in quick bursts as he got dressed.

Tiineke reached out to him. "Can't you stay here?"

"I can't. You need to be strong now. You'll be fine here, just stay inside. You need to be brave for the children." André stopped for a moment and held Tiineke in his arms. "I'll be back as soon as I can." He kissed her forehead and then tilted up her chin and kissed her deeply on the mouth. "I love you."

He picked up Elsa and held her for a moment, and then, kissing her softly on the cheek, handed her to Tiineke.

"You haven't eaten." Tiineke held his arm.

"I'll make a sandwich to take with me." He hurried out of the room.

Tiineke wrapped Elsa in a soft blanket and followed André down to the kitchen where he was talking to their sons.

"Now, Wim, you're the man of the house until I get back. Help your Mama to put up the shutters, and then both of you stay inside and behave yourselves, alright?" André slapped a piece of cheese between two slices of bread and wrapped it in some wax paper. He stuffed the sandwich in his pocket and leaned down to hug each boy quickly.

Wim straightened his shoulders, his face serious. "Yes, Papa."

Andréas stood without speaking, glancing up to the ceiling every few seconds as another squadron of planes roared overhead.

Another quick hug for Tiineke, and André was gone, pedalling his bike furiously towards the base.

Tiineke took a deep breath. "Alright, you two. Set the table for breakfast. I think we'll have a boiled egg today as a special treat. What do you say to that, Andréas? Would you like an egg?"

Andréas pulled himself back from his trance. "Yes, Mama."

"Right then. I'm going to get Elsa dressed and you get every-thing ready." Tiineke went upstairs and got Elsa dressed for the day. It was only 5 a.m. and the sky was still in the first pink-red freshness of dawn.

Everyone was silent until they sat down to breakfast.

Andréas tapped the top of his egg with his spoon. "Will we go to school today, Mama?"

Wim frowned at his brother. "Papa said we were to stay here."

Tiineke kept her voice calm and nodded. "Wim's right. Even though it's a school day, everyone will be staying home today. We'll do some lessons ourselves later."

The roar of another squadron passing overhead stopped all con-versation. They ran to the window and peered up. The shadows of thirty or forty airplanes darkened the morning sky. The house vibrated and a plate fell from the table to the floor with a crash, breaking into a hundred tiny pieces.

Elsa screamed, her shrieking competing with the roar of the engines.

"Hush little one. It's alright. It's alright." Tiineke took the child from her high chair and rocked her.

Wim put his hands over his ears. "When will it stop?"

Andréas watched the sky from the window as the sound faded. "They're gone now."

His words were barely out when the next roar began. The little boy ran to the door and opened it, stepping out on the doorstep.

Bang, bang, bang.

Andréas ran back in the house and slammed the door, his eyes huge. "They're trying to shoot the planes down."

Tiineke looked out and saw which direction the planes were coming from. "It's the squadron from de Kooy. They're chasing the German airplanes."

There was a hypnotic fascination in watching the planes engage in their unreal dance. Fire spit from one and then another. A ball of flame went dropping into the sea. A loud explosion came from the direction of the airport. *Kaboom.* Bombs dropping shook the earth and dishes rattled in the kitchen cupboards.

Tiineke shouted to Wim. "We have to put up the shutters." She pointed to her younger son. "Andréas, stay inside with Elsa."

Tiineke and Wim ran outside and clipped in the wooden storm shutters with shaking, clumsy hands. Once inside again, Tiineke ran up the stairs and pulled in the shutters. Back downstairs, they sat together in the living room.

Time passed, wave after wave of noise and destruction leaving them shaken and nursing headaches. Tiineke tried to engage the boys in lessons, having them take turns reading, but they were distracted in the gloom of the shut-up room. Tiineke read to them from the family Bible, and they played card games. At long last, darkness fell, and with it, quiet returned.

Finally, they heard the key in the door.

"Papa!"

Both boys ran to André as he came in. Ashen faced and grimy, he leaned down to hug them. Tiineke followed the boys to the front door.

"I didn't know if you'd be able to come home again." She held him gratefully, despite the sour smell of sweat and the grit covering his clothes. "Do you want some supper? I made soup."

"Yes, I suppose I'm hungry." He took off his glasses and rubbed his temples, settling in the living room. Andréas leaned against his chair, not leaving his side, while Wim sat at the kitchen table, watching.

Tiineke put a steaming bowl of soup on the table. "I've been listening to the radio. I just turned it off a few minutes ago because they just keep saying the same things over and over."

André moved to the table and, picking up his spoon, he nodded tiredly. "I heard some of it as well. They told the civilians to stay home until further notice."

"Thank God." Tiineke sat down at the table with him while he ate. "Will we be safe here?"

"Probably better than where we used to live. It's pretty far from the base and the airport, although the airport is pretty much gone. Fifteen airplanes gone between what was bombed on the ground and what was lost in fighting."

There was no further conversation for a few moments.

When André finished his meal, he nodded in the direction of the sofa where the boys had gone while their father ate his supper. "The kids should go up to bed. In fact, let's all get some sleep while we can."

In bed, Tiineke reached across the baby, nestled between them. She touched André, drawing comfort from the feel of his skin beneath her fingers, and gave voice to her real fears. "Will they be back tomorrow?"

"No question. It's a full-out invasion. We won't be able to hold out for long, but we'll fight as long as we can."

Tiineke was quiet for a few minutes. "If we were in Amsterdam, we'd probably be safer now, wouldn't we?"

André hugged her as close as he could. "We'll be alright."

He did not answer her question directly.

———

Dawn arrived too soon and they were shaken out of bed by the roar of the planes and dropping bombs. Elsa wailed from her spot between her parents. Tiineke was glad that André would be with them through the day.

It was impossible to sleep through the noise so they got up and went down together to start the day. Wim and Andréas were already up and standing on the doorstep, watching the planes overhead.

André pulled the boys back into the house. "Boys, come in."

Already it seemed normal to have the noise and shaking. Wim and Andréas started to lay the table for breakfast.

Tiineke watched the boys. "They're so adaptable."

André nodded. "Kids are."

For most of the day, André and Tiineke stayed close to the radio to listen to the bulletins as they came in. Rotterdam seemed to be a weak point.

"My poor parents." Tiineke hugged herself and shivered.

André put his arm around her. "They'll be alright."

"I hope so." Tiineke knew he couldn't predict how things would turn out anymore than she could, but it was comforting to hear him say it.

"Look, there goes another one!" Andréas was excited as a thick plume of grey-black smoke rose in the distance. He was getting more adventurous, standing out by the roadside to get a better view regularly shouting updates through the open front door. They all stepped out to see what was going on. The long, low wings of the German Junkers Ju 52s made Tiineke imagine a flock of buzzards skimming overhead, searching for prey. They heard a distant *pop-pop-pop* as the Dutch anti-aircraft guns spit into the air.

"I can't watch this." Tiineke went back in the house. She sat on the floor, playing with Elsa, while André and the boys watched the distant smoke and listened to the noise.

The days and nights passed. The news told of more locations that were now in German hands. Maastricht. Dordrecht. In the north, closer to home, the town of Sneek fell. On May 13, they heard that Queen Wilhelmina had been taken to safety. Princess Juliana and her family had left the night before.

"Listen," Tiineke said as they sat by the radio. "The ministers are leaving as well. 'Government in exile', they're calling it." She turned to André. "I'm glad the royal family is safe, but it feels a bit like being abandoned when the whole government leaves, doesn't it?"

"It's better, I think. At least we know that the Netherlands will still have a government of our own choosing."

She sighed and wrapped her arms around herself. "Yes, that's true, I suppose."

VII

Spring 1940

Tiineke dropped the dishcloth and ran with soapy, dripping hands to stand in front of the radio. She collapsed to the sofa beside André and clutched his hand. The boys stopped their card game and they all listened in horror.

Rotterdam had been bombed. The city was in flames and there were threats that the same would be done to Utrecht. In order to avoid unnecessary suffering, General Winkelman was surrendering.

"Rotterdam bombed." Tears flowed down Tiineke's cheeks.

André stroked her hand. "We don't know. Don't think the worst unless we know."

His words brought no comfort now. Tiineke continued to cry. "They're gone. I know it."

Andréas and Wim crept over to their mother and clung to her.

Andréas twined his arms around her neck and tucked his head against her shoulder. "Oma and Opa can't be dead."

"We hope not. We need to stay positive until we hear definite news." André squeezed his youngest son's shoulder.

"How will we know? The phones are cut off. I need to know!" Tiineke voice was shrill. She plucked at André's sleeve, sobbing.

Elsa woke up in her playpen and started to cry.

André stroke his wife's back. "Tiineke, Elsa needs you."

Automatically, Tiineke went to Elsa and picked her up, her moans subsiding as she as she rocked the small child. Pacing around the room calmed her, though her tears continued to slide down her cheeks and mingle with her daughter's as she pressed her face against Elsa's warm cheek.

Numbly, they continued to listen to the radio until the broadcast concluded.

Tiineke sat in her wing chair and closed her eyes. "It's over, then."

André stood and stuffed his hands in his pockets. "So it seems. I'll go in to work in the morning and find out what I can."

———

Each day, they listened to more reports of continued fighting in the furthest southwestern province of the country.

Tiineke stood, staring out the window after the latest news report. "I thought it was over."

André sat hunched by the radio. "Zeeland was exempt from the surrender."

Zeeland lasted three more days until it too was forced to surrender, and then it truly was over.

Finally, after several days, André came home from work carrying a small telex message.

The lists of casualties had been coming in from Rotterdam and he had been poring over each one as it arrived. With every list that did not have their names, he grew more hopeful, but then, on this day, at the bottom of the third page, he found them.

Jan Pol. Elsa Pol.

Tiineke took one look at André's face before he even said a word. "They're gone. I knew it."

He held open his arms wordlessly and enfolded Tiineke. "I'm sorry." He smelled the salt and sun in her hair. She smelled so *normal*. How was it possible?

He held her as she sobbed against his shoulder. The telex fluttered to the floor. Andréas stuffed it into his pocket, then both boys wrapped their arms around their parents, rocking, crying.

Tiineke disengaged herself from the arms of her husband and sons. She went out into the back garden and sat on one of the garden chairs. André followed her.

"Last summer we all sat here. It seems so long ago already."

André crouched beside her with his hand on her knee. "We need to hold on to those good memories."

When she didn't respond, André went back in to the house and addressed his boys. "We need to look after your Mama right now. We're all very, very sad about Oma and Opa, but Mama most of all, so we're going to do what we can to help her, right?"

He looked down at the tear-streaked faces of his sons.

Their voices were dull. "Yes, Papa."

———

For days, Tiineke worked on automatic. She was numb to all but the most insistent of attempts to break into her haze.

"Mama, Mrs. Pieck is here." Wim tugged on his mother's sleeve as she sat with Elsa sleeping in her lap. She gazed at him dumbly for a moment.

"Sorry, Wim. What did you say?"

"Mrs. Pieck, our teacher, is here to see you."

"Please show her in, Wim." Tiineke sat on, not moving.

Wim went back to bring her to the living room.

"Mrs. Meijer." The young woman lowered her voice when she saw the sleeping child and touched the baby's soft curls after shaking Tiineke's hand. "Good morning."

"I'm sorry for not getting up." Tiineke's voice was dull and listless. "Please take a seat."

"It's fine. I just wanted to come to let you know that school is starting again on Monday. We think it's important to get back to normal as soon as we can." Mrs. Pieck nodded towards the boys who stood leaning on their mother's chair, one on each side. "It's better for everyone, I think."

"Yes. Back to normal." Tiineke looked up at her and for a moment was puzzled about what this woman wanted from her. She rubbed her head before responding. "Good. The boys will be there." Tiineke subsided into silence and looked down at Elsa.

After a moment, the teacher turned to leave. "Well, that's all I came to say. I'm going around to all my students. Each of the teachers has taken part of the student list."

When Tiineke didn't respond, Mrs. Pieck turned to the boys. "We'll see you on Monday, then."

"Oma and Opa are dead." Andréas patted his mother's shoulder.

"Oh. I'm so very sorry. I didn't know." The teacher's eyes filled with tears. She touched Tiineke on the shoulder. "If there is anything I can do."

Tiineke blinked and shook her head. "Thank you. No. Nothing." She gestured to her oldest son. "Please see Mrs. Pieck out, Wim."

Wim did as he was bid, then returned.

"Mama, what shall we have for supper today?"

Tiineke sighed and looked at him. "We need to do some shopping, don't we?"

"I think so, Mama."

"Alright, boys. Get Elsa's carriage outside, please, Wim. Andréas, please get the shopping bags." Tiineke shook her hair back from her face and rolled her shoulders. "I'll just pin my hair up and then we'll go."

A moment later she came down the stairs. Her hair was tidy and she had put on a clean cardigan. Her voice was firm. "Do you need jackets?"

The boys spoke in chorus. "No, Mama."

Andréas took her hand when they went outside, skipping occasionally, and Wim pushed the carriage.

"I'm glad we're going back to school." Andréas nodded and then smiled. "I want to play football with my friends."

VIII

Spring 1941

"Mama, look here!" Andréas ran in, waving an envelope in the air.

Tiineke took it and read the return address. "It's a letter from your Tante Mary!" She put it aside. "I'll save it until Papa comes home and we can read it together. Off you go outside again, please."

Wim pleaded. "Open it now." After all these years, he still missed his Uncle Johan and loved to hear some news of him.

"Later. Go." Tiineke shooed the children outside into the warm spring sun. "Don't get into mischief!" She smiled as Wim took Elsa's hand and matched his pace to her small steps.

Later that evening, after their meager supper, Tiineke pulled out the letter. In fact, she had read it when she was alone, wanting to be sure there was nothing in it she wouldn't want the children to hear. One never knew these days.

André nodded to Tiineke before he rested his head back against the sofa. "Read it out loud for us."

Tiineke nodded and began.

Dear Tiineke, André, and children, I've been asking Johan to write to you for months, but it seems that he isn't going to, so I am finally finding the energy to do it. I suppose Johan is forbidden to contact you, but I haven't had those instructions.

Perhaps you've already heard, but the big news is that I have, at long last, had a baby. In fact, I have to admit that he was born last July. We hoped for so long and finally he is here. Yes, we are the parents of a fine boy, and we have called him Nicholas James, after my two brothers. I hope that their spirits will live on in our son. I can't imagine that they are both gone, fighting during those terrible five days last year. Tiineke, I'm sure you understand. My mother just stays in bed all the time now and my father tries to look after her, but he is hardly able either. I understand it. So here he is, a new life. Johan is over the moon and is very good with him, which is lucky because I'm so tired all the time. I hardly have the energy to even lift him.

Well, that's the news. Johan is fine and works a lot, and now he spends his free time with Nicky. Mama Meijer also works a lot and spends her free time getting the most out of the shops that the ration coupons can buy. She is good with Nicky too. I hope you are all well.

Love, Mary.

Tiineke looked at André. "What do you think?"

He hesitated and frowned. "It's great news, of course."

Wim huffed. "Is that all there is? A new baby?"

Tiineke smiled at his bored expression. "I'm afraid so."

The children moved into the living room and started playing with Elsa's blocks while Tiineke and André continued to sit at the table.

"She doesn't seem as excited as I'd expect, does she?" Tiineke reread the letter.

André shrugged. "Maybe she's just too tired to write more."

"Maybe." Tiineke furrowed her brow and folded the letter back into the envelope. "We'll have to send something, although I don't want to send any of our clothes along." She rubbed the swell of her own belly. "With our track record, we'll need those boy's clothes again. I'll hunt around tomorrow. We'll have to use some of our coupons."

"That's fine, we'll manage. How about sending a cheese along? And maybe some jars of the pickled herring. I hear that those are not so easy to get in Amsterdam as here."

"Great idea. I'll make up a box of little odds and ends."

Tiineke dismissed the uneasy feeling she had gotten from the letter and went to make a list of items she planned to put into a congratulatory package for Johan and Mary.

———

It was the next day at lunch.

"If I'm not here yet when you get home from school this afternoon, you can entertain yourselves for a little while, right? Make sure you are home in time to set the table and peel the potatoes."

Both boys together. "Yes, Mama."

Tiineke gave an extra stern glance in Andréas's and he smiled back at her. "I promise!"

He looked so innocent.

When the boys were safely at school, Tiineke took Elsa and went hunting for gifts for Mary and Johan's baby. Since milk was now being rationed, Tiineke was delighted that the shop owner agreed to give her a tin of dried milk powder without using her ration card. She was able to buy some smoked herring and a wedge of cheese as well.

When she got home with her purchases, the boys were home and busy with their chores.

"Well, this is great. I'm glad you stayed out of trouble and did as you were asked."

The boys exchanged a glance, then gave their full attention to their tasks.

"Is something going on? Oh, Andréas! How did you tear the leg of your pants...and how did you get all those scratches on your legs?" Tiineke knelt to examine Andréas's shorts. "What did you catch them on?"

He looked down at his pants as if surprised to see the tear. "I don't know."

She looked at him sharply. "You don't know how you tore your pants and scratched up your legs? I don't believe you. Stop what you are doing and stand here." She pulled him in front of her so that he was eye to eye with her. "I'll ask you again. What were you up to?"

André's key sounded in the lock.

"Papa's home!" All three children ran to the front door to greet their father, as they always did.

"Hello, hello. Yes, I see you too." André lifted Elsa, who wrapped her arms around his neck. He tipped forward to kiss each of his sons, then came into the kitchen, still carrying Elsa, with the boys on his heels.

"Hello." He kissed Tiineke on the lips, a quick kiss of greeting and then a second one, lingering a few seconds longer. "All well?"

She folded her arms across her chest and glanced down at Andréas. "Yes, I think so."

"Think?" He raised his eyebrows. "Did you have problems with your shopping?"

"No, I'll show you in a minute what I got. I think Mary and Johan will be pleased. No, I was about to hear from your son how he managed to tear up his pants and his legs." She looked down to Andréas where he hovered behind André.

André set Elsa down and turned to look at Andréas. Before André could ask anything, there was a loud knock on the door. *Rap-rap-rap.*

For a second, the whole family stood frozen, looking at each other. This was the type of loud knock that only the German police used. Visitors never knocked with such force.

André held up his hand and straightened his shoulders as he went to the door. "Stay here."

He opened the door.

"Good evening, sir." The German military police officer clicked his heels and nodded formally to André.

"Good evening. How can I help you?" André's voice was cool but polite.

"You have two sons, I believe?"

André gave one stiff nod. "I have."

"Well, sir, I'm sorry to report that they have been seen in a forbidden area. They were in an area of the dunes that is clearly marked with 'No Trespassing' and 'Forbidden to Enter' signs. They were seen climbing the fence and running away when the guards attempted to catch them." The officer's voice was firm and cold. "I must instruct you to punish the boys accordingly."

Tiineke stood with her hand at her throat. A cold trickle of sweat snaked down her back. André's back was ramrod straight. He was angry. *Please don't argue with the man.*

"What evidence do you have that the boys were my sons?" André voice was calm, the underlying anger apparent only to his family.

"They were recognized by one of my men. They have been seen in this area previously, and at that time, enquiries were made. There is no question that they were your sons. I expect that a sound thrashing should prevent this problem from recurring." The officer's eyes were steely.

André folded his arms across his chest. "In other words, you have no evidence."

"Do you refuse to believe me?"

"I suggest that your guards be a bit quicker to catch these boys, and if you do, and if they are my boys, I will then take the appropriate action. Until that time, there is nothing that I intend to do. If there is nothing else, sir, we were about to begin our supper." André took a step forward, forcing the officer to step back and out the door.

The officer flushed, his voice steely. "If the boys are caught, *we* will take the appropriate action." He nodded once and wheeled away, joining the two soldiers waiting outside, smoking cigarettes.

André stood for a moment at the closed door, listening to the receding footsteps, the hard boot heels ringing off the pavement.

Tiineke was tearful and sick with worry. "Oh, André, you've made an enemy there. Why didn't you just say that you would punish the boys and leave it at that?"

"They have taken over my country. They have taken over my workplace. They will not take over my home." André's lips were white against the red flush of his face. He turned on his boys. "Now you two. What were you doing in the forbidden area?"

Both boys sat quietly at the table, and for a moment, neither said anything, then Andréas stood up and dug into his pocket. He poured a handful of brass shell casings on to the table.

"We go in and collect these. We hear them shooting up in the dunes sometimes and then we go and look because they leave all the casings behind. Sometimes we even find a bullet that didn't fire properly."

Tiineke knuckles were white as she gripped the back of a chair. "Dear God in Heaven."

Wim bit his bottom lip. "I'm sorry, Mama. I knew we shouldn't have been there."

André's face drained of the flush of anger and was now pale. "How many of these do you have?"

"A whole jar full!" Andréas was very proud of his collection.

"So you've been several times."

"Uh, well, yes." Andréas blinked and he knew he'd revealed more than he had intended to.

André ran his hand through his hair. Pushing it back like that showed how much it was receding. He paced to the front window, then back to the kitchen. The silence was only broken by Elsa singing softly as she played with her blocks.

"I don't know how to say this in a way that will ensure that you understand. I could do as the officer instructed and 'thrash' you both, but I don't want to do that. I want you to understand what I'm saying now. You must *never*, ever, go there again. I don't know if you've seen anyone shot up there."

Wim was quick to shake his head. "No, Papa"

"I'm glad about that at least, but the fact is that these are not games. The Germans will probably kill you if you go there again. We've been lucky that they warned us. Can you understand me when I tell you that you must never go there again?"

Both boys nodded solemnly. "Yes, Papa."

"It was my idea. Wim said we shouldn't, but I wanted to." Andréas took a quick glance at his brother.

"I don't care whose idea it was. You should both know better than to go in an area that is forbidden. Again, we've been lucky that most of the soldiers around here are pretty friendly to us, but they don't have to be. They tell us what to do, and we do it. That's the way it is at the moment."

André's face was red again and his forehead beaded with sweat. He took a deep breath and reached out to put a hand on a shoulder of each of the boys. "We are living in times where you can't just play games. You have to be quite grown-up and responsible. It isn't Wim's job only, Andréas. I need to be able to count on you as well. I need to know that you are looking after yourselves for one thing, and also your sister and mother. That's your job when I'm not around, alright?"

Andréas's eyes were filled with tears. "I'm sorry, Papa. We won't do it again. I'll be responsible, I promise."

"I know you will." André ruffled his young son's hair and then turned to Wim. "I know your brother likes to get into mischief, but you're very sensible, Wim. You need to keep an eye on him and not let him lead you both into difficulty."

"Yes, Papa. I'll make sure from now on." Wim shot a look to his brother as if to say 'Are you listening?'

"Good boys. That's an end to it then. Stay far away from that area. I don't want to give them any excuse." He looked at Tiineke. "Let's have our supper."

Tiineke's throat was red where her fingers had remained unconsciously kneading her skin ever since the first hard knock on the door. She took a deep breath and turned back to her supper preparations. The cabbage was still slightly warm although the stove had been turned off just prior to the policeman's arrival.

She checked the potatoes. "The potatoes are almost cold. Shall I fry them?"

André sighed. "No, let's just eat."

They sat and ate their supper in silence, the food unappetizing and sticking in their throats.

———

They were settled into their routines. The boys went to school, Tiineke shopped for what little could be found, and André went to work. It all went on, yet nothing was the same. Airplanes overhead, noise, shouting, and the ever-present German soldiers kept the occupation intertwined with daily life. By now there were continual air raids as the Allies attempted to attack the German-held naval yards.

Usually the raids were far enough away to ignore, but one day the drone of the airplanes filled the air with a roar that meant they were close; very close.

"Boys! Come! Come *now*!" Tiineke yelled into the garden, scooping Elsa in her arms.

The whine and rattle of the approaching airplanes drowned out Wim's questions. Tiineke just kept yelling.

"Run for the dunes. Run!"

They joined their neighbours, all running for the dunes, as the first of the planes began their strafing. The target was the naval base, but experience had taught the villagers that the planes rarely only hit the target.

One of their neighbours reached out to take Elsa. "Here, give me the child!"

His wife put an arm around Tiineke to support her as they ran until they finally reached the towering piles of sand.

"When are you due?"

"Another six weeks." Tiineke panted and looked around to make sure both boys were safe.

The woman shook her head. "Not much of a time and place to bring in a new life, is it?"

Tiineke lowered herself to the sand and tossed her head. "Maybe it's just what we need."

They sat, quietly listening to the *rat-a-tat-tat* of the gunfire as the waves of planes continued to fire and the big guns around the naval base and on the beach responded. Slowly, the noise subsided as the planes wheeled away, heading back to England. A black ball of smoke filled the sky in the distance where one had gone down.

Someone spoke up. "I think we should be alright now."

Slowly, the villagers made their way back to their homes and businesses.

The neighbour reached for the little girl. "Do you want me to carry Elsa still?"

"No, thank you. She can walk. We'll take our time going back." Tiineke watched as her neighbour moved ahead of them.

The day was quiet now, but the breeze brought the smell of cordite mingled with the salty tang of the sea. The children played tag as they made their way back to the house. Laughter echoed through the dunes, replacing the staccato sound of gunfire.

As they got close to the house, Andréas froze, then called back over his shoulder. "Oh Mama, look!"

The walkway and garden was littered with broken window glass, the fragments glittering in the sun. They had to walk across it to get to the house. The crunch of the broken crystal underfoot had an alien feeling. It wasn't the walkway to their home they were crossing, rather a surreal landscape of unmelting ice. The slivers embedded themselves into the soles of their sandals.

Tiineke blinked back tears looking at the damage. "Get the broom please, Wim. You'll clear up down here. Andréas, come upstairs with me."

After surveying the rooms one by one, only the boys' room was undamaged. Tiineke turned to her son. "You stay here in your room with Elsa and look after her. You two can play while Wim and I clear up."

Andréas straightened up. "I can help you, Mama."

She put her hand on his shoulder. "You can help me most by looking after Elsa here where it's safe. That's just as important as clearing up the glass. Will you do that for me?"

"Yes, Mama. Come Elsa, I'll let you look at my shell collection."

Elsa grinned. "Can I have one?"

Tiineke gave a small smile as she went back downstairs. Children really were so adaptable.

When André came home from work, Tiineke was sitting in the big easy chair with a cool cloth on her forehead. The three children had been playing together at the table but they bounded over to their father when he came in. The room was dim because the light from one window was blocked by the cardboard Tiineke had nailed in front of the broken pane. Luckily, the side window was intact and the early evening light shone through.

He stroked her hair. "Are you alright?"

She took the cloth from her forehead and gave him a small smile. "I'm just tired. It's been a heck of a day and the baby is complaining about all this activity."

André touched her belly and felt a kick beneath his hand. "Yes, he wants out to see what's going on."

"I think you're right. I've made a salad for supper. We can fry an egg with it if that isn't enough."

"No, that's fine."

"Papa, come and see everything that happened!" The boys were hopping from foot to foot behind their father.

"Yes, alright, show me." André shrugged at Tiineke and turned to follow the boys.

Tiineke sat a few moments longer, and in the stillness of the evening she could hear their progress through the thin makeshift window covering. They took him around the house, showing him the three windows that had been broken and were now covered with cardboard. She could hear Andréas's voice, high with excitement as he pointed out where there were embedded bullets in the walls and in other places, long cracks.

The children were still excited when they came back in.

Andréas tugged on his father's arm. "After supper will you come down the street with us? Mr. deJong's shop has even more bullets stuck in the walls."

"No, I've seen enough. We'll have the evening inside and we'll have a game of cards." André was tired of the destruction.

The boys exchanged glances. "Even though it isn't a Saturday night?" Wim raised his eyebrows.

"A special treat." André patted Wim on the head.

———

Later, when the children were in bed, André and Tiineke talked.

"There isn't much spare wood around, but I'll see what I can find tomorrow to cover over the windows. The cardboard won't last long."

"I suppose having the glass replaced is out of the question."

"I suspect it will be a while before we can get that done, but I'll ask around."

André looked at Tiineke's flushed face, beaded with sweat. "It's getting hard on you to run for the dunes every time there is a raid, isn't it?"

"I'm not much of a runner these days."

"Shall we go to bed?" He wanted to hold her.

She nodded and slid under the covers.

In bed, he lay, spooning her, her back nestled against his chest and her bum against his crotch. He could feel himself stirring with desire and shifted a little away from her.

She spoke over her shoulder. "Let's have this baby first before starting another, shall we?"

He could hear the smile in her voice. "I'm sorry, but I can't help it. I don't need to do anything, I just need to feel you against me."

"Don't be sorry. The fact that you can still be aroused by me, despite the fact that I look like a baby elephant, I'll take it as a compliment." She reached behind her to pull him close again.

He lay listening to her breathe, her breath slowly deepening into a snore as she fell asleep, exhausted. He inhaled the scent of her as he remained pressed against her. The back of her neck was damp with sweat in the warm night and she gave off a slightly porridge-like smell. It was a comforting smell, uniquely her. He tried to capture the smell and feel of her, imprinting them inside his core.

In the morning he was awake already when she woke, but he hadn't risen.

"Aren't you getting up for work?" She nudged his thigh.

"Soon."

She lay on her back, and he raised himself on one elbow to look at her.

"You know how, when you are falling asleep, it seems like the world is finally quiet enough so that you can hear what your heart has to say?"

She looked up at him and smiled. "Yes, I know."

"It's when you realize the truth of things that maybe you don't really want to think about."

She reached up to touch his face. "What truth have you discovered?"

"That you all have to leave."

"Leave?" She struggled to sit up.

"Yes. Lots of people have been evacuated. Whole towns have been—look at Zandvoort. I've been selfish to keep you here when it is so dangerous."

They sat side by side, propped against the headboard, not speaking.

She took his hand. "Where you are is where our home is. Will you be able to leave?"

He shook his head. "Not a chance. The Germans wouldn't allow it."

"Then we don't go either."

"Tiineke, you and the children are my life. To imagine what might have happened yesterday, well, I can't bear it. You need to do this for them, and for me. I need to know you are safe."

"How can I manage without you?"

"How can I manage without *you*?" He kissed her forehead. "I don't know, but we'll have to until all this madness is over. It will be over one of these days, but until then, you need to be safe. I'll visit as often as I can." He stroked her belly. The baby was at rest.

Tiineke put her hand on top of his and frowned. "I can't go back to your mother's."

"No, I wouldn't ask you to. I'm going to write to Hank. I'm sure he'll take you in."

"Yes, I think so.

André turned his hand over to grasp hers. "We made the right decision all those years ago, didn't we? I don't regret a moment.

What a life we've had so far. I've been so happy, and we will be again. It's just for now."

She sighed. "We better get up. I can hear the boys talking. Will we tell them now?"

"We'll tell them when the plans are finalized. I'll write to Hank today." He gave her hand one final squeeze before getting out of bed.

Tiineke watched him get dressed. She knew that he was right. The children needed to be somewhere safe. *How, dear God, how can I leave him behind?*

IX

Fall 1941

Tiineke heard her husband's voice the moment he arrived.

"Where is she?" André didn't wait for a response as he bounded up the stairs of Hank's home.

"André?" Tiineke's heart pounded. She couldn't wait to see him after all these weeks.

"Here, Papa, come here." Wim took André's hand and led him to where his mother sat with the new baby in her arms.

"Meet your daughter." Tiineke held the small bundle out to him. "Marika, here's your Papa at long last."

"I'm sorry I wasn't here. I couldn't get the time off before now." André studied the tiny little girl in his arms.

Tiineke touched his arm. "You're here now. She hasn't changed that much in two weeks."

She didn't say anything about the overwhelming sadness she had felt at having her baby without her mother *or* husband by her side.

Tiineke rose from her chair. "Come, let's sit out in the living room so we can all be together. This room doesn't have the space for all of us. The house barely does." She laughed a small laugh.

Hank slipped his jacket and hat on. "I'm going out to find some fresh bread. I'll be back in a while." He left the family alone to enjoy their new baby.

"He's been so wonderful. He's partitioned off the attic into two rooms for the children and then he and I each have the two real bedrooms. He's so good with the boys. They love going out cycling along the canal with him." Tiineke's eyes filled with tears. "Even still, it's not the same."

"I know, I know." André held her close with one arm and his small daughter with the other. A small pair of arms clutched his legs. "Well, Marika, I'll give you back to Mama so I can give your big sister a hug." He handed the baby back to Tiineke and scooped Elsa up, swinging her above his head in his outstretched arms. She laughed and kicked her feet.

André laughed too. "Oh my, you are such a big girl. I almost can't do that anymore."

He sat down and the three children crowded around to tell him of their adventures in the new city.

Andréas gestured and chattered with excitement. "We started our new school. It's by the church, Janskerk, so it's easy to get to."

"I have two whole days here, so you'll have to show me later. Perhaps I even passed it on the way here from the bus station."

Wim tugged on his father's sleeve. "When can we come home, Papa?"

"I don't know, son. For now, you need to stay here and look after Mama and your sisters and brother."

Later, in bed together, André watched as Tiineke nursed Marika. "I have two German soldiers in the house now."

She looked away from her baby and studied her husband's face. "Oh my God. Are they alright?"

"Yes. I know them from the base. They're alright. Not bullies like some can be." He hesitated, then changed topics. "I can't believe how they've all grown in just a few weeks. Wim especially. He seems so grown up suddenly. To me, he looks more like thirteen or fourteen already, rather than not even twelve."

"I know. His legs stick out from under his trousers now. He needs new ones, really, but they'll have to do for a while yet."

André touched the baby's hand and she grasped his finger. "Are they behaving themselves here?"

"Yes, starting school has been good for them. It takes their minds off things. And as I said, Hank is really good with them. I think he was lonely and likes having us around, actually." She paused a moment. "It's funny, though. Until we came here, I didn't realize how much we used to laugh at home. I don't hear them laughing anymore." She pressed her lips together.

André gazed at the wall dreamily. "Do you remember standing under the lighthouse when Elsa was born?"

"Yes. We'll have to wait a while to take Marika there."

They sat, looking at the tiny baby lying in Tiineke's arms, remembering the starlit night, years ago.

The baby hiccupped.

Tiineke spoke, breaking the spell. "Hank sees Johan fairly regularly, you know."

"Oh yes, and how are they? How's their little one?"

"Hank is worried about Mary. He said she sleeps a lot. Johan gets the baby up and then your mother pretty much looks after him all day."

André tilted his head. "Has she seen a doctor?"

"The doctor just calls it the 'baby blues' and feels that she'll pull out of it in time."

André *tsk-tsked*. "Poor Johan. It isn't what he expected from life."

Tiineke shifted the baby to her other side. "He doesn't have your courage."

"He always wanted to make everyone happy. That's hard to do."

"Impossible to do, you mean."

"Yes, impossible to do."

Marika stopped hiccupping and fell into a deep sleep. Her fingers and legs jumped and twitched occasionally and she snuffled in the way of small babies. It was a comforting sound.

Tiineke put the baby in the cradle beside the bed and slid down beside André. He drew her close against him and kissed her deeply.

André awoke early after sleeping soundly for the first time in a long time. After breakfast, the children took him for a tour of the neighbourhood. The long row of tall, narrow houses fronted a canal where ducks swam contentedly. Small rowboats were tied up along the edge. They walked along the canal and crossed over to look at the school.

Elsa stamped her foot. "I want to go to school too."

Andréas patted her shoulder. "You're too small."

"Your Mama needs you at home. You're a big sister now, you know. You need to help Mama look after the baby." André squeezed her hand gently.

She looked up at him, her large blue eyes serious. "Yes, that's true."

It all seemed so peaceful. People were just living almost normal lives.

They crossed the Nieuwe Gracht and turned right to start circling back. On the corner were two German soldiers. One was examining the papers of a small man who stood with his head bowed. He wore a yellow Star of David on his jacket. The soldiers were yelling questions at him and he stuttered in response.

André hurried the children along, the moment of peace shattered.

After supper that night, Hank, Tiineke, and André sat at the table drinking *ersatz* coffee, the bitter drink that was at least better than nothing.

André recounted what he had seen, and turned to Tiineke. "Do you feel safe here?"

Tiineke hesitated, then nodded. "Yes. We see things like that as well. There aren't too many Jews around here—many have gone to work camps somewhere—but there are still a few. They always get a hard time from the Germans. It really upsets Andréas. Wim knows enough to keep his mouth closed, but I'm always worried that Andréas will say something he shouldn't. For the most part, we're left alone, though. There's no bombing here, so yes, it seems safer."

André watched her face as she spoke. He could see that she was worried, but he had to accept that it was a better place than Den Helder for them.

His visit was over too fast. They went as a family to the bus station, walking slowly.

André spoke quietly so that only Tiineke could hear him. "I'm not sure when I can come back. It's harder than I thought to get the time and permission, and even then, it's hard to get a place on the bus or train."

"I know. We'll manage until you can come back. Don't worry about us." Tiineke tried to smile.

"I think I'll cycle next time. It's only about 65 kilometres." André grinned as he emphasized the word *only*. "Here we are. I better get in line. You go on back now." He stooped to give everyone a hug and kisses.

Andréas clung to his father's jacket. "Can't we wait with you, Papa?"

"No, you go on home. This is no place for you to be." André glanced around at the crowds of armed soldiers pushing and talking in loud, abrupt voices.

One last kiss for Tiineke and his new daughter, then he turned decisively to the line-up.

"Come, kids. Wim please hold Elsa's hand." Tiineke turned away. André stole a last glance at her as she left. She held her shoulders and back stiff and didn't look back.

———

They fell into a routine again. Going to school, playing football, walking, and once in a while, a boat ride along the Binnen Spaame with a friend of Hank's. Tiineke shopped carefully to make the food stretch and only bought the absolute necessities for clothes. Andréas wore Wim's outgrown clothes. Elsa wore some of Andréas's. Tiineke recalled when she thought she would never dress a daughter in boy clothes. Times had changed. Once in a while, Tiineke received something for Wim from the mother of a boy who was older and bigger.

The time was marked by visits from André. He was even able to arrange to come for a few days over Sinterklaas.

"What news do you have?" Hank asked him one night after the children were asleep.

André rubbed his hands together to warm them in the chilly room. "I'm under German eyes constantly so you probably hear more than I do."

"A friend has a radio. I hear that things are very bad in the west. Everything is running short—food, gasoline, everything. You're lucky you still have your bike. I hear that they are starting to confiscate those as well now." Hank shook his head and crossed his long legs. "It's pretty hard to get much of a picture from the radio reports. A lot of it is in code. They're constantly saying things like, 'The cow has not yet delivered the milk', and even then, with the noise that the Germans transmit to block it out... well, it's hard to make much of it."

"We're lucky you were able to bring us the potatoes and ham. It's the first big meal we've had in a long time. And the skates you brought for the boys, they're thrilled with them! Even the drawing paper you brought for Elsa...you really found something for every-one. It was a good Sinterklaas." Tiineke swallowed the last of her coffee and set the cup aside. She didn't mention the Sinterklaas cel-ebration they had had just a few years previously with all the family around. There was no need.

The three of them sat silently for a moment, lost in their memories.

Hank finished his coffee as well and stood up. "It's bed for me. I'm lucky to have work here at the gas factory in Haarlem now, so I don't have any real travelling to do, but still I find I'm tired early."

"We won't be long behind you. I have to leave early tomorrow, so I may not see you again." André stood to say good night to his brother-in-law. Hank reached out his hand to shake, but André pulled him close to give him a hug.

"I can't thank you enough for looking after my family." André's voice was low in Hank's ear, and he choked as his eyes filled with tears.

Hank nodded. "They're my family too. I'll do my best with them until they can go home to you. I'm starting to make some connections with farmers in the area, so hopefully I'll start to organize the food supply better in the future." He broke away and went to his room.

André and Tiineke moved to the couch and sat close together, thighs touching. She began nursing Marika.

"Marika looks happy, anyway." André smiled a small smile.

"She sleeps a lot. Thank goodness she's still nursing, but even still, I don't think she's getting the nutrition she needs." Tiineke bent and kissed the baby's head, the soft hair tickling her nose.

"I was shocked to see how thin Wim is. He's so tall, he just looks like a beanpole."

Tiineke nodded with a smile, then the smile slipped away from her face. "Children are resilient. As long as everyone can stay out of trouble, we'll make it."

Tiineke knew her face must be transparent when André took a guess at her thoughts. "Is Andréas staying out of trouble?"

"He seems to have gotten in with a bunch of boys who run a little wild. Once in a while he comes home with something—potatoes or some scraps of wood for the stove. I've stopped asking." Tiineke's shoulders were slumped. Her once glossy hair was wispy and streaked with a few threads of grey now.

André put his hand on her knee and squeezed it without saying anything. He didn't chastise her for not managing the family better. Every day was an effort. He knew it himself.

Tiineke studied André. "You look tired. The ride is taking so much out of you. Especially now in the cold weather, it must be so hard. I don't ever remember a winter with so much snow."

"It's nothing. I'm fine." But his face was thin and drawn, the high cheekbones exaggerated by the deeply receding hairline.

Tiineke finished nursing and they watched Marika sleep for a few moments. Then Tiineke shivered. "We usually go to bed by now. It's easier to keep warm." She rose and led the way to their room.

In bed they could forget.

X

Summer 1942

"When is Papa coming?" Elsa's voice was whiny.

Tiineke sighed. "I don't know, sweetheart. His bicycle has been confiscated so he has no way to get here anymore."

Even at four years old, Elsa knew what 'confiscated' meant. Their own bicycles were gone as well.

The hot July days were making everyone cranky. Elsa flung herself on the sofa. "I want Papa."

"You have me, Elsa." Wim held out his hand to his sister. "Shall we go for a walk along the canal?"

Tiineke looked at him gratefully. "Would you, Wim? Andréas, you go along as well, but make sure you're home before Oom Hank so we can have supper as soon as he gets home."

Andréas glanced towards the kitchen, raising his eyebrows hopefully. "What are we having for supper?"

"Bread, and I have some soup made."

Andréas pulled a face. The same fare as most days. "Will we ever have real bread again?" The gritty black bread they received now was not the same as the bakery bread they'd had in Den Helder.

Tiineke smoothed her hand over his hair. "Someday."

As the day was warm Tiineke left the street door open, hoping to catch some breeze.

Bang-bang. A heavy fist thumped against the open door instead of ringing the bell.

"Hello?" A man's voice rang through the house and Tiineke came hurrying out.

"Yes?" It was a policeman. He was Dutch and had a kind-looking face. Tiineke breathed deep to slow her racing heart. Any authority at the door raised fear.

He looked down at a piece of paper, then back up at her. "Mrs. Meijer?"

"Yes. What is it?" Her heart throbbed and she felt nauseous.

It's probably nothing. The boys have gotten into some mischief.

She could smell the sweat from the policeman in his heavy uniform. From outside came the sound of pigeons cooing in the warm afternoon. Behind her, the clock ticked. Was it always so loud? Her thoughts tumbled and scattered.

The officer cleared his throat. "Your husband is Mr. Andréas Meijer, currently of Den Helder?"

"Yes, but he goes by André. Andréas is what we call our son." Tiineke stopped talking, knowing she was babbling.

He nodded as if she had said something very important. "I'm sorry to have to notify you that your husband was killed during an air attack on Rijkswerf Willemsoord."

Tiineke stepped backwards as if to distance herself from the news. She turned and sat down in the living room. He followed her in and continued. "His body will be interned in Den Helder. You will not be able to go for his funeral, I'm afraid." He had done this sort of thing before. His voice was sympathetic but professional.

Tiineke just gazed up at him. She had no questions. Her mind had stopped and she didn't know what to say or ask.

"That's all the information I have for you. In due course, the navy may send you further information."

He nodded once more, a slight dip of his head as if to punctuate his report, then touched the peak of his cap. "I'll leave you alone now. You have my sincere condolences, Mrs. Meijer."

He turned and left, closing the door behind him.

Marika's cries were what finally roused her. Her own eyes were dry and gritty as she rose and went to lift the baby from the carriage. As though she were in a dream, she went through the motions of sitting again and positioning the baby to nurse. It was only when she felt the tug on her breast that the dam opened. Soon she was sobbing, though she tried to control herself because she thought her milk would sour for her baby. Marika was hungry, though, and focused on her feeding.

When the baby pulled away, content for the moment, she turned her big blue eyes to her mother's face as Tiineke moaned. Finally, exhausted, the tears slowed. Tiineke sat in a stupor.

André had sacrificed the life that had been mapped out for him for her sake, for the sake of their family. She knew he'd often missed being part of his own family business. He had missed Johan and even his mother, and yet never complained, never even remarked on it. He had clearly loved their new life together and they had made the most of it, no matter how hard things had been.

She pushed away the cloud of guilt that had begun to envelop her. He had been happy with the decision and she had to hold on to that knowledge, and cling to the good memories. She closed her eyes and rested her head on the back of the chair. Marika slept now in her lap.

André...you were so good to me. So good for *me. How can I go on without you?*

The front door opened. "Mama, we're home!" It was Wim's voice, almost as if in response to her question.

You can go on because of them. Tiineke could almost hear André speaking.

She was leaning over the carriage, putting the sleeping baby down, when the three children blew into the room like a storm. She gave herself another moment looking down at the baby before turning to face them.

As she turned they fell silent.

"Mama, what's wrong?" Wim frowned and took a step towards her.

Her eyes filled with tears and she opened her arms to them.

"Your Papa." It was all she could manage before they engulfed her. She didn't need to say more. They knew. Even Elsa, at her young age, was a child of war. Death was a part of her daily life.

She released them and sat on the couch. They crowded around her, Elsa climbing on her lap and putting her thin arms around Tiineke's neck.

Andréas tugged Tiineke's sleeve. "What happened? Maybe it's a mistake."

"No sweetheart, it isn't a mistake. A policeman came to tell me." Tiineke was barely able to choke the words out. She cleared her throat, knowing that they needed to talk about it.

Wim was biting his lip, trying not to cry. "What happened?"

"There was an air raid. That's really all I know."

Andréas got up and wandered to the kitchen. He needed to be alone.

"Will we go to Den Helder for a funeral?" Wim's voice caught in his throat and his eyes filled with tears.

Tiineke could feel the shudders against her as Elsa continued to sob.

"No. The Navy will look after the funeral. We aren't supposed to go, and even if we could, how would we get there?"

"So we can't even say good-bye." Tears were rolling down Wim's cheeks now.

"Remember the last time he was here? We all walked with him for almost an hour while he pushed his bike. We said good-bye then. Don't you remember all the hugs he gave each of us?"

Andréas came back into the room. "He said we have to look after each other."

"That's right. And he said that we need to think of the happy times we had together. Always remember the good times. That's what he would want us to do."

Andréas stood, shivering, in front of Tiineke, then Wim stood too. He reached out for his younger brother and the two boys clung to each other in a tight hug. Tiineke wrapped her arms around Elsa and let her own silent tears soak into her daughter's hair.

Johan and Mary: 1934 – 1942

I

Summer 1934

Agatha nodded to Johan and Mary and flapped her hand in the direction of the warehouse. "I suppose you'll want to move into the rooms above." She peered at Johan and when he nodded, she continued. "We'll have to spend some time this week bringing you up to date on the bookkeeping, Johan." She read from a piece of paper where she had made a list.

Mary craned her neck to see the list. "What's that?"

Agatha's black brows pulled together in a frown. "Things to be done."

"Now that André and Tiineke have moved out, you mean?"

"I would prefer that we not speak of those people again."

Johan sighed. "Good Lord, Mama. You can't erase them as if they never existed. I'm angry with André as much as you are, but he's still my brother."

"He doesn't exist for me anymore." Agatha got up to remove the breakfast plates from the table.

Mary lifted her eyebrows to Johan and he shrugged in return. "She just needs time to adjust. I have to go. If I don't hurry, I'll be late for training, and Coach doesn't put up with that." Johan gave Mary a quick kiss and went to grab his boots from a hook by the door.

Agatha poked her head out the kitchen door. "Where are you going?"

Johan stopped with one hand on the door handle. "I'm off for my training. You know that. I go every morning now, Mama."

Agatha slapped the dishcloth against the door frame. "You can't seriously be considering staying with that. Everything's changed now."

"Nothing's changed for me. I can't just come and go as I like. This is a serious team, Mama."

Mary came and stood beside Johan. "Mama Meijer, I'll help you. I don't have a job yet, so there must be something I can do to be of more help than I have been."

Agatha's voice raised and she glared at Mary. "You? What are you trained to do in the business?"

Mary stepped back as if struck.

"Mama, Mary is a very intelligent girl and can be of great help if you'll only give her a chance. I'm sorry, I have to go." Johan hurried out and was pedalling furiously down the road a minute later.

Mary stood, not knowing if she should stay or go. "I guess I'll go out to get a paper to look at today's jobs, if you don't have anything for me."

Agatha tossed the dishrag on the kitchen counter and turned back to Mary. "You might as well come with me. I'll show you how to do some filing. I only hope it hasn't been left in a disaster."

She can't even say André's name. How sad.

Later that afternoon, Mary showed Johan what she had been doing in the small office in the plant.

"I'm amazed she even trusted me to file these invoices. She obviously thinks I'm a real idiot." Mary shook her head. "I didn't argue with her, though. She scares me too much for that."

"You aren't an arguing sort of person. That's one reason we get along so well. Neither one of us likes to argue, do we?" Johan kissed her forehead.

"She fully expects you to give up the football you know."

Johan snorted. "After I worked so hard to get on the Ajax team? I don't think so!"

"It would be awful if you did."

"I just have to figure out how to do both. I've done it before, worked in the business and played football. I've been lucky this last while that I could concentrate on the football because André was here, but I guess that's changed now."

Mary rested her hand on Johan's forearm. "Will you be able to manage?"

"Sure. And speaking of that, I better get to it. I'm supposed to be doing some inventory." Johan sighed, rolled his shoulders and picked up a clipboard.

"Can I help?"

"No, go on. I'll be over soon."

But when Johan slipped into bed beside Mary, it was late, and he was exhausted. Mary turned to him and put her arm across his stomach as he lay on his back.

"I thought you'd be asleep." He put his arm around her so her head rested against his shoulder.

"It's strange here. I'm still getting used to being up here instead of your old room." It was great, but even after three nights, it still felt odd. She shifted closer to him. He could feel the heat of her body through the thin cotton night dress.

"Do you like it, though? There's more space here. It's almost like having our own place."

"Oh yes, I do like it. The best thing about it is how far away from your mother it is here. We can make some noise knowing that she isn't just across the hall listening." Mary's fingers were trailing up and down Johan's chest.

Johan tsked. "I'm sure Mama wasn't laying there listening to us."

"Maybe not." Mary spoke without conviction. She propped herself up on one elbow and kissed him.

Johan took a deep breath and exhaled slowly. "I'm pretty tired."

"Too tired?" Mary's fingers moved down to loosen the cord of his pajamas. Her hand slipped inside the fabric and found him, already hard and waiting. "I don't think so."

Mary took the lead, kissing his throat and then moving downwards. Her tongue tasted the salty flavour of his sweat as she licked his nipple. Johan groaned, his exhaustion forgotten. He raised himself and pushed Mary back down. They kicked away the sheet and he pulled off her nightdress, their clothes landing in a heap on top of the sheet on the floor. For the first time in their marriage, Mary felt free to express herself in their lovemaking. Crying out as Johan entered her, she startled them both. He hesitated for a second.

Her hips moved to match his thrust. "Don't stop!"

Mary's abandon fuelled Johan's desire and they exploded together in a fury of passion.

"Oh my God. That's never happened before." Mary was suddenly a little bit shy again. She slipped her nightdress on again and threw the sheet back across the bed before sliding back in and snuggling close to Johan.

"I think we're going to like having our own place up here." Johan was groggy and on the edge of sleep, the sheet pulled up over his naked body.

Mary enjoyed the warm, musky scent of him. *Everything is going to be just fine.*

———

"Johan!" Mary nudged him. "What time is it?"

Johan blinked in the morning sun and looked at the clock. "Damn! It's late." He threw the tangled sheet off him, then flopped back down on the bed.

Mary pushed him. "What are you doing? Shouldn't you be going?"

"I'm already late. One day won't matter. We haven't started the serious training yet, we're just doing warm-up stuff and keeping limber. No, one day won't matter."

"Still, we should get up. I can imagine what your mother will have to say." Mary sighed.

Coming down to the kitchen, they found Agatha sitting, reading the early newspaper. Her breakfast plate showed she had already eaten.

"Finally." Agatha lowered the paper briefly before flicking it and raising it in front of her face again.

Johan and Mary glanced at each other and smiled quick smiles before getting their own breakfast.

Johan carried his breakfast to the dining room table. "I've decided that I'm going to spend the day getting up to speed on the books, Mama."

Agatha lowered the paper again. "Oh?"

"Yes. You were saying that you wanted me to review them so I think today would be a good day for that." He tried to maintain an innocent look.

"Hm. Well. That's good. I'm glad to see that you're starting to see that the business needs your attention." She folded the newspaper and got up to make a fresh pot of coffee.

Mary's voice held a smile as she glanced to the folded newspaper. "Did you see any likely looking jobs in the paper for me, Mama Meijer?"

Agatha raised one eyebrow. "For you? I hardly know what you'd be qualified for, so didn't look."

"Mama, you know very well what Mary is qualified for. We've talked about it before." Johan tried to take the sting out of his mother's words as he saw Mary flush.

"I'm not an employment agency. She can look for herself."

The smile slipped from Mary's face. "It's fine. Don't worry about it."

After breakfast, Johan and Agatha went out to the office in the plant.

"Why are you always so sharp with Mary, Mama?" A frown furrowed Johan's brow.

"I'm not sharp. I just say what I mean. She can take me or leave me. I am who I am and won't change now."

"Tiineke could stand up to you, but Mary is very sensitive. I want her to be happy. Can't you be a little kinder to her?" Johan's voice was pleading.

Agatha's glare pierced Johan. "I told you not to mention those people again."

"I'm sorry. It's hard to avoid mentioning them. But really, Mama, will you try to be a little softer with Mary?"

"I am who I am." She opened the file cabinet with a jerk.

II

Fall 1934

"No!" Johan flung away the newspaper. "I told you already, Mama. You can't commit me to anything in the mornings because I have training."

They were sitting after supper in the living room with the radio on. Mary was finishing the supper dishes.

Agatha folded her arms across her chest. "This is an important meeting with Lt. Cuypers. You need to be there."

"Why can't you understand this? We are in the season now and that means every morning I have training. It's like a job." Johan tried to be patient.

"*Like* a job." Agatha pounced on those words. "But *not* your job. Your job is in the family business."

"Mama, this is very important to me. I've already been spoken to by Coach because he's caught me yawning too many times. He thinks I'm bored or not paying attention."

"I can't do this by myself." Agatha's voice took on a wheedling tone. "I helped to keep the business going while I was raising children. After your father died, I don't know how I kept going, but I did, and I did it for you boys. Now it's all for you." Agatha put her hand on his arm.

"Mama, I know you worked long hours to keep it all together, and I'm grateful, don't think I'm not, but the football is important to me too." Johan took her hand and held it gently. "Please Mama, can't we make this work?"

She pulled away from him. "You say you're grateful but I don't see it. All I know is that, after all my years of sacrifice, I seem to be the only one still making the effort. You just fit me and the business in when you have some time."

"That isn't true. I do care about the business and I certainly care about you. You know that." Johan sighed.

"I don't know it. What I see is that you're too busy to come to important meetings."

"Fine, Mama. I'll just cycle out now to see Coach and explain to him that I'll be in late tomorrow morning. When Lt. Cuypers is here tomorrow, though, I'm going to let him know that future meetings will have to be later in the day."

In the quiet of their room that night, Johan told Mary about his meeting with the coach. "He was pretty angry."

Mary brushed the hair from Johan's forehead. "I'm not surprised, Johan. This is the season, this is what you've been working towards all these years. They expect you to be there."

"Everyone has commitments, though. It's an amateur team after all." Johan was now on the defensive.

"I know. What did he say exactly?"

"He told me that although I'm a great striker, he needs a centre forward that he can count on. He told me that unless I can start show-ing more commitment, he's going to keep me on the bench as part of the replacements. Right now he has me playing on the 'A' team." Johan's voice was full of pride. "The fact is that most of the fellows have jobs, but most of them aren't real. They work for companies that support the team so they just have to go in once in a while and show their face to get a paycheque, but really everyone knows that their primary job is to be on the team. Coach offered to find me a job like that." Johan flung himself down on the bed.

Mary sat down beside him. "So what will you do?"

"Well, obviously I can't take a job like that. I need to work here *and* be on the team. I already told Mama that tomorrow is a one-time only thing. She needs to schedule around my training and matches."

Mary tilted her head and raised her eyebrows. "You think that she will?"

"Oh yes, I'm sure of it. I've explained how important this is to me." He nodded and patted Mary's hand.

She smiled. *I hope so.*

———

The meeting next day between Lt. Cuypers, Johan, and Agatha was awkward at first.

"Mrs. Meijer, I have to tell you that we are very happy to have André working with us now." Lt. Cuypers smiled.

Agatha's face was blank. "Who?"

"André—your son—we're very happy to have him." Lt. Cuypers spoke a little bit louder, as if thinking Agatha was deaf.

Agatha sniffed and slid the order documents in front of him. "Are you ready to review the order now? My son, Johan, is prepared to show you the progress we are making."

Lt. Cuypers raised his eyebrows at Johan, who shrugged.

Agatha went back to the house at last while Johan finished meeting with the naval officer.

"You may have realized that my mother is very unhappy about my brother's decision. It has really thrown all of us into a difficult position."

The lieutenant sat back in his chair. "Well, I'm sorry about that. André had said something about it, but I didn't realize it was so serious."

"We'll get through it, and you don't need to worry about the order. You can see that the work is going ahead without problem." Johan waved out towards the shop floor.

"Time heals all. I'm sure your mother will get over this soon."

"Perhaps. Let's hope so." Johan shrugged again. "Listen, as you may know, I am very active in football and generally train in the mornings, so future meetings need to be in the afternoon. Will that be alright?"

"That's fine with me. I'm pretty flexible. It was your mother who asked for the meeting to be at this time. She was pretty insistent."

Johan clenched his fist, digging his nails into the palm of his hand, then forced it open again. He shook the officer's hand. "Feel free to contact me directly to arrange future meetings."

Lt. Cuypers hesitated before leaving. "Shall I give André your greeting?"

"Yes, by all means." Johan hoped his voice was more neutral sounding than he felt.

André should be here dealing with this, not me. He was selfish to leave. Johan could feel his face flushing as his anger grew.

"Good-bye then." Johan ushered out the officer before it became obvious how upset he was.

Week after week, Johan continued to juggle his football and the business. He collapsed into bed each night, exhausted, and struggled to get up early in time for training. He was too tired most nights for the attention Mary craved.

"Mary, I'm sorry. I'm just too tired. All I want to do is sleep." Johan turned his back to his wife, away from the hand she had been gently tracing across his chest.

Mary sighed. "I don't know how you can keep this up. I wish I could find a job. Maybe I could support us and we could move as well. Then you could just focus on the football."

"Don't be ridiculous. We wouldn't be able to live on any wages you could make, and besides, I told you before, I can't leave Mama alone with the business." Johan was too tired to soften the words, and fell asleep before Mary could respond.

———

It seemed like only moments had passed when Johan heard her through the fog of sleep. "Johan, the alarm is going. Time to get up." Mary nudged him.

He rubbed his eyes and sighed. "I just closed my eyes."

Mary got up with him. It was still dark outside in the cool fall morning.

She handed him his clean shirt. "Johan, why can't I help here more, since I can't find a job anywhere else? There must be something I can do, more than just standing behind the shop counter for a few hours. Can't I do something in the plant so you don't have so much to do when you come home later?"

Johan studied her for a moment. He knew she was right. She was perfectly able and it would be good if he could have an evening to just relax once in a while.

"Speak to Mama. She should start training you for some of the work." He cupped his hand under her chin. "I know you want to help. I appreciate it."

"The problem is that I have spoken with her. She just refuses my offers to help."

Johan raked his fingers through his hair and nodded before leaving the room. "Alright, I'll talk to her."

That evening, Agatha and Johan were examining some of the day's work. This was a job Johan did in the evenings, looking over the work to make sure that the quality was up to standard, and then bundling the accepted work into packages ready for the shipping man to load into boxes. Johan studied his mother as she ran her fingers over a seam on a sheet. Her hair was completely gray. Surely there was still some black in it before André left. She was getting old.

He was surprised at the idea. His mother had always seemed invincible.

She peered through her small round glasses, angling the fabric closer to the light. Her face was sculpted in hard, boney angles, and her nose seemed more hawk-like. She suddenly turned her head towards him and caught him studying her.

She straightened her shoulders. "What is it?"

"Why don't you let Mary help out more? This is a job that she could do during the day and then, if there were quality issues, they could be addressed right away with the machinist, instead of the next day."

"It's our name on this firm. This is a job for you and me, not some inexperienced girl who won't have the same care and concern that we have."

Johan laughed lightly. "Mama, Mary's name is Meijer now too, you know."

"It's not the same. This is your responsibility now." Agatha stepped closer to Johan and put her hand on his forearm.

Johan felt her thin fingers were frail, yet the grip was strong. It was as though she were clinging to him, as though it were he and she against the world.

Still, Johan pressed on. "Mama, she's not doing much else, she wants to help, and most of all, I could really use her help."

Agatha studied Johan for a moment. Her face was tight with worry, but it wasn't clear to Johan if she was worried about his health or about losing him, too. Her lips pursed and she nodded once.

She still clutched his arm. "Yes, alright, let me see what we can find for her to do to help out. You're right, of course. We should use her if we can."

Johan beamed at his mother. "Thank you, Mama. I appreciate it."

Mary was still sitting in the living room reading a book when Johan and Agatha went back in.

"Mary, Mama has agreed to start training you in the plant to help out." Johan put his arm around his mother to give her a little hug.

Agatha stood stiffly in the embrace. "Yes, we'll see if there is anything there that you can manage."

Ignoring the cold words, Mary smiled at Johan. She stood up and Johan moved away from his mother to reach for Mary's hand. Johan glanced back as he and Mary walked hand-in-hand towards the door to go up to their rooms above the warehouse and shivered at his mother's frown.

III

Spring 1935

Wham! Johan's football boots hit the wall as he flung them deep into the closet. He slammed the door and went into the living room. He threw himself down on the sofa and Agatha looked at him with a frown over the top of her morning newspaper.

"Why are you home so early? I thought your training always goes to noon."

Johan crossed his arms tightly. "You don't have to worry about my training anymore."

Agatha folded the paper and put it on the side table. "What does that mean?"

"It means I've been dropped from the team. You have your wish now." Johan stood and walked restlessly to stare out the window, his back to his mother.

"Why were you dropped? I thought you were such a star." Agatha wasn't sure what she felt. She was ecstatic that he would be able to focus on the business now, but at the same time offended that her son should be insulted in this way.

"Coach tells me that I just wasn't delivering the energy and drive that he is looking for. He needs to make places for others that can do better." Johan was still staring out the window.

"Well, perhaps it's for the best." Agatha picked up her paper again.

Johan turned to study her for a moment. "You just don't understand what this means to me, do you? You never have. Or worse, maybe you do."

Before she could reply, he left the room.

Johan stepped outside, planning to cross over to the factory where he knew Mary was working.

She's a trooper to put up with the stupid little jobs Mama gives her. This will kill her.

He knew the only bright spot in her weeks were the days when she could go and watch him play. She was so proud of him and glowed standing next to him in a crowd of people, happy to be close as people asked him questions or wanted to shake his hand after a good game. One of the happiest days of her life, she had once told him, was when Ajax won the National Championship. Johan had assisted on the winning goal. That night, after they made love, fuelled by adrenaline and excitement for the future they had talked again about moving to England.

His heart ached.

"I heard that there were scouts from England at the game."

Johan felt the fingers twined through his tighten their grip.

Mary eyes widened. "What would you do if you were asked to go there?"

"Mr. Van Loon could take over. He's very capable."

Mary small white teeth chewed her bottom lip. "Wouldn't your mother be furious, as she is with André?"

"It would be different. Someday we'd come back. My days as a footballer won't last forever and when we came back we'd have some money saved up to get our own place. We'd need more room because by then we'd have children to consider as well."

Mary squeezed his hand. "God willing. We haven't had any luck so far."

"Children will come. Don't you worry."

"Well, here's hoping the scouts were there, then."

"They probably would wait until the end of the season before making any kind of approach, but I've put the word out here and there that I'd be willing to move to England."

Johan was brought back to the present when a neighbour cycled by, calling out a greeting and tipping his cap.

Johan responded automatically. "Yes, good morning."

He abruptly turned at the factory door and marched down the street towards Vondel Park, where he and Mary often enjoyed a Sunday stroll. He would break her heart when he gave her the news. No scout from England would pick up a man who had been cut from the team. It was all over. Their dreams for the future. The thing she'd loved the most about him was finished.

Because of *her*. Because of Mama and her obsession with the damned family business. Johan picked up a fallen branch and whipped it aimlessly at the bushes he passed.

I knew I wasn't giving my all. Coach warned me. Why didn't I listen? I thought I could do it, even though I was always tired.

Johan could feel the bile rising in his throat as he thought about his mother and the business. He hated the thought of going in every day to work in the factory or shop without the happy release of his morning training with the team. He was born for the rush of playing in front of crowds, the cheering after a good move or a goal.

I could happily put a match to the business and watch it go up in flames.

He slumped down on a bench beside a pond and the ducks swam towards him, looking for crusts of bread.

"Sorry fellas, nothing for you today." Johan fluttered his hand at the ducks. "Nothing for any of us today."

As he watched the ducks swim and splash, the anger leaked out of him, leaving him exhausted and depressed. Finally, he threw his branch away and stood to trudge back home.

He stood back from the office for a few moments, watching Mary stamp the morning mail. She pounded the rubber date stamp into the ink pad, then carefully lined it up to stamp the date neatly on the top right corner of each document. Johan's eyes pricked with tears and a lump formed in his throat. She was an educated girl and should be working at a better job than this.

As if feeling his gaze, Mary looked up. First she smiled, then the smile melted away. Setting down the rubber stamp, she stood, and they met at the door of the office.

"What is it? What's happened?"

"I've been dropped from the team." Johan choked on the words. He had intended to be strong, but suddenly he was like a boy, needing the comfort of a hug. He held open his arms and Mary stepped in to his embrace. They stood for a moment, clinging together despite the glances of the factory workers.

"Everything alright?" Mr. Van Loon came up to them. His voice held a note of disapproval.

Johan mumbled. "It'll be fine."

Mr. Van Loon shook his head and made a tsking sound. "Maybe you should take a break, Mary."

Wordlessly, Mary and Johan walked out, clutching hands.

Despite just having returned from a walk, Johan led Mary away from the house. At a bench on a corner of the street, they sat down. The chirping birds and warm May sun were at odds with their mood. They both felt that their lives were forever changed.

Mary rested her hand on his knee. "Is there a chance to go back?"

"No, none."

"But if you gave up working for Meijer's..."

"I can't see it. Coach was quite definite, and besides, how could I give up working? We need to live somehow."

"But he once offered to get you a job like the other fellows have, where you only have to work a little, and still get a paycheque."

"It's too late. How could I do that anyway? That really would be like André. Where would Mama be then?"

"But what about *our* dreams?"

"We'll have to revise them, I guess. I don't know, Mary. I really don't know." Johan's voice was thick with tears.

"I'm sorry. We'll figure it out. It'll be alright." Mary patted his knee and shook her head, as if lost for words. She shifted on the hard bench. "I guess we better go back. Mr. Van Loon will be wondering what's happened to me."

"Yes, and I suppose I might as well go back to get in and help with the shipping. No point in waiting until later, like I usually do." Although all Johan really wanted to do was go to bed. Maybe when he woke up he'd find it was just a bad dream.

At noon, they went in together for their dinner. They usually had their warm meal at midday because Johan would be hungry after training. The smell of frying chops met them as they went in the house.

Agatha waved a wooden spoon at Johan. "Come now, I've made one of your favourite meals."

Johan scowled. "It looks like a Sunday dinner."

Agatha nodded. "I know you've had a disappointment and thought you'd like a nice dinner."

Johan shook his head. "It looks to me like you've done a celebration dinner."

"Johan." Mary touched his back. "Your mother's trying."

Johan twitched away and glanced down at Mary. "You give her a lot of credit."

Agatha set the platter of chops on the table with a loud clunk. "Eat it or not as you wish."

Agatha returned to the kitchen to pick up the bowl with potatoes. She paused and allowed herself a small smile before donning her neutral mask again and returning to Johan and Mary.

They fell into a routine. Johan slowly took over managing the plant while Agatha looked after the shop. Mary helped Johan and did a few hours with Agatha each day. After helping Agatha, there would be complaints to Johan.

"Your mother treats me like a fool."

"I think Mary shouldn't be asked to do too much. She can't cope well when there is pressure."

Johan did his best to referee between them.

"Just ignore her."

"Mama, I think Mary is quite able to deal with pressure."

Agatha pursed her lips. "No, when Mrs. Rypkema demanded a refund for the sheets because she imagined she saw a flaw, Mary just fell apart. I can't trust her to know how to handle customers."

Johan sighed and shook his head. "Mama, Mary told me about that and she said that as she was discussing the matter and looking at the flaw, you came along and told her to step back because you would handle it. She had been getting along fine."

Agatha waggled her finger. "I told her to step back because I could see she wasn't managing."

What Johan didn't say was how upset Mary had been about the incident.

"I can't ignore her. She embarrasses me in front of customers and scares me. I'm always watching what I say and do now because at any moment she might yell at me for something." Mary was in tears, her white skin blotched with red.

"Try not to let her get to you." It was all Johan could say.

"I wish I could find something outside the business. I'll keep looking." Mary sighed.

"Yes, something may come up."

Johan tried to be encouraging, but he noticed that she didn't seem to have the same energy for looking for a job. She did the mundane tasks assigned to her, and while Johan tried to give her more interesting challenges in the plant once in a while, she didn't take them up with enthusiasm. Mary rarely looked at the newspaper anymore. In the evenings, when the work was done, she would pick up the latest novel that she borrowed from the library, and bury herself in it.

They were in a routine, but it was a routine of drudgery and complaint.

IV

Spring 1937

'*D*ear Mary...'

She stopped reading for a moment to savour her mother's handwriting. The fine writing was slanted at an exact angle, the letters uniform with decorative swirls that added beauty without looking too artificial or ostentatious. Mary liked to take her time to read her letters from home. They sometimes felt like the only bright spot in her bleak life.

'*How are things with you? I was sorry to hear that you had another false hope with the pregnancy. I continue to pray for you.*'

Tears pricked Mary's eyes and she looked up at the muddy green wall of the bedroom. If she stared at it hard enough, she knew she could force back the tears that were so often close to the surface. The latest pregnancy disappointment was just another failure, something else she couldn't do. She had come to realize that there really wasn't anything at all she could do well. She mastered her tears and bent her head back to the letter.

'*Take heart, sweetheart. Things are starting to turn around finally now that the gold standard has finally been dropped. We see signs of it everywhere. Your brothers went last week to a concert from the local band called the Rhythm Giggers. Did you ever hear of them? It was to celebrate the replacement of the tram by a bus. Oh, it was a big event. It's so much faster now to get to Ede. Perhaps you and Johan can come this summer for a visit and see for yourself.'*

Mary almost laughed at that. Sure. Just like all the other holidays they had talked about and never taken.

'And now I come to the real reason for today's letter: Nicholaas has a friend who recently moved to Amsterdam. He works for Hagemeyer, the big trading house. Apparently, they have just done something with the stock exchange. I don't really understand it all, even though your brother did his best to explain it to me. What it means is that business is booming for them and Nicky's friend (Mr. Van den Schuur) needs a new secretary! They have a typing pool there, but he wants someone of his own to be a private secretary. I know it isn't really what you started out as in your career, but I remember you studied shorthand and typing. He is willing to meet with you so here is his name and office address. He is expecting to hear from you next week. Isn't that exciting? I know that you will be nervous after being away from a job for so long but you must do this. I know how unhappy you are working at Meijer's. Just go and talk to the man—for me.'

Mary studied the slip of enclosed paper with the name and address.

Her thoughts raced. *I can't, I'm useless. He'll see that in a minute.*

'Papa and the boys send their love. Hugs and kisses, Mam'

Mary hugged the thin paper close to her heart.

I suppose I'll have to go and talk to him just so Mama isn't disappointed in me.

Her mother still believed in her, she realized with some surprise. She carefully refolded the letter and returned it, along with the slip of paper, to its envelope. She slipped it into the pocket of a jacket hanging with the rest of her clothes. Someone would have to search very hard to find it there.

At supper that evening, however, Johan brought it up. "Mama tells me you had a letter today from your mother. Any interesting news?"

"Not really." Mary wasn't surprised that Agatha would have told Johan about her letter. Agatha told him about every little move she made. "My brothers went to some concert last week to celebrate the start of a bus route out of Wageningen."

"They have nothing better to do with their time, I suppose." Agatha gave a sniff of disapproval.

Mary didn't answer. She had long ago given up trying to defend herself or her family from Agatha's sharp comments.

"Johan, with that new order for fabric, I think we should look at the higher quality cotton." Agatha turned her attention to Johan and they carried on with a discussion about the business, dismissing Mary.

I'm not going to say anything about this job. It won't come to anything anyway.

Mary retreated into her own little world as she ate.

———

The following week, Mary made an announcement at breakfast. "I have to go to the doctor today."

Johan looked at her with surprise. "Really? You didn't say anything. Are you alright?"

She shrugged. "Yes, I'm fine. It's just a follow-up on some things."

Johan didn't pursue it, probably imagining they were woman things he didn't want to know about.

After Mary left the table, Agatha turned to her son. "She's forever at the doctor. She really can't be relied on to work steadily. Perhaps she should just rest more."

"I'm sure she's fine, Mama."

Agatha collected the breakfast dishes. "You go on to the office. Since Mary won't be around this morning, I'll come over for the mail and filing."

I hate having that girl poking around the business anyway. Johan and I don't need her.

———

Mary watched from the bedroom window and saw Agatha fol-low Johan to the plant. She carefully pinned on her best hat and smoothed her suit. She knew the dark green linen looked good with her fair features, but the suit was big on her now and hung off her thin hips.

Oh well, what does it matter? She twisted to look at herself in the small mirror above the set of drawers in their room. *I'm only going so I can tell Mam I did.*

Mary slipped out and mounted her bicycle quickly before anyone might see her. She didn't want any questions about why she was dressed up to go to the doctor. Her heart thumped and stomach rolled as she made her way towards the street of Oude Schans where the office of Hagemeyer was. The five-storey Montelbaanstoren clock tower was her landmark and she cycled steadily towards it. After all these years, she still didn't know her way around very well, and the noise and bustle of the busy Amsterdam streets frightened her. Luckily, she had given herself plenty of time to get to the eleven o'clock appointment. At ten-fifteen she locked her bike in a stand near the building and walked along the canal. Men called to each other as they unloaded barges on to horse drawn carts. There was a mist hanging over the water that intensified the smells of animals, men, and canal water. The murky layer clung to Mary's clothing and hair and left her feeling even sicker.

Her legs were rubbery as she climbed the steps to the second floor office. What was she doing here? This was crazy.

She asked the young man at the front desk for Mr. Van den Schuur and sat on the wooden chair she was directed to. She suddenly had to pee and wasn't sure she could hold it.

At that moment, a tall man with white-blond hair entered the front office, and in a few long strides, came over to her. She stood as he held out his hand to shake hers. He had a wide, friendly smile and his breath smelled faintly of peppermint as he spoke.

"Come in, Mrs. Meijer. Did you have trouble finding us?" He led the way through the frosted glass double doors to a room where five women were busy typing.

A couple of the women glanced up, then continued on with their work. Mary trailed after Mr. Van den Schuur, feeling awkward in the room of such efficient, professional women.

He led her to a small office and gestured for her to sit down at one of the two leather chairs at his desk. As she settled herself, gripping her purse tightly on her lap, he stacked a few of the papers that cluttered his desk.

He smiled and waved his hand at all the papers. "I'm sorry, it's a bit of a mess here. I just can't seem to get my head above water long enough to get organized."

She smiled tentatively, not certain if she should acknowledge that he looked quite disorganized, or if that would seem rude.

He leaned back in his chair. "So, you're Nicky's sister. We were great friends at school."

"I've been away from home for three years now, so I don't know any of his university friends." Mary's face flushed. "I may have heard the name Van den Schuur in passing." She didn't want him to think that he hadn't been such a friend of her brother's after all.

He laughed. "Well, if anything, he might have mentioned 'Marty', but I'm not sure he would have talked much about some of our adventures anyway. So I understand that you are working at your husband's business at the moment."

Mary nodded. "Yes, I do, although he and his mother do most of the work. Well, of course they also have machine operators."

"So you have time on your hands?"

"I do. I'm not sure what you've been told, but I haven't worked as a secretary before. At my first job, I managed an institutional laundry." Mary almost blurted the words out, determined to get the true facts out so she could end this and go home again before they started to wonder where she was.

"But I think I was told that you did train for shorthand and typing, correct?"

"Well, yes, but I never really used it."

Mr. Van den Schuur leaned forward and lowered his voice. Mary leaned forward as well, creating an air of conspiracy.

"I'll tell you a secret: we're in the same boat then, because I studied agriculture at university in Wageningen, and now here I am in a trading house for technical things. I studied business as a secondary degree and I just got very lucky that I met up with the right person who thought I would manage here nicely. So if I can do it, why not you?" He leaned back again.

Mary gazed at him without speaking.

"So what I'm looking for is someone to come in just three days a week to help me with my correspondence and report writing. Perhaps do some filing as well." He pushed some of the papers into another pile, helplessly. "What do you think? I can't pay a lot, but we can start out and then review after three months to see how we suit each other."

"Are you serious?" Mary heard the tremble in her voice and felt dizzy. She took a deep breath to clear her head.

He laughed. "Yes, of course I'm serious."

She stammered. "Yes! Yes, I would love to work for you."

He stood up. "Well, that's great. I'll get them to move a small desk just outside my door here. Everything will be set up for you to begin on Monday. Would that suit you?"

Mary stood as well, her hand cramping in the tight grip she still had on her purse. "Yes, that would be fine."

After bidding farewell to Mr. Van den Schuur, Mary cycled home slowly. How was it possible? What would Johan say? Would he be happy? She wished she had told him she was going for this interview. Her forehead wrinkled in an anxious frown all of the way home, and she had a crashing headache by the time she got there.

Agatha glanced up when Mary walked in. "Well, what did the doctor have to say?"

Mary ignored the question. "Has Johan come in for his lunch yet?"

"Yes, of course. He can't wait for you and your odd schedules. He's a working man." Agatha sniffed.

"Perhaps I'll go over and talk to him in the office, then." Mary spoke more to herself than Agatha.

Agatha raised her eyebrows. "You're going to the plant dressed like that? It's a very fancy outfit for going to the doctor."

Mary flushed, remembering she was in her good suit. "Perhaps you're right. I'll go and change first."

She escaped to her room, hearing Agatha clicking her tongue as she fled.

In their bedroom, she stared in the mirror as she unpinned her hat. When she'd left this morning, she'd had no sense she would actually get a job. Now that she had it, she wasn't sure how she felt. It had been years since she'd had a real job, and especially this job. Working as a secretary...it was very different from her previous work.

She sat on the bed, tears filling her eyes.

I can't do this. Why in the world did I even go there this morning?

Brushing the tears away, she stood again, and mechanically changed into her everyday clothes. A pleated skirt, sweater, and matching cardigan, putting away her dressy black shoes and pulling on socks and her comfortable loafers. Coming down the stairs, she turned towards the plant instead of the house.

Johan saw her coming and stood to meet her at the door of the office. Pulling her inside, he closed the door.

"Are you alright? I was worried when you weren't back by lunchtime."

She looked up at his pale face and thought about how it used always to be tanned from being outside all the time.

"I'm fine." She licked her dry lips and hesitated. She felt light-headed and could imagine how pale she must be.

"Are you..." Johan left the question unfinished.

For a moment, she didn't understand, then she felt herself flush. "No, I'm not pregnant. I'm sorry if you had your hopes up."

"It's fine, it's fine." He patted her hand, then dropped it and returned to his chair behind the desk. "So everything is alright?"

"I didn't actually go to the doctor."

"Oh?" Now Johan's forehead wrinkled. "So where did you go?"

"I had a job interview."

"A job interview? Well, that's wonderful. Why in the world didn't you tell us? How did it go?"

"I didn't really think it would amount to anything so I didn't want to get you, or your mother, excited."

"Well? It must have gone alright for you to be telling me now." Johan waved at Mary to go on.

She smiled. "I got the job."

Johan leaped from his chair and came back Mary and hugged her. "But that's marvellous. What sort of a job is it?" He released her and led her gently to the chair across from his at the desk.

"It's a secretarial job, three days a week." Mary was still hesitant to speak of it.

"Secretarial? Well, that's interesting. How did you hear about it?" Johan was shaking his head as if bemused.

"Mama set me up. It's for a friend of Nicky's."

"Ah. Yes, well, that's great."

Mary frowned. "It's not some sort of charitable thing. He really needs someone to help him."

Johan reached across the desk and squeezed her hand. "Yes, of course, I believe it."

Mary stood up. "Well, I just wanted to tell you. You're alright with it, aren't you? I'll still be able to help you here in the office as well."

"I'm fine with it. It's what we've been hoping for, isn't it? Don't worry about your work here. Mama can help out more again. I think she'd like that anyway, so yes, it's a great thing all around, isn't it?"

Mary wandered slowly out of the plant and back to the house. The breeze blew wisps of her fine hair around her face where it had come loose from the pins. She brushed them away in a daze, trying to adjust to the idea of the new life ahead of her.

———

"You've what?" Agatha looked up from her darning, the needle poised in the air and the sock, over its mushroom-shaped block, frozen in her other hand, waiting to be stabbed.

Mary pushed her hair behind her ear. "I've gotten a job."

Agatha's hands fell to her lap still gripping her darning. "What sort of a job could you possibly have gotten?"

"It's for three days a week as a private secretary."

"Private secretary? Ha." Agatha barked a short laugh. "What in the world qualifies you for that? I have to look over all the filing you do to make sure it's done right."

Mary shrank a little deeper into her chair. She looked down at the cheese sandwich in the plate on her lap.

"So what company is hiring you as a *private secretary*?" Agatha's tone was scornful.

Mary picked up the sandwich without bringing it to her mouth. "Hagemeyer."

"Why all the secrecy? I knew when I saw you in your good suit that you hadn't just gone to the doctor."

Mary lifted one shoulder. "I don't know."

"Hmph. And when do you start this new job?"

"Monday. I'm sorry for the short notice. I'll make sure the filing is caught up before that."

"Don't bother. Johan and I will manage just fine." Agatha smirked.

Johan came in a few minutes late for supper, carrying a large bunch of red and yellow tulips which he presented with a flourish to Mary.

"To celebrate your new job. Congratulations sweetheart."

Mary smiled and straightened her shoulders. "Thank you. I'll have to write to Mama after supper to give her the good news." Mary gathered the flowers in her arms and turned to find a vase in the kitchen.

Agatha's words followed her. "Your mother! Ah, that's how you got the job. I wondered."

Johan chided his mother gently. "Mama, please. Mary is very capable, and if she found the job through a connection of her brother's, what of it? That's how the world works."

Agatha made a moue of disapproval with her mouth. "So you say."

———

Monday morning was bright. The spring sunlight filtered into the bedroom early and put soft stripes across Johan's face as he lay on his back, sleeping. His snores were comforting to Mary. She sat propped up, looking down on him. His blond hair seemed a little thinner than when she first met him, but still full and soft. His brow had a crease in it she hadn't noticed before, and she traced it gently with her finger, barely touching his skin. But it was still enough to wake him, and his blue eyes opened. They were dark and clear, and he smiled at her.

"Good morning. You're awake early." His teeth were white, his smile boyish.

Mary leaned down to kiss his forehead. "When you're sleeping, you look like the boy I fell in love with."

He tapped the tip of her nose with his finger. "Only when I'm sleeping?"

"Yes. The rest of the time you look worried and distracted with things." She answered honestly.

He sat up in bed and took her hand. "It isn't the life we had planned, is it?"

"No. Perhaps life never is."

He studied her a moment. "What will you wear today?"

"I'll wear my navy blue suit and save the green one for later in the week. I can't go in wearing the same thing again." She slipped out of bed to start dressing. "I'll see today what people wear. Hopefully I don't need a suit every day."

"I'm sure that won't be expected. But if so, well, you'll be making your own money. You can buy some new clothes, if necessary." Johan stood behind her and kissed the back of her neck.

She turned to face him. "I don't suppose I can keep my money. I'll have to give it to your mother."

"Well, she might be looking for some contribution to the household, I suppose." Johan nodded. "But we'll make sure you keep a good portion of it."

"That would be nice. We'll see." Mary wasn't as confident.

At seven-thirty, Mary was on her bicycle. She tried to comfort herself as she navigated through the early morning traffic.

These streets will be familiar after a few trips.

A horse and cart swung out in front of her, and she swerved to avoid it. She gripped the handlebars and felt perspiration soaking her white cotton blouse under her arms. *I won't be able to take my jacket off now.*

The smell of fresh coffee emanated from the cafes as she passed. Businessmen with their newspapers in front of them were sipping their early morning coffee before going into work. A woman in a white apron was sweeping the curb in front of a shop and called out a cheerful "good morning" to Mary as she cycled past. The city was starting to look prosperous again. Coats of fresh paint were being applied to window frames that hadn't seen paint in a few years. The sound of hammers and saws mingled with the sounds of the traffic as new construction blossomed and old buildings were repaired.

Mary parked her bicycle gratefully in the space beside the Hagemeyer building, along with all the other bikes. She was hot and sweaty after her ride.

Maybe once I start making some money I'll take the tram instead.

Sitting in the front office, waiting for Mr. Van den Schuur to come for her, Mary was seized with another wave of nausea. What was she doing here? Mama Meijer was right, she couldn't do this.

She began to rise with the thought of leaving when Mr. Van den Schuur walked through the door.

"You're bright and early, Mrs. Meijer. I can see we will get along just fine." He beamed at her. "So, this morning you get the royal treatment of being escorted in, but when you come on Wednesday, you'll be one of us and just come right in. I'm going to leave you here in the capable hands of Mrs. Smit, who will show you where everything is and how it all works, alright?"

From that moment until the end of the day, Mary was instructed first by Mrs. Smit, who was only a few years older than herself, and then by Mr. Van den Schuur, finishing the day back with Mrs. Smit. At half past four, Mrs. Smit pulled open her desk drawer and removed her purse.

"Well, that's it for today. You look exhausted. It's a lot to take in at first, isn't it?" She squeezed Mary's hand once before standing up.

Mary rubbed her head. "I have a headache. I haven't learned so much in one day since I was in school."

"Well, you did just fine and really seem to catch on." Mrs. Smit nodded and smiled. "Don't worry, you'll be in the swing of things before you know it."

Mary put her head in through the open door of Mr. Van den Schuur's office to say good night to him before leaving.

He smiled at her. "So we haven't frightened you away? You'll be back on Wednesday?"

Despite the headache, she grinned. "Yes, absolutely. I'll see you on Wednesday."

Mary's head cleared as she cycled home with renewed energy.

Mama Meijer is wrong. I can *do the job.*

Memories of her old job began to filter back to her. She thought about the system she used to have to keep track of certain things that needed to be done each week. She could do that here, too. She could create a colour coding system to keep track of the weekly reports that Mr. Van den Schuur needed to submit. Her mind raced with ideas. The confidence that had been slowly drained from her over the past three years fluttered.

Her legs pumped and she navigated around a parked automobile effortlessly.

V

Fall 1939

"Look!" Mary's eyes were shining as she came in the house. She opened the small canvas bag and proudly displayed the paper sack inside filled with sugar.

"Fantastic! Mama, maybe you can bake one of your jam rolls now that Mary brought home all this sugar. What do you think?" Johan turned to his mother with a pleading look.

Agatha sniffed. "So how did you manage to get this much sugar?" Her tone of disapproval made it sound like Mary must have done something illegal.

Mary chose to ignore Agatha's typically critical tone. "Mr. Van den Schuur got in a few kilos and divided it among all the staff so we can have it in time for Sinterklaas. One of the benefits of working for a trading company, I suppose."

"Since sugar is being rationed, I'm surprised he would be so irresponsible." Agatha turned away.

Mary rolled her eyes at Johan and he gave a small, tight smile. Mary felt herself flush. She knew that Johan didn't like any criticism of his mother, even such a small, spontaneous gesture. She closed the bag again, the joy of her gift faded.

After supper, the three of them sat together, listening to the radio. Premier deGeer was being questioned about the reports of impending war. After the sinking of the *Simon Bolivar* by German mines, everyone was jittery.

Mary laid her hand on Johan's leg. "He keeps insisting the reports are false. Is it true, do you think? Can we remain neutral?"

Johan looked up from his newspaper, but before he could respond, Agatha cut in.

"The government knows what they are doing. We just keep at our work and mind our own business, the same as always."

"Mr. Van den Schuur doesn't think so. He said—"

Agatha waved her hand. "Mr. Van den Schuur! What does he know? You put far too much store by what he has to say. I don't understand your hero worship of that man."

"Mama's right, Mary. It's tiresome the way you refer to him all the time." Johan frowned and went back to his paper.

Mary jutted out her bottom teeth and chewed her top lip slightly. "I didn't mean anything by it." She picked up her knitting again.

Tears pricked her eyes and she felt the lump in her throat. She focused on thrusting the one needle through the pale blue stitch on her other needle.

During those early days of December the smell of baking filled the house. Agatha had actually whistled as she kneaded the dough, and although she never mentioned it to Mary, it was clear Agatha was pleased to have the extra sugar for baking.

The celebration of Sinterklaas was quiet but even Mary enjoyed it. Treating themselves to the fresh baked cookies and cake and opening the small gifts had been nice, but this time of day was the best, when she and Johan were alone in their rooms.

"I wish I could see my family." Mary held the journal her parents had sent her, stroking the tooled forest green leather of the cover.

Johan brushed a kiss across her forehead. "We'll make a plan to go for a few days this summer. I promise. Come to bed now."

Mary smiled, setting down the journal. "Yes, definitely. We'll go this summer." She was secretly putting aside a little bit of money from her earnings. She had gotten a raise a year ago but hadn't mentioned that at home. She wanted to save the money and then simply get the train tickets as a surprise for Johan. She had the money saved up already, but still she would keep it secret until the right time. She was sure that even Agatha's probing eyes hadn't discovered her old sock with the money, pushed into the toe of a rarely worn shoe. Even if Johan decided he couldn't spare the time, she would go by herself. It would have to be early in the summer, perhaps even May.

Mary slipped into bed and Johan moved across to his own side of the bed. He always warmed up the cold, clammy sheets for her by laying on her side for a few moments while she got ready. Now she tucked herself in to him, inhaling his scent. She trailed her hand down his chest as he lay on his back.

"You seem in such a good mood these days. I'm glad to see it." Johan took her small, thin hand in his. He rolled over on his side to look into her eyes. His look was languid and he started to guide her hand down his body.

Mary took a deep breath. "I went to the doctor yesterday, Johan."

"You did?" His brow furrowed. "Is everything alright? Did he give you a new tonic? Is that why you seem to be feeling better?"

"No, he didn't give me a tonic. He gave me the results of a test."

"A test? What sort of a test?"

"A pregnancy test."

Johan pushed himself up on one elbow now to study her face, waiting without asking anything.

She smiled. "Johan, I'm pregnant."

"Oh my God." He slid his arm under her neck and pulled her close to him.

She laughed as he squeezed her to his chest. "Careful you don't crush me! Or should I say, us."

"Mary, after all this time. I can't believe it. What wonderful, wonderful news." Mary felt the wetness of tears on her neck. "I thought... well, I thought it wasn't going to happen." His voice was choked.

"I know. I felt the same way too. But here we are. The baby is due in July. The doctor thinks we shouldn't tell people about it for another month."

They lay again, looking at each other.

Johan's blue eyes were watery, the tip of his nose red. "He's not sure?" He frowned.

She couldn't keep the smile from her face, despite the words of warning. "He's sure I'm pregnant, but until we pass the three-month mark, anything can happen."

Johan nodded, his face serious. "Ah, I see. Alright. Nothing will happen, though. I'll look after you. You need to quit work, of course."

Mary had known this would be his reaction. "I talked to the doctor about that and he feels quite confident that I should keep working for now. He thinks that daily cycling and routine will be good for me. Just sitting at home and worrying would be worse."

Johan was silent for a moment. "Let's leave that for now. At the moment, I just want to hold you and dream of the future."

Mary drifted off to sleep finally, feeling happier than she had in a long time.

———

Mary came downstairs the next morning. Johan had gone down earlier and she could hear his voice in the kitchen, speaking with his mother, as she came through the door. Mary felt good. The morning sickness that had plagued Tiineke hadn't affected her yet. She hugged their secret to herself as she went into the kitchen, a small, private smile on her lips.

Agatha nodded at Mary. "So you're finally pregnant."

Mary gasped, feeling as though a cup of cold water had been thrown at her face. She looked at Johan, who was beaming at her.

"I thought we weren't going to say anything yet."

"That doesn't include Mama." He looked surprised.

"I see. Of course not." She looked at Agatha. "Yes, Mama Meijer, I'm finally pregnant."

Agatha managed a sour smile. "Well, I know that Johan has wanted a child for quite some time, so congratulations. It will be good to have a son to bring into the family business."

Mary raised her eyebrows. "Would a daughter be allowed to be part of the business?"

"Yes, of course. If she is capable, then of course." Agatha set down her coffee cup and glanced at Mary. "You'll be putting in your notice then, I assume?"

Johan responded before Mary could say anything. "We're still discussing that."

"Oh?" Agatha raised her thick, black eyebrows.

"The doctor thinks it best if I continue with the exercise and routine." Mary turned her back to Agatha. "Are you making pap for breakfast?" Mary picked up the wooden spoon to stir the bubbling porridge. "It smells good, and I'm certainly hungry."

Mary knew she was just deferring the inevitable as she cycled to work that morning. Her early morning burst of energy had quickly dwindled and she actually felt very tired already. She knew she wouldn't be able to keep working for much longer. So far, the winter had been mild and she could still cycle, but she could smell snow in the air as she pedalled briskly to keep warm. Once it started snowing, she would have to take the tram and the idea of the extra time that would take didn't attract her. She'd make it until the end of the year, another three weeks. It was more the point of standing up for herself than anything else. She had her money saved up for her trip home in the summer, and that was all she really needed. The cold slithered up her sleeves and she thought longingly of the flowers and mild breezes of May and June. It would be wonderful to just go and spend a few weeks at home. Her parents would love it and to see her brothers again...would she even recognize them by now? Yes, she looked forward to spring.

VI

Spring 1940

They sat in stunned silence, chairs pulled close to the radio. Mary kept her hands crossed on the large swell of her belly, fingers laced tightly as if to protect the baby within. Since she had finished work four months previously, she had lost all energy as though all she had went to the growing child. Now, tears streamed down her face. She stopped asking 'how can this be happening?' No one had an answer. For once, even Agatha had nothing to say, she just sat, pale and tight-lipped, her black brows pulled into a deep 'v' of anger and fear, stark against her white skin. There was no talk of opening the business today; no employees had shown up for work. With every new wave of airplanes passing overhead, all three winced and looked up at the ceiling, not knowing if it would stay in place above their heads.

"Maybe they're bypassing us to go to England," Johan had said uncertainly when the first waves of aircraft woke them at dawn. By the six a.m. news, the family was clustered near the radio, and the truth became clear.

"The Germans are attacking our airfields. We are under attack without a declaration of war." The usual calm of the radio announcer was edged with stress. Bulletins were coming in moment by moment. They listened in horror at the report of damages at Ypenburg and the complete occupation almost immediately of the Ockenburg airfield.

Equally quick was the occupation of Valkenburg but there the stories were mitigated by the news that the airfield was under construction and some of the German planes had sunk into the soft ground. In Amsterdam they were too far away to hear the bombs dropping, but the continual swell and fading of passing aircraft kept them on edge throughout the day.

Eventually Agatha pulled herself away from the radio to prepare breakfast.

"You need to eat something." Johan brought Mary a plate of toast and boiled eggs to the table.

Mary sat down to the food. "It seems wrong, somehow, to just do ordinary things, like eat breakfast."

Agatha carried in the teapot and set it down. "It's the only way. You just keep going."

Johan hesitated and then blurted out. "I wonder what André is doing."

Agatha threw a black look at him. "Don't waste your time thinking of others. We need to discuss our own plans. The factory will be open tomorrow, so today you'll need to go around with messages to the employees to tell them so."

Mary glanced at Johan, then to Agatha. Her mother-in-law's lips were pressed together in a rigid line, white and bloodless, tiny lines creasing around her mouth in the effort.

She was worried about André too. Why couldn't she just admit it? What a stubborn woman.

I'll never be like that with my child.

Mary rubbed her belly.

Johan left to cycle around to the employees. When he came back, the three of them gathered again in the living room by the radio.

Mary clung to his arm as they sat side by side on the sofa. "What are people saying?"

"You look pale. Here, stretch out on the sofa. Shall I get you a cup of tea?" Johan was delaying his answer.

She pushed his hand away as he stroked her forehead. "I can't keep track of what's going on from the radio reports. What's going on, Johan? What's going to happen?" Her voice hitched as the tears began again.

"It's impossible to say, really. Of course, they're coming in from the east, so there will be lots of...action...there." He tried to soften the words.

"Fighting, you mean. Oh God." She moaned. "My brothers are both in the reserves. They joined a few months ago. Mama told them they were too young, but they insisted, and they were taken on."

"Yes. I remember you telling me. Probably it won't be too bad. The Germans are almost like distant cousins to us Dutch. They won't treat the Dutch badly." Johan voice was soothing.

"Don't speak nonsense." Agatha spoke now. "The Dutch are fighting for our country, and anyone in the way of the Germans might be killed. It's a war." Her voice was harsh and loud.

Mary sobbed.

Johan put his arm around her and spoke sharply to his mother. "Mama, there's no need to think the worst. Let's just wait and see."

Mary rested her head on his shoulder and wrapped her arms around him, clinging to him. Her arms were thin, but held him tightly.

Johan stood and pulled his wife gently to her feet. "Mary, why don't you go up and lie down. All this constant listening to the news isn't doing you any good. Go up and I'll bring you some soup later."

She drifted up to her room. *I'll sleep, and maybe when I wake, it'll all be over, and I'll find it was just a bad dream.* She made her way up the steps to their rooms, touching the walls on either side of her for support. It seemed that the world as she knew it was disappearing before her and she felt she might collapse.

Mary slept as much as she could. When she couldn't sleep, she lay in bed, cocooned in the feather duvet, thinking and remembering.

It was lunchtime the day after the Germans began their attack.

Johan tried to encourage her to come down to eat. "Mary, will you get up now?"

She turned her head away. "I'm tired."

"I know, but it's better for you and for the baby to get up and walk around a little. Come down for your lunch."

With a deep sigh, she allowed him to pull her from bed and help her dress.

Agatha looked Mary up and down when they came into the kitchen. "Well, you finally are up. Can you please prepare the supper? We have a factory to run."

"Supper?" Mary was groggy and hardly understood what was being asked of her.

Agatha was impatient. "Yes, supper! Peel the potatoes and start the chicken to roast at four o'clock."

When Johan and his mother returned to the factory after lunch, Mary took her tea and sat by the radio. The reports kept coming in, but still it was confusing, and Mary didn't know what it meant to her family. "Germans were in Maastricht. The Grebbe Line was holding so far but was under heavy shelling."

What is the Grebbe Line? She should have paid more attention to the reports in the newspaper over the past weeks, should have asked more questions. Mr. Van den Schuur used to talk to her and explain things so she understood, but since she'd left work she had become disconnected with the world, and Johan and Agatha became impatient with her questions, so she had stopped asking them.

With a jolt, Mary realized the time and forced herself away from the radio to the kitchen.

In the factory, very little work was being done as the staff, including Agatha, listened to a small radio in Johan's office.

Mr. Van Loon clasped his hands and shook his head. "The north is finished. They'll be in Sneek tomorrow."

One of the female machinists dabbed her eyes with her handkerchief. "It's really just delaying the inevitable. We should surrender now. Why should so many people die over this?" She was a mother and was clearly worried about her eighteen-year-old son going out to join the fighting.

They closed early and the staff went home for the night, though they would definitely be back in the morning. Agatha was firm on that point.

"We need to keep things normal. We have a big order that we need to work on."

Everyone nodded and agreed. Normal was best.

Supper was barely finished when Mary went back to bed, claiming exhaustion. Johan went up with her for a few minutes to tuck her in. The bed was warm and inviting. It was still light outside, and the spring evening filtered in through the window. Birds sang their last songs for the evening.

On May 13th Queen Wilhelmina left by ship for the safety of England. Princess Juliana and her family had already left and were enroute to Canada.

"Everyone's leaving. There's no hope." Mary voice was a whisper as they listened to more radio reports.

"They have to leave. The queen will continue to run things in exile." Agatha snapped as if Mary had said something disloyal about the royal family.

Mary didn't respond. Her thoughts were not on the queen but on her own mother. What was going on there? There was no way to find out. They didn't have a telephone and it seemed as though the telephones were out all over, anyway.

She went back to bed.

At nine-thirty that night, Johan came up to their room to check on Mary. She was awake and looked at him dully as he stood beside the bed.

He sat on the edge of the bed. "Are you alright?" He stroked her hair back from her face. Her forehead was greasy and damp with sweat. Her face was pale even against the white pillow.

She turned her red-rimmed eyes to his face. "What's happening?"

He hesitated and took her hand. "Radio Bremen just announced that they've taken the Grebbe Line."

She blinked at him. "What does that really mean?"

He patted her hand. "It's just a matter of time now when it will be over."

"I wish it was over now. I want to talk to my mother." She started to cry.

"I know, I know, sweetheart." Johan bent over and gathered her into his arms.

She put her arms around his neck. She smelled warm and musky. Johan felt a lump in his throat. She wanted her family and he was determined to find a way to make that happen.

He stroked her damp back and neck. "I've been distracted with everything for a while. I'm sorry. We'll be alright. I'll look after you. Can I get you some tea or water?"

"No. Nothing." She lay back down. "I just want to sleep until it's over."

He kissed her forehead and left her to go back down to the radio and his mother.

———

It was after lunch on May 14ᵗʰ. Mary walked across the gap to the factory to join Johan and Agatha. She couldn't listen to the radio any longer and had switched it off as soon as they had gone back to work after lunch. Then she had suddenly felt the need to be near Johan, and decided to take a flask of coffee to him.

She stopped and sniffed the air. A faint acrid odour of smoke drifted on the wind. There was a fire somewhere.

There was no work going on. It was midafternoon, yet the factory was eerily still. A radio was on and all the employees were clustered around. A woman was sobbing. Mary stopped, afraid to go on. Johan looked up to see his wife.

"Mary." Johan's eyes were filled with tears. He held out his arms to her as he walked to meet her halfway across the floor. "My God it's awful. They say that negotiations were underway. It's unbelievable." His voice choked.

"What's happened?" Mary pushed out of his embrace with a hand on his chest, the flask of coffee still clutched in her other hand.

He looked surprised. Whatever it was, he'd thought she already knew. "Rotterdam. The Germans have destroyed it. Bombed it to pieces. What's left is burning. It's destroyed."

"My God." She tasted bile and put her hand in front of her mouth to stop from throwing up. She was dizzy and thought she might faint.

"Sit down." Johan pulled her into a chair.

"Are we next?" Mary was suddenly afraid for her baby. The numbness she had felt for days was suddenly gone, replaced by terror. "Will we be blown up too? Should we get out? Go to my parents?" She was on her feet now, her voice growing hysterical.

Agatha came over to them. "Be quiet! We have a duty to stay calm and in control."

"Mama." Johan pleaded with his arm around Mary's shoulder.

Agatha shook her head and jerked her head at Mary. "Take her out of here. Put her to bed."

Johan led Mary back to the house and sat her down in the chair by the window. "Shh now. We'll have a hot cup of tea. There's no need to panic. They won't come here. We aren't important to them. Rotterdam is an important port for the Germans. They won't come." He went into the kitchen to boil water for tea, returning with a small glass of Genver.

Mary turned her head away. "I don't want it. I'll be sick."

"Please try, for me." He pushed the glass towards her again, and like an obedient child, she drank the liquor, feeling it warm her.

"Better?"

She felt some colour returning to her cheeks. "Yes. Was it true? You don't think we'll be bombed too?"

"Absolutely. There just wouldn't be any point."

But Mary could see the uncertainty in his eyes. Who could really know what would happen?

———

"I can't eat." Mary pushed away the half-consumed bowl of pea soup.

Johan slid it back in front of her. "You need to keep up your strength for the baby's sake."

She sighed and picked up her spoon again. "I feel sick. Don't you?"

Agatha sniffed. "We all feel sick, Mary, but you need to keep going as best you can. There is no point in lying down to die."

"You're so strong, Mama Meijer. I don't know how you do it." Mary ate a few more spoonfuls of soup before pushing away the plate. "I just can't manage anymore supper." She was almost in tears.

"Alright. Leave it for now. You did alright." Johan picked up her bowl and took it to the kitchen. "Will we go and hear what the latest is?"

"I can't listen anymore. I'm going to bed." Mary got to her feet and started to clear the rest of the table.

Agatha took the dishes from Mary's hands. "Leave it. I'll do it. Johan will help me."

Without arguing, Mary went out to go up to their room.

Johan called after her. "I'll be up shortly to check on you."

At seven-thirty, Johan went up and woke his wife. "It's over. Winkelman was just on the radio and said the Dutch have surrendered. It's over, sweetheart. We're safe."

The glazed look on Mary's face slowly cleared. She sat up and reached for Johan as he sat on the edge of the bed.

"Thank God." She started to cry, clinging to him. He was strong and solid in her arms. It seemed to Mary that she was coming out of a long illness and despite the swell of the baby and the new full and heavy feel of her breasts, Mary felt weak and fragile.

"We need to put this behind us now and get you back to good health." Johan stroked her back with one hand, holding her against his chest with the other.

"Please, somehow, will you reach my parents to find out how everyone is? I know they don't have a phone, but the shop on the corner of their street does."

"First thing tomorrow morning, I'll get on the telephone. Hopefully some sort of communication is still working out there."

"Promise you'll keep trying until you find out?"

"I promise. Now you can sleep easier, knowing the worst is behind us." He laid her down again.

"Yes. I feel better already." She tried to smile at him, reaching out to touch him again as he stood to go back downstairs. "Thank you for looking after me."

He held her hand for a second. "The worst is behind us."

"It's confirmed then. There's nothing else to know right now, so we should all turn our attention to the work." Agatha snapped off the small radio in the factory and clapped her hands to punctuate her message. Back to work. Back to normal.

The small group of machinists shuffled back to their machines, talking and distracted.

One of the women settled on her seat, picking up her material to start hemming. "Was it all worth it?"

Mr. Van Loon's back was rigid. "We couldn't just let them walk in and take us over without a fight. No one should control us."

"Don't we do it every day of our lives? Let other people tell us what to do and when to do it?" The woman glanced towards Agatha, then looked down at her work when Agatha gave her a sharp frown.

Mr. Van Loon's voice was cold. "The difference is you have the choice to leave at any time."

The woman bent her head and said no more.

In the office, Johan was on the telephone. He had been making call after call. Many numbers simply gave the *beep-beep-beep* of a disconnected line, but finally he got through to a local police station in Ede.

Johan hesitated but steeled himself to ask the questions. "I'm trying to get information about my wife's family. They live in Wageningen. I know the city has been evacuated, but is it possible to find out how they are?" Johan gave the names of Mary's family members and then waited as the man flipped through papers.

"Are you sure? I'm sure it's chaos there. Is it possible there is a mistake?"

Johan listened for a moment in silence as the police officer spoke.

Agatha had come in to the office and looked up from her clipboard and list of invoices. She frowned and spoke even before he had fully disengaged. "What is it?"

Johan hung up the phone. He rested his head in one hand, fingers pressed to his forehead, thumb digging in to his cheekbone.

"Well?"

When he did look at her, his eyes burned with tears. "Mary's brothers. Nicholas and James. Both of them." He choked and stopped.

Agatha rose to stand beside him. She rested a hand on his shoulder. "Both of them what?"

"Both of them gone. Killed in fighting on the Grebbe line. Oh my God. How can I tell Mary?" He buried his head in his hands, tears welling.

"You better go and do it now. Did you hear anything of the parents?"

"They aren't on the list of dead, wounded, or missing, so presumably that means they're alright. As alright as they can be with both their sons gone." Johan paused, breathing deep to steady himself, then spoke again. "I wonder how André and the family are doing. Den Helder took a real beating."

"Who?" Agatha turned back to her filing.

Johan walked with slow steps out of the factory and into the house.

Why can't Mama let the past with André go? She's so hard.

Mary was in the kitchen, chopping vegetables for soup. She looked up when Johan came in. His forehead beaded with sweat.

"Johan?" Mary put the knife down on the counter. "What is it?" She moved towards him.

He opened his arms wordlessly to engulf her in a hug.

"What is it? Tell me!" She pushed back against his chest. The dark circles shadowing her eyes made her pale face ghostly. Her fair hair lay flat against her skull. The shock might kill her.

Tears slid down Johan's cheeks. "Nicholas and James. I'm sorry, Mary. I'm so sorry."

Something inside of her shut down. She shook her head and tried to step back. She swayed as his words stabbed her.

Johan half-carried, half-led her to a chair at the dining room table. "Come and sit down. You've had a shock. Are you faint?"

She didn't speak, but stared at him. Finally, a small word. "No."

"Oh, Mary. They were brave. The police officer who gave me the news told me that they were with a major named Jocometti who led a counterattack, despite all odds. They were so very courageous, fighting to defend their home and country."

"Brave? Courageous?" Mary flushed. "What does any of that mean or matter? They were *children*!" She beat his chest with her fists. "They were my brothers. Oh my God. Mama and Papa, what about them?" She was sobbing now.

"I asked, and they aren't on any lists, so that means that they are safe." He held her awkwardly, he on one chair and she on another.

"Mama will die. James was her baby. He couldn't do any wrong in her eyes. And Nicholas...Papa was so proud of him. Papa thought he'd be a lawyer." Mary couldn't take it in. The futures that, only days ago were so bright and promising, gone now. Snuffed out. "Why? Why?"

"I don't know." Johan shook his head. "Would you like to lie down? Come, I'll help you upstairs, bring you something to drink."

Mary pounded his shoulder. "The worst is over. That's what you said."

"I'm sorry." He let her strike him.

Finally, she stood, and Johan supported her up the stairs to their room. She shuffled along like an old woman. Upstairs, she sat on the edge of the bed, and now and then she shivered. Johan removed her shoes and laid her down, fully dressed, under the feather duvet. When he returned ten minutes later with a tray of tea and toast and a small glass of gin, she hadn't moved. She stared at the ceiling.

"Come, get something in you. Please."

She sat up obediently and took the glass from his hand. He guided it to her mouth. "Drink now."

She drank, coughing as the fiery liquid burned its way down.

"How about a nibble of toast? Could you manage that?"

Again, she took it from his hand obediently, chewing mechanically, drinking some tea when he told her to drink. She was an automaton, drinking and eating without knowing what she was doing. The person who was Mary had withdrawn from the field, receding somewhere deep into her core.

Finally, Johan let her lie back down and tucked the warm duvet around her again, despite the warmth of the spring day.

"I'll be back shortly to check on you, but for now I better go and help Mama out. Is that alright? Will you be okay?" He stroked her damp hair.

Mary just looked at him.

"Try to get some sleep, alright?" Johan gave her a final touch on the top of her head, then left her to go to the office.

VII

Spring 1940

"**I** went down to watch them arrive, you know." Hank ran his hand across one of the towels without seeming to realize it.

Johan looked at his old friend curiously. "Really? Why?"

"I'm not really sure. I suppose I was hoping I'd see people throwing old tomatoes at them. Of course, I wouldn't have the nerve to do it myself, but still...I was hoping."

"And? Were people throwing tomatoes?" Johan spoke quietly as he shook out and refolded towels. He and Hank were in the shop and Johan was getting it ready to open again. It had been closed for a week and smelled musty and damp.

"You'd never believe it." Hank punched his fist into his other hand. "People were lining the street, waving as the German trucks drove down Middenweg. How is it possible?"

"People do what they need to do. You just push down your feelings and accept the new reality."

"After what happened in Rotterdam...how can people just accept it?" Hank's parents had been amongst the dead in Rotterdam. He was flushed and grinding his teeth.

Johan thought of Mary's two young brothers. "And not just Rotterdam."

"That's right. So how can we just accept it?"

"We all make sacrifices. It's just the way it is. You just say to your-self, 'This isn't what I wanted, but it's how it is,' and you carry on to make the best of it."

"But at what cost? Those people that waved cheerfully as the enemy drove into Amsterdam, someday they'll have to pay a price. Perhaps just something as simple as their neighbours not talking to them any longer, or perhaps something more. Don't you think so?" Hank swivelled towards Johan, his gaze piercing.

Johan looked at Hank and then back to his work. "You're prob-ably right. I don't know."

Hank shook himself. "I'm sorry. I didn't mean to take out my anger on you. You and Mary have enough to think about without me going on at you." He stooped to straighten out a stack of linens. "Good news about Tiineke and André, anyway. Thank God they're all alright."

"Yes, that is great news. Do me a favour, though, and don't say anything in front of my mother." Johan sighed deeply.

"Don't tell me that after everything that's gone on, she's still so angry? I would have thought that a war would put things into per-spective for her."

"Her perspective is that she's washed her hands of them and doesn't want to hear about them."

"I'm sorry, Johan, I know she's your mother, but it's just crazy to be like that. Now is the time for us to pull together. My God, I can't stop thinking about my parents, wishing I had them with me. So many mothers have lost their sons, and yet she just wastes hers." His voice choked and he turned to stare out the window.

"I know. I tried to talk to her when I found out that André was alright, but she wouldn't talk about him." Johan threw down his towel. "Let's leave this and go in to Mary. Maybe seeing you will help her a bit."

They stepped through the adjoining door in to the house. The tick-tock of the clock hanging on the wall was loud in the quiet of the room.

Johan called out to his wife as they came into the living room. "Mary, look who it is. Hank is here to see you." The afternoon sun flooded the room in a defiant blaze of spring light and warmth.

"Mary." Hank stepped quickly over to her and held out his arms. She looked up and seemed to pull herself back from a long way away. She stood to greet him, wordlessly stepping into his embrace and they stood holding each other, her tears soaking his shoulder.

Hank's eyes filled as well. "Mary, I'm so sorry. Your brothers were fine young men. I remember you talking about them and I know how proud you were of them."

"Oh Hank. Your parents. Both your parents. It's just too awful. Have you talked to Tiineke? I should write her a letter, but just haven't been able to yet." Mary's voice was broken and almost incoherent as the words stumbled over each other.

"Yes, I managed to speak with her. André has some pull at the base and they reached me at the warehouse office. I'm sure she's just the same as you. She asked about you and mentioned writing. Meanwhile, she asked me to tell you how sorry she is."

Johan stood by awkwardly until finally Mary took a deep breath and loosened her arms from around Hank's neck. Hank stepped back and took out his large white handkerchief, wiping his eyes and blowing his nose. Mary sank back into the chair, and with that, seemed to slip away again as she turned her head to look out the window.

Johan shook his head once, then turned back to Hank. "I'll put the kettle on for tea, shall I?"

Hank nodded and cleared his throat. "Yes, tea, always a good thing."

Johan brought in the tea tray and tried to change subjects. "So what about your job? Will you continue on there?"

"For now, I suppose. Who knows what will happen in the future, but it sounds like the idea is that everything stays as normal as possible." Hank shrugged. "Mary, are you feeling alright, with the baby, I mean?"

Mary continued to gaze out the window with a blank stare, her lids slightly lowered. Her hands were flat on the armrests of the chair.

Johan reached over and put a hand on her knee. "Mary, Hank was talking to you."

She started and turned. "Pardon me? I didn't hear you."

Hank pointed to the swell of her belly. "How is the baby? Are you feeling alright?"

"Oh yes. Fine." Her voice was listless.

"Is he moving yet? I remember how exciting that was for Tiineke when she first felt the baby moving."

Johan smiled gratefully at Hank.

"Moving?" Mary seemed to struggle to understand the questions.

"Yes, we've felt the baby moving quite a bit, haven't we, Mary?" Johan answered for her. "He seems especially busy in the evening and keeps Mary awake if she tries to go to bed early, doesn't he, Mary?"

"Yes." She turned back to the window.

They heard the front door open. Johan stood. "Ah, here's Mama, home from afternoon service."

"Mrs. Meijer. Hello." Hank held out his hand to shake Agatha's as she came in to the room.

Agatha nodded. "Hank. It's a long time since we've seen you."

Johan couldn't tell if she sounded happy about that or disapproving. "Were there a lot of people in church, Mama?"

"Yes, it was filled. Difficult times bring everyone back. You and Mary should have come. I think it doesn't look well on the family when you aren't there. People notice."

No question this time. Disapproving. "Mama, you know Mary isn't up to it at the moment. I'm sure people would understand."

Hank stood. "It's time I was going. Johan, it was good to see you." He bent over to kiss Mary on the forehead. "I'll be writing to Tiineke tonight. I'll give her your greeting."

Johan winced. He could almost feel his mother's scowl.

Mary didn't respond.

Hank shook Agatha's hand again, then Johan's.

Johan gripped Hank's arm. "Come again. It's good to see old friends."

"I will."

VIII

Summer 1940

"He's absolutely beautiful!" Hank gazed down at the sleeping baby. "Congratulations again, Johan. Mary, I won't keep you awake by standing here all afternoon. You must still be tired." Hank bent to kiss her cheek as she lay propped against several pillows.

Johan watched Hank with Mary. He couldn't help but compare her to what he recalled of Tiineke when she first gave birth in this very bed. Tiineke had been tired but healthy and happy looking, glowing with a flush of pride and joy. Mary was frail and pale. Although it had been several days since the birth, she still looked exhausted.

Hank ventured a similar opinion when he and Johan were back downstairs in the living room. "Mary doesn't seem very well."

Agatha snapped and fidgeted with her newspaper before finally laying it on her lap. "I've told her she needs to get up and get back into a routine. She's spent so much time in bed these past few weeks her body is wasting away." Agatha's voice was sharp with irritation.

Johan nodded. "Mama's right, and I've told Mary as well, but she just tells me she can't, and goes back to sleep. She only wakes up long enough to eat a little and do what needs to be done for the baby."

"Nicholas James. It's a nice name for the little fellow." Hank changed subjects.

Johan crossed and uncrossed his legs. "Yes, I thought it would make Mary happy to name him for her brothers. I think it does, but on the other hand, it's a constant reminder of them. Maybe it wasn't such a good idea. Really, I'm just at a loss to know how to help her." He was both irritated and frustrated.

Hank's brow furrowed. "Maybe you should talk to the doctor."

"What nonsense!" Agatha slapped the rolled newspaper against her thigh. "You've indulged that girl far too much, Johan. She has responsibilities now and it's high time she start to live up to them."

Hank blinked, then turned back to Johan. "So what do you think of Netherlands's chance against Belgium?"

Johan jumped on the subject, glad to have someone to talk to about soccer.

Agatha lifted the paper in front of her face again.

———

Later, Johan walked outside with Hank. They stood talking, Hank sitting on his bicycle and Johan with his arms crossed across his chest. He shivered despite the warm summer evening.

"Johan, you're a lucky man. A beautiful wife, a handsome son... make sure you look after them." Hank spoke with mock sternness, as a father might.

Johan grinned. "He is handsome, isn't he? I'll tell you, he has good kicking legs."

"Ah, he'll be a famous footballer then."

"I hope so." The grin faded from Johan's face.

Hank touched Johan on the shoulder. "Seriously though, don't you think you should talk to a doctor about Mary? She seems so frail, and I always had this thought that new mothers were supposed to be hearty."

"Mama knows best. I'll leave it for now." Johan shrugged. "I won't hold you longer. You don't want to linger on the streets these days."

"I'll come again soon so I can see how your young man grows." With that promise, Hank pushed off, waving as he pedalled into the lowering sun.

Instead of returning to his mother, Johan went upstairs to Mary. She was curled on her side but Johan couldn't tell if she slept. She didn't move at his entering the room.

Johan stepped over and looked down at his small son and saw that his eyes were open and he was fidgeting.

He leaned down and lifted the small baby. "Are you awake then, Nicky? Come and sit with Papa for a few moments."

Nicholas started to cry and Johan bounced him up and down. "This isn't good enough, is it? I think we need to change you don't we?" Johan looked at Mary again and still she didn't move. Johan listened to her breath. *I know you're awake.* It was as though she was holding her breath, hoping that he didn't call her.

"Alright, let's see how we men manage this then, shall we?" Johan carried Nicky into the front dressing room where a change table had been set up on top of an old dresser.

Nicholas watched as Johan fumbled with pins and buttons. "Now, here you are, all dry and comfortable again. We did it!" Johan was inordinately proud of himself with his first experience of changing a baby. He lifted Nicholas back up against his shoulder, and the baby nestled against him, gurgling and sucking on his fist.

"Shall we go down and see Oma and let Mama sleep for a bit?"

Agatha looked up when Johan and Nicholas came in to the room.

"Her Highness is still resting then?" She nodded towards the warehouse.

"I don't mind. It gives me time with Nicky. I changed him."

"Did you?" Agatha frowned. "You shouldn't have to do that."

"Mama, he's my son too. Why shouldn't I help look after him?" Johan laid the baby on his knees and touched the small waving hands tenderly. Nicky grabbed one of Johan's thumbs in each hand

and held them tightly. Johan could feel a lump rise in his throat. *This is my son. What is in store for you in the future?*

It seemed as if Agatha had heard Johan's question. "It's good to have a new Meijer in the family. Someone that we can plan for in the business."

Johan could taste bile in his throat. "The business. Mama, not everyone is cut out for this business you know."

"Cut out for." She scoffed. "What does that mean? He'll learn the business at our knees and by the time he needs to be ready, he will be."

Nicholas started to cry. One fist found its way into his mouth again and he sucked furiously before crying again.

Agatha stood up and looked down at the crying baby. "Well, Papa, that's one thing you can't help with. His Mama will have to stir herself to feed him."

Johan rose, bouncing the baby as he walked, stroking the small back. "Alright now, no need to be so upset. We'll go now and find Mama."

They went back across the courtyard to the warehouse.

"Mary." Johan spoke quietly as he came back in to the room.

Mary stirred slightly.

"Mary. You need to feed Nicky."

There was a deep sigh and Mary turned over on her back and opened her eyes to look up at Johan. "Already?"

"I'm afraid so." Johan leaned down as Mary pushed herself into a sitting position in the bed. He handed Nicky to her and kissed her damp forehead, all in one movement. "Did you sleep well?"

He watched as she opened the buttons of her night dress and settled the baby at her breast. Johan could feel himself stir as he glimpsed the engorged nipple. He stepped back so Mary wouldn't notice. The last thing he wanted was for her to feel pressure from him, although he was longing to hold her and make love to her again. It had been months now and he felt the physical ache from not being with her.

"Yes, I suppose so. I just can't seem to shake this exhausted feeling, though, no matter how much I sleep." She didn't look up at Johan, but studied the baby as he suckled.

Johan watched Mary's face as she watched Nicky. She wore a small frown, as if she were looking at something mildly interesting, but not connected to her.

Johan took a deep breath. "Mama thinks it would be best if you forced yourself to get up more."

She looked up at him, her eyes filled with tears. "Johan, please don't make me. I'm just so tired. I'll be alright in a few days, but just now, all I can do is sleep."

He was contrite. "Don't worry. You just rest up and regain your strength. I can help out with Nicky. In fact, I enjoy it."

He touched the soft white hair on the back of the baby's head as he fed. All feelings of arousal gone now, he simply gazed with pleasure at the sight of mother and child.

Johan reached for Nicky when it was clear he had finished feeding. "Here, let me take him."

Mary rested her head against the pillows. "You don't mind?"

"No. Not at all. You get some rest."

He lifted his small son and smiled as Nicky opened his eyes briefly before closing them contentedly. By the time he was downstairs and in the house, the baby was sleeping soundly in his arms. His mouth fell open slightly as Johan placed him in the baby carriage positioned near the window. Johan could smell his faint milky breath as he leaned down to kiss the baby's forehead, then he pulled the white gauzy netting over the carriage to keep any insects away that might come in with the summer breeze.

Agatha huffed and shook her head. "So she's still not getting up then?"

"No, there's no point now. She'll get a good night's sleep and I'm sure she'll feel better in the morning." Johan's tone was defensive.

Agatha smiled suddenly, a rare upturn of her pursed lips.

"That's fine. Just the three of us then for the evening." She glanced towards the sleeping child. "Put the news on and I'll get the coffee." Agatha had a small, precious supply of coffee and they treated themselves to one cup each in the evening.

Johan drew the heavy dark brown velour drapes. There was a time when people often left the drapes open on a summer evening to catch the fresh breeze, heavy with the fragrance of flowers. These days all drapes were drawn tight before the first light went on. Even if sympathies lay with the Allies, no one wanted to make their home a target for English bombers.

They listened to the news in silence for a while.

Agatha drained her coffee cup. "Do you hear? De Geer is meeting with Hitler in peace talks. Soon all this rationing nonsense will be over and we can go back to normal."

Johan sipped his coffee slowly. "I hope you're right."

"Of course I'm right. You'll see." Agatha stood to snap off the radio.

Johan smiled. "You generally are, aren't you, Mama?"

"Look, the young man is awake." Agatha stood over the carriage and reached in to pick up Nicky. He cried in surprise and Johan stood to take him.

"I'm fine. He'll settle down in a moment." Agatha turned her back to Johan and walked around the room, jogging Nicky gently. His cries faded to a whimper and then to a quiet gurgling as he became accustomed to Agatha's arms and scent. After a few moments he began fussing again.

Johan watched his mother with his son for a moment and then, finishing his coffee, he stood. "I better take him up. He'll need changing and he might be hungry again. He didn't really feed for that long earlier. It's time I went up, anyway."

He stepped in front of Agatha and reached for the baby. Agatha hesitated for a moment and then transferred the child to Johan.

Agatha looked at the baby and smiled. "Yes, we'll say good night then."

Johan studied his mother for another moment before turning to leave. He shivered and held his son closer, trying to shake off the shadow that seemed to enclose him.

IX

Winter 1941

When Nicky was six months old, Agatha began feeding him cereal and pureed vegetables.

Mary watched Agatha prepare the food. "Are you sure he can have those things already?"

"Yes, I'm sure. He needs them. Here, let him sit on my lap and we'll see how he likes it."

Mary sat listlessly and watched as Agatha used a small egg spoon to feed a little bit of cereal to Nicky. His face puckered and his tongue smacked against the roof of his mouth as he experienced the new texture. He smiled up at his grandmother and tried to grab her glasses. Agatha took another spoonful and waved it under Nicky's nose. His mouth opened and she popped in the cereal. Waving his arms, he opened his mouth without prompting as soon as he had swallowed. Agatha used her left forearm and hand to pin down his arms while she gave him another spoon of cereal. He rocked and hummed, his small hands opening and closing, yet not fighting against being trapped by Agatha.

Mary picked at a loose thread on her skirt as she watched them. "You're good with him."

Agatha glanced up to pierce Mary with her gaze. "I've had enough practice."

"I know. You and Johan are doing so much to help me. Nicky doesn't really need me at all." Mary's voice was despondent.

Agatha barely listened to Mary. Instead she stroked Nicky's cheek. "That's enough cereal for now. In a couple of days we'll try some carrots." Agatha put Nicky on Mary's lap. "What he needs you for is the rest of his feed."

"I'll take him upstairs. He'll be ready for a nap when he's finished so I might lie down for a bit as well." Mary wrapped a soft flannel blanket around the baby to protect him against the January chill for the walk across to the warehouse.

"Will we see you for supper?" Agatha's voice was edged with criticism.

Mary hesitated, then nodded. "Yes, I'm only going to lie down for a little, while Nicky is. I'll come down to peel the potatoes if you want me to."

"That would be helpful." Agatha bit back any other harsh words. *It would be easier if she stayed out of the way.* That girl was nothing but a weak and lazy child, and the less seen of her, the better.

Agatha went through to the factory where Johan was in deep conversation with Mr. Van Loon.

Johan paused when he saw his mother. "Mama, is Mary looking after Nicky?"

"Yes. They've gone to lie down. Nicky had his first cereal today."

"Oh, you said you were going to try him on it. How did it go?"

"Fine, as I knew it would." Agatha turned to look over at the receiving area. "And now, what about here. Did the shipment of new material arrive?"

"Mr. Van Loon and I were just talking about it. No, it didn't come in. Since the textile rationing went in place in August, it's gotten worse and worse. You just can't rely on things coming in as they should anymore." Johan gestured for the plant manager and his mother to follow him in to the privacy of the office and closed the door.

Johan perched on the edge of the desk and folded his arms in front of him. "I think it's time we faced the fact that we need to let some of the staff go. With the raw materials so unpredictable, we never know if we'll have work or not."

Agatha sighed. It was the Depression years all over again. "Alright. Let's keep two on and let the others go."

By the end of the day there were only two men remaining. Johan had let one woman go and the other two men. Mr. Van Loon, of course, would be kept on. He could maintain the machines to ensure they stayed in good working order for when they were needed again.

Johan grumbled when he came into the house for supper. "I'm not good at this sort of thing."

Agatha shook her head. "No one's good at letting people go."

Mary was standing at the counter, cutting vegetables. Johan gave her a quick kiss on the cheek, then picked up Nicky from the playpen.

Johan held his son, gazing down at the big blue eyes. "I hate it. How did André manage it? I never realized then what a rotten job this could be."

Agatha's back stiffened. Even now, she couldn't bear to hear André's name. What a waste of all those years raising him to be a man.

Conversation at supper was subdued. After the dishes were done, Mary hovered in the living room. "I'm taking Nicky up and I'm going to bed as well."

Agatha made a show of looking at her watch. "At seven o'clock? I don't know why you bother getting up at all."

"Mama's right, Mary. Why don't you come back down and we'll have a game of cribbage?"

Mary's voice trembled and her eyes welled with tears. "I know the two of you want to listen to the news. I'm not interested and I'm tired. I'm going to bed."

She lifted the baby from the blanket on the floor where he had been playing.

"Good night, my boy." Johan kissed him as Mary held the baby towards him. She turned away to leave the room.

Agatha snapped her fingers. "Am I permitted to say good night to my grandson?"

"Yes, of course." Mary turned back and held the baby down towards Agatha.

Instead of just kissing him as Johan had done, Agatha reached up to take him from Mary. For a fraction of a second Mary held him tight, then let go as Agatha pulled gently. Agatha held the child on her lap and spoke with him.

"Now, sweetheart, have a good sleep. Tomorrow, perhaps, I'll take you for a walk, if the sun is shining a little bit. We need to get you big and strong, a true Meijer."

Mary stood by, her shoulders slumped, waiting until Agatha handed the boy back to her.

"Now you can go." Agatha waved her hand.

Without a word, Mary turned and stopped only long enough to gather the blanket and tuck it around Nicky protectively.

Johan had his back to Mary while he twisted the knob of the radio, edging it back and forth until the sound became sharp. He didn't see his wife and son leave.

The routine was set. Johan and Agatha listened to the news and discuss the day while Mary and Nicky went to bed. Night after night.

X

Spring 1941

"It's crazy. Just crazy!" Hank kicked the ball against the back wall of Johan's garden a little harder than he meant to.

The ball rebounded, striking Johan in the shin. "Ouch! The ball isn't a weapon, my friend."

Hank retrieved the ball and kicked it over to Johan. "Be quicker, then. I remember a time when you would have fielded that easily." Hank lost interest in the sparring and threw himself into a garden chair beside the playpen where Nicky stood rocking back and forth, clinging to the top rail.

"I mean, really, how can this little fellow grow up properly with all this rationing? Bread, milk, and now, potatoes. There are farms producing milk and potatoes all around Haarlem where I live, and yet we can't have it. Doesn't it worry you? Make you angry?" Hank poked Johan in the shoulder with his bony finger.

Johan stepped back and massaged his shoulder, scowling at Hank. "Yes, of course it does, and please, keep your voice down. You never know who's listening or what they will make of what you say. You just need to figure out how to manage within the rules. There's no other choice. Mama says we need to just bear up, and she's right. Sometimes German soldiers come in to the shop and buy things. We can't afford to alienate them, you know."

Hank glowered and opened his mouth to say something, but instead took a breath and changed the subject. "How's Mary doing? I thought I'd see her this afternoon."

Johan shook his head. "She's lying down."

Hank glanced at his watch. "At two o'clock on a Sunday afternoon? The sun is so nice today, there's a promise of spring in the air. She should be out here, enjoying it."

"Don't tell me about it. I can't do anything to encourage her. She sleeps so much, it's unbelievable. If I say anything too stern to her, she cries. Mama has lost complete patience with it all." Johan sighed deeply and sat hunched over, forearms resting on his legs, hands folded. He stared down at the ground, as if to find answers in the old stone cobbles.

Hank hesitated and then ventured: "Well, at least she seems to be looking after Nicky alright. He's a cheerful little fellow."

Johan barked a short laugh. "Ha! Now that he's weaned and eating real food—which, by the way, Mama got him doing—Mary hardly seems to notice Nicky. Between Mama and I, we do pretty much everything. I take him over to the plant with me most mornings, Mama takes him in the afternoons to go to the shops, and then I have him again in the evenings until it's bedtime."

Hank furrowed his brow. "Is that true? You must be so worried about her."

"We're certainly frustrated. I think we've been really patient with her, but enough is enough. My mother shouldn't have to carry such a big burden at her age. She has enough to think about without raising a baby." Johan's voice was hard. He sat back in his chair and looked at Nicky. His face softened. "You aren't to blame are you, son? You're such a good-natured child despite everything."

"What does the doctor say? By now you've had her to see the doctor." Hank smiled at the baby and then turned back to Johan.

"Oh, the doctor. Please. Who has time and money for doctors? I took her once and he said it was just baby blues. I'm not taking her again. She just needs to set her mind to getting up and getting into the routine of being a mother." Johan knew he was letting his impatience show but couldn't help himself.

"I don't know, Johan. I've heard of this 'baby blues' before. She should be past it by now, shouldn't she? I would take her again, if I were you."

"Well, when your wife has it, by all means, go to the doctor." Johan closed his eyes for a moment, then looked at Hank. "I'm sorry. I didn't mean to be such a bear. I know you mean well. It's just that things seem so difficult between Mama and Mary right now. I wish Mary would make an effort, that's all. It's almost like she goes out of her way to provoke Mama. Listen to this..."

"I wrote to Tiineke to tell them about Nicky."

Johan had been holding Nicky up in the air like an airplane, but now brought the baby back down and held him close. He glanced at his mother before mumbling a response. "That's good. I'm sure you were excited to share the news with her."

"It wasn't that so much. It was more a matter of finally giving up waiting for you to do it. You should have written to your own brother." Mary looked up from the vegetables she was chopping.

Agatha clanged the lid of the potato pot on the kitchen counter. Nicky began to wail.

Johan tried to soothe the baby. "Shhh, it's alright, shhh."

"If you two don't have anything better to chatter about, then please go elsewhere to do it. I don't have the patience for all this gossip while I'm trying to get supper made." Agatha spit the words at Johan before turning her back on both of them.

The small flare of energy left Mary as quickly as it had come.

"I'm sorry, Mama Meijer. I won't say anything further to distract you." She resumed chopping the vegetables.

Johan took Nicky through to the other room without a word.

"Why would she want to provoke my mother like that? After everything that Mama does for us."

"I don't know. As you noted, I'm not an expert on women." Hank leaned back in his chair and crossed his arms.

Johan gripped Hank's knee and squeezed it once. "I didn't mean anything with that. You know I didn't. You grew up with a sister, at least."

"I'm afraid I honestly don't know. Maybe she just feels overwhelmed by your mother. Perhaps that was her way of fighting back. I know Tiineke often felt upset by your mother, which is why they moved out, right?" Hank shrugged and held up his hands with an air of bewilderment. "Speaking of my sister, she and the kids are going to move in with me."

Johan straightened up. "Have they been evacuated from Den Helder?" This was news he hadn't heard. He heard more about his brother than he let on to anyone, through the naval connections at Meijer's. Although the business had slowed down, Meijer's still had a contract with the shipyards in Den Helder for some basic linen. The yards were now under the control of the Germans, but in many ways it was just business as usual.

"Not officially, but it's just too dangerous for them now. I've taken over the whole house where I'm renting and doing some remodelling to accommodate everyone. I could really use some help, actually." Hank shifted in his chair to study Johan's face.

Johan flushed and turned his gaze on his young son. "Don't look at me. I have enough to keep me busy."

They both knew that Agatha would not allow Johan to help work on something to benefit his brother, or worse yet, Tiineke.

"Well maybe once they're settled, you and Mary will bring Nicky over to meet them." Hank nudged Johan with his elbow. "It would be good for Mary, I think, something to look forward to."

"We'll see." Johan shrugged. They both knew that it was unlikely to happen. "So how are you going to manage with so many extra in the house? Especially now that you lost your job in Amsterdam."

"It won't be easy. I knew the job at the warehouse wouldn't last long. Business was getting really slow, anyway. Joining in the strike in February just gave them an excuse to let me go." Hank nodded, one corner of his mouth turned down.

"Did you strike? I didn't realize." Johan was not really surprised, knowing his friend's thoughts on the occupation.

"Of course I did. Don't tell me you didn't. The whole country was striking, for God's sake. The way the Nazis are treating Dutch citizens...it isn't right. Even though I lost my job, I'm glad I did."

"Really? What did it gain us?" Johan gestured towards the neighborhood. "If anything, it made things worse, all those retaliations. You lost your job. What good did that do?"

"I've been lucky. I got a job at the gas works in Haarlem so I don't have to go so far now. It all worked out." Hank was quiet for a moment. "Don't you ever feel that you just need to stand up for yourself or others, even if you don't win your point in the end?"

"No, I don't. Not when it's pointless. I didn't go out to strike in February. As Mama says, my responsibility is to look after my family. The store was closed, but it was closed anyway, and there was only Mr. Van Loon and I working at the plant that day, so whether we went on strike or not wouldn't have even been noticed."

Hank shook his head slowly and touched Johan's arm. "Sometimes I feel I don't even know who you are anymore. Where did that fearless football striker go? The guy that other players on the field would try to take down just to get him out of the way?"

"Life isn't a game." Johan shifted away from Hank's touch.

Hank laced his hands together. His voice was sad. "I know that, I just thought that you had the courage to go and make the big visions and plans come true."

"Plans change." Johan realized he had had this conversation once before. He stood up and picked up his son.

Hank stood as well. "I better get going. Seriously though, it would be great if you would come out for a visit. Some time when André is down for a few days. It's been too long that you and your brother have been apart. It's time to build bridges, before you live to regret it." Hank rested his hand on Johan's shoulder for a moment.

Johan shrugged Hank's hand off. "They made their choice."

Hank sighed and followed Johan. They had to go through the house to get out since the back yard was still locked and barred, years after Agatha had lost her chickens.

Hank patted the handlebars of his bike. "I hear they're starting to confiscate bicycles these days. I try and stay off the main roads when I can. I'm not giving up my iron horse."

Johan patted Hank on the shoulder. "It's good to see you, even if we don't always see eye to eye. It feels like I'm so taken up with 'Mary problems' and with just keeping things going with the business that I don't have much time for myself. Good thing I have this guy to bring sunshine to my days." Johan held Nicky on one hip and tickled the child under his chin, making him giggle.

"You're good with him. It's nice to see. I'll be back when I can. Give my greetings to Mary." Hank hopped on his bike, pedalling away quickly.

———

Mary stood at their upstairs window and watched Hank cycle away before turning her attention to Johan and Nicky. She felt removed from them. Her heart didn't catch as Johan set Nicky down on the sidewalk. *Shouldn't I feel more than this?* She looked on while Johan held the small child's hands, steadying the boy as he wobbled on his baby legs. Johan took a small step back and Nicky stepped forward, the dimpled knee stiff and awkward. He moved his other leg up and then swayed before balancing again. He shrieked with joy and Johan laughed.

"Good boy! Clever boy! You'll be walking on your own in no time, won't you?" Johan lifted the boy to give him a hug.

Mary's gaze shifted as she saw Agatha arriving home from church. Her navy blue Sunday hat was pinned rigidly to her hair, the steel grey bun protruding from underneath. She marched up to Johan and Nicky, her voice mingling with theirs.

"Come see Oma now, little one. Have you been out walking with Papa? You've gotten some sun, haven't you?" She reached to take the child from Johan's arms, and for a moment, the three of them were a tangle of arms, voices, and laughter.

Nicky brings out the better part of her.

The three of them went in to the house, the door closing behind them. Mary sighed, knowing she should go downstairs and join them. She should help to make the Sunday dinner, such as it was. A few small potatoes if they were lucky. Perhaps a piece of fish. It didn't matter. She wasn't hungry.

Make an effort. Come on, Mary, make an effort. It was what Johan was constantly saying to her these days. Why? Perhaps later she'd feel like writing a letter to her mother. Poor Mama. She knew from her father's letters that her mother was in bad shape. She hadn't gotten over the loss of her two sons and now slept as much as Mary herself did. She didn't write letters to Mary anymore, so her father wrote once in a while. She could tell how hard it was for her father from those occasional cryptic notes. They were just a matter of form:

"Lief Mary—How are you? Are you getting enough to eat? You must be so happy with your son. Someday we'll see him, God willing. Your mother sends her love."

Mary could recite the letters by now. There was never any news to tell. No concerts or happy events to talk about. It was one long effort of getting through one day and then the next. Mary could read it all between the lines.

———

"Johan, thank you for arranging this. I can't tell you what it means to me." Mary reached across the desk and touched Johan's warm hand as her husband dialled the office telephone. "I can't believe you and Papa organized this between you."

She pulled the bulky cardigan around her and seemed lost in the cloud of grey wool as she waited for Johan to get the call connected. She didn't know if it was the damp spring morning or the fact that it was the anniversary of her brothers' death that made her feel chilled to the bone.

Johan smiled at her. "It was a bit of a challenge, I admit. Since your parents don't have a telephone, your father really had to hunt for somewhere to take the call. Luckily, the family doctor has a telephone. Ah, here we are. It's ringing."

Mary felt her heart flutter and suddenly she was nauseous. She hadn't spoken with her mother for so long. Her face flushed and suddenly she felt overheated in the big sweater and threw it open.

Johan jumped a bit and held the receiver away from his ear as Mary's father bellowed into the telephone. "Hello, sir. Yes, we can hear you just fine."

Mary smiled a small, rare smile as she heard her father's voice from across the desk.

"Alright, I'm putting Mary on now. My thoughts are with you on this sad day. Here you are now." Johan handed the receiver over to Mary. "Do you want me to stay?"

Mary shook her head. She wanted to be alone with her parents.

Johan nodded and left.

Mary put the receiver to her ear and the tears welled as her father spoke. "Hello *Meisje.*"

She indeed felt like the little girl her father was calling her. "Papa? Oh, Papa, it's so good to hear your voice. Is Mama there with you?" Mary needed to hear her mother more than anything else in the world.

His voice boomed through the receiver. "Yes, she's here. I'll put her on. Take care of yourself and give little Nicky a hug from his Opa."

And then Mary heard the sound of the telephone being passed over. "Mama...Mama. Oh God, I wish I was there with you!"

Raspy breathing came through the line. "Sweetheart." There were seconds of breathing again as if her mother couldn't find the words. "I wish you were here too." It was all she could seem to manage.

Mary could tell how diminished her mother was. Gone was the woman who pushed her to do so many things—join the track team, play the piano, take on jobs she didn't have the confidence to do. The soft, uncertain voice was that of a frailer, older woman. She sounded so tired and dazed.

Still, it was her mother.

"Mama, I can't believe it's a year. Sometimes I just imagine that the boys are still at home and doing all their normal things. I dream of that and sometimes, when I wake up, just for a few minutes, I think it's real."

Her mother started to sob. The sound triggered something deep inside Mary, and the dam that had been holding her feelings at bay burst open.

"Oh Mama, Mama." Mary was inarticulate as she too, sobbed. She pressed the receiver to her ear and together she and her mother cried. At last Mary's breath hitched and she felt herself calming. She heard the rumble of her father's voice behind her mother's sobs as he tried to soothe her her.

Johan, who had been hovering just outside the office door, came in and handed Mary a large clean, white handkerchief. "Shall I take the phone?"

"No!" Mary clung to the receiver. "Mama, I'm so glad Papa is there for you. He'll look after you. He knows what you need." Mary's voice was stronger than it had been in some time. Johan flushed and looked a little stung, but stepped back again to let his wife finish.

"Mama, say good-bye to Papa for me. I need to go. You understand, don't you? I love you both. Good-bye, Mama." Mary kept the receiver at her ear even as she moved to hang up, her head bending towards the telephone itself. "Good-bye, Mama." She hung up and her voice became a whisper. Good-bye."

Mary turned to her husband, standing in the doorway. "Thank you, Johan." Her eyes filled with tears again as she gazed up at him.

He held out his arms to her and she stood up and stepped in to his embrace. She clung to him and cried against his shoulder.

"I do understand, you know." His voice was gruff.

"You're good to me. Thank God Nicky has you for a father."

"Mama has taken Nicky out to the park. Why don't you have a little rest and then get cleaned up for supper?" Johan steered her towards the door.

"Yes, that's what I'll do." She felt a sense of peace. She believed she was stronger now, more able to think. She came down well before supper. She felt hot; almost feverish. She wore her favourite green suit.

Agatha put down the beet she had been cutting up. "What in the world are you all dressed up for?"

"I'm going to cycle over to Westerkerk for a few moments, if I have time before supper."

Agatha tilted her head, then seemed to recall it was a special occasion for Mary. "Ah, yes. You have time if you make it quick."

Johan was in the living room with Nicky. "Do you want me to go with you?"

"No. I just want to say a prayer for the boys. I'll go on my own. You don't mind do you?" Mary kissed him on the cheek.

Johan stood up with Nicky and held him out to kiss his mother and for her to give him a kiss in return. "No, of course not. Take as long as you need. Supper can wait a few moments, if necessary."

Mary pinned on her hat and looked at herself critically in the mirror. The suit hung on her. She'd lost so much weight. She seemed to be seeing herself clearly for the first time in a long time.

Bouncing Nicky on his hip, Johan watched Mary cycle past the window. "I think your Mama is going to be alright."

Nicky pointed out the window. "Mama."

"Hey, Mama! Nicky just said Mama for the first time!" Johan grinned and spun his son around, making him laugh. "Wait until I tell your Mama, Nicky. Won't she be pleased?"

At supper, Johan tried to get Nicky to say 'Mama' again for Mary. She was stilled dressed in her good suit and a flushed, feverish look coloured her cheeks and forehead. Her hair was tidy and pinned up, a wispy tendril brushing her right temple.

Johan tickled Nicky's cheek. "Honestly, he said it."

Mary looked from her son to her mother-in-law. "He should be learning to say 'Oma' instead. Mama Meijer, you have done so much for Nicky and for me. I never really thank you, but I should, because I *am* grateful."

Agatha looked surprised.

Johan squeezed Mary's hand. "That's a nice thing to say, isn't it, Mama?"

Agatha nodded but frowned. "I just do what needs to be done."

After supper, Mary put on an apron and helped clear the dishes. Johan came in to the kitchen where the women were working.

"Now the rain has cleared away, it's a fine evening. I think I'll take Nicky down to watch some football practice. Unless, Mary, you would like to come along. Then I'll wait."

"No, you two go." Mary set down the tea towel and put her arms around both of them. She kissed Nicky's forehead, then kissed Johan on the lips. "Good-bye. Have fun."

Johan stood uncertainly for a moment, unaccustomed to Mary's demonstrative behaviour.

"Well, if you're sure then." Johan slipped Nicky's small sailor suit jacket on him, and carried him out.

Mary went to the living room to watch them until they were out of sight, then came back to the kitchen. "Nicky reminds me of Andréas with that jacket on. The same white-blond curls."

Agatha flinched. "Hmmph. He looks like himself. If anything, he looks like Johan at that age."

"Yes, he's a Meijer through and through. All of us kids—my two brothers and I—we all have the English genes." Mary was oblivious to the tense of 'have' versus 'had'. She went on almost dreamily. "We always had fine, strawberry blonde hair when we were children, and skin that would burn in five minutes of sun. I don't know how it is that Johan with his blond hair can still get as brown as a berry. It's a nice combination and you're right, Nicky takes after him."

After the dishes, Agatha and Mary sat for a while in the living room. Agatha read the paper while Mary sat and stared out the window. Routinely, she looked at her watch. The room was quiet aside from the loud ticking of the clock.

Mary looked around the room, feeling as though she hadn't really seen it a long time. "You miss the radio, I suppose, now that it's been confiscated."

Agatha rattled the newspaper. "I don't miss it much since the AVRO radio studio was taken over by the Germans in March. There was nothing worth listening to anymore. Between Blokzijl's Nazi propaganda and Wagner, we're better off without it."

The clock chimed seven o'clock. "Well, Mama Meijer, I'm going up. Good night." Mary came over and formally shook Agatha's hand. On impulse she bent over and kissed Agatha's cheek.

Agatha's hand moved to her cheek and she flushed. "Good night."

Mary glanced back one last time and saw her mother-in-law's hand still resting against her cheek and her face puzzled.

When Johan returned, Agatha had just made a pot of tea. Johan put Nicky down in his playpen and the boy promptly fell asleep, his thumb in his mouth and his arm curled around a small, well-worn teddy bear.

Agatha took a sip of her tea. "Well, Mary really seems to have come out of herself. The transformation is unbelievable. Can you imagine that she kissed me good-night?"

Johan coughed and sputtered before swallowing his mouthful of tea. "My goodness!"

Agatha nodded. "Yes."

Johan sat back and enjoyed his tea. "I think that it really helped her to talk to her mother for a bit today. I wish I had thought of it sooner. I think, too, that getting this anniversary of the boys' death behind her is a big thing."

"Well, I can honestly say that I actually enjoyed her company this evening, even though she was so oddly dressed up. Really, Johan, the girl often doesn't have much common sense."

"I thought she looked lovely tonight. It was nice to see." Johan set down his cup and saucer. "I better get his bottle sorted and then get this young man up to his bed." Johan lifted Nicky up and cradled him.

He murmured to the boy as they went across to the warehouse and up to their apartment. "Better days ahead, my son." The door to the bedroom was closed, and Johan moved quietly in the outer room as he undressed his young son. Nicky woke in the chilly air and cried out.

"Shhh. Mustn't wake Mama." He expertly changed the baby's diaper and dressed him in his soft blue pajamas, then sat in the rocking chair and fed the boy a bottle of warm milk and water he had prepared before coming back to the room. By the time Nicky had finished the bottle, he was almost asleep, snuffling softly. Johan picked him up again and before laying him in his own small bed, he cracked the bedroom door. It was fully dark now with the curtains pulled closed. He listened for a moment but didn't hear Mary moving.

"Mary? I'm just putting Nicky to bed. Did you want to say good night?"

No answer.

He closed the door again. "Sorry, little man. Mama must be asleep already. You'll get your kiss from her in the morning." He laid Nicky in the crib and tucked the flannel blanket around him. It was still cool at night, so he pulled the white knitted blanket over him as well. Mary's mother had knitted that when she found out that Mary was pregnant. It seemed so long ago already.

Johan started to move towards the door to go back down to the living room and his mother, then on impulse turned back to the bedroom. He slipped inside and went to the bed. He wanted to give Mary a small, light kiss. She had been so much better tonight, seeming at peace for the first time in so many months. His eyes adjusted to the dim light as he made his way to the side of the bed. He stopped. Mary wasn't there. He pulled open the curtains a crack to let the late evening light in. No, she definitely wasn't there. He opened the curtains fully and glanced around the room. There was no sign she had been there to undress. The usual scattering of hair pins on the dressing table was missing and her white nightgown was laid on the back of the chair where she had put it this morning upon rising.

Maybe she was in the bathroom. No, he recalled the open door as he passed on his way up the stairs. His brow furrowed and his heart pounded. What was going on? Perhaps she decided to go for a walk—but if she did, surely she would be home by now. Thoughts tumbled over and over in his mind. What, where, why?

He rushed from the room and was almost at the stairs when he happened to glance into the warehouse loft. In the middle of the floor he could see the legs of a toppled chair.

There shouldn't be a chair there. What's going on?

Johan felt as though his body moved without his direction. He crossed the landing and went into the warehouse, turning the corner towards the toppled chair.

"No." He moaned and grabbed for Mary's legs, trying to support her hanging body. He couldn't lift her. He couldn't reach for the rope to untie it. He had no knife to cut her down. Finally he let go and fell to his knees, crying.

"Mary, Mary, *why?*" He covered his face with his hands, his eyes burning, his throat swollen, sobbing her name.

At long last, he stood. He made his way down the stairs and across to the house. For a moment, he stopped in the kitchen and splashed water on his face, using the still-damp tea towel to dry himself, then went into the living room.

"What's wrong?" Agatha frowned. "Did you two have an argument?"

"Mary's dead, Mama." Johan broke down again as he fell onto the sofa.

"Dead? How is that possible? She was perfectly fine two hours ago." Agatha spoke in a no-nonsense voice as if to say that Johan was being foolish and must be mistaken.

"We need to call the police, I think, Mama." Johan's voice was broken.

Agatha stood. "The police? I don't understand."

"Mama, Mary has killed herself."

Agatha slapped her open hand against her leg. "That selfish, miserable girl!"

Johan rose and raked his hand through his hair. "I'll go through to the shop and telephone them now."

It was after midnight when it was finally quiet again. The police were gone. Mary was gone.

"What will I say to Nicky?" Johan sat on the sofa with his eyes closed and head back.

Agatha shook her head. "He's too young to understand. You don't have to say anything."

"I don't just mean now. I mean for the years ahead. He'll want to understand why his mother did this." Johan opened his eyes and sat up.

Agatha spoke without hesitation. "We say that his mother's heart stopped. She wasn't well. It's the truth."

"It's not the whole truth, is it?"

"It's all the truth he needs to know. What's done is done. Why upset him with things he can't change?"

"I suppose you're right." Johan was exhausted, but wasn't sure he could go upstairs, sleep in their bed.

Agatha rose. "I'm going to bed and you must also. Nicky will be awake as usual tomorrow, and you need to be strong for his sake now." Agatha's steely gaze brought Johan to his feet and propelled him towards the door.

The words were automatic. "Good night, Mama."

'Good night'? What is good about this night?

XI

Winter 1941

"Oma! Oma!" Nicky waved his fists when he saw his grandmother, bouncing on Johan's hip. He had learned the word 'Oma' and could say it very clearly now, along with the rest of his small vocabulary. The word 'Mama' had withered and faded from lack of use.

"Yes, Nicky. I'm coming." Agatha dried her hands and engulfed Nicky's two fists in her own hands. "He's cold." She reached to take the child from Johan and looked at her son. "How was it?"

"Well, it's good to see that even in these times, Sinterklaas can still make it to Amsterdam. It was fine. I think Nicky's still a bit young to understand it all, but he liked seeing the big white horse, and being around all the children in the concert hall was fun for him."

"You see? Life goes on as normal if you make an effort." Agatha nodded.

Johan was troubled. "I'm not sure I would call it normal to see all these kids lining the street in their Youth Stormer uniforms."

"There has always been scouting in one form or another, this is just the latest version." Agatha peeled the jacket and sweaters off Nicky.

"You're probably right." Johan hung up his own jacket. "I guess I'm just not in the mood for it all. Somehow it felt ominous and threatening. I was glad to come back home."

"Well, of course you were." She looked down at Nicky. "Now, young man, you sit right here in your own chair and watch Oma make the supper." She set the squirming boy into his high chair and gave him a crust of black bread to gnaw on with his six teeth.

Johan made a pot of tea and sat at the small kitchen table beside his son and watched as his mother chopped a carrot and onion for the soup. "Are those still from your own garden?"

"Yes. You didn't think I'd grow much out there, but we didn't do too badly. I still have quite a bit lying under sand in the shed out there. It's better than what can be bought in the shops." She was quite proud of the garden she had put in after the chickens had gone, all those years ago.

"At least you can shop as you like. The Jews aren't so lucky."

"There's nothing we can do about that, is there? It'll all blow over sooner or later."

"Hopefully it'll be sooner rather than later." Johan felt weary of it all. "I saw Mr. and Mrs. Rosenbloom today on my way to the parade."

"Oh yes? Were they there also?" Agatha asked without much actual interest.

"No, they weren't going to the parade. They were going to the American embassy to try and get emigration papers. You know he had his textile permit withdrawn in November. He can't make a living anymore." Johan pressed his fingers to his forehead. He had a headache after the afternoon in the noise and crowds.

"Oh yes, I remember hearing that. All Jewish textile merchants are in the same boat, it's not just him." She scooped up a bit of bread from the floor where Nicky had dropped it and blew on it to remove any dust before handing it back.

Johan was irritated. "You think it's better because he's not alone in his misery?"

"What's wrong with you? Don't you have enough to think about with your own business without thinking about someone else's?" Agatha turned to look at him, then began picking the meat off the soup bone.

Johan cocked his head and studied his mother. *She's oblivious to what's going on outside these walls.* "The Rosenbloom kids can't even go to their old school anymore."

Agatha slammed the knife down on the counter and turned to Johan with her arms crossed. Nicky dropped the soggy bit of bread again and his bottom lip began to tremble.

"Why are you so obsessed with what the Rosenblooms are doing all of a sudden? Haven't you learned yet to mind your own business? That's the way to manage through these troubles." Agatha's lips were pursed in a thin, tight line.

Nicky began to cry, a small whimper born of tiredness and upset at the tension. Agatha stepped forward to lift him out of the high chair, but Johan picked him up first.

Johan looked at his mother, his forehead wrinkled. "You *know* what's going on, you just don't care, do you?"

She pointed to the child. "I care about what's important, and so should you."

Johan turned and carried Nicky in to the living room.

Agatha could hear their voices—Johan's quiet rumble and Nicky's high-pitched squeals, happy again as his father helped to stack wooden blocks in a tower.

I won't see that boy hurt. He'll take over from Johan when the time comes and until that time he needs to be protected. I can protect him. I will protect him. Agatha knew the business would be in good future hands with Johan and Nicky, as long as Johan didn't act foolishly right now.

XII

Summer 1942

The peal of the telephone in the quiet office startled Johan out of the semi-doze he had fallen in to. It was a warm afternoon and despite having the window open along with the doors of both the shop and the factory, there wasn't so much as a breath of air slipping through to break the oppressive closeness of the afternoon.

"Hello, Meijer's." Johan made his voice sound brisk and business-like.

"Johan, it's Hank." There was a pause.

"Hank? What is it? What's going on?" Johan felt his stomach churn. Hank had never telephoned before and the thought flitted across Johan's mind as to how Hank had even found a telephone to use.

"Johan..." Hank stopped, his voice choked.

Johan stood at the desk, the receiver gripped in his hand. Through the glass wall he could see Mr. Van Loon glance up at the movement in the office. The older man's brow furrowed and he pointed to himself and then to Johan in a gesture of 'Do you want me?'

Johan shook his head. He turned his back to block out Mr. Van Loon's gaze.

"Hank, please. What is it?" Johan could hear the quiver in his own voice.

Hank tried again. "Johan...it's André."

Johan fought to keep control of his voice. "He's been hurt?"

"There was an attack on Willemsnoord. The base was hit quite badly. There were several casualties. I'm sorry, Johan, André was one of the men killed."

"Dear God." Johan was numb. It didn't seem real.

"I thought you'd want to know."

"Yes, of course. Thank you." Johan knew there was nothing else to say, but still he gripped the telephone in his hand. "How's Tiineke?"

"You know. She's trying to be strong for the kids. It's hard because they can't even have a proper funeral, so I think they're having a hard time accepting it. Andréas especially seems to be having a difficult time. Wim is stoic; he seems to have really grown up and is trying to help Tiineke, but Andréas, well, he just seems to have withdrawn." Hank paused. "There is going to be a memorial service in the Nieuwe Kerk on Saturday afternoon, just in case you and your mother want to come. Two o'clock, and then we'll have people back here to the house. You're both welcome, and I know Tiineke would like to meet Nicky, finally."

"Thank you for the information. I'll talk to Mama. I'll have to see." Johan felt he was talking about a stranger, a business acquaintance perhaps. Not André, not his own brother.

Hank's voice became brisk. "I'll have to go now. I'm using the minister's office here at the church. I just finished making the arrangements and he said I could use his telephone."

That solves that mystery. Johan caught the irrelevant fact and held it. "Yes, of course. Thank you again for letting me know." Johan's ear was hurting where he'd pressed the phone against it. "Good-bye, then." Johan began to replace the receiver, then lifted it again.

"Please tell Tiineke I'm sorry! Tell her..." But it was too late. Hank had disengaged.

Johan cradled the receiver and noticed it was wet with perspiration. His hand was cramped from gripping so hard. He stretched and flexed it a couple of times.

He turned and stood, looking out through the glass. Mr. Van Loon had been surreptitiously watching and now he came forward with a clipboard in his hand.

"Johan, do you have a minute to discuss this order?"

"Come in." Johan sat down and waved to the other chair so Mr. Van Loon sat as well.

Johan tilted his head back and looked at the ceiling. Mr. Van Loon waited without speaking. .

Finally, Johan broke the silence. "It's André."

"Oh?" Mr. Van Loon didn't prompt any further, sensing what was coming.

"He's dead." There, he'd said it. Johan was practicing before he went in to tell his mother.

Mr. Van Loon shook his head and closed his eyes for a moment. When he opened them again, they were shiny and he blinked rapidly. "Do you know what happened?"

"There was a raid on the naval base. That's all I know."

"I suppose that's enough to know." Mr. Van Loon nodded. "So much sadness in our country, now. I'm sorry for your loss. If there is anything I can do..." He trailed off, knowing there really wasn't anything that could be done to help ease Johan's pain.

"No, nothing. Unless you feel like telling my mother." Johan made a small attempt at a smile.

Mr. Van Loon licked his lips. "No, I'll leave that to you."

"Yes. Yes, I better go do it." Johan stood and walked out of the office. Perspiration trickled down his forehead, and he mopped his brow as he walked. His stomach churned and he felt lightheaded.

Agatha had just laid Nicky down for a nap. He slept in Wim's old room now, beside her own room. Johan had moved back in to his old childhood room. It was easier in the winter and saved on electricity when they were all in the same space. Johan didn't admit that he couldn't bear to go up the stairs to the warehouse anymore, where he always imagined Mary's hanging body.

His mother sat in the chair by the window, winded after her efforts climbing up and down the narrow steps. She looked up when Johan came in and frowned.

"What are you doing here? Surely you haven't finished the monthly invoices already?"

"Mama, I have some bad news to tell you."

She sighed deeply. "Don't tell me someone else who owes us money has suddenly disappeared or gone out of business? We had two like that last month and can't go on. People should pay their bills."

"No, Mama, it's not about the business."

The puzzled expression on her face remained for a moment, then cleared. She flushed, then began to pale.

"It's André, Mama. I just had a call from Hank to tell me that André's been killed in an attack at Den Helder." Johan sat on the edge of the sofa and reached out to take Agatha's hand. "I'm sorry, Mama."

She pulled her hand away abruptly and held it in a fist on her lap. "Well. And what does that mean to me?" She turned her head and stared out the window.

Johan gripped her shoulder, forcing her to look back at him. "Mama!"

"I told you as I told him on the day that he betrayed me by leaving here. He means nothing to me anymore. Nothing!" Her voice was shrill. She stood.

Johan looked up at her, his eyes wide. "Where are you going?"

"I have laundry to do." She marched out to the small room behind the kitchen, letting the door swing closed behind her.

Johan sat back on the sofa. *Should I follow her?*

He rose and called to her. "Mama, I'm going for a walk." Not waiting for her reply, he went out into the sunny afternoon. He strode quickly until he reached Vondel Park where he found a bench and sat down.

"Mary." His voice was barely above a whisper. "Where did we go wrong?"

At the sound of his voice, the ducks on the pond fluttered and settled at the far side of the water. He remembered sitting on this very bench after he had proposed to Mary. Life had been so good.

"The best days of my life." He spoke aloud. He and André had been the best of friends, he had had his beautiful girl promising to

marry him, his football career shining like a beacon ahead of him—
life was so full of promise that day.

"Thank God for Nicky." He looked up through the shady branches
to the blue sky. He suddenly yearned to see his young son, to hold
him tight and feel the downy softness of the boy's skin against his
cheek. He sighed, rose, and made his way back home. The groups
of German soldiers patrolling the area and lingering on the streets
outside of shops were like murders of black crows. They oppressed
Johan with their presence. He was exhausted by the time he reached
home again.

His mother was sitting in the living room with a damp cloth on
her forehead.

"Are you alright?"

"I'm fine. The heat has given me a headache." Agatha refolded
the cloth and put the cool side across her eyes.

Johan longed to talk about André. He wanted to remember all
the good times they had shared, and even wanted to talk about the
past few years. Why couldn't she forgive? What had André's life been
like, cut off from his family?

It's no good. She'll never talk about him again.

He turned away from her. "It must be about time for Nicky to get
up from his nap. I'll go and get him."

"Yes, do." Agatha remained in her chair and Johan glanced back
to see her press her hand against the cloth.

Upstairs, Johan sat on the edge of the bed and tickled his son
under the chin. The blue eyes opened and a big grin spread across
the boy's face.

"Papa!" Nicky was delighted to be woken by his father for a
change.

"Hello, son. How about giving your Papa a hug? I really need
one." Johan held out his arms and Nicky crawled onto his lap, reaching up to put his arms around Johan's neck. Johan breathed deeply
the slightly musky smell of the boy's damp skin. His hair was tousled
and the curls poked out in a mass of tangled silky blond tendrils.

Johan kissed Nicky's neck and held him close. Tears pricked behind his eyes and suddenly he couldn't hold them back. He squeezed his eyes shut, his forehead creased in a deep frown. Tears trickled down his cheeks, wetting Nicky's skin.

"Papa hurt?" Nicky pushed back against Johan's chest and sat on his lap, facing him. His small hand reached up to touch his father's face, his own face puzzled. He had never seen his father cry and he was frightened.

"Papa's hurt inside." Johan touched his chest. "Inside here."

Nicky leaned forward to kiss his father's shirt where Johan had indicated. "All better?"

"Almost." With an effort, he smiled at his son. "I'm going to take you to meet your cousins." Johan said it knowing the word was unknown to the child.

Nicky smiled and clambered off Johan's knees. He reached for his shorts and waved them at Johan.

Johan smiled a little more easily this time. "Life goes on, doesn't it?"

He proceeded to get Nicky dressed.

The Meijers: 1942 – 1945

I

Summer 1942

Johan hoped his bicycle wouldn't be gone by the time he returned. He locked it up amongst several others in a secluded spot behind the church. He was early and carried Nicky in his arms for a short walk along Korte Annastraat before returning to the imposing rectangular building. He was nervous about meeting Tiineke.

Johan looked down at his son. "What if she tells me to go to hell?" Immediately, he felt guilty. "Don't repeat that to Oma, alright son?"

Nicky smiled, his skin glowing and flushed from the sun and air he had gotten on the ride over from Amsterdam.

Johan lifted up his son. "Well, we might as well go in."

He carried Nicky to the door, then decided to let him walk on his own. He set the boy down and Nicky grasped two of Johan's strong fingers as they walked side by side into the church's dim interior. Johan stopped for a moment to let his eyes adjust. There was a small knot of people clustered in the first few rows. Heads turned as they heard Nicky's chatter and the *clump-clump-clump* of his clumsy footsteps. Hank rose and came to greet Johan, holding out his hand.

"It's so great you came." Hank enclosed Johan's hand with both of his. "Come, sit with me." Hank put a hand against Johan's back and gently propelled him forward.

Johan scooped up Nicky and carried him. As they reached the pew and Hank moved in to reseat himself, Tiineke turned to glance back. Her eyes were swollen and red and, as she saw Johan, her mouth opened in an 'O' of surprise. She rose and moved out of the pew to meet him.

Johan handed Nicky to Hank. "Please take him."

Hank took the child without a word. Johan opened his arms and Tiineke stepped into the embrace.

"It's so good that you're here." Johan felt her tears against his temple and his own began to fall.

"I'm sorry. So sorry." He felt himself clinging to her.

"Yes." It wasn't a time for words, for expressions of pain or recrimination. She patted his back.

I should be comforting her.

But Johan didn't know how.

Organ music started and the minister arrived. Tiineke whispered in his ear. "We'll talk later." She returned to her seat.

Johan sat down and Hank let the squirming Nicky crawl back over to his father.

Johan looked at his son. "Hush now."

Nicky nodded solemnly. He sat on Johan's lap, resting against his father's broad chest, with his thumb in his mouth. Johan knew that his mother would have automatically pulled the thumb away, but he left the child to his comfort and put his arms around him, lacing his hands together in front of the boy.

After the service was over, the small group made their way outside. The sun blazed and people blinked in the sudden brightness.

"So this is Nicky." Tiineke cradled her own baby with one arm and reached out to touch Nicky's soft curls with her free hand.

"Yes. Nicky, this is your Tante Tiineke." He looked up at Tiineke. "He's not quite sure what an aunt is, I think. He's used to the idea of 'Oom' Hank, but an uncle is quite different than an aunt."

"He's lovely. He reminds me of Andréas at that age."

The children stood clustered around Tiineke awkwardly. They were still and quiet.

Andréas stepped forward first and put out his hand. "I'm Andréas." Johan shook the boy's proffered hand.

Tiineke poked Wim and he stepped forward also to shake hands. "Hello, Oom Johan."

"Wim, you're a young man already. You're almost as tall as I am." Johan had a hard time adjusting to the thought that this tall twelve-year-old was the same little boy with whom he had played football so often.

"And here is Elsa. Come Elsa, meet your Oom Johan." Tiineke pulled the small girl forward from behind her. Elsa clutched Tiineke's skirt to avoid having to shake hands. She peeked uncertainly at him with a swath of Tiineke's skirt held in front of her like a curtain.

Johan held up his hand. "Leave her. I hope we can get to know each other over time."

Nicky squirmed and wriggled to get down and Johan set him on the sidewalk. He toddled over to see Elsa and suddenly Tiineke had both little children holding on to her leg. Elsa released her grip on Tiineke's skirt and smiled at Nicky.

Tiineke caressed the boy's curls again. "I think they'll be friends. Now, if I could walk I would say we should go back to the house for tea." She looked up at the few other people still clustered around her. "Please, friends, you're welcome to come to the house."

There was a small group of people who had remained close to Tiineke, wanting to say a few words to her. Hank's house wasn't far from the church and they slowly made their way back there. Johan carried Nicky again and talked quietly with Hank while other people walked with Tiineke.

"They are mostly neighbours." Hank nodded towards a couple who walked with Tiineke. "She hasn't made many friends since coming to Haarlem. Their life really was in Den Helder. It's been so hard for her with André so far away, and now gone forever. I suppose her life there is done now."

"I probably should be going home." Johan felt uncomfortable going back to Hank's house. He could go now, knowing he had done his duty.

"She'd be hurt if you did. Johan, you've taken the first step, that's the hard part. Come on."

Johan kept walking, pushed along as if by the tide.

Only a few people came in. Those that did seemed happy to drink someone else's tea, saving their own precious rations for themselves. Once a cup of tea was consumed, they all left until only family members remained.

Elsa sat with Nicky in a corner, playing with some of her toys. Wim and Andréas sat together nearby, Wim flipping through a book.

Tiineke rested her hand on Johan's arm. "I was so sorry to hear about Mary." Johan bit his lip and then took a breath and nodded. "Thank you. It already feels so long ago."

"We didn't hear too many details."

Johan swallowed. "No. Her heart stopped. That's the official explanation."

Tiineke's brow furrowed. "Was she ill?"

"Tiineke, if you don't mind, we're just trying to put it behind us. I know you're trying to be kind, but I just can't talk about it."

"No, I understand. I feel the same way. What else is there to say other than, 'They aren't here anymore'?" Tiineke touched his hand.

"Why haven't you visited us before, Oom Johan?" Andréas had moved closer, unobserved.

Tiineke held a finger to her lips to shush her son. "Andréas, don't be rude."

"I'm not!"

"It's alright, Tiineke. Andréas, your father and I had a sort of falling out quite a long time ago." Johan turned his hands palm-up on his lap.

Andréas scowled. "So if Papa was mad at you, then why are you here now?"

Hank jumped in. "Andréas Johannas! Now you really are being rude.

Johan put his hand on Andréas's shoulder. "I don't really think your Papa was mad at me, and in fact, I wasn't really mad at him, either."

The young face was puzzled. "I don't understand."

"It was your Oma that was mad at Papa." Tiineke pulled Andréas towards her and looped her arm around the child's waist. "Since your Oom Johan lives with your Oma, he can't really go against what she wants because then there will be big arguments in the house."

Johan nodded. "That probably sums it up."

Andréas put his hand on his mother's shoulder and continued to study his uncle. "But you're here now. Won't there be big arguments now, or is it alright now that Papa is dead?"

"Dear God, save us from curious children." Tiineke sighed before Johan could say anything and pushed Andréas away. "If you have finished your lemonade, then all you children can go outside for half an hour." She turned to Johan. "Is it alright if Nicky goes with them?"

"Yes. He never gets to play with any children, so this is a wonderful treat for him." Johan watched Elsa patiently pile up blocks for Nicky to knock down.

Tiineke stood to herd the children out the door. "Andréas, you're in charge of Nicky, and of course, Wim, you're in charge of everyone. You can go as far as the park at the end of the street, and no further. Go, now."

The children dashed from the house, leaving a vacuum of silence in their wake.

Johan could hardly meet Tiineke's eyes. "Tiineke, you're being very kind to me. Over the past few days I've been thinking over and over again about how I should have made contact. Mary told me to, I just didn't listen." He shifted his gaze to the window, then back to Tiineke. She looked steadily at him and waited until his eyes were back on hers before responding.

"André didn't blame you. In fact, he always felt responsible for leaving you in an impossible situation." Tiineke's voice was choked.

Johan leaned forward and reached for her hand. His voice was thick. "I was angry with him for a long while, because I did blame him. After a while though, I understood. Still, by then it was a habit just to stay apart."

"It was easier. Yes, I know. André understood. You were always the peacemaker in the house, but this was one argument you couldn't fix." She squeezed his hand, then gently pulled herself free from his grip.

"Your children are so handsome. Wim is the image of André." Johan needed to break the tension.

"Wim is the image in looks, but Andréas has his spirit." Hank joined in now.

"Do you think so?" Tiineke looked a little surprised by the comment. "I often thought, in fact, that he was like you, Johan. He loves to laugh and has such energy. You used to laugh so much and make *me* laugh when I first knew you."

Johan could feel a lump in his throat. "Those days are long gone."

"Isn't it funny how it goes. These past years, that's one thing I remember so clearly about André. He really enjoyed our life. I remember him laughing often, and even singing once in a while, if you can call it that." Tiineke smiled a small secret smile of remembrance.

Hank squeezed his sister's shoulder. "You did that to him, Sus. You and the children brought that out in him."

Tiineke smiled through her welling tears. "I believe you're right."

Suddenly Johan felt a fresh sadness for the loss of a brother he hardly knew. He stood up. "I better collect Nicky and head back. Let's hope the bike hasn't been confiscated or stolen by now."

"Come, we'll walk together to the park." Tiineke rose also.

Hank propelled them out the door. "You two go. I'll clear up here, and look after Marika. She's been so good to sleep through these past couple of hours, and it looks like she'll sleep on for a bit longer."

Johan took Tiineke's arm and linked it through his. "I'm very glad I came today."

"Yes, so am I. André would be pleased to know that, if nothing else, his death has brought part of his family back together again. The children would really like it if you and Nicky would come again. Elsa seems thrilled to have a young cousin, and the boys would enjoy getting some football tips from you."

"I'm sure Hank does a great job of giving football tips." Johan was not sure yet about what he wanted to do about keeping in touch.

Tiineke glanced at him and withdrew her arm, pulling away. "Look, here they are. Children!"

They came pelting over to her. She gave them each a hug, including Nicky. "Everyone alright?"

Wim stuffed his hands in his pockets. "Yes, Mama, we're alright. Can we go home now?"

"Yes. Your Oom Johan and Nicky are going back to Amsterdam now."

Andréas scuffed the ground with his toe and then looked up at Johan. "Will you come again?"

Johan put his hand on the boy's shoulder. "Would you like me to?"

Andréas tilted his head and narrowed his eyes, studying his uncle. "Wim told me that you were a famous footballer. Will you teach me?"

Johan looked at Wim. "Do you remember you and I playing football together?" He was surprised and pleased.

Wim shrugged one shoulder. "A little. Mostly I remember Papa and Oom Hank talking about you."

"Ah. Well, Andréas, I was never famous, but I probably do have a couple of moves I can dig up to teach you, if you like."

Andréas nodded. "We have practice on Wednesday afternoons. Come then."

"I'll see what I can do. It depends on how busy work is, but if I can, I will."

Satisfied with that, Andréas and Wim ran ahead and disappeared into the house. Tiineke held Elsa's hand and Johan carried Nicky. Elsa kept making faces at Nicky to make him giggle.

Tiineke was quiet as they walked together and then she stopped. She faced Johan and gave him a piercing look. "Don't let them down, Johan. The boys can't take it. Either be in their life or don't, but not halfway."

"I'm sorry, Tiineke, I didn't mean to do that." He bit his lip under her scrutiny, then took a deep breath and nodded. "I'd like to be part of your family. I want Nicky to grow up knowing his cousins. He can learn from them. Things I can't teach him, and certainly Mama can't teach him." In his mind, Johan could see Tiineke leaning down and giving each of the children a spontaneous hug, even though they had only been parted for a short time. "If I can be here Wednesday, I will be. If I can't, I'll send a note. Sound okay?"

"That's fair. It'll be good for the children to have you and Nicky in their lives. Their family is so small. It's something nice in an ugly world for them." Tiineke turned to follow as her daughter skipped ahead of them.

Johan strapped Nicky in to the seat on the front of his bike and climbed on. As he pedalled away, he felt better than he had in a long time, despite the gnawing ache in his heart left by his missing brother.

II

Spring 1943

"Kaboom! Kaboom! Five times Kaboom!" Andréas jumped and spread his arms wide each time he shouted. "Could you hear the explosions, Oom Johan?"

"Quiet now, your baby sister is sleeping." Johan tried to calm his young nephew. He didn't want any neighbors hearing anything of the conversation, even though everyone was talking about it.

Tiineke gestured for her son to be quiet. "Oom Johan's right. Settle down now, Andréas."

"Well, tell us!" Andréas sat on the floor close to Johan.

"I really couldn't hear anything. It's too far from our house, but I know someone who did hear it. It's as you said: five big explosions, and then part of the registry building fell in."

"And the Resistance injected the guards with something to put them to sleep, didn't they?" Andréas already knew all the details, but he couldn't stop talking about it.

Johan nodded. "That's right. They came in dressed as policeman, apparently."

Wim couldn't understand his brother's excitement. "I don't know why you think this was so wonderful. Twelve of the organizers were taken out to the dunes in Overveen and shot. It's not like they got away with it."

"I know they did. They were heroes. During the school holidays, I'm going to walk there and put flowers down for them." Andréas folded his arms.

"You will not!" Tiineke waggled her finger at him. "You have no idea what you're talking about. Heroes indeed! Stay away from there Andréas, I'm warning you now!" She glared at him.

"Your mother is absolutely right, Andréas. It's fine to read about these things in the newspaper, but leave it at that. Don't even talk about it outside of these walls." Johan put his hands on the boy's shoulders and looked seriously into his face.

Andréas glanced from his mother to his uncle and knew when he was beaten. "Yes, alright. I understand." He put a finger to his lips. "Loose lips sink ships."

Tiineke looked out the window, then back at Andréas. "Go on outside for a bit. The rain has stopped and you boys can take Elsa out. Why don't you see if you can find any pieces of coal. You did such a good job of that last week."

The children put on their jackets and boots. Wim's wrists and thin forearms stretched out from under his sleeves and the jacket pulled tightly against his shoulders and chest.

Johan laughed. "That Andréas. One minute he is a nine-year-old and the next minute he seems more like nineteen!"

Tiineke sighed and shook her head. "I know, it's true. Thank goodness for Wim. He's so steady and never gives me a moment of worry. His clothes are too tight and even his boots are too small, but he never complains."

When the children were safely out of earshot she stood and went to the bookshelf. Opening the world atlas, she pulled out a poorly printed paper and unfolded it. She glanced out the window to ensure no one was coming before handing it to Johan.

"Have you seen this copy of 'Trouw'?"

Johan's eyes widened in shock. "Yes, I've seen it. 'Loyalty'—it's a good name for a Resistance newspaper—but what are you doing with it? How did you get a copy?"

"Andréas brought it home the other day."

Johan looked up at Tiineke and shook his head. "Good Lord. So dangerous!"

"But look what they say! We know that all Jews are supposed to report for work camps by April tenth, but this paper is telling them not to, that their lives will be in danger. Do you believe it? Andréas had some Jewish boys in his class in Den Helder. What will they do? Andréas is so worried." Tiineke was close to tears. "The world has gone crazy."

Johan handed the paper back to Tiineke and she folded it back up and returned it to the atlas.

He lowered his voice despite being alone with Tiineke. "I don't know what to think, quite honestly. I suspect there is something to it. You hear so many rumours. I have Jewish friends as well, but they've disappeared somewhere." He motioned towards the atlas. "Be careful with that paper. I stay away from it all. I'm just not good at hiding things or lying. Even when I was making up stories to tell Mama about where I was going when I first started to come here to visit, Mama could see right through me. I was almost glad the first time I heard Nicky call you 'Tante' and then I knew I had to come clean. He doesn't have any other aunts so the moment my mother would hear him say that word, she would know the truth. She knew anyway, I'm sure. The evening I came out for Wim's semi-final match I told Mama I was going bowling with some old school chums and you should have seen the look she gave me."

Tiineke laughed, then looked startled to hear the sound. "Bowling! Have you ever even been bowling? Why would you say that? Now that sounds more like the Johan I used to know!"

Johan laughed as well. "I went bowling once. I hated it, but it was all I could come up with to explain going out at that time of day. I'm quite sure she didn't believe me."

"I can imagine. And how is it now that she knows the truth?"

"She's furious, but she doesn't say too much. She slams things around—the pots take an awful beating—and she makes up all sorts of reasons to keep Nicky from coming out with me, but other than that, she keeps pretty quiet about it."

Tiineke raised an eyebrow. "Times have changed for everyone, then."

"Yes, there was a time she would have absolutely forbidden it. You know, I think she's afraid. After losing André, she doesn't have the courage to take the chance, in case I do the same thing and leave her."

Tiineke hugged herself. "Some lessons in life have to be learned the hard way."

"Yes, I suppose so. She never imagined that André would actually leave. She's not used to being wrong."

Tiineke looked at Johan with raised eyebrows and he could read in her face that she wasn't sure if he was being sarcastic.

Johan felt defensive. "She's getting frail-looking, you know. Even she can't buy enough food anymore with all this rationing. She had some stored vegetables and that helped for a while, but they're gone now. She pretends she isn't hungry and gives her portion to Nicky and I."

"Yes, I know how it is." Tiineke rose and went to the kitchen, then returned with a bag containing a few potatoes. "Here, take this along with you. Hank has some connection to a local farmer who has been helping out a little."

After glancing inside he thrust the bag back at her. "No, absolutely not. You have more mouths to feed than we do, and by the look of Wim and Andréas, they need a lot of feeding." He set the bag down on the table when she didn't take it back. "Thank you, though. You're very kind. André was a lucky man." Johan checked his watch. "I had better be going. I never know how long I have to wait until I can get a train. It's a real nuisance not having my bike anymore."

"You'll come back for Wim's birthday? It's hard to believe he'll only be thirteen. He seems so much older with his height and serious ways." Tiineke stood to look out the window.

Johan could tell by her smile that the children were returning. "I'll do my best to make it. You know how it is..." He trailed off, not needing to explain about the hazards of travel these days.

She nodded and smiled a grim smile. "We'll hope for the best."

Johan knew Tiineke and the kids enjoyed his visits. He thought that somehow he provided a link to his brother. Once in a while he caught her looking at him, and he would realize he had said or done something in a similar way to André. He didn't mind. If it could help them cope, he was glad for it.

———

Johan didn't make it back for Wim's birthday but he sent a letter and a book entitled *A Man For The Ages* through the mail. Inside the book was a carefully inscribed name: "Property of André Meijer, 1920". There was a note with the book.

"I remember this was a real favourite of your father's. It was a bestseller at the time and it seemed to have a big effect on him. I hope you like it."

Wim clasped it to his chest. "This was Papa's." His eyes were shiny.

Tiineke tousled Wim's hair even though she knew he was getting too old for it. "Yes, that's very special, isn't it?"

"Please, can I see it?" Andréas had a small furrow on his forehead and his lips were pushed out in a jealous pout.

Wim handed the book over but kept a sharp eye on his brother. "You can hold it for a moment, but then I want it back. It's mine."

Reluctantly, Andréas handed it back after touching the inscription and opening the book to random pages. "Well, you can have it. I don't like books anyway. I'm going to be a famous footballer and finish with school as soon as I can."

Elsa glanced at it, then lost interest. "It's boring." While she liked listening to stories and enjoyed it when Tiineke read aloud from the Bible each evening, she preferred Andréas's wild entertainments. He always thought up good games.

———

"It's too hot, Andréas. I don't want to play anymore." Elsa sat down on the front step.

Andréas jumped up and down. "Come on, just a little while longer."

He kicked the football towards her and she caught it, putting it on her lap and wrapping her thin arms around the ball. She was hungry and the warm July afternoon made her tired.

Andréas turned to look up to the sky where a squadron of planes roared overhead. He shaded his eyes and as they banked towards the south, then pointed at them and nodded. "They're going to Amsterdam."

Elsa stood up and moved beside Andréas. "Will Oom Johan and Nicky be alright?" She tugged on his shirt.

Andréas answered with confidence. "Oh yes. Oom Johan will make sure."

———

Tiineke looked up from her darning when Elsa drifted into the house. "Mama, when will we see Oom Johan and Nicky again? We haven't seen them for so long."

"I know. It's hard for them to get here, but I had a letter to say that they have borrowed a bike and they are definitely coming for Andréas's big football match. They'll spend the whole day here." Tiineke stroked her daughter's hair, pushing stray wisps behind her ear.

Elsa pulled away to fling herself down on a chair. "Where's Wim? How come I couldn't go with him today?"

"He and your Oom Hank are collecting some things and you would have been in the way. Why don't you take your sister and the three of you go to the park?" She pulled her daughter to her feet.

Tiineke wanted Elsa out of the way when Hank and Wim arrived home. She didn't want to attract attention to the supplies they were bringing in to build the small hiding place. Hank had managed to hide a few materials at work they could use to build a very small room under the floor of the dining room. Technically, Wim was far too young to report in for work camps, but his height and mature look might put him at risk. Hank had also managed to acquire a radio they could listen to and hide in the space.

Elsa sighed, but obediently wheeled the baby carriage out. Tiineke could hear her outside. "Mama wants us to go to the park."

Andréas bounced the ball. "Great idea!"

Tiineke stuck her head out the door and called to them. "Andréas, don't leave your sisters alone. You stay with them and come home together."

Andréas waved an arm to show he heard, then dropped his ball and kicked it ahead of him, running along behind it. Tiineke knew from experience that this didn't mean he would pay attention, and hoped that he would do as she said. *Oh André. That boy needs a firm hand, and Hank can't manage him.* She often spoke to André. He was always with her in spirit.

The project of carving out the space beneath the floor was well underway when the children came home again.

Hank had insisted the children must know about the space, so when they came in to find the room full of dirt and cut-up floor boards, Hank sat them down.

"Now listen, this is a family secret. This hiding space is for emergencies and it could mean life or death. Do you understand me?" Hank waited for Elsa to nod solemnly and then looked to the boy.

"Yes, of course." Andréas sniffed and straightened his shoulders. "I could have been helping you."

Hank put his hand on Andréas's shoulder. "I know you could have. You're a strong young man and I know I can always rely on you, but too many people attract attention. It was safer for just Wim and I to go with our small handcart, as if we were dumping some refuse."

Andréas thawed a bit, mollified. "You can trust Elsa, too. You won't say anything will you?" He looked sternly at his young sister.

"I won't say anything." Elsa didn't add that she didn't have friends of her own, anyway. Her brothers were her friends.

By the time they sat down to their supper of potatoes, the table was back in place and the space hidden beneath a throw rug. The earth had been moved out to the back garden and spread carefully around the plants and bushes. The walls of the hiding place were supported with scraps of wood and canvas. It wouldn't be a place to spend any length of time in, but it would do for an emergency.

"Can we listen to the radio?" Andréas paced around the room with excitement.

Tiineke looked out at the evening sky. "Not until we put up the blackout curtains, so we have to wait a little longer."

They spent some time reading and then, as dusk slowly fell on the summer evening, they gathered around the kitchen table in the safety of their blacked-out home to listen to Radio Orange. Over the BBC, they heard their own Queen's voice speaking to them.

Andréas poked Elsa. "They *did* go to Amsterdam. I knew that's where the planes were going!"

Tiineke and Hank exchanged a look as they listened to the report of the bombing of Amsterdam.

"I'll try to reach Johan tomorrow. I'm sure they're fine. It sounds like the north of Amsterdam is affected, not where they are." Hank's face reflected the worry Tiineke knew was on hers.

Elsa tugged on Tiineke's sweater. "Listen, Mama, she's talking about the Princess Margriet. I wonder if she's beautiful." Elsa's face was dreamy as they listened to the story of the baby princess living in safety in Canada.

Andréas pushed his sister scornfully. "Of course she's beautiful. Princesses are."

Everyone laughed.

At the end of the broadcast there were a number of strange statements. "The cow jumped over the moon. The grass is ready for cutting. The milk is not sour." Elsa giggled to listen to them.

"They're secret messages to the underground." Hank explained as he snapped off the receiver. It was an odd-looking, pieced-together apparatus.

"It's wonderful that your friend was able to build this. Did it cost you a fortune?" Tiineke ran her hand across the top of the machine.

"Not too bad. It's worth it, just to be in touch with the world again, isn't it? Now, let's put it away into the hiding place." Hank pulled aside the rug and pried open the trapdoor, then closed off the space and covered it after putting the receiver inside. "Not a word to a soul about it, right?" He looked at each person in turn.

Solemn nods and ascensions answered him.

———

"Was Papa a good student?" Andréas had recovered from his pique at Wim receiving the book for his birthday. He had read it as well, although it had been a struggle for him. Democracy was a big subject to understand.

Johan nodded. "He was rather. I should say, he was a good student for the subjects that interested him. He loved anything that he believed could be applied to business. Mathematics, reading and writing, economics, things like that he was very good at. Sports, not good at all." Johan laughed a little, remembering André's grumbling about the mandatory physical education periods.

"Papa must have liked working in the family business." Wim chewed thoughtfully on a blade of grass. They were stretched out on the ground after having spent an hour practicing football.

"Yes, he loved it. He enjoyed meeting the customers, he liked to solve problems in his bookkeeping—there was never a stray credit or debit whenever he was done. He wasn't that good with mechanics at first, but under Mr. Van Loon's tutoring, he even became very good at that."

Andréas sat back, resting on his hands, looking down on his uncle. "Do you love it too?"

"I have to admit that I do not. Your Papa had such a skill for it all. For me, it is drudgery. I'd much rather be out here playing football." Johan smiled at his young nephew.

With a puzzled expression, Andréas studied Johan. "So why did you work there and not Papa?"

Johan sighed. Here was this thorny question again. Obviously, André hadn't discussed it all with the boys, so was it right that he now do so? Johan didn't know what to say.

"Your father and mother wanted a different life for all of you as a family. Our Mama—your Oma—was very disappointed with that choice and because she was angry with your Papa, they didn't speak again. Since the business had to continue, I stepped in and took your Papa's place. Come now, break time is over. Let me show you this move that every striker should know." He sprung up and started dancing forward with the ball.

"Hey, you fellows!" A German soldier called over to them. "How about a little game, you three against us?" The German waved to include himself and a second solder. He smiled in a friendly way, his blond hair and suntanned face giving him the appearance of a happy young man on holiday. He was already rolling up his uniform shirt sleeves in anticipation. The other soldier looked younger and clapped his hands, grinning at Johan and the boys.

Andréas had been holding the ball in his hands and he now dropped it to the ground. "I'm going home." His eyes narrowed and he pulled his brows and mouth into a fierce scowl.

Johan rested his hand on Andréas's shoulder. "Wait, listen now, we don't want to upset them."

"I am not playing with *them*." Andréas stood with his feet planted, arms crossed across his chest.

"Come boys!" The soldier waved his arm in a 'come on' gesture.

"You're not going to let these guys chase you away, are you?" Wim faced his brother, goading him just a little.

Andréas's face flushed dark. He stooped to pick up the ball.

"No way."

Johan flashed a grateful look to Wim. He walked forward and spoke briefly to the soldiers to outline the pitch and goals.

The soldiers played well, but for them it was a diversion on a boring afternoon. For Andréas, Wim, and Johan, it was an outlet. They played with an intensity and drive with which the Germans couldn't compete. Finally, the German who had first suggested the game put up his hands.

"You have the game." He laughed. "Your sons are very good. They play as men."

"My nephews." Johan corrected. "Yes, they do."

"Thank you for the game." The second soldier bowed his head politely to the boys.

"We have to go." Wim put his hand on his brother's shoulder, turning him from where he stood, glaring.

"Good afternoon." Johan turned to follow his nephews. The sport was won, but it felt like a hollow victory.

III

Fall 1943

"**M**ama, you need to eat something. You can't keep giving your portion to Nicky."

Agatha's hair was completely silver-grey now. The ramrod posture she had always maintained was gone although she still carried her chin in the air. Her lips were thin and bloodless and her skin looked sallow and stretched across her high cheekbones.

"I do eat. Nicky is a growing boy, though, and needs more than I do."

Johan didn't have to look in the mirror to know he too had lost weight. His belt was cinched tighter than it had been since he was a teenager. He sighed and didn't say anything more. He was glad that three-year-old Nicky still had a look of general good health. He was small for his age, but aside from that, he was happy and healthy, unlike some of the other children in the half-day pre-school that he attended twice a week. The church-run school gave the children a glass of milk, which was part of the reason it was so well-attended.

Agatha rose, then paused before picking up her empty plate. "I heard that men who join the Landwacht get special privileges."

Johan glanced at her across the sparse dinner table. "You aren't suggesting I join the NSB? You know that's the Dutch Nazi party, don't you?" He couldn't believe what he was hearing.

She looked down and gathered up the rest of the plates. "I'm not suggesting anything. I'm just making conversation."

Johan spoke through clenched teeth. "Rationing is everywhere. We're all equally hungry, whatever the political party."

After his mother retreated to the kitchen, Johan sat watching his young son. He stood and picked Nicky up just to hold him for a moment. They stood in front of the window and looked out at the rain falling in the last of the muddy grey light. A woman and two children pushed a wooden cart along the road. They were all wet and pushed slowly. The young boy trailed behind the cart, holding it with one hand, barely lifting his feet. He wasn't pushing so much as holding it as a blind man might stretch out his arm to hold the shoulder of the man in front of him. The woman's legs were bare and in the bleak light of dusk, Johan imagined they looked blue with cold. Between the woman and the girl, who looked about thirteen years of age, they struggled to guide the awkward wooden cart, oblivious of the deep puddles they splashed through. The woman's headscarf was soaked through and clung to her skull, making her look sleek and feral. The girl had a hooded rain coat on, although it was too large for her. Johan knew instinctively that the coat belonged to the mother.

The family were foragers who most likely had travelled a long distance during the day simply to find enough food, coals, or wood to keep them going. They and those like them were a common sight these days. As the trio passed the window where Johan stood in the gloom, hugging Nicky, the boy outside turned his head towards the window for a moment. Johan shrank back, even though he knew he probably wasn't really visible in the darkness of the room. He held Nicky closer for a moment, feeling the warmth of his son against him.

Where will it end? What will become of you? Johan shivered as he felt the weight of his responsibility. *How do I keep you safe and teach you right and wrong in this crazy world?*

"Dark time, Papa." Nicky squirmed down out of Johan's arms so he could go around the room, pulling closed the heavy drapes. Nicky lisped a popular little song that reminded and encouraged people to black out their homes. Together, Johan and Nicky drew the drapes, closing out the sight of the wretched family making their way up the street.

Once the curtains were drawn, they went back into the kitchen, where Agatha waited.

"Mama, I know you are just trying to look after things, as you've always done." Johan put his hand over hers as she stood staring out of the kitchen window, resting her hands on the counter for support.

"I don't know what to do anymore. I have money in the bank, but can't buy the food we need." Her voice was husky with anger and frustration. They walked together back to the living room.

"I know. I'm going out to see Hank on the weekend. Being out in Haarlem, he seems to have some contacts with access to food. He told me he can get some potatoes and bread for us. He probably has friends who are farmers out there." Johan's voice was soft.

"Hank. So now that family is to be our support, is it?" Agatha's tone was bitter.

Johan stepped in front of her and tilted her chin with his fingers to force her to look him in the eye. "Mama, there's nothing wrong with Hank, and if he can help us, I am glad to take the help."

"And *her*—I suppose she'll be happy to help me. That will make her feel good." Agatha pulled away from him.

"Tiineke has enough to think about looking after her own family. This is between Hank and I." Johan sighed and shook his head. "Mama, Sinterklaas is coming up. Let's try to make a small celebration for ourselves here. We need to keep things as normal as possible, isn't that what you're always saying?"

"I don't like you seeing them. Yes, if we can get some help with food, fine, and I have the money to pay, don't forget. But for the rest, all the time that you spend with them, I don't like it and it is confusing for Nicky." Agatha had voiced this point of view before, but now there was an air of desperation in her voice.

"Mama, I'm not going to stop seeing André's family. I think it helps the boys for me to be around a little bit."

"Why? They have Hank. He seems to be able to do everything for them, so why do they need you?" Agatha waved her hand dismissively.

"I remind them of their father. Hank can't give them that. I tell them stories of when André and I were young. I talk about you and Papa."

Agatha snorted. "I can just imagine."

"Mama, I tell them about the business and how you and Papa built it up. I tell them about how you continued to make a go of things, even after Papa died, just as they are experiencing now. I think it helps them and I intend to keep going to visit when I can. It really isn't often anymore with the way transportation is, so don't make a big fuss."

"I tell you—"

"And I'm telling you, don't go on about it." Johan stood. "We're going to bed. Come, son."

Johan held out his hand to Nicky and they left the room without a 'good night' from Agatha.

———

"Papers!" The soldier snapped at Johan while another stood by with his rifle at the ready.

Johan pulled out his wallet and showed them his identity card.

"What is the purpose of your travel to Haarlem this morning? Why do you have all this material with you? Textiles are rationed."

The soldier barked out his questions and comments without giving Johan time to answer. He pushed a sausage-shaped finger into the small bolt of fabric Johan carried, nearly causing Johan to drop it on the wet cobbled street. Beside them, the waiting bus belched black diesel fumes.

"I have a special permit as a textile merchant. I do business with the government. I'm going to a meeting in Haarlem." Johan told the lie and hoped he wouldn't be questioned too much further. He knew he wasn't a skilled liar.

The soldier fingered the fabric, more gently this time, as if he would like to have it. He glanced at his partner and saw him watching through narrowed eyes. Johan knew that if this soldier was on his own, he would have taken some or all of the material.

Finally, he barked again. "Pass!"

Johan mounted the bus, sitting down with relief.

After three years, he still couldn't get used to all the soldiers with their loud, aggressive voices, yelling and prodding people with fingers and rifles. It was getting worse. As the Resistance movement grew, retaliations and general aggressiveness from the Germans escalated as well. No one, however innocent, was safe. Anyone could be in the wrong place at the wrong time, Johan knew.

In Haarlem, he walked with his bundle under his arm, moving briskly along Jansweg.

"Oom Johan's here!" Andréas had been watching for him and called out happily as he opened the front door.

Johan shook hands with Hank and kissed Tiineke on the cheek. "I know I'm a little early with Sinterklaas, but here you go, Tiineke. I thought you might be able to make something with this for the girls." He handed her the bolt.

"Thank you Johan. It's perfect. The girls never get anything new because I need to use all my ration coupons keeping the boys in clothes. Elsa, won't you love a dress made of this?" Tiineke showed the material to the little girl hovering at her side.

"Oh, Oom Johan! It's so beautiful!" Elsa's eyes shone.

Johan turned to Wim and Andréas with a smile.

"What's this in my pocket?" He pulled out a small wooden box. "Look, it unfolds." Johan opened the catch and emptied the small game pieces on the table, then flipped over the wooden box to reveal the chess board.

"It looks old." Wim fingered the small, finely carved pieces.

"This set belonged to your Papa and I. We would take this out with us sometimes when we made a bicycle trip for an afternoon. We had some nice times with a quiet game of chess by the side of a river or in a park."

Andréas picked up one of the castle pieces and turned it over in his hand. "Will you teach us to play?"

Johan was surprised. "Didn't your Papa teach you?"

"He taught me, but it was a long time ago and I don't really remember. I think the chess set was left in Den Helder." Wim picked up a black and a white knight and waved them in a mock battle against each other in the air. He nodded to his brother. "You always wanted to play cards or go outside for football."

Andréas put the castle down and sat at the table. "Well, I want to learn now."

Johan spent the afternoon teaching the boys about the game of chess.

"It's about strategy. You need to think ahead to imagine what your opponent might do if you do this or that. You have to see that if you move your knight this way, then Wim will probably use his queen to take it. That might be alright though, as a sacrifice, because then you can use your queen to take his, right? Sometimes the sacrifice is worth it for the achievement of the greater good or strategy." Johan moved the pieces around the board, explaining the moves. After a while he left Andréas and Wim alone to play together.

"He really catches on fast, doesn't he?" Johan nodded at Andréas.

Hank watched the boys before turning back to Johan. "Oh yes. They're both very clever. If Andréas sets his mind to something, there's no stopping him. Wim is more methodical in his approach to life, whereas Andréas is passionate. He flares up like a fire when he is interested and then moves on to something new, where Wim will stick to it more."

They had walked out to the kitchen and now Hank took out a canvas bag from under the sink and handed it to Johan.

"Apples, potatoes, carrots, and bread." Johan peered in the bag, inhaling the delicious scent of the produce. "I can't take all of this. There are only the three of us."

"Actually, Andréas brought home the potatoes—don't ask, I have no idea where he got them. As well, I'm lucky. I have some good contacts and sometimes I can get more than other times. This was a good week, so take it. I don't know when I'll see you again, so you'll have to make it last."

"Mama is an expert at making things stretch. Between this and the ration coupons, we'll have plenty for a good long time. It'll really make a difference. Thank you, Hank."

Hank leaned back against the kitchen counter. "How is your mother?"

"She's alright. She's really showing her age. She's good with Nicky, though. I don't know where I'd be without her to look after him. He adores her, so for the most part, I leave her to look after him. I know it brings her happiness."

"She could enjoy a house full of grandchildren if she wanted." Hank cocked his head as the sound of clicking chess pieces and murmur of voices filtered back to the kitchen.

"I know. She can be a hard woman." Johan shook his head.

Johan stopped at the door before leaving to give each person a hug. "I don't know when I can get back, so enjoy Sinterklaas and I'll see you when I see you." He clasped Wim. "You're so tall now. I'm sure you're just about the same height your Papa was."

The thirteen-year-old awkwardly hugged him in return.

"And you, mister. I'll look forward to a good game of chess with you next time, alright?" Johan was surprised at the fierce hug Andréas gave him. His heart squeezed as he hugged him back. Johan knew that, for Andréas, he was a surrogate father and he liked the feeling. He was proud of this bright, energetic boy.

"Bring Nicky next time!" Elsa demanded as Johan hoisted her up for a big hug.

"I'll do my best. Thank you again for this." Johan held up the bag of food with his left hand as he shook hands with Hank.

"No problem. We'll be in touch." Hank clasped Johan's shoulder.

"Johan, thank you for the fabric. We'll see you next time." Tiineke gave Johan a quick hug, then closed the door behind him as Johan set off towards the bus station and home.

IV

Spring 1944

"Americans bomb Nijmegen!" The newspapers screamed the story. *"Eight Hundred Dead!"*

"The Nazis are making the most of this, aren't they?" Hank threw the paper down in disgust.

"God, it's an awful thing." Johan shook his head. "Did they do it on purpose, do you think? What would be the point in that?"

"I'm sure not." Hank automatically lowered his voice.

They were sitting in a small café in Halfweg. As the name indicated, the small village was halfway between Haarlem and Amsterdam. They had each taken the electric tram to the village and met in the café.

"I heard on Radio Orange that the Americans made a mistake. They couldn't see because of some cloud cover. They thought they were over Germany."

Johan lifted an eyebrow when Hank said he had listened to Radio Orange, but didn't ask any questions. He was just grateful Hank seemed to have contacts that he and his mother didn't have.

"Hank, these contributions are making all the difference for us. I can't tell you how much I appreciate the help." Johan tipped his head to indicate the canvas bag between his feet.

"I know. Things are getting desperate, especially for you folks in the city." Hank nodded.

"They fenced off Vondel Park now, you know. People were cutting down the trees for fuel. It is damned cold in the house these days. Nicky goes around bundled up in so many layers, he can hardly move. My mother has him looking like some little roly-poly clown. It's only at night when you peel the layers off like an onion that you see how thin he actually is." Johan could feel a lump form in his throat.

"It's the same here. Wim and Andréas go everyday along the train tracks, along with everyone else, and look for fragments of coal. They're out there early in the morning before school. There have been some pretty fierce fights over any bits that are found. You see grown men fighting with women or children. It's really awful. People are doing whatever they have to, just to survive. I think it's why we hear of so many resistance fighters being captured. Neighbors turn in neighbors for the promise of some food or fuel. We're living in impossible times." Hank blinked and stopped talking, taking a quick look around him.

Following Hank's lead, Johan glanced around as well. "I better get back. Mama is terrified every time I leave the house these days. I never tell her when I'm meeting you because I think she'd have a heart attack while she was waiting for me to come back. She thinks I'm just out for a walk."

Hank laughed. "So you think. Don't kid yourself. Your mother always knows what's going on and is always fully in charge, whether you admit it or not."

Johan laughed as well. "You're probably right."

"So we're agreed that next time you'll come out to the house? I don't like meeting out in the open like this. People see you with a sack of anything and you become a target." Hank stood and narrowed his eyes as he studied the people around them.

"Yes, of course. I'll just make an arrangement that I'll stay overnight. Getting back before curfew could be a problem." Johan put the bag against his chest and buttoned his overcoat over it. He held in in place with his left arm pressed against his stomach. "Listen, I'm really grateful that you can manage to help out like this. The rations just don't go very far these days, do they?"

Hank patted Johan's shoulder. "As long as we have anything to share, we'll share it."

They shook hands at the tram stop and Johan climbed aboard. He looked out the window as they pulled away and watched Hank cross the street to his own stop. Hank looked thin, despite the long wool coat he wore. Johan saw Hank tuck his scarf tighter against his throat, stuff his hands into his deep pockets and lean against the post as he settled to wait for his own tram. He had a shift at the gas works that evening and would probably go directly there now. Johan knew that Hank was lucky to still have two shifts a week. Homes these days were only allowed gas for two hours a day.

———

The weeks passed, although winter seemed endless. Snow and freezing rain made the poorly heated homes feel even colder.

"Hello, hello!" Johan forced some energy in to his voice.

Tiineke could see in a glance that Johan was weary after the journey from Amsterdam on this miserable March day. "Shall I make you some ersatz coffee?"

Johan pulled a small face. "No, thank you. I'll leave it for now. You're in the middle of a game. Don't let me interrupt, I'll just sit and watch for a bit. Hank's not home yet?"

Resuming her seat at the table, Tiineke shook her head. "No. He should be here in another hour or so."

Johan sat on the sofa and leaned back, closing his eyes and starting to doze. Tiineke put her finger to her lips to let the children know they should let their uncle sleep.

The weak winter sun gave them just enough light to finish their card game. Tiineke didn't feel like playing cards, but it took their minds off the cold and kept the children inside, where it was safe. She didn't like it when the boys were off wandering by themselves. Tiineke glanced over to the sofa where Marika was asleep, wrapped in a warm woollen blanket.

"Yes!" Elsa snatched the card Andréas had just discarded.

Renny deGroot

Tiineke frowned at Elsa and held her finger up. "Shh."

Wim chuckled at Elsa's delight. "You don't have much of a poker face, do you?"

Elsa pouted. "We aren't playing poker."

Andréas squeezed his sister's hand. "That's right, we aren't. I like it when you laugh."

Elsa gave him a big grin in reward.

Rap-rap-rap. The sound of someone knocking on the kitchen window shocked them all, then Tiineke ran to the window and swung it open. Johan had awoken with a start, disoriented, but he quickly followed Tiineke into the kitchen.

A young boy stood outside the window. "*Ratzia!*" And then he dashed away without waiting for an answer or giving more information. Tiineke heard his urgent message a few houses down again as she was closing the window. "*Ratzia!*" The boy dashed along the back gardens, giving his warning where he knew young men and boys lived.

A raid! These raids were commonplace now. The Germans would target a street or neighbourhood and sweep through like locusts, searching for radios, hidden Jews, or young men to send to labour camps.

"Quickly!" Tiineke ran back to the living room. The children were already pulling the trap door open and Wim was folding himself down inside the hiding place. The radio was already there, kept there any time it wasn't being used. There was a small sack of potatoes there also, and Wim didn't have much room, but quickly settled himself without comment.

Johan helped as they flung the rug back across the trapdoor and Tiineke, Andréas, and Elsa went back to their card game. Johan took Wim's spot at the table. They heard the clang and clatter of a heavy metal truck stop outside the door and the distinctive *clump-clump* of many boots landing on the pavement as men jumped down from the back of the truck.

Tiineke's heart was in her throat, waiting for the bang on the door, and even though she was expecting it, she jumped when it came.

Bang-bang-bang. "Open the door."

"Stay here." Tiineke held her hand up, pinning Andréas and Elsa in their seats with her look.

Johan stood back with the children. Tiineke threw once more glance at her brother-in-law, knowing this was his first raid.

She answered the door. "Yes, sir?"

The Nazi officer stepped in to the room. His mouse-grey wool uniform smelled damp and musty. The peaked cap was incongruously crisp and new-looking and he wore it at a rigid angle that made him look even taller than he was. His high turned-back cuffs made the wrists and hands that held an official piece of paper look almost delicate.

He moved further inside to make room for the three soldiers who accompanied him. They took up positions behind their officer like a row of crows, standing silently with only their eyes flicking around the room as they waited for him to speak.

The officer barked. "Names?"

"I'm Tiineke Meijer, and these are my children." Tiineke waved in the direction of Andréas and Elsa, ignoring, for the moment, the baby, who was beginning to whimper on the sofa.

"I'm Johan Meijer, Mrs. Meijer's brother-in-law. I live in Amsterdam, but am visiting for a couple of days." A frown crossed the officer's face and Johan stopped talking.

The officer stepped closer to the table where the two children sat, pale and still. Elsa looked only at her mother, her large blue eyes filled with tears of fear. She trembled as if she were cold.

Andréas stared up at the officer, making eye contact defiantly.

Please don't say anything. She knew how much Andréas hated the Germans. *Don't be rude!* She looked at her son, hoping to transmit her thoughts to him, but he refused to look at her.

"Names?" The officer barked again to the children. Tiineke took a breath to answer, but the officer held up his hand to stop her from speaking, instead snapping at the children. "Well?"

Andréas answered smartly. "Andréas Johannes Meijer."

"Elsa." The little girl's voice was barely above a whisper.

Dear God, he was going to ask where Wim was. They had practiced for this very thing. He was visiting his grandmother in Amsterdam. Would that be questioned now if Johan was here? Tiineke's mind raced. *He's only fourteen, though. Why would they be looking for Wim specifically? He isn't old enough that he should be reporting in for a work camp.*

Maybe they're looking for Hank.

Oh dear God, no! She had sometimes wondered how Hank came to have the food and other little extras he brought home. Oh God, all that black market activity. *What have you done, Hank?*

"Papers!" The officer turned back to Tiineke. He was being very thorough. She was surprised they hadn't stormed through the rest of the house yet, in search of Hank.

With shaking hands, she pulled the identity papers for all of them from her handbag and handed them over. Marika was crying now and Tiineke picked up the baby and handed her to Elsa.

"Hold her, please."

Elsa seemed grateful to be holding her baby sister. Tiineke heard her murmuring softly to soothe the baby, and Marika's cries subsided into a soft snuffling.

Johan also pulled out his identity papers to show who he was and that he was considered 'essential' to the German war effort with his work at Meijer's.

The grim, square-jawed officer gave Johan's papers a cursory glance and handed them back. He spent much more time studying Tiineke's identity cards and comparing them to his official piece of paper. He turned and nodded to the soldiers. One stepped forward in front of Tiineke to separate her from her children. She frowned. Johan automatically moved to her side and put his arm around her shoulder. The soldier stepped back to guard both of them.

"What—" And then Tiineke screamed as the two other soldiers stepped over to Andréas. They roughly pulled him to his feet to stand in front of the officer.

"Andréas Johannes Meijer, you are charged with spying..." The rest of the words were lost as Tiineke screamed.

"No! No! No! He's a boy, just a boy. He isn't guilty of anything!"

Johan reached out a hand in the direction of his nephew. "There must be some mistake!"

The officer gestured with his head, and looked at his men. "Take him outside."

Elsa cried and reached out to cling to Andréas's shirt. "Andréas!"

Her small hand was pried loose and the two soldiers gripped Andréas's arms.

"Be brave, Elsa." Andréas touched his sister's cheek before he was pulled away.

"No, no, no!" Tiineke tried to push past the guard in front of her. Her way was barred. He lifted his rifle and aimed it at Tiineke and Johan.

Johan kept his arm around Tiineke. Tiineke could feel he was as helpless as her. *I wish Hank were here. He would know what to do!*

"Where are you taking him?" Tiineke pulled against Johan's grip. The soldiers had Andréas outside now.

Elsa sat sobbing and clinging to Marika, who wailed in sympathy.

The soldier guarding Tiineke stepped back a few paces towards the door, still training his weapon at her head.

"*Where are you taking him?*" She lunged away from Johan and followed the soldier until they were both at the door. She peered past him into the darkness outside. The blacked-out headlamps of the truck gave off a dim, ghostly light. She could just make out that they had lifted him into the back of the truck. The two soldiers had set their rifles on the floor of the truck and were in the process of climbing in themselves.

In the pale light Tiineke could see Andréas's small, white face looking in her direction. Did she see his hand rise in a farewell wave? It was impossible to see through the darkness and her tears.

Suddenly, quick as a fox, Andréas leapt out of the truck again. He leapt as only a ten-year-old boy could leap—over the shoulders of the two surprised soldiers, twisting in mid-air to land in a crouch.

Then he was running. He ran, dodging, zig-zagging down the street. There was a stunned silence, then the head officer started shouting at the soldiers.

"Get him, you idiots! The prisoner is escaping!"

One of the soldiers lifted his rifle, then the other did as well. Shots rang out, the sound of the gunfire shocking in the stillness of the night. A woman screamed and flattened herself against the wall of a shop a few doors away. People took cover, doors slamming in their haste to get inside.

"Andréas. Andréas." Tiineke moaned. Her heart was pounding and she would throw up in a minute, she knew.

The soldier who had been guarding Tiineke and Johan ran to the cab of the truck and switched on a spotlight. The bright light revealed the street. Tiineke, unguarded now, ran out into the street as well.

"No!" She ran with Johan a step behind her.

One of the soldiers got there before them. He knelt and turned over the small, crumpled boy. Andréas was covered in blood, his face slack and pale. Tiineke threw herself down on the wet, dirty cobblestones of the street. The soldier stood up, turned, and walked back to report to the officer.

"Dead, sir."

The officer made a note on his form. "Shot while trying to escape."

He gestured to his men to get back in the truck. "It doesn't matter. He would have been executed anyway." He got into the passenger side of the cab and waved his hand at the driver to move on. The truck drove slowly around Tiineke where she knelt in the street, sobbing and cradling the boy in her arms. The lumbering truck disappeared around the corner and the night slowly fell quiet again, except for the sound of Tiineke's keening.

Johan crouched beside Tiineke. He tried to raise her and she shook him off. He knelt beside her in the mud and she turned to him then, leaving Andréas's head resting in her lap. She balled up her fists and hammered on Johan's chest.

"How could this happen? Why? He's only a little boy." She sobbed.

Johan caught her beating fists and held them gently against his chest. Slowly, she stopped fighting him and, exhausted, dropped her head, resting it against his chest. Johan released her hands.

"Why, why, why." She saw him as he was only moments ago, laughing with his sister. *Oh André, I've only just barely survived you leaving me. I can't do this. I just can't.*

"Come, let's get him inside." Johan stood up, trying to raise Tiineke again.

She stayed where she was, rocking and hugging Andréas's small body to her. Suddenly Wim was there as well.

"Mama. Oh my God, Mama." Wim was crying. Elsa stood at the door. She had put Marika into her carriage and the baby was wailing from inside the house.

"I didn't know what was going on. I heard a lot of noise but I stayed quiet, the way you told me to." Wim hands were before his mouth as he sobbed. "I should have come out. Maybe I could have saved him."

Tiineke finally looked up. "No. Then I would have had two dead sons." She lifted a hand to him. "Help me."

Wim helped his mother up while Johan picked up the small, inert body.

Tiineke shivered violently. Wet dirt clung to her legs and skirt. Her hands and cardigan were covered in blood. Her arms hung at her sides as Wim gripped her around the waist and propelled her towards the house.

The neighbors were coming out now, slipping out of their homes again like pale rabbits from their warrens.

The woman next door called to them. "I'm so sorry. He was a fine boy."

"Thank you." Tiineke's voice was formal. They reached the front door. The woman took a step as if to come into the house, but Tiineke didn't want anyone else. Perhaps this neighbour said something to cause the Nazis to come for Andréas. Who was a friend and who wasn't? Tiineke didn't know anymore.

Elsa threw herself, sobbing, against her mother, oblivious to the blood staining her mother's sweater. Tiineke gently pulled away. She looked at her hands and went to the kitchen to wash them. She peeled off her cardigan and threw it in the kitchen garbage, then scrubbed her hands and arms in the ice cold water. Hot water was a luxury they seldom used anymore. Tiineke took the pot scrubber and scoured her hands and nails. Her hands took on a raw, angry, red colour and still Tiineke rubbed and scoured them.

"Mama, I can't get Marika to stop crying." Elsa stood at her mother's elbow.

"I'm coming now." Tiineke finally dried her hands on the blue checked tea towel.

Tiineke looked at Elsa, then took the damp tea towel and wiped the child's cheek. The towel came away red, but Elsa's face was clean again. Tiineke dropped the towel into the garbage on top of her cardigan. They went together to the living room and Tiineke picked up Marika. Almost immediately the crying slowed down and she hiccupped a few times before subsiding into silence.

"Shh, you're alright. You're alright."

Wim knelt on the floor beside the sofa where Johan had placed Andréas's body. He rested his forehead on the edge of the cushion so his curls mingled with Andréas's.

My boys are so beautiful. Tiineke sat down in silence in the armchair and tucked Marika in the crook of one arm, leaving room for Elsa to climb on her lap and nestle herself under the other arm. Tiineke continued to shiver as she sat there, looking in silence at her sons.

Johan sat on a chair at the table a little distance from the family. He looked down at the table, not able to watch the silent anguish of the mother and siblings.

Johan's eyes fell on the deck of cards, Andréas's hand laid down as though he would resume playing in a moment. Johan felt the lump in his throat rise and the hot tears began. He buried his face in his hands and cried. Images of the boy's proud defiance as he stood between the two towering soldiers returned to him, and Johan felt the child had known what was coming. His concern at the time had been not for himself, but for his young sister. His last moments had been to give her words of comfort.

Finally Johan rose and got two blankets. One he laid over Andréas, leaving his face uncovered, and the other he tucked around

Tiineke and the girls. Both the girls were asleep and Andréas looked as though he lay sleeping under the blanket. Wim sat on the floor with his back resting against the chair where his mother sat. The four of them made a small human island. Still no one spoke. Words were not big enough to capture the horror of what had happened. Johan returned to his chair and waited.

The door burst open.

"Dear God, what's happened?" Hank stormed into the house. "I met Mrs. Van Rood on the corner and all she said was 'hurry home' and 'it's so awful'. I could hardly understand her through her crying."

Wim stood now and put his arms around his uncle. "I should have helped. I was hiding. I should have been doing something." He moaned as he wept. It was as though with Hank's entrance, the spell was broken, the numbness replaced by a storm. Hank patted Wim's back, then gently pushed him away.

"I'm sorry, Hank. Andréas has been shot." Johan reached out and gripped Hank's arm.

"How can that be? Where is the doctor?" Words tumbled from Hank as he crossed to where Andréas was lying. Hank knelt and put his hands on Andréas's cheeks. The marble-like cold told him.

"No." The protest came as a long groan. He turned to his sister who still sat, stunned and silent.

Johan picked up Elsa from Tiineke's lap. The child was awake and crying again. Tiineke looked up at her brother and finally stood, slowly, as though she had aged twenty years in the past hour. She still held her youngest daughter, who was gazing around solemnly.

"Oh Hank." It was all Tiineke could manage.

Then Hank had his sister, along with the baby, engulfed in his embrace, and Tiineke started to sob. She rested her forehead against his shoulder and cried.

Johan went in to the kitchen with Elsa. "Will you help me make some tea for your mother?"

Distracted momentarily, Elsa allowed Johan to put her down and she started to assemble cups and saucers. Johan closed the blackout curtains in the kitchen and lit the stove, using a little of the precious gas to boil water. He made a pot of tea, and with Elsa's help, took it back to the living room.

He poured a cup for Tiineke. "I wish I had some brandy to put in it."

"No. This is fine. Thank you, Johan." With the release of her tears, she was a little calmer again. Her face wasn't quite as white. Already, she was coming back to realize she still had three other children who needed her.

With the tea came the explanations to Hank, the horror of the retelling a catharsis for them all. During the night, they alternated between crying and calm and finally, exhausted, they got ready for bed.

Tiineke realized that Andréas was laying on the couch which had been intended for Johan's bed. She took a deep breath. "Do you want to sleep in Andréas's bed?"

"No, no! I'll be fine here in the big chair. It's only a couple of hours until day anyway."

And so Johan sat with the body of his nephew through the night, not sleeping. Just thinking. Remembering the boy, and the boy's father, and from there, remembering more. He thought about his and André's boyhood years. When he had been Andréas's age, all he could think about was football, cycling, and perhaps school. How did Andréas go from those things to being a spy? He had no doubt that it was true. The Resistance would have been able to use a boy like Andréas to go where adults couldn't go without rousing suspicion.

As morning broke, Johan went around and opened the heavy curtains. Pale sunlight filtered through the windows and lay on Andréas's waxy face. The illusion of sleep had passed.

"I'll run out and get the minister. He'll help to make the arrangements." Hank had walked into the room quietly while Johan stood, looking down at his nephew.

"Yes, alright. I'll make a bit of breakfast, shall I?" Johan felt helpless.

"Leave it for a bit. It'll give Tiineke something to do when she gets up." As he was about to leave, Hank turned back to Johan. "Will I have the minister call your mother as well?"

"Would he?" Johan felt some relief. He was in no mood to talk to his mother at the moment.

"Yes, I'm sure he will." Hank put on his jacket and left, closing the door softly behind him.

By midday, the parade of people had come and gone. The minister had led them in prayers, and Andréas's body had been taken, arrangements for the funeral made. The family sat at the table eating some black, gritty bread with a thin smear of jam. Elsa was making small figures with her fingers to make Marika laugh.

"Here is a bunny, hop, hop, hop." She held two fingers up like rabbit ears and bounced her hand along the table in front of Marika, both of them giggling. The others watched in silence.

Children are resilient.

In the quiet aftermath of the people, the knock on the kitchen door sounded loud.

Tiineke held up her hand. "I can't take anymore kind neighbors."

"Stay, I'll get it. They don't know me. I can be rude and tell them to go away without a problem." Johan gently pressed Tiineke back into her chair as he rose.

He opened the kitchen door but there was no one there. He looked down and saw a large basket on the step. Looking up and down through the back gardens again to be sure, he didn't see anyone.

"There is no one there, but someone has left this." Johan carried the heavy basket in and set it on the table.

"There's a note." Tiineke took the note out of the sealed envelope and opened it. "'*Your son was a good man. He'll be missed. RVV*'"

Johan shook his head and furrowed his brow. "RVV?"

Hank nodded. "It stands for 'de Raad van het Verzet.' 'The Council of the Resistance'. They're quite active around here. I've heard of them. They do a lot of good work."

Johan chewed his top lip. "I feel like I live in a different world in our little enclave in Amsterdam."

Hank's voice was sharp and face grim. "Don't kid yourself. The groups are everywhere and probably just as active right next door to your Meijer's."

Wim had opened the basket and was pulling out the contents. "A sausage and look—half a cheese!" They hadn't seen food like this in a very long time.

Tiineke pushed it away from her and rose to walk to the window. "Blood money." She gazed out the window blindly. "I don't want it."

Hank went to her and put an arm around her shoulder. "Did you really read the note Tiineke? He 'was a good *man*' it says, and they're right. He was more of a man than many twice and three times his age. He made his own choices."

"That's the point. He wasn't a man, he was just a boy. He did things for a lark, not knowing where they could lead!" She sobbed. "They used his spirit of adventure, they took advantage of him!"

Johan took out his handkerchief and blew his nose. "Tiineke, I'm not sure that's true. I remember how much he hated the Germans." Johan recalled how Andréas had not wanted to play football with the two soldiers.

"You're wrong, Oom Johan. And Mama, *you're* wrong." Wim spoke up now. "He didn't hate the Germans. Remember, Mama? His closest friend in Den Helder was a German boy. What he hated was having people come in and take over our country. He felt that everyone deserves the freedom to live their own lives. We talked about it a lot. Freedom. That was why he did what he did. Not for a lark, although I guess he probably did love the adventure, knowing Andréas."

"You knew about it? Oh my God, Wim, are you involved as well?" Tiineke was almost hysterical.

"No, no, Mama. I didn't know for sure. At first he was just running messages and he told me a couple of things, but then he stopped talking about it. I suspected he was involved but I didn't ask and he didn't tell. And no, I'm not involved. I don't have that same spirit." Wim cast his eyes down on the ground now, as if in shame.

Tiineke grabbed Wim by the shoulders and shook him.

"Promise me, promise me you won't get involved!"

"It's alright, Mama. I won't leave you. I promise." Wim spoke with a wisdom beyond his years.

There was a moment of silence before Elsa spoke up. "Mama, please, may I have a piece of cheese?"

Hank looked at Tiineke. She sighed and turned back to the food on the table. "Yes, sweetheart. It is a gift from Andréas, isn't it? He would want you to enjoy it, I'm sure."

V

Fall 1944

The kitchen door slammed open.

"Johan, what in the world are you doing?"

Johan raced into the living room where she sat dozing in the chair, Nicky playing at her feet.

"Mama, the allies are landing!" Johan held a poorly printed piece of paper. Across the top was printed 'Liberation Special'.

"Where did you get that?" Agatha frowned. She had made it clear she didn't want the Resistance newspapers in the house.

"Did you hear me? It's almost at an end!" Johan ignored her question. He scooped up Nicky and danced around the living room. The boy laughed. "Thousands of them have parachuted in around Nijmegen. It'll be over soon, I'm telling you! People are out in the streets celebrating."

"Johan, please calm down." She passed her hand across her forehead, her fingers pressing down. "I have a headache."

Johan was contrite. "Shall I get you some water?" There wasn't much else he could offer her.

She shivered and pulled her sweater closer around her. "No. No water, thank you, just some peace and quiet."

"I'll take Nicky out for a walk."

Agatha rested her head on the back of the chair and closed her eyes. "Be careful. I hope you're right that it's almost over, but it isn't over yet, so please don't stay out for long."

"We won't. Let's go, son" Johan grinned at the boy and held out his hand.

————

Johan held the child's hand tightly as they walked along. On the streets, people were in a frenzy of activity. Radio Orange had reported the night before that the British were in Breda. It was true, the Allies were coming! The word was everywhere.

"Here you are, little one." A woman with an arm full of flowers handed one to Nicky. People were chatting and laughing, even though the German patrols could be seen as usual.

Nicky tired quickly and the unaccustomed crowds frightened him. He whimpered. "Papa, I want to go home."

When they arrived home again, Agatha was preparing their supper of mashed potatoes and carrots. Rations allowed them fifteen hundred calories a day, but it primarily consisted of potatoes and other vegetables. Even with this allowance, they often couldn't find the required food. Without the supplements they continued to get from Hank, they would have been feeling the hardship more than they did. Even with the help, Johan could see the toll the deprivations were having on Agatha. Her hair was white now and the skin of her hands almost translucent. The veins showed blue under the white skin.

Looking up, Agatha turned and leaned against the counter. "Well?"

"It certainly seems to be true. People are going mad out there." Johan patted Agatha on the arm.

"Oma. For you." Nicky handed his flower to Agatha.

She wiped her hands carefully on her apron and took the flower from him. "Very nice, Nicky. Thank you." She turned to Johan. "It would have been good if you could have found a bit of butter to bring home instead of flowers."

Johan shook his head. "Unfortunately people aren't standing on the street corner handing out butter." He knew she was being sarcastic. It was her way of saying 'don't believe all this celebrating'. "Mama, I know you don't believe in being positive, but for once I'll ask you to say nothing. Let us believe. Don't tarnish Nicky with your negative thinking, please." Johan sucked in his breath to control his flash of anger.

She looked at him in surprise. "I'm not being negative, I'm being realistic. If you are realistic about something, you won't be disappointed."

"So we're disappointed. At least we would have had some hope and good feelings for a short time at least."

Agatha turned back to the supper preparation without saying anything further.

Johan glanced at her stiff back and retreated to the living room. He knew that since Andréas had died, he himself was different. He was ready to argue with her about anything and everything. The war had soured him.

———

A week later it was obvious that Agatha had been right. The war wasn't over yet. All the rumours were just that.

"What's that, Papa?" Nicky pointed as his father carried a box into the living room.

"A radio." Johan looked at his mother.

Agatha stepped back, her eyes narrowed. "Where did you get that?"

"The black market is alive and well. There are all sorts of things available for sale because the NSB have been leaving in droves for Germany. They are leaving their goods piled up in front of Central Station when they find they don't have room on the train."

While the ordinary Dutch citizens had been out celebrating at the rumours of the arrival of the Allies, the Dutch Nazi Party had taken flight.

Agatha hugged herself. "It's dangerous to have a radio in the house. You know they aren't allowed."

"We haven't been raided yet, so I doubt we will be now. Besides, I think we can find a hiding place in this big house, just in case. There's enough room around here to hide a dozen radios. I want to listen to Radio Orange myself, not just hear it secondhand from other people." Johan began to set up the radio in the corner of the living room.

Agatha sniffed but kept any further argument to herself. That evening, the old habit of listening to the news started again. The broadcast was only fifteen minutes long, but Johan felt connected again to the real world.

I've been living in a vacuum for years.

He tucked the radio away after the first night. Night after night, they listened to the news. On September fifteenth, hopes soared again as they listened to war correspondent, Robert Kiek, as he described the liberation of the city of Maastricht. "Maastricht is a sea of orange!"

Johan looked at his mother with a grin. "You see?"

"It's a good start."

Hank reached Johan by phone the next day. "We're being evacuated; we have to leave the house. Tiineke's in a state and quite honestly, I don't know what'll happen here. There are rumours that the gas plant is being closed, which means no work for me. The moment that happens I'll be sent to a German labour camp. I'm thinking of diving." Diving meant Hank would go into hiding rather than risk being picked up and sent to a camp.

Johan passed his hand across his forehead, then the hesitation passed. "How can I help? Does Tiineke want to come here?"

"No, I've found a place for her and the girls, but if you could take Wim, it would ease her mind.

She's so afraid for him. She's worried that he'll either be sent to a camp just because he's a big, strapping boy, or that someone will think that he's like his brother and he'll be suspected."

"Right. He better get here as quick as he can, then."

"Do you want to check with your mother first?"

Now Johan was strong and certain. "Absolutely not. Send him here."

"Alright. With the railway strike, it's pretty chaotic, but I'll get him there somehow, and I'm sending some food with him, whatever I can lay my hands on, but listen: make it last as long as possible, because with this strike, food is going to get really scarce."

Johan sent Nicky to the back garden to play after he hung up with Hank.

His mother was in the kitchen, rinsing off some vegetables she had grown in her little garden.

"It isn't a lot, but it's something anyway." Agatha spoke with a touch of pride as she showed Johan a few small onions.

Johan rolled two small onions in his hand and lifted them to his nose to inhale the spicy scent. "Store them. We'll be glad of them when the winter comes." Johan set the onions down and took her two hands in his. "Mama, I was just on the telephone with Hank."

"Oh?" Agatha was wary.

"Mama, Wim is coming to live with us."

"No." Agatha turned back to the vegetables and resumed brushing them with a stiff brush.

"Mama, I wasn't asking you. I'm telling you that he's coming here. I've told Hank to get him here as quick as he can. They have to leave the house. That part of Haarlem is being completely evacuated."

"This is my house, and I told that family long ago that if they left, they left for good."

"This is your house is it? So what am I? A lodger? If that's the case then perhaps Nicky and I should find new lodgings. Somewhere that can also accommodate Wim." Johan's face heated and sweat prickled under his arms.

Agatha leaned on the counter. She wasn't accustomed to having Johan take a stand like this.

"Of course this is your home also, but I expect you to respect my wishes."

"Well, Mama, I think I've been doing that all my life. It's time that you respect mine." Johan felt his neck muscles ache. "Look, your grandchildren didn't betray you." Johan's stress on the word 'betray' was deliberately sarcastic. "It's sad that you can't find it in your heart to forgive Tiineke, or the memory of André. I think you're the one losing out with that position, but that's your choice. But the children, Wim, had no say in the decision."

When Agatha continued to silently look down at the vegetables, Johan went on. "Mama, you can choose what to think and feel, but I'm telling you that Wim is coming here and I expect you to treat him civilly. He has lost his father, his brother, and now his home. He's a kid, and he deserves our help and kindness."

With that, Johan turned away and called Nicky inside.

"Come on, Nicky. I have a great surprise for you. Your cousin Wim is coming to live here, so let's go up and see how we can rearrange some things."

"Yay!" Nicky was thrilled. "Is Elsa coming too?" Elsa was by far his favourite cousin.

Johan smiled. "I'm afraid not. You'll have to make do with Wim."

Agatha heard them continuing to talk as they left to go upstairs to the bedrooms.

Johan's voice floated back to her. "Perhaps, since my room is larger and can easily have two beds, we should switch, you and I. What would you think of that?"

The child's response was lost as the door to the stairs closed behind them, but she could hear his excited chatter.

Agatha poured a glass of water for herself and sat down at the table. She thought back to when Wim was Nicky's age.

He was my pet and hope for the future. Everything I worked for was to be carried on by my sons and their sons.

What was it all for? She knew Johan hated the work. Even after all these years, she knew that he found it drudgery. Business was just not for him. Maybe Wim was the answer. She started to imagine what the boy would look like by now, ten years after she had last seen him. Perhaps it would be easier to work with him and train him for the business. He could work with Johan. Johan had become so difficult lately.

Agatha's secret fear was that she wouldn't have the strength to go on for much longer. She didn't say anything to Johan, but aside from the constant gnawing hunger, she had developed a pain in her stomach. She wouldn't bother going to a doctor. There was no point. Whatever would happen would happen, and she would bear it. She had lain awake nights, though, unable to sleep through the pain, worried that the moment she was gone, Johan would sell the business. Her life's work. Gone without thought. Perhaps she could change that if only she had enough time to see Wim grow to be a man. The thought was suddenly comforting.

Yes, perhaps it's all for the best.

———

Wim arrived early in the evening, just before curfew.

Johan was amazed. "How did you manage to find a bicycle and get it here without it being taken away?"

"Oom Hank dug it up somewhere and he told me all the back roads to take. I had to go off and hide a couple of times because of troops, but I made it."

"Your mother's alright?"

"Yes, they're all fine but they're sharing one room with some other woman, so there was just no way for me to stay." He shifted uneasily from one foot to the other, glancing around the old kitchen where he had started his life. "Oom Hank said he'd telephone you tonight at eight o'clock to check if I made it."

"Alright, I'll go in to the office for the call." Johan took the satchel from Wim and gave him a quick hug, then stood back and looked at the tall boy. "It's good that you're here."

Nicky was squirming with excitement. "Come and see your room. Papa gave us his room and you and I are sharing. It's a nice room with a window looking on the garden." He tugged Wim's hand to go upstairs.

"Give him a moment to get settled, Nicky." Johan turned his son around and pushed him towards the living room. "Let's first go in to say hello to Oma." Johan led Wim in to the living room.

Agatha sat in her usual chair. Her lap was covered in socks she was darning for Johan and Nicky. She put down the one she was working on and looked up at Wim. They gazed at each other without speaking for a moment. Agatha's eyes flickered over to Johan for a second.

Johan narrowed his eyes and knew she could read his message. *If you say anything rude, I'll never forgive you.*

She held out her hand to the boy. "Forgive me for not standing. You can see I'm in the middle of my work here. I'm glad you made it here safely."

Wim took her hand and then bent down to kiss her—once, twice, and again, in the usual Dutch greeting.

"Thank you for having me here." Wim spoke formally. "I remember you just like that, sitting in that chair."

"Can you remember so far back?" Johan was surprised.

"Oh yes. I can remember many things. Oma, you used to take me for walks. I remember that."

"Oma sometimes takes me for walks too." Nicky piped up, not wanting to be left out.

Agatha picked up her darning. "Nicky, you should take Wim up to help him unpack."

With that, Wim was part of the household.

Later, Johan spoke briefly with Hank. "Yes, Wim arrived here just fine, and my mother behaved herself, so all is well."

"Alright, well, I'm leaving now. You're on your own from here, I'm afraid."

"I understand. Look after yourself, and we'll see you when it's all over."

"God willing." And the line went dead.

Johan sat in the darkness of the empty office for a few moments. They'd been lucky up to now that Hank had been helping to supplement their rations with farm produce. Johan had paid for the goods, but these days cash money wasn't worth anything.

I'm going to have to figure this out. I need to establish some trading relationships. We have a warehouse full of fabric that isn't being used right now. That must be worth something to someone.

Johan decided that he would start asking a few questions the next day. He knew the black market was thriving, but he hadn't been involved before now. The whole thing may be over soon with the Allies pushing forward, but it wouldn't hurt to start making some inquiries just in case.

With Hank gone, I need to look after this family in a way I never have.

VI

Winter 1944

"Alright Wim, try it now." Johan knelt back and made a circling motion with his hand.

Wim sat on the stationary bicycle in its homemade wooden frame again and pedalled furiously. The radio flickered to life and the BBC broadcaster could be heard introducing the nightly Radio Orange program.

Johan clapped his hands. "Wonderful!"

Agatha peered at the machine. "Well, I must say I'm surprised you got that working, Johan."

Johan perched on the edge of the sofa in order to hear better. "Wim, are you alright to keep going for a bit? I'll take over when you need me to."

"I'm alright for now." Wim puffed out his words in short gasps. Hunger and lack of outdoor activity had taken their toll on his stamina.

They sat huddled around the radio, listening to the latest reports as Wim pedalled the bicycle, generating enough electricity to power the radio. They were in almost total darkness, with only the light from one candle casting a ghostly light on the scene.

Wim sputtered. "The one good thing is that I feel warmer than I've felt all day."

After a few minutes, Wim and Johan traded places, the sound dying out until Johan got enough speed to power back the radio.

When Johan was tired, they switched places again, and then again. Nicky climbed on Wim's lap and curled up against his grown-up cousin. Wim wrapped his arms around Nicky to warm him up. The gas and electricity had been shut down completely for months now. They had a homemade kerosene stove sitting on top of their normal stove. On it, they cooked their meals, such as they were.

"This is a good way to work off those lead pancakes we had for supper." Johan tried to joke.

Agatha sniffed. "We're lucky to have those pancakes."

"I know, Mam. I'm just teasing."

Johan went out each day with fabric under his jacket and met with black market dealers with food to trade. It was just about the only commodity worth having. Their rations allowed for one loaf of bread and one kilo of potatoes a week but it was never enough to keep them going. Agatha learned how to make flour from tulip bulbs and from that they made pancakes consisting of the tulip bulb flour and mashed sugar beets.

"Okay, that's enough of that for one night!" Johan declared when the broadcast was over. He and Wim were exhausted from the exertion of pedaling the bicycle generator.

"We'll get back in good fitness after a few days of this I'm sure." Johan stretched and flexed his muscles. *It's either that or we'll die trying.*

It was early on the morning of Christmas Eve. Johan came down from the warehouse above the factory with a roll of fine wool that they sometimes used for custom orders of blankets or cushion covers.

Agatha tried to take the bolt away. "You're not taking that out. When this war is over, we'll need our inventory to get up and running again. You can't just give it all away."

Johan gently pushed her aside. "Mama, if we don't live through the winter, we won't care about getting the business up and running again."

He put on the old fedora hat and coat that had once belonged to his father. The outfit made him look older, and there was room under the coat to carry the material or food that he would get in return trade. It was getting dangerous to be out on the streets now, despite his permit to work. All work had stopped without electricity and gas. The Germans needed men to dig trenches and build fortifications so they snatched up any man that seemed able-bodied. Johan pulled the hat down low and picked up his father's old walking stick as well.

"You shouldn't go." Agatha clung to his sleeve, her voice querulous.

"I'll see you later, Mama." And he left.

He walked for hours that day, most of the way to Haarlem and back, but returned home, triumphant.

"For Christmas supper, look what I have!"

They crowded around. Like a magician, Johan pulled treasures from his pockets, one by one: two eggs and two apples. For supper on Christmas Day, they shared the food amongst the four of them, and gave thanks for the change from tulip bulbs and beets.

Day after weary day. Week after exhausting week. The coldest winter in recent memory felt that much colder by bodies starved of protective fat and in houses lacking in heat. Agatha's shed had long since been burned as fuel in the stove. Next, Johan and Wim broke up every wooden packing case in the warehouse and after that, they broke up all the shelving. Finally, Johan started on the furniture up in the old suite above the warehouse.

"Imagine, this is where your mother and father lived when they first got married." Johan pushed aside his own memories of Mary and then he and Wim hacked and sawed at the chest of drawers.

"It's pretty gloomy-looking." Wim looked at the drab walls.

"I suppose it is."

Agatha had taken Nicky out with her earlier to collect their weekly rations.

"I'll take him to the soup kitchen for a meal."

"Yes, and get something yourself, Mama, please." Johan looked at the thin old woman that his mother had become. She was more bird-like than the strapping tower of strength that he had always known.

"We'll see." Johan could hear a little of her old spirit, with her chin raised and shoulders stiff.

Now, while Agatha was out, Johan and Wim worked at chopping apart the furniture. Johan knew that the chest of drawers had belonged to Agatha's mother and she would secretly be heartbroken to lose it, but there was no choice.

"This is good, hard wood. We'll make it last as long as we can." Johan hefted one of the old boards.

They had a small fire ready to light in the stove when Agatha and Nicky arrived home. Johan wasn't going to say anything about the source of the wood for the fire if Agatha didn't ask. Lately, she seemed content enough to let Johan manage things.

"Look!" Agatha was almost cheerful. "We had to stand in line for more than five hours, but the Red Cross was at the kitchen giving out some flour and margarine!"

"My God, that's wonderful! I was starting to worry." Johan picked Nicky up and peeled the woolen hat off him. "How are you, son? You're half frozen, aren't you?" Johan held his young son.

Agatha stroked the child's curls. "He's a good boy. He didn't complain. Show your Papa what you collected while I was standing in line."

"Look, Papa!" Nicky slid out of his father's arms and took him to the small hall by the door. Piled on the floor were a few small sticks.

"Good man! Where did you find these?"

Agatha explained for Nicky. "The old trees by the canal were cut down in the night and there were some sticks in the gutters that somehow hadn't been collected."

Johan made a tsk-tsk sound. "Ah, those beautiful old trees. Well, I'm surprised it didn't happen before now."

Suddenly, Agatha swayed. She stumbled in to the living room and just made it to the sofa where she sank down. "I'm alright, just a little lightheaded."

Johan knelt beside her and took her thin hand in his. "Did you get anything to eat while you were out?"

"Yes, both Nicky and I had a bowl of cabbage soup. At least I think it was cabbage."

Johan nodded to his nephew. "Wim, light the stove."

Agatha fluttered her hand weakly. "Johan, don't be extravagant. It's too early."

Wim stood, hesitating, looking at Johan.

Johan stood and pointed to the stove. "Light it."

Wim knelt down to get the stove going.

"Mama, there's no point arguing with me. You and Nicky are both frozen after that long day outside." Johan put up his hand to stop her when she looked like she was going to say something further.

Agatha nodded and closed her eyes. She slumped on the sofa, her face white and lips blue. Johan pulled a blanket from the back of the chair and lifted his mother's feet on to the sofa and covered her.

"Lay back now and relax for a bit. I'll get supper ready." He expected another argument.

She nodded again. "Thank you."

Despite everything, somehow they made it through the winter. When it was too dangerous for Johan to go out in the streets anymore, he dressed in some of his mother's clothes and went out as a woman.

Agatha's eyes were shiny with tears the first time he told her he would wear some of her clothes. "I'm sorry, Johan. I should be the one going out."

"Mama, you're not up to it. I won't allow it. You stay in bed, and I'm going out to see what I can find."

Nicky looked at him with big round eyes when he saw his father dressed up in his grandmother's clothes.

"Why are you dressing like that, Papa?"

Johan hesitated. He wanted to shelter the boy as much as possible, and yet these were serious times, and he needed Nicky to understand that.

"It's dangerous for men to go outside right now because the Germans would like to take us to help them with their work. I don't want to go away and help the Germans, so I need to hide like this."

"Will this keep you safe, Papa?"

"Yes, I believe it will."

Nicky looked thoughtful for a moment. "Alright. I'll look after Oma while you're away."

"Good for you." Johan ruffled his son's shaggy honey-gold mop of hair.

Johan met with his black market contacts and if they had anything to trade, he took it. Sometimes it was a tiny bit of real tea, an incredible luxury after drinking the pressed herb tablet dissolved in water that passed for tea these days. Always he tried for some flour, but often he would have to come home satisfied with tulip bulbs and the sickening sweet beets.

In April, Operation Manna was implemented. Hundreds of huge Lancaster bombers flew overhead at tree-top level, dropping food. American Flying Fortresses followed with more food. Flour, powdered eggs, and biscuits were dropped. Even candy and chewing gum fluttered down in small parachutes. Johan, Wim, and Nicky all went out together to collect food. When they got back, Johan made some real pancakes.

"Come and eat something, Mama. It's just a matter of time, now. This time it truly is just about over."

Agatha was lying on the sofa under a blanket, despite the mild spring day. "Yes. Yes, just about over."

———

Johan was hunched near the radio while Wim was on the bike-generator on May fourth. He stopped peddling for a moment when they heard the news over Radio Orange.

It's over! The Germans have surrendered.

Wim pedalled again furiously as they began to lose power to the radio. After the broadcast was over, they heard people out in the streets.

Wim ran to the window. "Look!"

People were pouring out into the streets as the news spread. Carrying red-white-and-blue flags and small orange pennants, people called and laughed and danced. Even though there were still German soldiers out in the streets as well, the neighbourhood seemed oblivious to them.

"It's over! It's over!" The cry was everywhere.

"Mama, come out and see!" Johan tried to get his mother to come outside.

Agatha shook her head. "I can see what's going on from the comfort of my chair."

He left her again to go out with Wim and Nicky.

"We made it, boys." Johan was jubilant. The streets were full with thin, pale, ghostly-looking people. Teeth looked overly large in gaunt faces as they grinned and laughed with unaccustomed excitement. People were crying as much as they were laughing.

"If only Piet had held on a few more weeks."

"I wish Papa were here now."

"Poor Tante Mien would have been so happy now."

All around them people talked about those who hadn't made it through the winter of starvation while they rejoiced with those who had.

Wim was subdued after the first shouts of joy. Johan put his arm around the boy's shoulder and gave the skinny boy a quick hug. "Andréas helped to bring this day about. We'll never forget him."

Wim smiled sadly. "Yes, you're right."

"Come, let's go back in to Oma."

The three of them went inside to sit with Agatha. Johan got the kerosene stove running and boiled some water. From the back of a kitchen cupboard he pulled out a small tin box. He spilled out the small horde of black tea leaves into the pot, then carried the teapot and good cups and saucers in to the living room.

"I've been saving this last bit of tea for a special occasion. I would say this is it."

They each sat quietly with their own thoughts, savouring the tea, even young Nicky. The fragrant, slightly floral aroma of the steam was a joy. Agatha closed her eyes as she breathed deeply.

Nicky put his small hand on her knee. "Are you alright, Oma?"

"Yes, child. I'll be fine."

Johan didn't comment on the future tense of her response but studied her closely. He saw how thin and frail she was. She had been losing her hair over the past few months so that now he saw flakey scalp where there had once been thick, wiry, black hair. Her yellow skin was thin and sagged across bony cheekbones. She had heavy dark circles surrounding her eyes, obvious even behind the protection of her glasses.

"We have to fatten you up a bit, Mama." Johan frowned.

"Well, not today son. The tea was a treat, but now I'm going to bed." She seemed to struggle getting out of the chair.

Wim stood. "Shall I help you up the stairs, Oma?"

"Certainly not." She took the walking stick she had been using for several months now and made her way to the stairs.

Wim glanced at Johan, and Johan made a gesture to hold him back. He knew his mother wouldn't appreciate any help.

They listened until, after what seemed an age, they heard her steps above them. She had made it to her room. Now they could all go to bed, to sleep in the knowledge of a better tomorrow.

VII

Summer 1945

Johan stood in the living room and stared at the doctor who had just come down from Agatha's bedroom. He tried to swallow down the lump in his throat. "Are you sure, Doctor?"

"Yes, I'm afraid so, Mr. Meijer. Your mother is in her last hours. She won't make it through the night."

Johan took out his handkerchief. "I knew she wasn't well—who among us is?—I just thought that once she got some good food in to her, she'd be alright again."

"I'm afraid not. She's clearly been ill for quite some time, but I think that her sense of duty as much as anything kept her going. With the end of the war, she feels her duty is done." The doctor shook his head and squeezed Johan's arm. "She's asking for you. There's really nothing more I can do here. I've made her comfortable, so you'll find her a bit groggy perhaps. I'll leave you now. Fetch me when it's over." The doctor was practical and had other patients to see.

Johan saw the man to the door and then stood for a moment taking a couple of deep breaths. Finally he went out to the garden where the boys were kicking around the ball in the fading light of evening. "Wim, will you continue to look after Nicky please. I'm going to sit with Oma for a while." The boys had already said good night to their grandmother and Johan didn't see any reason to tell them they had most likely said their final good-bye. She wouldn't like the fuss.

Within two hours it was over. She had spoken to him as he held her hand. Until the end she was demanding and insistent. She took longer and longer pauses between words, but still, she persevered until she had said all that she needed to.

"I did it for you. Don't let it all be for nothing." Agatha's voice was little more than a whisper.

Johan brushed a thin, grey tendril of hair off her forehead. "Mam, don't think about those things. Rest now."

She clutched at his hand with surprising strength. She had always amazed him with her strength and willpower. "Don't let me down."

He knew what she wanted. A promise. He sighed. There would be no freedom for him. "Alright Mama. I won't sell the business."

Agatha paused once more and gathered strength. She was determined. "You give me your word now."

"Yes, Mama. Please don't worry anymore." His tears fell and he mopped his face with his wet handkerchief. He bent close to hear her last words.

"You're a good boy."

He sat with his head bowed by her bedside, drained and exhausted, her bird-like claw of a hand still resting in his.

It's the end of an era.

He opened his hand and let her go.

"Where are the flowers? We've left them behind. Wim, run back and get them. Your mother will like to have flowers for her new house." Johan stood and turned his face to the sun as they waited.

Wim bolted back to the house to get the large bouquet of yellow sunflowers and bright pink and red gerberas with a few sprigs of spicy, fragrant freesias.

When they started walking again, Wim turned to his uncle. "Won't you lose business by closing the shop on a Saturday? I didn't think we'd go until tomorrow."

"We might lose a bit of business, but if the customers really want something, they'll come back. Helping your mother and uncle move in to their new home is *family* business, so it's more important."

Johan turned to Nicky, who skipped along beside them, kicking a football along in the warm summer sunshine. Johan smiled at the sight of the boy's renewed energy and healthy appearance after only a few weeks of proper food. "Isn't it wonderful, Nicky, that your cousins will be living so close by now?"

They walked across the Bloemgracht Bridge and turned down Nassaukade. From there, they turned on to Hugo de Grootkade where they could walk along the water to the street they were looking for.

Nicky pulled on his father's sleeve. "Will they stay here always?"

"Well, certainly for a long time. Your Tante Tiineke and Oom Hank have bought this house together so Oom Hank can be close to his new business." Johan tousled Nicky's hair before the boy skipped out of reach again.

"It'll be handy for you too, Wim. You can easily go over to see your mother and sisters now." He saw a cloud pass Wim's face.

Wim hesitated, then nodded. "Yes, it'll be easy."

Johan stopped and put his hand on Wim's shoulder to stop him as well. "Wait for a moment. What is it, Wim?"

"Nothing. Nothing at all. I'm very grateful to you for giving me a home and looking after me all this time."

"Wim, would you rather move back with your mother and sisters?" The thought only just occurred to him.

The tall, slim boy looked his uncle in the eye, then down to the ground. "No, I'm fine living with you. I know that you count on me to help you with Nicky and the shop."

Johan gripped his nephew's upper arm. "Wim, don't live your life trying to please everyone else. Now, tell me honestly what you would like to do."

"Honestly? I'd like to go back and live with my mother and the girls. I can still help you, though." The boy flushed and bit his lip.

"Then that is what we shall do. It sounds like the house should be big enough for everyone. The inheritance that came from your great aunt in Rotterdam has come at the right time for your Mam and uncle to get a new start. Your uncle made so many connections during his years of black market trading that opening his own business in import-export seems perfect for him."

"What about you, Oom Johan? You once told us that you hated working in the business. Maybe you should sell it and get a new start for yourself?" Wim was emboldened by his own courage.

Johan was quiet for a moment. "No, Wim. Before your Oma died she had me promise that I wouldn't sell the business. She felt strongly that it was the Meijer heritage and that I have a duty to maintain it."

Wim looked at his uncle. "But even though you don't like it? You'll keep it going?" He was amazed.

"I made a deathbed promise, Wim. One day your generation can decide what you want to do with it."

Nicky skipped back to Johan and Wim. "Come on! Come and see, Papa. Look at the fire engine!"

They watched for a moment as a fire truck passed them, clanging the bell.

Nicky pointed to the receding truck. "I want to be a fireman when I grow up, Papa."

"Well then, Nicky, that's what you shall be. Whatever you want to do in your life, you are free to choose, and I'll help you as best I can."

"Maybe I'll be a footballer." Nicky scooted off, he and Wim dancing the ball between them.

Johan smiled. "That would be good, too."

Acknowledgments

Many books, internet articles and individual memories went into the writing of this novel. Some specific resources include: Simon Kuper's *Ajax, the Dutch, the War: The Strange Tale of Soccer During Europe's Darkest Hour*, 'wm0zart' youtube video of the commemoration of the *1943 Amsterdam Population Registry attack*, Margaretha Kidd's article *The financing of the Resistance in the Netherlands 1940-1945*, Henri A. van der Zee's *The Hunger Winter: Occupied Holland 1944-1945* and the many memories shared by residents of Holland Christian Homes, Brampton, Ontario.

Special thanks to the family reminiscences shared by my mother, Johanna deGroot-Meijer (who, thank goodness, was only ever supportive of my dreams) RIP; father, Pieter deGroot (who inspired the love of story-telling in me) RIP; uncle Marinus deGroot, aunt Gre deGroot and most of all my uncle Jan deGroot and aunt Marja deGroot – in whose living room in Heiloo, The Netherlands, this book was first germinated – during an evening of laughter, love and family stories.

On a personal note, I'd like to thank the following for their contributions in terms of readings, suggestions and general support and encouragement: Max deGroot, Anne-Marie Dick, again - Marja deGroot and her daughter-in-law Janneke deGroot (for research assistance and contributions to authenticity), Margaret Doherty, Marg Dowling, Shanaaz Akbar, Holly Beyea, Ron Base (for early encouragement), Jo Anne Daynard, John-Charles MacKinnon, Tiffany Maxwell-Graovac (Editor, Teacher and Cheer-leader), Sharron Elkouby (for yet another editing project for me) and Jimmy Carton (research assistant, sounding board and the best story teller I know). Couldn't have done it without you, folks!

Manufactured by Amazon.ca
Bolton, ON